FIVE HIGHLY ACCLAIMED AUTHORS BRING YOU THE MAGICAL SPIRIT OF VALENTINE'S DAY

MARY BALOGH won the *Romantic Times* Award for Best New Regency Writer and its Reviewer's Choice Award for Best Regency Author in 1985 and 1989. She lives in Kipling, Saskatchewan, Canada.

SANDRA HEATH is one of Signet's most talented new writers and the author of the highly popular *A Christmas Courtship*. She lives in Gloucester, England.

CARLA KELLY was the winner of the 1989 *Romantic Times* Award for Best New Regency Author and the 1990 *Romantic Times* Reviewer's Choice Award for Best Regency Novel. She lives in Monroe, Louisiana.

EDITH LAYTON has won a total of seven awards for her romance novels and has been elected to the *Romantic Times* Romance Writers Hall of Fame. She lives in Jericho, New York.

CAROL PROCTOR was nominated for the *Romantic Times* Best New Regency Author Award in 1990. She resides in Forth Worth, Texas.

A REGENCY VALENTINE II

Five Stories by

Mary Balogh

Sandra Heath

Carla Kelly

Edith Layton

Carol Proctor

A SIGNET BOOK

SIGNET
Published by the Penguin Group
Penguin Books USA Inc., 375 Hudson Street,
New York, New York 10014, U.S.A.
Penguin Books Ltd, 27 Wrights Lane,
London W8 5TZ, England
Penguin Books Australia Ltd, Ringwood,
Victoria, Australia
Penguin Books Canada Ltd, 10 Alcorn Avenue,
Toronto, Ontario, Canada M4V 3B2
Penguin Books (N.Z.) Ltd, 182–190 Wairau Road,
Auckland 10, New Zealand

Penguin Books Ltd, Registered Offices:
Harmondsworth, Middlesex, England

First published by Signet, an imprint of New American Library,
a division of Penguin Books USA Inc.

First Printing, January, 1992
10 9 8 7 6 5 4 3 2 1

 REGISTERED TRADEMARK—MARCA REGISTRADA

PRINTED IN THE UNITED STATES OF AMERICA

Contents

A Task for Cupid
by Carol Proctor

SHE WAS A SMALL stout woman with softly waving hair which was not yet quite white. Her full cheeks, common-looking turned-up nose, and cherubic aspect might have seemed best suited to a farmer's wife, as she herself was fond of remarking. Of course, one would have suspected that she was a lady, if only because of the high-necked black silk gown she wore, or the fine lace cap upon her head, or the great ruby which sparkled upon her finger.

It was something less obvious, though, that proclaimed her true position. Perhaps it was the determined set of her chin or the ramrod stiffness of her back, even when seated, but whatever it was, one always was aware that she was a marchioness. The fact was even more obvious this morning, as she was surveying her visitor with an air of disapproving hauteur.

This person, a tall and darkly handsome young gentleman, dressed quietly but correctly in a dark blue tailcoat and fawn-colored inexpressibles, was pacing about distractedly, paying little or no attention to the room's other occupant. When he paused by a window to gaze through it with unseeing eyes and ran a hand through his already disordered curls, the marchioness could preserve her silence no longer.

7

"I never imagined that a grandson of mine could be so indifferent to appearances," she said acidly.

He cast startled eyes upon her, as if he had forgotten that she was also in the room, which, as a matter of fact, he had. Seeing that she finally had his attention, she clarified her statement.

"If you choose to make a public spectacle of yourself and provide the servants with ample opportunity for speculation, I would prefer that you do it elsewhere, rather than under *my* roof."

He turned to her, and the despair in his eyes smote her conscience. She ignored the feeling. The last thing the boy needed was to wallow in her pity.

"Grandmother, I—" he began tentatively.

She cut him off ruthlessly. "I have seen lovesickness often enough to be able to recognize it. Refusing a perfectly good dinner last night! I shall be fortunate if my chef does not leave. It is hard enough to persuade him that his talents are appreciated, buried in the country."

He swallowed. "I am sorry, Grandmother."

She could have wept, but she steeled her heart against it. "I am out of patience with these melancholy looks and these heartrending sighs. I am well aware that this excessive display of emotion has become fashionable recently, but as for myself, I have no sympathy for it. In my day, when a gel jilted a gentleman, he would have been too proud to wear his heart upon his sleeve. If your grandfather were alive, I should hate to think what he would say—"

"But, Grandmother—"

"Please have the goodness not to interrupt me when I am speaking. As I was saying, if you wish to remain here with me, you will rid yourself of that gloomy countenance. You will eat your dinner instead of just pushing the food around on your plate, and perhaps we can fill you out again. And you might care to try for some sport with Lord Gonville. A few days of hunting would help to put the roses back into your cheeks."

She clearly had taken him by surprise. He was too perplexed to speak. Seeing it, she pressed her advantage. "Yes, and while you're with me, you will attend every dinner and ball in the county. I am not about to have it said that some chit out of the schoolroom has bested Denzil Huntingford."

"But, Grandmother, you're mistaken."

He spoke gently, but she could feel an icy fear clutch at her heart. It was even worse than she had imagined. She spoke gruffly. "Well, if it's that sort of affair, then of course we need say no more about it, though once one has reached the age I have, there is little about the world that can shock or surprise."

He was frowning in puzzlement. "I don't quite understand you." He shook his head. "No one has jilted me, although it might be better if she had. Then I might finally give up hope."

Now it was her brow that was furrowed. "What are you saying?" she demanded. "Are you in love or are you not?"

The dark eyes were filled with pain. "Yes, I am, though nothing will ever come of it. She's the most beautiful, the most admirable girl in the world. She has scores of admirers."

Her features had relaxed somewhat, but her voice was still sharp as she asked, "Just who is this paragon, anyway? Would I know her family?"

He shrugged. "I suppose so. Her name is Amabel Penworth."

"Amabel Penworth!"

Her tone surprised him. "Yes. Do you know her?"

"Of the Oxfordshire Penworths?"

"Yes."

"Her father is Sir Roger Penworth?"

"Yes, do you know him?"

He was looking at her curiously but blankly, and she decided that he was not enacting a subtle plot to enlist her help. "Her mother was a bosom bow of your mother's," she told him. "Amabel is my godchild."

She saw that she had been justified in presuming his innocence, for there was no mistaking his genuine surprise. "Your godchild! How was it that I did not know of this?"

For the first time during this interview, she allowed a corner of her mouth to curl upward. "Considering that I have over a dozen godchildren, it's hardly surprising. Besides, you did meet her here once, and as I recall, you wanted nothing to do with her. In fact, you insulted her."

It was hard to say whether he were more shocked or angry. A flush had risen to his cheeks. "I would *never* dream of insulting Miss Penworth. Nor could I so easily forget having met her. I am persuaded that you must be mistaken," he concluded stiffly.

"A grandmother's memory is always a little too long for a grandson's convenience," she observed. "As I remember it, she wanted to set up housekeeping with you, but of course you were twelve or so and wanted nothing to do with dolls, or with a seven-year-old girl."

By now he had caught the mischievous twinkle in her eyes, which was so great a part of her charm. Her expression was that of a lively school-girl once more, and it was possible to understand how the late marquess had fallen in love within minutes of meeting her. Denzil gave her a reluctant smile. "You're roasting me, of course."

"No, every word that I say is true."

Hope began to dawn in his face. "Then you truly are her godmother? Then you actually may be able to—" His face clouded over. "No, I don't suppose so."

She gave a sigh of exasperation. "I wish you would stop this beating about the bush. I assume that this visit you are paying did not spring strictly from the warm regard in which you hold me. I cannot help you unless you ask me, my dear. Nor can I do anything until I know what has occurred. Now, has she refused to marry you or not?"

"Refused to marry me!" He gave a bitter laugh. "I've hardly even spoken a word with her."

All at once she understood, and it made her so angry that she had to spring up from her chair, quite startling her grandson. "Denzil, do not tell me that this accursed shyness of yours has kept you from speaking to her!"

"Of course it has!" His gaze had dropped ashamedly. "I've never been able to talk to any girl—you know that. Being in love has only made it harder. She's so beautiful that all I can do is stare at her."

Lady Witley was now the one doing the pacing. "I *knew* that this would happen. Why, haven't I warned your father a hundred times—"

"It's not as if I haven't tried. But just to exchange a word with her, I would have to shove through a crowd of her admirers. The worst part, though, is knowing when I got there I would have nothing to say."

She grimaced. "Yes, I know. You'd stand there like a dolt, gaping at her, and she probably would imagine that you didn't have all of your faculties. I know your father's own education was neglected, but that was all the more reason to see to yours."

He gaped at her. "His education? Why, Father is one of the most renowned classical scholars in England!"

"That's just what I mean," she replied cryptically. "I never could understand what Maria could see in him, though—but that is all beside the point. The problem is what may be done now. I suppose you know the sort of reputation you've earned with your remoteness. I am surprised that anyone ever invites you to cross the threshold."

He looked troubled. "If you mean that ridiculous sobriquet they've seen fit to bestow upon me—"

" 'The Female-Hater'? Why, yes, that is the one I was referring to, even though it would seem more fitted to an octogenarian than to a boy of twenty-four."

"But you know that I'm not like that, Grandmother—"

"Yes, I know that, and I also know that you are generally liked and respected by your own sex, but had you considered that excludes half the world?"

Denzil, long accustomed to his grandmother's old-fashioned frank speaking, hardly even noticed her shocking choice of words.

Her eyes suddenly softened as she looked at him. "Yes, I know all about you. I know that you've never refused to subscribe to any charity that asks you and that you've been active in several of the reform societies. I myself see no harm in uniting with different classes of persons in order to achieve a good end, and I believe that you will do the title more credit than your father ever has done—"

He could not let these words pass. "Grandmother, I think that you are—" he began, flushing slightly.

"Well, there is no point in our quarreling about it," she said agreeably, seating herself once more. "Now, the thing is that you have come for my advice. I say, go to the gel, tell her you're in love with her, and be done with it."

"But, Grandmother, I can't. That's just what I've been telling you—"

"Nonsense!"

"I'm afraid to speak to her and I don't know what to say."

She shook her head. "Your grandfather would be beside himself, were he here today. Why, he was the most silver-tongued, the most charming ..." Her voice faded as a reflective smile played across her face.

"Well, I wish he were here," said Denzil unhappily. "Perhaps he could give me lessons, tell me what to say to her—"

"Yes, he could." She gave a huge unconscious sigh. The two sat in silence for a moment, before she raised her head and fixed her grandson with a level gaze. "You really *cannot* talk to her, can you?"

He shook his head. "No, I don't know what I expected you to do. I suppose you're right in saying my education was neglected, but it is too late to change that now."

"Are you certain that you're in love with her?"

He shrugged. "As sure as I can be. There's just something about the way she tilts her head ... and her laugh ... and she has the most beautiful blue eyes—but it's hopeless, of course."

"Perhaps not."

He looked up abruptly.

Her face was grave, but her eyes were glowing. "What is it?" he asked eagerly.

"Go back to London," she advised him. "I have an idea, but there is something that I must do first."

Another look at her countenance informed him that further questions would be useless. "I'll give Chase the order to start packing now."

She gave him the delightfully mischievous smile again. "You might as well wait to leave until after we have a bite of nuncheon. But by all means leave me alone, for I have a letter to write."

He obediently rose and exited, leaving her to stare for a minute after that tall, spare figure. The Honorable Denzil Huntingford, heir to the Viscount Dore, and Miss Amabel Penworth. It would be a good match. The Penworths were an old and respected family, and Amabel would have a considerable fortune. More than that, it dearly would have gratified the heart of her only child, Maria. She removed the miniature which always hung about her neck and gazed at it fondly. It was twenty-two years that Maria had been gone, but she still could feel her presence, still could see those laughing dark eyes which were so like her father's. It was almost as if the painted visage were making a request of her, and when had she ever been able to refuse Maria anything? There was a fullness in her eyes, but she blinked it away and lifted her chin.

"Very well, my dear," she whispered, "I'll arrange it—as long as I am sure that it is the best thing for both of the children."

A month was to pass, an interminable month. As the days and weeks multiplied, the hope which his grandmother had raised began to wane. London was cold and dreary at this season, which exactly suited Denzil's mood. It seemed only fitting that most of his acquaintances should be out of town. He shunned the ones that weren't, preferring to be alone with his own black thoughts. The knowledge that Amabel was also in the country did nothing to make him feel more optimistic. She doubtless was flitting from one house to another, pursued by all her court. He had been an idiot to think that the marchioness could magically find a way out of all his difficulties for him. Her silence could only mean that she had failed.

Despairing, he threw himself into other activities. The problem was that he found his mind wandering during discussion about the current disturbances and the legislation which would be necessary to improve conditions. Too often his thoughts were dwelling upon a pair of blue eyes, or thick curls of dark gold, or upon soft white shoulders. He would shake his head and try to turn his attention to the matter at hand, but he never was successful for long. Even casual observers began to remark that Mr. Huntingford seemed quieter and more preoccupied than usual. By the time the meeting concluded, his heart generally would be even heavier than when it began. In this dark mood, he considered going home to Dore, though it would provide few diversions. Upon reflection, he decided to wait to hear from his grandmother, if only for politeness' sake.

Therefore, he felt no real elation when he returned to his chambers one day in late November and discovered a letter marked with her cramped but forceful handwriting. He was to be startled by its contents. After the briefest of formalities the marchioness came right to the point. "I have started events in motion," the missive read. "Please have the goodness to come to Witley immediately. Prepare for an extended stay and write to your father that you will be spending the holidays with me." She did not elaborate and Denzil could not help feeling irritated. What if he didn't like the scheme which she so carelessly had begun? He wasn't a child, after all. She should have consulted him. He had half a mind not to obey this peremptory summons.

He heaved a sigh and gave his head a little shake. It was a grandmother's way, he supposed, to always picture one as if he were still in short coats. She undoubtedly was not *deliberately* trying to insult him, and after all, he had asked for her help. She was the only female who didn't render him tongue-tied in her presence. If he spurned her offer of aid, he was not likely to get another.

Accordingly, he gave Chase the necessary orders and sat down to write the required letter to his father.

The advantage of bachelorhood was that one could depart at a moment's notice. Denzil arrived at Witley Castle two days later. It was late in the evening and he was tired, but he was not surprised to be informed that the marchioness wished to see him immediately. Indeed, by now his own curiosity was such that he would have been disappointed if she hadn't.

After giving his hat and coat to the waiting footman, he went upstairs to her chamber. She was already in bed, but she still had on her dressing gown of a heavy brocade, and there was an open book by her side. She greeted him with warmth as he crossed the room, took her by the hands, and gave her a peck on the cheek. There was no mistaking her air of suppressed excitement.

In response to a gesture from her, he drew up a gilt-and-embroidered chair and seated himself by her bed. She smiled into that expectant countenance.

"Well, my dear, I think you will be happy when you hear what I have to say. The Penworths are coming to stay with me for three weeks!"

Dismayed, he started up with a cry, knocking over the chair as he did so. "Amabel here? Oh, I do not think that—"

"You are not required to think," she told him severely, though the sparkle in her eyes belied her tone. "Now, sit down and I will tell you what I have planned."

Meekly he righted the chair and again seated himself as she continued.

"That amount of time should be sufficient for you to woo her. There will be dinners and entertainments, of course, but I have invited no other guests, so you will have every opportunity to spend uninterrupted time with Miss Penworth."

"But, Grandmother, I should not—"

"I believe that in three weeks you should come to know each other well enough to know your own minds, and if you should find that you did not suit, at least we all no longer will have to suffer this lovesickness of yours."

"Did not suit! Oh, never, but—"

She gave him a disapproving frown. "You've lost more weight, haven't you? Well, I must contrive to fatten you up before her arrival. Skeletons are not the most attractive suitors. She might well reject you out of hand."

"But, Grandmother!" The note of heartfelt anguish stopped her flow of words. She lifted her brows and gazed at him. He swallowed painfully.

"It will do no good to have Ama . . . Miss Penworth here. You might shut us up together in the tower for a week and it still wouldn't make a difference. I couldn't think of a thing to say to her. I know I couldn't."

Her visage softened. "Bless you, child, did you think that I had not taken that into account? The Penworths do not arrive until January. The holidays would have been better, of course, but they were already engaged to stay with some friends in Shropshire. In any case, that gives us more time to work."

He stared at her, uncomprehending.

She leaned forward and patted his hand in a grandmotherly fashion. "I mean to teach you how to woo Miss Penworth. After all, I was married to one of the most smooth-tongued suitors of my day. I think that I am well qualified to instruct you."

His expression of dismay was almost comic, but she did not appear to be amused. "I am quite serious, Denzil. We both agreed that your education had been neglected. Well, I intend to supply the deficiencies."

"It's the maddest scheme I've ever heard!" His outburst was involuntary, but it drew from her an austere look.

"I have had quite enough with these 'could nots' and 'would nots' and 'will nots,'" she informed him coldly. "If you truly love this gel, as you say, then you will be willing to make an effort to win her. No one is entitled to happiness who is not willing to work for it."

He gazed silently into those clear gray eyes. After all, what did he have to lose? The worst that could happen would be that he would appear a fool in her eyes and give her a distaste of him. Surely that was no worse than the current situation, wherein she didn't even know that he was alive. What other choice did he have?

"Very well, Grandmother. I will try."

A smile lit her features. "Excellent. You had better go to your chamber, for it is late and we will want to get an early start in the morning."

"As you say." He rose and replaced the chair. "Good night." What had he let himself in for now? He abruptly recalled several veiled comments the late marquess had made about the marchioness's penchant for wild schemes. He had been a child at the time, too young to understand. He heaved a small unconscious sigh as he exited the room.

She expelled a breath as the door closed behind him. It had seemed a near thing for a minute. His cooperation was essential. Well, her scheme was falling into place quite nicely now. As long as she could convince the boy to speak to Amabel, all would be well.

By the end of a week, the strain of the endeavor was beginning to tell on them both. Though Denzil did his best to comply with her suggestions, his growing pessimism was obvious and it could not help but damage the marchioness's own hopes.

She had decided to begin with the most crucial problem of what he would say to Miss Penworth. To that end she had given him poems to commit to memory, poems of the sort which the late marquess had applied judiciously during his own courtship.

Not the sort to waste any time herself, she worked on a piece of embroidery as she sat in the damask-covered wing chair and listened to him. When he had finished his recitation, she gave a gentle sigh and then spoke.

"Well, at least there is no fault with your memory, anyway. I think that perhaps that piece was not suited to . . . to your own particular style. Why don't you try the Herrick instead—and this time, try to imbue it with feeling."

A darksome look crossed his face for a moment, but then he drew in a deep breath and obediently began: " 'What conscience, say, is it in thee, When I a heart had one, To take away that heart from me, And to retain thine own—?' "

She visibly cringed. "No! You mustn't use that singsong tone. The words have some meaning, you know, and you must say them as if they do."

He frowned at her, perplexed.

She sighed again. "For example, the word 'conscience' should be emphasized. Say 'What *conscience* say, is it in thee—' "

He screwed up his face, but made an obedient attempt. " 'What CONSCIENCE, say, is it in—' "

"No, no, you mustn't scream it that way. You'll frighten the poor gel out of her wits."

It was his turn to give a sigh of exasperation. " 'What conscience, say, is it—' "

She put down her embroidery. "If you are going to whisper, she most likely will not be able to hear you."

Goaded beyond endurance, he glared at her. "Grandmother, I—"

She silenced him with a look. "Just try it once again. It's such a short and simple poem. All it requires is that you deliver it with expression. You say you're in love with this chit. Well, pretend that I am she."

His silence was eloquent. She scowled at him. "Well?"

"Well, it's difficult to deliver it with *expression* if you continue to interrupt me."

"Go on, then." She took up her embroidery once again.

This time he was allowed to recite the poem from beginning to end. He did so without making any major mistakes, a fact which made him feel some justifiable pride. One glance at his grandmother's face, though, was enough to inform him that no applause would be forthcoming.

She sighed once more and laid down her embroidery again. "I think that perhaps we could use a rest," she said.

By the time they resumed their lessons that afternoon, the marchioness had decided that it would be of little use to continue working on the poetry that day. Accordingly, they focused upon other areas in which she thought Denzil might profit from instruction. Fighting against irritation, she had to admit that her grandson showed little aptitude for any aspect of courtship. She sighed to herself, concealing her impatience, though her aspect became increasingly grim as the day wore on.

"Kiss my hand, Denzil," she commanded him abruptly.

Startled, he complied, bowing over it correctly, though stiffly.

"No, no, no—I mean kiss it as if I were Miss Penworth."

He repeated his performance without any perceptible alteration.

She repressed another sigh. "No, you have not the way of it. To begin with, you must meet my eyes."

With some difficulty he managed to obey.

"Good. Now, as you bow over my hand, your

eyes must not leave mine, but must gaze at me with a warm, rapturous sort of look—"

His skepticism was obvious.

"Well, I know that I am not Miss Penworth, but you must use your imagination. I want to see that you can do it properly when she comes. Now, try it—no, no, look into my eyes!"

He tried to meet her eyes, failed, kissed her hand, and popped back upright in the same manner as originally. He ran a distracted hand through his hair. His grandmother muttered something under her breath which he did not quite catch. "I beg your pardon?"

She shook her head, then gave him a weary, beatific smile. "It was nothing," she lied. "I think that perhaps we have done enough for today."

He could not disguise his relief, and broke into a delighted smile. "I'll go out for a ride, then."

"Fine."

As she watched him retreat across the Turkish carpet, she wondered to herself how a gentleman as polished and suave as her late husband could have produced a grandson who, despite all his virtues, had no address whatsoever. She shook her head again. The task, which had seemed so simple, was rapidly becoming a herculean one. Well, perhaps some fresh inspiration would strike her on the morrow.

By the end of another week, no fresh inspiration having struck, Lady Witley was near to desperate and Denzil was becoming mutinous. As a sign of rebellion he had appeared in trousers this morning and she had been forced to send him back upstairs to change. She was conscious of a pounding in her head as she listened to him recite:

" 'When in the chronicle of wasted time I see descriptions of the fairest fights—' "

She shuddered. "Please take your mind from Gentleman Jackson's saloon. *Wights*! 'The fairest wights.' "

" '—the fairest wights, and beauty making beautiful old rhyme—' " He cut off the poem abruptly. "I'm sorry, Grandmother, but it simply doesn't make any sense!"

"Denzil—"

"No, it simply doesn't, and 'in praise of ladies dead'—well, I'm sorry, but that seems repulsive to me. I can't imagine that Miss Penworth would wish to hear about it."

Her temper was beginning to rise in spite of her efforts to control it. "You mustn't read things out of context or they won't make any sense. I assure you that Miss Penworth—"

"I think Miss Penworth will assume that I'm a complete idiot if I come jabbering away at her with all this poetry nonsense."

"Nonsense! Nonsense indeed—why, I'll have you know that your grandfather—"

"But I'm not my grandfather and never will be."

"You have never spoken truer words." Glaring at that abruptly woebegone face, she was stricken by a sense of remorse.

"You're right, Grandmother. I ... I appreciate all you have tried to do for me." He shook his head, dropping his eyes. "I suppose it's all been for nothing. I might as well go."

"No." She crossed over to him with an agility that belied her years, and taking one of his arms in hers, hugged it comfortingly. "We were all made differently. That's as it should be. We will find another way for you to woo Miss Penworth."

He looked at her dubiously.

"Perhaps you are better off not using the poetry. Your own words would suffice. You could tell her that her eyes are like stars—"

He shook his head.

"That her aspect is like the sun—"

He shook his head again.

"That—"

"No, Grandmother." He spoke firmly. "I have no gift for making pretty speeches and I will only look foolish if I try."

She clung to his arm silently. So this was it, then. She had done her best. He patted her arm. "I am sorry."

"There must be no more of this leaving non-sense," she said mechanically. "I have invited you for Christmas and I intend for you to stay."

"Whatever you say." He leaned over to kiss the top of her head gently. He would have released himself and left the room, but she clutched him with a sudden thought.

"Wait."

He looked at her with no real hope.

She was apparently studying the design of the marquetry in the floor. He paused for a moment and then prompted her. "You were going to say?"

"Hush!" With an effort, she had managed to produce deep creases between the fine brows of that cherubic countenance, an expression which only the initiated could recognize as a scowl of concentration. "Yes, I think that might work . . . I see no reason why . . ." she was muttering to her-self when she broke off abruptly and turned delighted eyes upon him. "I have it," she announced.

He would have instantly demanded what she meant, but she indicated the sofa. As soon as he had helped her onto it, he seated himself beside her and looked at her questioningly. She patted his hand reassuringly.

"You were the one who gave me the idea," she said, assigning credit where it was due. "You yourself said that you were not one to make pretty speeches—and you aren't, of course. I should have seen that sooner."

He cleared his throat. "I agree with you, but this still leaves me with nothing to say to Miss Penworth."

Her eyes twinkled. "That's the beauty of it—you won't have to say anything."

He frowned. "Do you mean you are going to pretend that I am dumb?"

"Of course not!" she exclaimed testily. "What a buffle-headed notion." Before he could spring to his own defense, she added. "No, what I meant is that you will *hardly* have to speak to her. The role you will play is perfectly suited to your temperament."

"The role I will play—?" he began suspiciously.

"Yes. I don't know why it didn't occur to me before. I suppose I simply haven't had enough mental exercise of late."

He was abruptly befogged in a cloud of misgivings. "Grandmother, this scheme of yours—"

"It will serve admirably to conceal your weaknesses, and—"

"But—"

"Please, how often must I ask you not to interrupt me while I am speaking?" Seeing him silenced, she continued, "Since you are twenty-four, that would make Miss Penworth—let me think—yes, nineteen. Yes, I can see no flaw in my plan."

It was with a sense of dread that he asked her, "Grandmother, exactly what is your plan?"

She hesitated for a moment, absentmindedly fingering the stiff black silk of her skirt, before beginning slowly, "It is true that a smooth-tongued suitor who is able to pay a gel flowery compliments with ease will always make himself popular. There is one other type of gentleman, however, that a young gel almost never can resist."

He kept quiet as she paused, and then resumed. "I suppose it is just something in their natures. They are invariably intrigued by a silent but masterful man. Perhaps it is because they do not know what he is thinking. And since you are already rumored to be a female-hater, it must prove simply irresistible." She glanced at the dark and handsome countenance beside her. "Particularly given your obvious attractions."

"Do you really think so?" he asked eagerly. His face fell. "I don't know if I could pretend to be that sort of person, though."

The corner of her mouth rose slightly. "I should think it would be a great deal easier for you than what we attempted earlier—after all, you're already silent."

His brows drew together in a frown. She anticipated his objections. "You will not have this sort of opportunity again," she said gently. "What sacrifice would you make to win Miss Penworth?"

"Anything." He spoke without thinking, and realized suddenly that he'd already given her his answer. She smiled serenely at him, but there was a dangerous sparkle in her eyes. He abruptly remembered his grandfather's warnings about her madcap schemes and felt a chill of fear.

"That's a good boy," she said, patting his hand again.

*   *   *

She was in favor of beginning her new instruction immediately, pointing out that they had already wasted a good deal of time, but Denzil was firm. He was already suffering from mental fatigue, and besides, it was nearly time to change for dinner.

She submitted rather rapidly, which surprised Denzil somewhat. Perhaps she was learning not to treat him like a child, after all. It was with the happy sensation of having won an unexpected victory that he changed into the required dark tailcoat, white satin vest, and pantaloons. The marchioness insisted upon observing the formalities, even though they were by themselves.

He went downstairs in the same chipper mood, which was buoyed even further by the delectable smells wafting from the kitchen. For once, he felt that he would be able to do justice to the culinary masterpieces that awaited.

It wasn't until he had already finished the *potage de poissons à la russe* as well as the *turbot à l'anglaise* and was beginning upon the *rond de veau a la royale* that the misgivings began. He glanced across the table at his grandmother, but she was applying herself serenely to her veal. She never had been one to subscribe to what she termed "the idiotish notion" that females should display indifference to their food.

He made an effort to ignore his forebodings and to concentrate upon his meal instead, but it was too late. His conscience had awakened and his appetite could not help but be affected.

It had been one thing to try to learn to tell Amabel the things that truly were in his heart. It was quite another to assume a false role, to pretend to be someone else in order to make her fall in love with him. Surely only a cad would sink so low?

By the end of the meal he had resolved to speak to his grandmother immediately. She forestalled him by excusing herself and saying that she had a letter to write. He was left to wrestle with his own doubts for the rest of the evening.

After spending a troubled night, he rose with the intention of confronting his grandmother and telling her that he wouldn't fall in with her little scheme. She had already breakfasted by the time he came downstairs, so he found her in the morning room, working on her embroidery again. She gave him a sunny smile as he entered the room, and put down her work thankfully.

"I shall be glad when winter is over and I am able to occupy myself outdoors once again. I can't tell you how I detest needlework! There was a time when the rawest weather wouldn't deter me, although now these old bones . . . But how are you this morning, my dear? Ready to begin?"

He stiffened at the phrase which had greeted him every day since his arrival. It was clear that the inquiry about his health was only a formality, as his grandmother never waited for a response. The irritation he felt only served to strengthen his determination.

"No, my lady," he said coldly. "I have decided that I will not participate in this charade. I will not marry a lady who cannot love me for myself."

"Tush!" she exclaimed mildly, seemingly not at all offended. "How can she love you for yourself if you never exchange a word with her?"

His face darkened slightly. "It is all this *pretense* that I object to—and I resent the assumption that she is so shallow she can only be interested in someone who behaves like a character out of a novel. If appearances are all that matter to her, then I would be—"

She gave an amused sniff. "Appearances! What do you gentlemen know of appearances! Would you have fallen in love with her if you had only seen her with her hair uncurled, in a drab and unfashionable gown, and—"

He began to protest hotly, but she waved a negligent hand at him. "Oh, I know that you think you would, but the truth of the matter is . . . Well, it is useless to argue about it after all. Let me assure you, from my years of observing the traffic between the sexes, that no romance would ever blossom without some attention to appearances."

He scowled at her. "Be that as it may, I am not a child and I know my own mind. I have no intention of going along with your plan, and you can't make me!" It struck him rather forcibly as he spoke that he might have chosen a more fortunate turn of phrase, and he wished that he hadn't felt it necessary to thump his fist on the little pie-crust table for emphasis.

The smile had vanished from her face. She was regarding him with the same severity she had when, as a ten-year-old, he had smashed her favorite Chinese vase during an impromptu game of indoor cricket. "Well," she remarked dryly, "I never had any intention of doing so—in fact, any efforts I made would be useless without your full cooperation." She lifted her chin slightly. "I am sorry to hear that you have such a poor opinion of me—as if I should wish to practice deception upon an innocent young girl, and my own goddaughter at that! No, I merely hoped that I might give you the means—"

"Grandmother—"

She was not about to show him any mercy. "—to become acquainted so that, in time, you might come to know each other and *possibly* form a sincere attachment. I was under the impression that you lacked a way to do so yourself, but of course—"

"No, Grandmother, you—"

"—you are free to leave immediately. As I no longer have your interests to consider, I shall go ahead and invite Lord Hereward. The Penworths tell me that he is constantly in her train, and naturally they would find it a most acceptable match."

At the mention of this rival, a charming and wealthy earl some ten years senior to himself, Denzil could feel his last bit of resistance crumble. On the last occasion that he had seen Amabel, the earl had remained by her side for most of the evening. He could picture her now, that lovely face upturned attentively to the earl's, as her bewitching laugh floated over. "You needn't do that, Grandmother. I am sorry that I said what I did. I am staying."

She looked keenly at him, and only the late marquess would have been able to distinguish the remote twinkle in her eyes as she spoke. "You are certain, then? It would be rather embarrassing if you backed out just before their arrival and left me with no means of entertaining Miss Penworth."

"I will stay for the duration, I promise you," he said ponderously. He hesitated for a moment, then looked up to meet her eyes diffidently. "You promise that I shall have to play this role for only a little while? That I may be myself as soon as we begin to be acquainted?"

Her face softened as she gazed at him. "That has been all I ever hoped for . . ." She paused for a moment, then began again. "You have so many wonderful qualities, my dear. Any gel would fall in love with you in a minute. All you have to do is to believe that." She shook her head gently.

"You must also give Miss Penworth credit. A young lady who is perceptive is able to look beneath the surface to see the man she loves."

He found her words enigmatic, but knew it was useless to ask for any explanation. "Very well," he said resignedly. "I suppose we might as well get started, then."

Her eyebrows shot upward and she did not bother to conceal her smile. "Your enthusiasm overwhelms me," she commented wryly.

If he had imagined that his conscience had been troubled before, he was to discover, as his lessons began, that he had only scratched the surface. Once her triumph was assured, his grandmother had fallen silent for a few moments, her face screwed up in thought, though she subsequently informed him that she was merely deciding where to begin. "It is such a very simple thing for you to learn, after all. I am sure that you will have the knack of it in no time."

He was about to express his own reservations when she said abruptly, "Ah, well. Pretend that I am Miss Penworth and ask me to go driving with you."

His dismay was obvious. "But, Grandmother, we're not going through all that again. You know that I can't manufacture pretty compliments as—"

"Hush! Stop acting as if you're pigeon-witted, for I know you're not. Simply pretend that you are asking the young lady out for a drive, nothing more than that."

"But isn't it rather cold for—?"

"Imbecile!" He halted his words instantly, dreading worse epithets. She glared at him in some exasperation. "Hmph. I suppose it is not your fault, after all. I think it would be best if you

left the room and returned to discover me here—
it will give you a fresh start."

This, to Denzil's way of thinking, seemed to be
going to extreme lengths, but then it was hardly
any more ridiculous than all the poetry he'd mem-
orized. With a sigh, he obediently rose and exited.
Once outside the door, he straightened himself,
cleared his throat, and reentered the room.

"My dear Miss Penworth," he exclaimed, con-
gratulating himself for this touch of realism.

"Yes," said his grandmother, looking up.

He could feel his confidence beginning to ebb.
"I was wondering . . . that is, if you're not doing
anything else . . . I would be most obliged to you
. . . if you would wish to . . . that is, I should be
honored if you would care to take a drive with
me."

"When?" she said flatly.

He had reddened and was beginning to perspire.
He fingered his collar unconsciously, as if trying
to get more air. "Whenever . . . that is . . . I had
thought that we might go this afternoon. Of
course, if it is not convenient for you, I shall
understand. I daresay that you may already have
some other plans, given—"

"Stop!" The marchioness's face was drawn up
in a grimace, her hands covering her ears. "I cannot listen to this any longer. You've hardly given
the poor gel any option but to refuse you. Sit down
and I will show you how the thing should be
done."

With that she rose and swept from the room in
a rustle of stiff black silk, returning seconds later
and executing a commendable bow. "Miss Penworth. I am going for a drive and I should be honored by your company. The carriage will be ready
in forty-five minutes." She bowed again, not at all

creakily, he thought. She then turned on her heel and stalked magnificently to the door. He gaped after her.

"You observe my method? The chit wasn't given a chance to say no." She recrossed the room and seated herself once more. "Now, you try it, and please close your mouth. You look quite idiotic with your jaw hanging open in that way."

He was too taken aback by her performance to resent her tone. "I should try that? But what if she doesn't wish to go for a drive with me?"

Using all her fortitude, she prevented the sigh which was rising within her from escaping. "That is *her* problem, not yours. Now, go."

Incredulously, he did as she asked. Upon his entrance, he tried to duplicate her words as exactly as possible. It would have been far too sanguine to assume that she would be pleased with the result, nor was she, but there was a certain gleam in her eyes that suggested he might have done worse. She directed him to repeat his words with more assurance this time.

By the end of half an hour's work she declared that his performance could hardly be bettered and that he showed an aptitude for the role that was quite startling. "At this rate," she declared confidently, "we shall have you readied before their arrival without any difficulty. I might even venture to guarantee that nothing now will prevent my campaign from proceeding as planned and that you will receive a positive response to your proposal on Valentine's Day."

"My what!"

She had allowed herself to be carried away by her enthusiasm and so had made the unforgivable mistake of saying too much too soon. She quickly tried to repair the damage. "If you should wish to do it then, of course. I merely had thought that it would be an excellent opportunity—young girls being as romantic as they are—but of course yours would be the final decision . . ."

"Grandmother . . ." he began warningly.

She patted his arm reassuringly. "It all will be in your hands, of course. I only mean to give you the help you will need to make your initial acquaintance with Miss Penworth. Everything will be up to you after that. Naturally I would be willing to help with advice whenever you should need it, but you will be the one to decide whether or not to act upon my suggestions."

There was nothing that he could object to in these words, so he stared at her silently, gazing into that blandly smiling countenance with a sinking heart. He told himself that now, for the first time, he knew what it was to be truly uneasy.

His misgivings were not to be allayed during the ensuing weeks, though they passed quickly. He dutifully assisted his grandmother in observing the rituals of Christmas—helping to hang the mistletoe bough, overseeing the preparation of the Yule log, receiving the wassailers with hospitality. He was courteous to the guests who came to share the traditional joint of beef and plum pudding, though even the least observant of the visitors could not fail to notice that his mind was elsewhere. Boxing Day passed, and New Year's Eve, and suddenly it was January.

The knowledge that his instructress had pronounced him ready to commence his courtship in no way relieved his apprehensions. In fact the very aptitude of which she had boasted had begun to trouble him. He did not fear that he would forget his lessons upon Amabel's arrival: his worry was that he had learned them too well. He had fallen into the habit of acting his part all the time. It had carried him through the Christmas party quite easily, though he was dismayed to learn later from his grandmother that the two young ladies present had showed signs of being smitten with him. If he depended on his role so greatly already, wasn't it unlikely that he should find the courage to desert it after Miss Penworth's arrival? And such being the case, how was Amabel ever to come to know his own character? He could not give credence to his grandmother's reassurances. Amabel would have to be possessed of supernormal powers to see through the facade. His situation had begun to seem more hopeless than when he had embarked upon this masquerade. He would have given up and gone home in despair, but he had promised the marchioness that he would stay. He was tormented by dreams of Amabel, with her blue eyes smiling up at him beguilingly, or of her waltzing off in the arms of Lord Hereward, with never a backward glance for himself. He would awaken with his heart pounding, and at such times his baser side whispered that he would be justified in practicing a little deception upon Miss Penworth in order to win her hand. He told himself that he was worrying unnecessarily, that surely his grandmother must be right. As he began to feel comfortable with Amabel, he naturally must reveal his true nature.

These were the sorts of arguments with which he comforted himself a few days later on the snowy afternoon when the Penworths' traveling carriage appeared in their drive. He had taken to sitting by the front windows with a book, in this case, *The Sportsman's Directory*. He was reading, with no real interest, what to do "if a dog is seized with a Hovering in the Lights," when, glancing up, he saw the carriage. Remembering his grandmother's dictums, he rose and carefully checked his appearance, then went to her room to quietly inform her of the visitors' imminent arrival. He had slipped into his part almost without thinking, and the marchioness regarded him with a look of approbation.

"You'll do very well," she remarked reassuringly. "I shall want to change my gown before I see them, so if you would, please go downstairs and greet them for me."

Two months ago, such a command would have terrified him into fleeing the house. Now he simply made his way downstairs silently, stoically.

All his training had not prepared him for his first sight of Miss Penworth, however. She was the first to enter, as she swirled impetuously past the butler and into the room. She was a beautiful picture in a Russian wrapping-cloak over a heavily braided carriage dress of dark blue wool, with a fashionable high-crowned silk bonnet of the same shade resting atop her golden curls.

"Godmama! Oh, Godmama!" she called, smiling.

Then she happened to glance up the staircase and, seeing Denzil, halted abruptly. Their eyes locked together and for a moment he thought that his heart would stop. He drank in every detail of her face, from the full, slightly parted lips to the candid eyes which were the color of the sky on a cloudless spring day. She had the freshness of a flower which has unexpectedly pushed its way up through the snow, and suddenly his conscience began to sound anew. She clearly was an angel, and how could he have thought of deluding her?

In the next instant the clamorings of his conscience were to stop in an equally abrupt manner.

"Here, Belle, I must protest this treatment—you're making me look the shabbiest sort of escort." The deep masculine voice, the jocular tone, and particularly the casual nickname he used to refer to Miss Penworth all caused Denzil's spine to stiffen even before Lord Hereward appeared in the doorway. The earl was not above the average height and his coloring was undistinguished, but his well-dressed figure boasted a powerful muscularity and the charm fairly exploded from those sparkling gray eyes, crinkled now in amusement. Amabel seemed to be recalled from her trance by this arrival. She turned to her suitor, laughing.

"Oh, Herry, how ridiculous you are! I am just looking for Godmama, but I suppose that she is still upstairs." She looked back at Denzil, a question in her eyes.

Aware once again of appearances, he now proceeded down the rest of the staircase. "She sent me down to bid you all welcome. She will be here herself in a moment. I am her grandson, Denzil Huntingford."

To his sorrow, though not to his surprise, Miss Penworth apparently did not remember having met him before. "I am pleased to make your acquaintance," she said formally, while her eyes searched the floor above him for a glimpse of her godmother. "And this is Lord Hereward, who has been kind enough to escort us here."

The latter, who had been regarding Denzil through his quizzing glass, now took his hand and shook it heartily. "I've met Mr. Huntingford before, my dear. He's one of that group which has proposed that child labor be regulated. You've no idea of the abuses, intolerable! If the bill comes to the House of Lords, you may be assured that I will support it, Huntingford.''

Drat the man—did he have to be quite so likable? "It's not a bill yet, my lord, and I fear that the real fight will be in the House of Commons, though I appreciate your support, of course," Denzil was replying rather mechanically when the two senior Penworths entered.

The plump, though still attractive lady who was obviously Amabel's mother brightened as she caught sight of Denzil. "You must be Denzil Huntingford," she said, stepping forward to take him by the hands. "Why, I haven't seen you since you were twelve years old, I think! I am Clara Penworth—your mother was my dearest friend." She peered up at him intently. "You haven't much of a look of her, I think—except for your eyes. Ah, yes, they are precisely like my dear Maria's." There was a little catch in her voice as she spoke, and her husband, a burly individual with craggy, good-humored features, stepped up to join her.

"There, now, that's enough of that, my dear. Don't go on so or you'll start sniveling and embarrass the poor lad more than you have already. Sir Roger Penworth, at your service," he continued, addressing the latter part of his speech to Denzil and gripping him firmly by the hand. "I think we've met at Brooks's, haven't we, Huntingford?"

Denzil had time to do no more than nod in reply when a cry from Amabel interrupted the conversation. "Godmama!"

"My dear!" The marchioness was descending the stairs regally. "How are you all, my dears? And, Lord Hereward, what a pleasant surprise! How is your delightful mother?"

The usual sorts of greetings were exchanged,

though Denzil did not notice that when his grandmother pressed her cheek against Amabel's, she
also whispered something in her ear. As soon as
the bustle had died down a bit, the marchioness
directed a servant to show the guests up to their
rooms so that they might refresh themselves after
their long journey. Although her parents accepted
the offer gratefully, Amabel declared that she was
not in the least tired and that she meant to remain
and visit with her godmother. The marchioness
took her hand and patted it, saying, "Then perhaps you would care to join me in the drawing
room for tea. Lord Hereward, your presence is
required also, for I know that you can tell me all
the latest *on-dits.*"

Personally, Denzil would have preferred that his
grandmother demand to know what Lord Hereward was doing there uninvited and show him the
door, but he was to appreciate the cleverness of
Lady Witley's strategy in a few moments. While
she kept the amiable earl engaged in conversation,
Denzil was free to claim Miss Penworth's entire
attention.

His shyness would probably still have prevented
him from speaking, but fortunately Miss Penworth
was at no such loss. She chatted easily about what
an impressive and intriguing structure the castle
was and what a length of time had passed since
she last visited it. It was almost easy for Denzil to
say that he would show her around it after breakfast the next morning. With a sense of unreality,
he heard her demure assent and realized that, for
better or worse, the scheme was launched at last.

Denzil was startled when his grandmother rang
for the tea tray to be withdrawn. It seemed that
he had been in conversation with Miss Penworth
for only moments instead of well over an hour. To

Denzil's great relief, as they all rose Lord Hereward regretfully declined the marchioness's invitation to remain for dinner.

". . . for I told Lord Gonville that I should arrive in time for dinner tonight, and I greatly fear that I shall be late already." Here he turned a winning smile at Miss Penworth. "But how could I turn down an opportunity to escort such beauty, particularly when my journey lay nearby?"

She returned his smile, and Denzil felt a stab of pain. "It was most kind of you to do so, although your fears about the weather happily proved unfounded. I hope that you will be warm enough on your way over to the Hall."

"Goodness, did you *ride* all the way here?" inquired the marchioness.

"Actually, no. I meant to, but the wind was simply too brisk when we started out this morning. I found myself forced to take shelter in the Penworths' carriage instead."

"And where is your carriage, then?" asked Denzil, trying not to betray his ire.

"Oh, I sent it on to the Hall with my man inside—it probably arrived ages ago. I can't say that I regret it, though. It was delightful to spend those hours in such charming company."

An irrepressible laugh escaped Amabel. "Oh, Herry, you are the most shameless flatterer."

"Never!" he was beginning in protest, but the marchioness cut him off.

"Will you be staying with Lord Gonville for some time, then? We should so like to see you again."

The gray eyes rested appreciatively on Amabel. "I will be staying for . . . for some weeks, I imagine. My duty should rightfully call me to London in February, but then, I am a sad, light-minded fellow, not at all like Mr. Huntingford here."

"Well, in that case we will certainly expect you and Lord Gonville to join us for dinner while you are here. And if you are going to be here in February, you must be sure to come to our Valentine's Day ball. I mean to have half of the county there."

"A Valentine's Day ball—what a marvelous notion. Nothing could prevent me from attending it."

Denzil felt sick to his stomach at the thought of having to compete with Lord Hereward for Amabel's attentions. Why on earth did his grandmother have to be so hospitable? It would mean that all their efforts had been for naught. He saw the exchange of smiles between Lord Hereward and Amabel and knew utter misery.

Perhaps the marchioness was able to read something of his emotions in his face, for she said, "Please let me have my carriage brought around for you, Lord Hereward. I am afraid that with the sun dropping, it will soon be quite bitter."

His mind now recalled to the thought of departure, he shook his head. "No, thank you, Lady Witley, it is but a short ride, after all. I should be there well within the hour." Accordingly, he replaced his coat and hat and took his leave of them, asking Miss Penworth to remember him to her parents.

"A most delightful gentleman, is he not?" remarked the marchioness after the door had closed behind that powerful figure. Denzil wished she would keep her mouth shut. Neither did Amabel's answer reassure him.

She gave a light laugh. "He certainly is most amusing. I never need fear that a party will be *dull* if he is present."

Denzil came to himself just in time to prevent a sigh from escaping. It would hardly fit in with the picture he was trying to present of himself as a strong-and-silent man.

He had no difficulty recapturing the role at dinner, for all he could do was to gaze helplessly and speechlessly at the vision of loveliness opposite him. It was fortunate the marchioness had decided to dine *en famille* tonight, so that at least there was no one else to observe his stupefaction.

His dinner partner, Lady Penworth, appeared entirely indifferent to his inattention. She was one of those women with the happy ability to maintain a conversation with no assistance whatsoever. All that Denzil had to do was to nod every now and then or to make some sort of noise to assure her of his continued presence. She chatted on obliviously, as she shared with him anecdotes about his mother in her salad days.

It was a subject that normally would have interested him, but at the moment he had eyes and ears for no one but Amabel. He still hardly could believe that he was in such proximity to her. Although he knew it was rude to stare, he could not prevent his gaze from returning again and again to her. She was beautiful, that was certain, but it was her liveliness that made her so enchanting, he thought as she addressed a teasing remark to her godmother. She turned to her father at that moment, and her eyes happened to intercept Denzil's. Again, it seemed that time stopped and that everyone else in the room had vanished. He did not know if he were breathing or not, but somehow the air about him seemed to become thicker. It was over in an instant, as she politely turned her gaze upon her father in response to a question. Denzil sat stunned in his chair. Had he dreamt that look? Or was it truly possible that something so deep could pass, without words, between two people in a matter of seconds?

To him it seemed that the rest of the evening went by swiftly, covered as it was by a rosy sort of glow. Still tired from their journey, the Penworths decided to retire promptly, a suggestion which his grandmother welcomed. ". . . for I keep very early hours myself—I have become quite a countrywoman now, and I am not quite as young as I once was."

"Oh, Godmama." Amabel leaned down to give her a peck on the cheek before going upstairs. "Good night." She smiled shyly at Denzil. He managed to nod at her.

All his current happiness had not made him forget his grandmother's transgressions. He turned quickly to her.

"What is it, Denzil?" she asked wearily.

"I want to know what you meant by inviting Hereward to come here and dangle after Miss Penworth. I thought you meant to help *my* courtship!"

Her voice was grave, but there was a light far back in her eyes. "I told you that I meant for you and Miss Penworth to come to know each other. Surely you would not wish to marry her and have her discover later that she preferred Lord Hereward?"

He flushed. "You needn't mock me."

"I am sorry." Her features relaxed into a smile. "I could hardly forbid him from my house, after all."

He was struggling to express his fears. "But . . . but, dash it, the fellow's much too *charming*—and it's clear that Ama . . . Miss Penworth has a partiality for him."

She smiled again, but decided to take pity on him. "Yes, she does, as do we all, but had you considered that the adjective 'amusing' would not be the most felicitous choice to apply to someone you were considering as a future spouse?" She saw that her words had taken effect, so now she rose. She patted his cheek. "For my part, I think we have made a most promising start." She left him thoughtfully silent behind her.

He could not know that when she made her way upstairs and opened the door to her room, she encountered a visitor sitting disconsolately in a gilt-and-embroidered chair. "Amabel!"

"Oh, Godmama, I am sorry, but I simply could not wait to speak with you."

Denzil prided himself on having adjusted well to country hours, so it was still early by the time he had risen and dressed himself and made his way downstairs. He was not surprised to see the marchioness there before him, but he was startled to see Amabel seated beside her, chatting animatedly. To have breakfasted alone with the object of his affection would have been an ordeal for one still so painfully shy, but it was quite another matter to do so under the benevolent eyes of his grandmother.

As before, Amabel proved herself equal to holding up more than her end of the conversation, and Denzil again was able to relax. There was no difficulty in slipping into his role, indeed he began to feel as if he'd been doing it his whole life. As they finished their meal, however, he could feel his tension begin to mount. For the first time, he would be alone with Amabel. His throat constricted at the thought. He knew that he wouldn't be able to get a word out when they were together. She would probably think him a complete dolt!

With no real enthusiasm, he was pushing the remains of his eggs about on his plate when the marchioness spoke. "You children needn't remain here to keep me company. I know that Denzil has promised you a tour of the castle, so off you go. I have some business to take care of myself."

He looked up at Lady Witley, the despair written in his eyes. She gave him a calm and steady look. "If it is not too inclement, you might show Miss Penworth the tower—all our visitors seem to enjoy it."

"At last! As I recall, you never would let us in it when we were children. You were afraid that we might fall."

The marchioness turned her gaze away from Denzil and back to Amabel. "Denzil knows it well. He will take good care of you."

Thus forced, Denzil had no choice but to rise. He shot his grandmother another anxious glance, but she merely nodded at him. He must remember what they had practiced. "Allow me, Miss Penworth," he said, drawing back her chair. "If we are to visit the tower, you will need a wrap, for it is cold."

The marchioness interrupted. "If Amabel has no objection, she may use my old cloak. I learned to keep it always by me during the first months of my marriage. Despite all our modern contrivances, the castle is still a dreadfully drafty place."

Amabel took the cloak from her readily, then turned to Denzil. He helped her on with it, then offered her his arm. As she laid hers upon it, his heart began to pound. It was extraordinary that such a commonplace thing could have such an effect. His only hope now was to cling to the role he had rehearsed. He set off silently as his grand-mother called, "Enjoy yourselves, children."

For a few moments he feared that this expedition would prove to be the realization of his worst nightmare, as, despite his efforts, he could not produce a word. Fortunately, after they reached the Great Hall, Amabel gave a sigh and began.

"I can't tell you how relaxing it is not to be a member of a large party. It seems one never has a moment alone or unplanned. I am so glad that Godmama did not invite other visitors." She laughed suddenly. "Oh, dear, how selfish and odious I sound—just like the young ladies who are 'bored' with entertainments before their first Season is half-over."

"You could never sound odious. I, too, am glad that there are no other visitors." The words coming out of his own mouth took him by surprise, as did the low, feeling tone in which he uttered them. Such a moment might well have purchased them another fifteen minutes of silence, but fortunately Amabel did not seem at all conscious.

Lit only by the weak rays of winter that struggled in through the narrow vertical windows, the Hall seemed quite gloomy to Denzil, an effect which was enhanced by its tomblike chill. But Amabel was all admiration. She exclaimed over the flagged floor, the timbered ceiling, and the massive chimneypiece. She seemed to delight in the ancient tapestries on the wall and the enormous banquet table, and asked, "Does the marchioness ever use this room?"

"Yes." He paused, and decided he might amplify the statement. "She held her Christmas celebrations here, as a matter of fact."

From this simple beginning, it seemed almost natural that she should inquire about the details of their holiday and the role that he had played in the traditional festivities. The conversation flowed so easily that he hardly noticed as, lost in their own world, they passed through a half-dozen passages. It was almost inevitable that they then should proceed from discussing the marchioness's care of her tenants to the topic of Denzil's own home, Dore, and that eventually this direction should lead them to the subject of the need for reform. Miss Penworth was soon discovered to have her sympathies in the right place, and so all constraint was forgotten. It was at the end of ten minutes' tirade that he realized he had entirely forgotten his part, and so he retreated again into silence. If such sudden reticence seemed odd to Miss Penworth, she affected not to notice it.

They were in the yellow drawing room when her hand abruptly tightened on his arm. He looked down at her questioningly. "Oh, I don't care about seeing the portrait gallery," she said. "Please, may we go to the tower now? I have been wanting to ever since Godmama said that we could."

Meeting those frank blue eyes just inches from his own caused an electric shock to go through him. He couldn't have replied even if he'd thought of anything to say. So instead he merely lifted his chin, turned his face, and they proceeded in the direction of the tower.

The passageway that led to the tower was bitterly cold, and as they approached it, they were hit by a draft that ruffled Denzil's hair and sent the tails of his coat flying. Miss Penworth regarded him with some concern. "It *is* cold. Shall we go back and get your greatcoat?"

He shook his head. "It won't take us long to climb it." With an effort he swung open the heavy oak door, and they were in the tower itself.

She involuntarily glanced at the remains of the structure above them, through which the gray sky could be clearly seen. "What a pity it was damaged. I suppose it was Cromwell."

He nodded and led her to the bottom of the stairs that circled up inside the outer walls of the shell. The absence of inner walls made their climb a treacherous prospect, as there would be nothing to stand between them and a sheer drop to the ground.

She put a tentative foot on the first stone step. "I wonder why they never rebuilt it?"

"Hadn't much use for it, I suppose."

"Yes, and then even with the Restoration, it took quite some time for many families to repair their fortunes. What a difficult time it must have been! Still, I suppose that it was fortunate that the entire castle wasn't ruined."

He decided it would be permissible to attempt a mild joke. "It was lucky that Cromwell's men hadn't more gunpowder."

He succeeded in winning one of her delightful laughs with this sally, and it warmed him far more than any greatcoat could have done. In fact his happiness was such that he failed to register that they were climbing too rapidly and not paying enough attention to their footing on the damaged stone steps. Since the remains of the stairs were far too narrow to permit more than one person at a time, he followed behind her, simply intent on keeping up with his fair visitor.

"I cannot wait to see the view at the top—I am sure it is magnificent. We *can* go all the way to the top, can't we?"

He had begun to notice that the snow, although not recent, had left this section of the stairs damp. It was likely that they might encounter ice as they continued to climb. "Miss Penworth ..." he began, intending to warn her.

It was then that it happened. A pigeon, which had found a sheltered nook in the wall, was startled by their approach and flew out at Amabel with a great rush of wings, startling her. At that instant she was putting her foot upon the next, shadowed stair, which unfortunately was half-coated by ice. She let out a cry, her foot slipped, and she was falling backward. A moment later she was pressed against the wall, caught in arms of wiry strength, and both she and Denzil were gasping for breath.

It took several minutes for them to regain their equilibrium. When she did at last, she left that comforting grasp reluctantly, forced by her realization of the impropriety of lingering there.

"Are you all right?" Denzil asked hoarsely. His shortness of breath was caused by more than fright. His terror had been abruptly replaced by a sensation of bliss as he held her in his arms. He felt he might happily have done so forever.

"Y-yes." Her voice was shaking. "Thanks to you."

He still held her hand, and now he squeezed it gently. "Do you feel steady enough to go back down yet?"

She hesitated only for an instant, then nodded.

"I will go down first. You follow behind me. Keep one hand on the wall and the other upon my back for balance. Don't be afraid to take hold of the fabric. Tell me if you need to stop and rest." He studied that drooping figure narrowly. "Are you ready?"

She nodded, and he began slowly down, taking one step at a time. He could feel the tentative hand on his back, and he would wait until she had descended to go down the next step. Once or twice her hand tightened on his back as her foot met a gap or a loose stone, and he could hear her sharp intake of breath. He would stop immediately, turn to take her hand, and pat it reassuringly. "Do not worry. I will not let anything happen to you." After he was certain that she was calmer, he would start down again, and with such slow but sure progress they eventually reached the bottom of the stairs. Amabel was trembling. He held her hands in his in order to provide her with some much-needed support.

"Y-you saved my life. I don't know how I—"

"It was nothing. Let me take you back to the drawing room. You will feel better after a cup of tea."

She nodded, and they proceeded on their way. She was leaning heavily on his arm, and it occurred to him that the shock had taken a greater toll on her than he had previously suspected. "Perhaps you had better lie down in your chamber instead."

She offered no protest, and he was escorting her to the great staircase when they met the Penworths coming down. Denzil gave them a brief summary of the incident. Not attempting to mask their concern, they thanked Denzil briefly, and supporting their daughter on either side, began to help her to her chamber.

If Denzil thought that he would hear no more about the episode, he was soon to discover that he was mistaken. There was hardly another topic permitted during dinner, although the marchioness, reading his discomfort in his face, made valiant attempts to turn the subject. The Penworths were embarrassingly grateful to him and insisted on praising his heroism in a way most distasteful to him. The most painful aspect of it, though, was the glowing look he encountered whenever he met Amabel's eyes. She apparently had cast him in the same sort of epic role as had her parents, and it made him feel the lowest worm on earth. It was heavily ironic that he should be the recipient of such admiring glances from the object of his affections when their relationship was based entirely upon deceit, but he was far from deriving amusement from the situation. Instead, his heart grew heavier with every exclamation of thankfulness, and finding that all his protests and denials were disregarded, he at last fell into a gloomy silence. When he spoke privately with his grandmother in her chamber later, she remarked that he had enacted his role in a masterly way that evening.

". . . for if I'd been a young gel, I might have fallen in love with you myself this evening. The way that you ignored them when they were singing your praises to the skies! Nothing could have been more certain to convince her of the nobility of your character."

"Of the . . ." He was speechless for a second. "Well, it's certainly a pity, then, that I feel the most arrant rogue that ever lived."

"What nonsense!"

He shook his head as he paced across the carpet gloomily. "No, it's true. First, I deceive her as to my true character. Then, because she suffers a slight mishap, Sir Roger and Lady Penworth act as if I had saved her from the jaws of a lion. It's clear that any credit I have with her is false."

She directed a shrewd look at him. "You did not arrange for Miss Penworth to slip so that you could catch her—in fact, according to your own account, you were about to prevent such an event occurring. Don't you consider that you acted bravely in the circumstances?"

He shrugged, then continued his pacing. "I only did what anyone else would have done. If I'd had any real nobility of character, I'd have paid more attention. I'd have called a halt to the expedition before anything could happen." He ran a distracted hand through his curls. "All their gratitude makes me feel a scab about the deception. I can't imagine things coming to a worse pass."

Although she herself never would have been so vulgar as to shrug, she made a movement that suggested it. "My own feeling is that matters were arranging themselves quite nicely. I had thought to myself that there was not going to be any need to wait until Valentine's Day to ask Miss Penworth for her hand." He flushed and was about to speak, but she cut him off ruthlessly. "If this lionizing is all that bothers you, you needn't worry. Lords Gonville and Hereward are invited for dinner tomorrow night, and the Penworths can hardly carry on in front of them." She nodded at him. "As it is now, I am weary. Good night."

Beside himself with shock, he followed her implicit command and left the room. It wasn't until he was outside the door that he realized he might have upbraided her for her perfidy. To invite the two more eligible bachelors in the vicinity to come dangling after Amabel—and one already on terms of intimacy with her! He could not imagine what would have led his grandmother to disregard his sentiments in that fashion. Seething with annoyance, he completely forgot the plan he had been considering, that of going to Amabel in the morning and confessing his dishonesty.

* * *

Instead, after breakfasting alone, he went for a brisk gallop, ignoring the inclemency of the weather. The exercise served to take the edge off the worst of his anger. As little as he wished for the company of Lord Hereward and Lord Gonville, it was wise of his grandmother to invite them, in light of events yesterday. Since through his own deceit he had induced a state of hero worship in the girl, it would be almost criminal of him to keep her away from the rest of the world for a month. As his grandmother had said, if he asked for her hand now, he could not doubt that she would accept. She had less idea of his true nature than that of the man in the moon. Perhaps the society of others would open her eyes somewhat to his defects.

Although such reflections calmed him, they did not induce any happiness in him. Upon returning, and learning that Miss Penworth meant to keep to her chamber this morning, he reclaimed *The Sportsman's Directory* and sought his own room, though he had scant interest in such matters as "How to Take Woodcocks by Draw-nets, &c."

He was not to see her until dinnertime, her family feeling it best for her to rest and recover herself before the party that evening. It was a larger affair than Denzil had anticipated, including besides Lord Gonville and Lord Hereward, the Kennicott family, on whose girls he had made such an impression before, as well as the Bentons and some other neighbors.

Although he had found the Penworths' accolades mortifying the day before, it was as nothing compared to the agony of having the incident made generally known and having to endure the soulful gazes of the two Kennicott girls. It was fortunate that he was seated by Amabel instead of either of these damsels. She was far too well-bred to carry on about his exploit in company, and instead seemed content to resume their interrupted discussion on reform. He might gladly have conversed with her about it all evening, but he turned his attention to Mrs. Kennicott, on his other side, halfway through the meal, as politeness dictated. This lady, who had overheard part of his conversation with Amabel, could not help but remark in a disapproving way what an unusual young lady she was. To her dismay, Denzil agreed with her warmly, and he might have expanded on the statement had she not quickly turned the subject.

In an outright act of provocation, and certainly ignoring the claims of rank, the marchioness had seated Lord Hereward on Amabel's other side. Denzil could not help but notice that in contrast to his own quiet discussion with her, their conversation sparkled. Amabel was much more animated and her laugh rang out frequently, although she never permitted it to reach an unladylike volume. With Mrs. Kennicott in sole command of his ears, Denzil was not able to determine what it was that amused Amabel so. He was rather beginning to regret his own nobility in delaying his proposal and thinking that perhaps it might have been wise to have seized the opportunity yesterday.

Despite his pique, he found it impossible to preserve any sort of stiffness with Lord Hereward after the ladies left the gentlemen to their port. Hereward praised Denzil's rescue and expressed his frank envy in a manner calculated to disarm even the most rapacious enemy. When after one glass he winked at Denzil in a friendly way and suggested that they delay no longer in rejoining the beautiful Miss Penworth, Denzil felt a stab of jealousy, but found himself powerless to resent the earl. As they rose, he knew real despair. What hope was there of Amabel's holding out against Hereward's charm when he himself was unable to resist it?

The rest of the evening was to prove scarcely more happy for Denzil. It did not surprise him that the marchioness should call on the two Kennicott girls to perform after supper. The younger was an accomplished pianist and the elder had a superior voice. There was nothing unusual, either, in the fact that they chose to perform a series of ballads, all dealing with the topic of love. What did catch Denzil unawares, though, was the fact that the fair songstress chose to ignore the rest of the audience and to direct the entire song, feelingly, to him. It was impossible to tell whether everyone else were aware of the fact. Lord Hereward was certainly preoccupied with Amabel. In any event, Denzil himself felt humiliated. He sank lower and lower in his chair as the songs went on, in a futile attempt to become invisible. Just when he thought that he would have to spring from his chair and leave the room in order to escape Miss Kennicott's eloquent gaze, his grandmother came to his rescue.

As they were all applauding the end of one ballad, Lady Witley turned to Amabel. "You haven't honored us with a tune, Miss Penworth. I am sure that music must rank among your accomplishments."

Amabel laughingly denied having any particular skill. "I am sure that I could not fail to disappoint after hearing someone of Miss Kennicott's ability."

Lady Penworth could not bear to hear her offspring carry on in this vein. "Now, my dear, you know that you have a very pretty voice."

Lord Hereward joined in the argument. "I'll swear that she has, for she delighted us all in Shropshire. May I not persuade you, Miss Penworth? I'll venture to accompany you, if you wish."

She smiled at him and Denzil felt a stab of pain in his heart. "Now, how could I be so unhandsome as to turn down such a generous offer? I shall consent only if you are willing to join your voice to mine, however." She addressed the rest of the company. "Lord Hereward is a most gifted performer."

The marchioness took charge of the situation. "I am sure that we would all enjoy hearing both of you."

"Now you have put me on my mettle. I accept the risk of embarrassing myself, only in order to have the signal pleasure of joining my voice to yours."

"You should be ashamed of yourself, Herry," Amabel said severely, and Denzil thought that if she had been holding a fan she would have rapped the earl playfully on the arm with it.

Lord Hereward escorted her to the instrument, the Kennicotts having yielded their place. There was a brief minute's delay while the two held a whispered conference, which sickened Denzil. Surely it was unnecessary for those two heads to be quite so close? When they reached an agreement and Lord Hereward seated himself with a flourish, Denzil soon discovered that the worst suffering was yet to come.

Amabel seemed a capable, if not exceptional performer, her voice rendered pleasing by the unpretentiousness of her delivery. Lord Hereward, it was obvious, did indeed possess a fine voice, which moreover showed the benefits of training. It was not the quality of the music which nauseated Denzil so much as the looks which passed between the performers. There were little conspiratorial smiles and raisings of the eyebrows, and though he was trying not to let his jealousy run away with him, Denzil could swear that he saw the earl wink once at Amabel. It was all too apparent that they stood on terms of great intimacy, and Denzil, grinding his teeth, could not help torturing himself with the picture of all the countless duets they must have performed together while in Shropshire. It was no wonder that they had those odious nicknames for each other.

By the end of the evening, all his scruples had once again vanished. It was evident that the earl was capable of using every underhanded trick that he could in order to win Amabel. It was practically Denzil's duty to keep such an artless girl from falling prey to a hardened man of the world like Hereward. As much as he disliked any form of dishonesty, and as much pain as it would cause him personally, he must be willing to abandon his own code of ethics in order to safeguard this lovely innocent.

With such a resolve, he threw himself into his role. It enabled him to decline with tolerable composure Lord Gonville's invitation to join their shooting party on the morrow, instead of telling him that what he wished for least was more of Hereward's company.

Hounded by jealousy, Denzil would have been all too happy to confer with his grandmother after the party had broken up and ask her what steps he should take next in this masquerade. Owing to the lateness of the hour, it was not to be. He rose the next morning without a clear plan of attack in mind, but determined to continue his pursuit of Amabel. He could not have foreseen the surprising turn of events that lay before him.

The day had dawned bitterly cold, turning the half-melted snow into a glaze of slippery ice. Riding was out of the question, it was clear. He felt a stab of disappointment. A gallop always served to clear his mind, and he badly needed some sort of perspective on his problems.

He was not a man who could bear to be idle for long, and though the marchioness and Sir Roger and Lady Penworth seemed perfectly happy to sit in the yellow drawing room and chat about persons unknown to him, there was little sport for Denzil in such an activity. His ever-alert grandmother waved him from the room, bidding him go and find Amabel, ". . . for I am afraid that she must think us sadly dull. All my dependence is upon you to contrive a scheme for her entertainment." He needed no other push. If he meant to fix his interest with Amabel, there was not a moment to lose.

He found her toying on the pianoforte in a desultory fashion, her mind clearly elsewhere. She started at his footsteps, but quickly recovered herself and looked up at him with a smile.

"I am sorry to have interrupted you. I will go."

"No, please don't. I wasn't accomplishing much anyway. Last night reminded me that I should practice, but my wits are too scattered this morning."

He would have given a great deal to know the cause, but he contented himself with remarking how much he had enjoyed her performance.

"Thank you. Her . . . Lord Hereward is such an

accomplished musician that he never fails to make
his partner appear to perfection."

It would have provided an adequate cue for a
polished compliment, but without any at his command, Denzil instead remained silent for a
moment, grinding his teeth.

Amabel did not seem discomposed in the least,
for now she rose and extended a hand to him. "Do
you mean to continue our tour today? I should be
delighted if you would."

It was within Denzil's abilities to murmur an
assent, and so he did. He offered her his arm and
they began on their way.

The until-now-neglected portrait gallery was
accordingly visited, and to Denzil's relief, Amabel
did not try to trace a resemblance to him in any
of his ancestors. He was his father's child and had
little in common physically with the Witley
family.

He saw nothing odd in the fact that she made
little comment about the other rooms they passed
through, and it wasn't until they reached the
armory that it occurred to him that she was still
in a pensive mood.

"Are you tired? We could return downstairs."

She shook her head. "No, I'm sorry. I was only
thinking how pleasant it was not to be forced to
make conversation continually. That is one of my
favorite things about you—you dislike idle chatter
as much as I, and so we may be comfortable
together without speaking."

It was the most abruptly personal statement she
had ever made, and it caught him by surprise. At
first he was pleased by the compliment, but as he
reflected upon it he felt a renewed sense of guilt.
Whatever affection she felt was for the strong,

silent stranger he portrayed rather than for himself.

He hadn't long to think about it, though, for now, awakened, she began to take a real interest in the armory. "How well I remember this," she exclaimed. "Do you know—I am sure that it will sound nonsensical to you—but I used to be afraid to be in this room by myself when I was a child. I was frightened of the suits of armor and I thought they might come alive."

Her hand tightened around his unconsciously, and without thinking, he patted it. There was some faint stirring of memory he could not quite draw forth. Amabel's little shiver recalled him to the situation at hand and he abandoned the effort, towing her gently from the room. "We needn't remain here. There is still a great deal to see."

There was a preoccupied look upon her face, as if she were struggling with the same effort of recall as he had been. "Denzil ..." she began slowly. He did not even notice her use of his first name.

"There is somewhere I would like to go—if we can find it. Perhaps she has refurbished it now, but at one time there was a nursery."

The nursery. Denzil hadn't thought of it in years. "Well, we can try to find it," he remarked in his practical way, and leading her to the stairs, they began to climb.

When they reached the third story, it took many turnings down one passageway and another, and retracing their steps, until they found the room they had been seeking. They looked into each other's eyes with a superstitious fear.

"Go ahead," Denzil urged.

"Oh, but what if it has changed?"

Seeing that she truly was reluctant, he grasped

the handle and with some effort was able to open the door. She tiptoed in silently, with Denzil just behind her. A sigh escaped her, and Denzil himself drew in a sharp breath.

It was as if he had taken a step back through time and become a child again. The room was unaltered in any way. The same faded draperies were still tied carelessly back, as if someone expected the children to be returning with their nanny at any minute. The toys of generations were stacked along shelves, in boxes, and in corners. It was apparent that the room was cleaned at regular intervals, even if they were somewhat far apart. Neither Denzil nor Amabel had a regard for any lingering dust, however. She spied a favorite doll and with a glad cry crossed the room swiftly. Denzil noticed a familiar hobbyhorse in another corner. He made his way over to it and was reaching out his hand when he suddenly realized how ridiculous he must look.

Amabel had no such scruples. She had picked the doll up and was turning it lovingly in her hands. "How well I remember you! I called you Susan, I know. But how sadly uncurled your hair has become. And the gilt lace is coming unsewn from that elegant gown. You haven't had a little girl play with you in a while, have you?"

Denzil had glanced over at her as she was speaking, and suddenly he froze into place. There was something oddly familiar about the way she was kneeling with the doll and crooning to it. The memory that had been nagging at him came rushing to the surface. He could see her now, a skinny and not terribly lovely child, with pale, straight hair, her eyes too large for her thin face. "I remember you now!" he exclaimed, taking an involuntary step toward her.

She looked up at him, startled, and he realized that he might have chosen his words better. "I . . . er, that is, I had forgotten until just now that you had come here for a visit as a child."

She might properly have been incensed, but instead she merely rose, raising an eyebrow. "Had you? What do you remember?"

It was only natural that he should approach her in order to carry on the conversation better, and so he did, without giving the matter any thought. There was another memory traveling upward from the depths of his unconscious. "I . . . I remember you holding that doll and . . . and you used to sing to it too, I think, and . . ." A picture of the armory rose to his mind. "The armory! That was it—I found you there one day, didn't I? You had wandered in by accident, and when you noticed the armor, you were too frightened to move."

"I thought that if I held still, they would too."

"You told me that. And then everyone came and made the biggest stir. You'd have thought I'd done something remarkable by finding you."

Her face was grave except for a suspicious light far at the back of her eyes. "And you told me that I was a silly, stupid old girl and that you wanted nothing further to do with me."

He looked aghast at her. "I couldn't have said that!"

"You did. And you also said that even your dog was smart enough to come when it was called."

"You're not serious?"

She nodded.

Well, that was it. He had made certain that she knew of his defects, very certain indeed. All hope of a romance was surely at an end now. He grimaced with the anguish of it, closing his eyes briefly, but when he opened them, she was still standing there, quite close to him, regarding him steadily. "Amabel, I . . ." he began.

He had no idea what he had been going to say, for suddenly the strange sensation began. The air became too thick to breathe, he was aware of the rapid pounding of his heart, and of a warmth spreading over him. All he could see was Amabel's face, just inches away from his. "Amabel . . ."

In the next instant she was in his arms and he was kissing her. He had never known such happiness in his life. She was molded to him; she might have been made for him. It was all perfectly natural and all perfectly right. He abruptly realized what he was doing, and the shock enabled him to thrust her from his arms.

Amabel was becomingly flushed, and there was a dreamy expression in her eyes, but she did not appear otherwise discomposed.

"Amabel!" He could not for the life of him think of what to say.

"I love you."

What a cad he was, taking advantage of this lovely young girl. Now was the time, if ever, to tell her about his deception. "I . . . er, I love you too."

When he reflected upon it later, his actions seemed even more heinous than they had at the time. He had given this innocent an entirely false picture of his character. He had seized her during a moment of nostalgic weakness and done what no gentleman should do to a lady to whom he was not actually affianced. It was no wonder then that she had made the surprising declaration: she was doubtless giddy and could have no real idea of what she had said. Still, it was obvious that her affections were seriously engaged, and by a total fiction! Though the action had been unpremeditated, he could not have done anything more in character with the person he was portraying. He spent a sleepless night, and the only comfort he could find was in the certainty that Amabel would probably be too mortified to see or speak to him when she thought over the incident.

He was to be disappointed. At breakfast, she did pinken becomingly when in his vicinity, and her smile was rather shyer than usual. There was no mistaking that glow in her eyes, though. My word! She probably considered herself as good as affianced to him already. He could not face the guilt a moment longer. As soon as they had finished eating, he turned to his grandmother, who had been observing the lovers with a look of satisfaction.

"My lady, although I do not wish to take you away from your guest, there is a matter of some urgency that I need to discuss with you."

She raised a questioning eyebrow, but seeing the desperation in his face, she complied. "Very well, my dear. Amabel, I depend upon you to entertain your parents and amuse yourself for a short while."

Amabel blushed again, which only heightened her beauty. "I am happy to, Godmama. I have neglected my music since I have been here. I shall go and practice."

Denzil felt as if he would burst by the time he and the marchioness had made their laborious way up to her sitting room. He seated her and she regarded him with some complacency.

"So, when are the banns to be announced? I did not know that you had it in you, my dear. I thought it would probably take the entire three weeks for you and Miss Penworth to make up your minds, and here you are, smelling of April and May. Of course, it took the marquess only five minutes, or so he always said. I have hoped"—here she smiled at him fondly—"to see my first great-grandchild before I die."

He was too unhappy to even try to interrupt her. She noticed that he was sitting with his head sunk in his hands. "Why, whatever is the matter?"

He lifted his face. "Oh, Grandmother. I have done the most terrible thing."

Without any more encouragement than that, he proceeded to pour out his story. As she listened, her brow darkened and then grew stormy. "Fiddle-faddle! You've been listening too much to the nonsensical notions that people are trying to bring into the fashion. Why, what every girl wants most is to be kissed—by the right gentleman, of course. And if you both love each other, why shouldn't you say so? If I were you, I should be glad that Amabel does not subscribe to these missish notions, particularly given your own . . ." Here she was forced to pause to struggle for words, giving him the opportunity to break in.

"But don't you see, Grandmother? That is what I have been telling you. She is not in love with *me*. She is in love with some pattern of perfection who does not exist."

"We all fall in love with an ideal," his grandmother murmured softly, but Denzil did not catch her words.

"If I had any sense of honor, I would go to her now and confess exactly what I have done. She will hate me and probably never speak to me again, which is less than I deserve."

"Denzil." The marchioness's voice was surprisingly soft. "Are you so certain that you have been acting a part? You are in love with Miss Penworth, or at least you told me so."

He stared at her unbelievingly. "How can you ask me that question? You were the one who gave me all those lessons and who said how well I learned them! You know very well that I am not brave, or strong, or certain of myself. You know I am not the type of gentleman that ladies swoon over."

"It is true that you were not certain of yourself," she said slowly. "Do you imagine that everyone else is?"

She was talking in riddles. It made his brain ache to listen to her. "Well," he said dully, "if you have no further suggestions for me, I might as well go downstairs and get this over with."

There was a sudden alarm on her cherubic face. "Do you mean to tell Miss Penworth that you do not really love her?"

"If I loved her, could I have deceived her in that fashion?"

"Then I do have some advice for you—wait."

He gazed at her hopelessly.

"You have more than a week left with Miss Penworth before Saint Valentine's Day. You still have time to let her come to know the true Denzil Huntingford."

He shook his head unbelievingly. "I do not understand why you always mention Saint Valentine's Day—as if it is not just a day like any other. You seem to think it has some magical property which will make everything right."

She smiled wisely. "When you have lived as long as I have, you too will have faith in the sort of miracles Dan Cupid can work. Remember, I once felt the sting of his arrows myself."

Well, if she was going to be poetic, there was no

sense in trying to prolong the conversation. "You'll want to return to your guests . . ."

She leaned forward and grasped his wrist painfully. "Listen carefully, my grandson. If you hold Miss Penworth in affection, you will give your love every chance. Love which is not tenacious cannot survive."

More than her words, the painful grip made an impression. "I will try," he said heavily.

The ensuing days took on a nightmarish quality for Denzil. Although he most longed for the opportunity of spending every waking minute in Amabel's company, the love shining out of her eyes served as a constant reproach to him. He would resolve to be himself when they were together, but his own consciousness of guilt rendered him more and more taciturn and therefore more like the character he had resolved not to portray any longer. There could be no more comfortable talks together, for he was simply too aware of his own transgressions to relax when he was with her. To his own horror, he saw himself withdrawing from her more and more, to the point where he was beginning to avoid her. The worst part of it was that such remoteness apparently served to intrigue her all the more. There was no corresponding coolness in her manner. The same adoring look greeted him whenever his eyes chanced to meet hers.

He was able to rest only fitfully at nights. Lady Penworth commented upon his haggard appearance at dinner one evening, asking solicitously if he felt quite the thing. The corresponding concern upon Amabel's face made him feel even lower than he had before. In his despair, he thought that perhaps the only honorable course would be to leave the castle and return to London. He might have done so had it not been for the dinner party given by Lord Gonville a few days before the ball.

Although he was quite racked by guilt, it had not yet so far induced in him a self-sacrificing desire for more of Lord Hereward's company. This reluctance helped to keep him miserably silent in the carriage ride there, though none of his four companions seemed to notice. Amabel was breathtakingly lovely in a gown of blue, elaborately flounced about the bottom and cut quite bare over the shoulders. Denzil ground his teeth at the thought of the compliments Hereward undoubtedly had waiting.

As it turned out, however, it was not Lord Hereward who was to cause Denzil the most discomfiture, but rather the elder Kennicott girl. When they were paired during a game of charades, she made quite a fool of herself over him, going so far as to take his hand and press it to her in a most embarrassing way, in the guise of acting out her part. Quite apart from his own mortification, Denzil was annoyed at the amused glances which passed between Amabel and Lord Hereward. They obviously were enjoying themselves at his expense, and he knew who was to blame. How dare Hereward take advantage of Denzil's helplessness in this situation? It was not his own fault if he looked like a blushing idiot. Well, if Hereward meant to cut him out, he would find that Denzil, too, had some underhand methods at his own disposal.

He tried to keep his countenance grimly impassive when they made their good-byes and, as usual, Lord Hereward lingered far too long over Amabel's hand. When the earl said he hoped that he might have the honor of the first dance with

Amabel at the upcoming ball, Denzil could keep silent no longer. "That dance, my lord, is already promised to me." The masterful tone of his own voice surprised him.

Whatever Amabel thought of this fiction, she at least did not contradict him, but affirmed that it was so. Not at all discomposed, the earl asked for the second instead. There was little Denzil could say to that.

Denzil was angry and preoccupied on the carriage ride home, and so missed the glances that Amabel shot him under her lashes. Dash it, his grandmother was right. All policy's allowed in war and love, as she had said. He would play his part to the hilt, would follow every one of his grandmother's suggestions. He meant to win Amabel, and he was not going to let a few scruples get in his way.

Accordingly, he conferred with the marchioness early the next morning. If she was surprised by the sudden pliancy of his mood, she at least was wise enough not to reveal it. She carefully delineated all her plans for his Valentine's Day campaign as he took eager notes. The problem didn't occur to him until after she had finished.

"But this means I'll have to leave and go to London," he said with a frown.

"No. You may send your man for the flowers. The fact that you went to the trouble will mean more than your actually going—how fortunate it is that I never have kept flowers in my greenhouse!"

"But . . . the other . . ." He began to blush and could not quite finish the sentence. Fortunately, she understood what he meant.

"Go over to my *secretaire* there and open it. On

the top shelf on the left you will find a box. Bring it over to me."

He followed her instructions. When he brought the small dark blue velvet box over to her, she took it from his hands and opened it. Inside, there was a ruby sparkling in a delicate setting of gold. She removed it from the box and handed it to him.

"It was your mother's," she said. "Your father gave it to her upon their engagement. "I wrote and asked him to send it here so that you might use it, if you wish."

Denzil was turning it over in his hand. "My mother's . . ."

"Yes. Of course, you may go to London and select something else if you would prefer, but this one has such sentimental associations . . ."

He looked up abruptly and saw that his grandmother's eyes were bright. "No. I should like to give her this one, if she'll have me." He stooped down to kiss the plump cheek. "It was wonderful of you to think of it, Grandmother."

For the first time in his memory, she extracted a handkerchief and applied it to the corners of her eyes. "It was nothing. You never knew your mother well, but you remind me of her a great deal. You have her sweetness—and her strength."

He did not know what to say, so he merely stood there awkwardly until she handed the box to him and gave him a tiny push. "There, you had better go before I make a complete fool of myself. I need to recover myself a little before I go back downstairs, and you have a great deal to do."

It was fortunate, perhaps, that his preparations required a certain amount of Denzil's time during the next few days. If he had spent too many minutes with Amabel, his resolve might have crumbled. If he had thought about it, he might have become ashamed of the web he was weaving. He had no doubt that his grandmother was right and that no girl could be immune to these sorts of romantic touches. The marchioness had added an enigmatic remark, however. She had said that she was revealing all this information because she wanted to be sure that he would do this sort of thing for Amabel *after* their marriage, and that it would be much more important *then* than it was now. He had no idea what she was talking about, but he agreed readily to comply. Anything that would bring Amabel happiness must be his premier object. Although he knew he was undeserving, he would try all his life to be worthy of her.

On the morning of Saint Valentine's Day, Amabel awakened to the noise of something tapping against the glass. Rising, she put on her wrapper and went to the window to investigate. When she opened it, she could see, in the early-morning light, a man's figure, the arm poised ready to throw. She focused on it and saw that it was Denzil. He dropped the handful of pebbles he had been about to toss as he gazed up at that luminous countenance.

"Good morning."

"Is that you, Denzil?"

"Yes, I'm sorry to wake you, but I wanted . . ."

"What?"

He hesitated. He had no wish to wake the other occupants of the castle by shouting, but he needed to speak with her. There was an empty trellis beside her window, the roses having been tied down for the winter. It was a short distance to the second story.

"Wait," he said, and indicating the trellis, began to climb up it.

"Be careful," called Amabel as she nervously surveyed the rickety structure.

In a few moments they were face-to-face. "I'm sorry to have wakened you," he explained, "but I wanted to be sure that I was the first person you saw today."

Amabel remembered the time-honored method of choosing a valentine, and she blushed with pleasure, but she was not given leisure to ponder it.

"Look outside your door," he continued.

She went to her door and opened it, discovering a lovely nosegay of pink roses accompanied by a lace-edged card, which said simply, "With all my heart, from your valentine." The tears started to fill her eyes. She pressed the flowers to her nose and inhaled appreciatively before returning to the window.

"Oh, Denzil, they are beautiful."

Standing there with her locks disordered, her face still flushed from sleep, she nevertheless looked more lovely to Denzil than she ever had before. The same magnetic pull that he remembered had him in its power now, but this time it was entirely delightful. Their faces were just inches away, and without thinking at all, he leaned forward to kiss her. Her lips were warm and receptive, and for that moment time seemed to stand still. It was fortunate that he was on the trellis, for all of him cried out against ending that kiss, but he was forced to, in order to tighten his grip. He gazed into her eyes, and they spoke volumes to him, without her ever uttering a word.

"I want every dance with you tonight," he said huskily.

She blushed a little deeper. "You know that is

not possible. What would people think?" The words recalled her to herself suddenly. Here she was in her bedroom, wearing only her wrapper and a shift, and kissing a man, even though he nominally was outside it. She tightened the wrapper about her, still clinging to his roses in the other hand. "I must go. What if someone should see us?"

"What if they should?" he agreed gravely, but his eyes were shining with an exhilaration she never before had witnessed. "Good-bye for now, then." He descended the trellis rapidly, and upon reaching the bottom, blew her a kiss. Feeling that there was no point in observing the proprieties by now, she returned it softly. She watched him until he disappeared from sight, then closed the window against the cold. She walked over to her dressing table and laid the roses on it dreamily. I suppose I might as well dress, she thought, I certainly won't be able to fall back asleep.

When she came downstairs an hour later, she found him at the breakfast table with the marchioness. He did not say a word about the earlier episode, but merely greeted her politely, though his eyes betrayed his feelings. The marchioness welcomed her also, in an abstracted way, ringing the bell as she did so. "I cannot promise you a great deal in the way of breakfast. The toast is burnt, the eggs are underdone, there are no kippers, and the coffee has not come, though I sent for it a quarter of an hour ago. It makes me think I was foolish beyond belief to plan a ball for Saint Valentine's Day. All the servants are busy woolgathering, their minds on love knots and such, no doubt."

"I think it was a wonderful notion, myself," said

Amabel. She caught the warm look in Denzil's eyes as she spoke, and it kindled a flush in her own cheeks.

"Be that as it may, I don't know how I am going to be sure that everything is done before the guests arrive." Here she began to rise. "I suppose I must see to that coffee myself, for no one has come . . ."

The others would have protested, but at that moment a servant appeared with the steaming urn. "Hmph," commented the marchioness as she seated herself once more. As soon as the servant had departed, Amabel turned to Lady Witley again.

"Godmama, the ball does not begin until nine, so you have plenty of time to prepare. I shall help you in any way I can, also."

"Oh, but you should be enjoying yourself."

"And I will, at the ball. Now, just tell me what needs to be done. You must have some rest today, so that you may receive all your guests."

Though Amabel had no regrets about her rash offer, the project was to take up most of the rest of the day. Although the marchioness conferred with everyone personally, she was well content to let Amabel be her legs and see that her orders were carried out. From the stables to the kitchens, there were details to be superintended. The elderly butler was not capable of seeing to all of the arrangements; moreover, he clearly was quite as exasperated with the rest of the servants as the marchioness was.

There were floral and other offerings arriving all day for Amabel from those suitors fortunate enough to be invited to the ball; but, busy as she was, they went almost unnoticed. It was Lord Hereward who immediately upon his arrival at the ball that evening was unkind enough to charge her with neglect.

"Don't be silly, Herry," she said rather impatiently. "You know I could not possibly wear red roses with a gown this color."

He ran an admiring eye over her. She was looking particularly beautiful tonight in a gown of rose-pink silk with flowers embroidered about the hem and sleeves and neck. She had an elegant figure, which the simple lines of the gown could not help but accentuate. Her color was high and her countenance animated; she was sparkling this evening.

He removed a quizzing glass from his waistcoat and inspected the flowers she carried. "Since we are such old friends, I hope you will not mind my asking—just who was the gentleman fortunate enough to select the appropriate color?"

"Oh, it was Denzil—Mr. Huntingford, I mean," she replied, her blush betraying her. She did not look at Lord Hereward as she spoke; indeed, she had hardly glanced at him during the whole of their conversation. He turned his quizzing glass toward the sight which seemed to hold her interest. It was the object of their discussion himself, supporting his grandmother as she received her guests.

"Lucky devil," murmured Lord Hereward with a wry smile.

"What?" Amabel asked, still distracted.

"When am I to wish you both happy?" the earl asked in an undertone.

She turned to him, startled, her eyes wide. "Herry, if you dare . . ."

"I shall be silent as the grave, I assure you," he said. He smiled gently at her. "Besides, you are forgetting that you have promised me the second

dance. I shall expect to find you *unoccupied* then."
He bent formally over her hand and went to rejoin
his friends.

Amabel's dreamy state was noticed by others
among her suitors, though fortunately none of the
rest had as certain an idea of the cause. It was
hardly remarkable that when the musicians struck
up, she would be escorted to the floor by Mr.
Huntingford. After all, she was a guest at the castle and he was the marchioness's grandson. If they
did exchange some rather warm glances, it would
take an idiot to infer much from that. She seemed
happy enough to dance with Lord Hereward and
Lord Gonville and her other admirers, while Huntingford did his duty by his grandmother's female
guests.

It was not difficult for Amabel to act happy;
indeed, she was happier than she had ever been
before in her life. Her only difficulty lay in trying
to remember the proprieties and in forcing herself
to tear her eyes away from that tall dark figure as
he moved about the ballroom.

Her card had filled quickly and it was with disappointment that she thought of his expressed
desire to have every dance with her. Surely he
might have managed two, anyway. Of course, as
Lady Witley's grandson, he was one of the hosts
and must look after *all* of the guests. She tried to
ignore her sense of loss.

With no lack of partners, the hours passed
swiftly enough for her. Soon it would be time to
go in to dinner. The first strains of a waltz were
beginning when Denzil suddenly materialized in
front of her. Her hand was already in that of her
next partner, who happened to be the youthful
Lord Mollison.

"Mollison, glad I've found you. Your groom

wanted to speak with you. Something terribly urgent he has to say regarding your horses."

Lord Mollison, whose life revolved around the care, feeding, exercise, and general health of his splendid pair of match-bays, turned pale, gulped, and abandoned Amabel with scarcely another thought.

Denzil bowed to her. "May I?"

She nodded as she placed her hand in his, but whispered, "Was that the truth or a fiction?"

"The truth is that no man could ever have a lovelier valentine than you." The words were coming to him glibly, almost too glibly, he thought. He could no more stop now than stem the tide of the ocean. She felt utterly marvelous in his arms as they waltzed. Taking a deep breath, he steered her out of the pattern and through a door. It took just another few steps to reach the garden. There was no difficulty in finding their way, for the night was clear and the moon was full.

Although the day had been unseasonably warm, the night was chilly, but neither of them noticed. There were no obstacles now, Denzil thought. The ring was in his pocket. He took her by the hands and gazed into those shining blue eyes. "Amabel, I love you," he heard himself say.

"I love you too."

It had been quite easy. With another short sentence he could make her his forever. Those eyes were so beautiful, and so trusting. Why did they have to be so trusting? Of course, he could make it up to her later, after they were married. "Amabel, I would . . ." He fell silent.

"Yes?"

He could not meet those eyes, so innocent, so blinded by a false love. Would she ever be able to forgive him if she found out the truth even years later? He must not think of that now.

"Amabel, I . . ."

"Yes?"

All the months of guilt came crashing down upon him. God help him! He loved this girl too much to take advantage of her. He dropped her hands. "Amabel, I . . . I have to confess. I have deceived you."

It was not what she had been expecting to hear, and her eyes flew open in surprise. Now that he had begun, the words came pouring from him like a flood.

"I haven't been honest with you from the beginning. I came to visit my grandmother in the autumn to tell her that I was in love with you. Because of her affection for me, she invited you and your family here and spent all the weeks that led up to your visit in teaching me how to woo you. She was the one that decided I should try to fascinate you by pretending to be a strong and silent man. The more we were together, and the more deeply I loved you, the more I realized how wrong it was, but I could not seem to stop."

He drew in a ragged breath. "After that day we . . . after that day in the nursery, I knew I had let the masquerade go too far. I tried my hardest to keep my distance from you, but I found that I couldn't. I knew that it would be best if I were to leave the castle and not trouble you again, but, God help me, I lacked the will. And seeing how intimate Lord Hereward was with you the other day at dinner inspired my baser self to keep with my grandmother's original plan."

He shook his head wildly. "I am not the man you think me. I am not masterful, or mysterious, or fascinating. I hope that someday you will be able to forgive me. My grandmother . . . well, she is an old lady, and sometimes they have odd notions."

He was breathing heavily, his heart pounding, as he stared at her, waiting to see how she would react to his revelation. To his astonishment, one corner of her mouth turned up, then the other, and she began to chuckle and finally laugh aloud.

"Amabel . . ."

Her laughter was becoming harder and harder. The news must have made her hysterical. "Amabel . . ." he said, concerned.

She had practically fallen down on a nearby bench. Her amusement was causing her to produce great unladylike whoops. The tears were beginning to stream from the corners of her eyes.

He could not decide. Was this simply the result of overstrained nerves, or had she never taken him seriously at all? "Amabel!" He gave her shoulder a little shake.

She tried to contain herself but failed. He was forced to merely stand silently by until she exhausted herself. Eventually her laughter subsided into chuckles, which gradually became only occasional, and she began to fight to regain her breath.

Denzil had felt a complete fool for the past five minutes. Clearly his grandmother had been wrong. This was his payment for listening to the schemes of an addled old woman.

"Well," he said coldly, "shall I show you back to the ballroom now, or would you prefer not to be seen in my company?"

"Oh, Denzil!" There was real remorse in her eyes, and she rose and kissed him in a manner which left him in no doubt whatsoever as to her feelings. He held her in his arms, feeling dazed,

and scarcely believing his own good fortune.
Could it be that she had forgiven him already?
Whatever this meant, he had to ask the question
now. He lifted his lips from hers and gazed into
her eyes. "Amabel, will you marry me?"

"Yes."

Such a moment naturally required a celebration, and they both had similar ideas about what
was called for. After a few more moments he again
came to himself and released her. She looked in
his eyes and read his thoughts at a glance.

"I am sorry that I worried you so. It's just that
the situation is so ridiculous. Godmama came to
see me last autumn also. She happened to mention
that you had been staying with her, and somehow
... well, I don't know how it happened, but I
ended up by confessing to her that I had loved you
for years."

"For years!" he repeated, astounded.

She smiled. "Well, ever since you rescued me
from the armory, I suppose. You were my childhood picture of Sir Galahad—even though you
wanted nothing to do with me. I thought it might
be just an infatuation that I would outgrow, but
when I saw you in London, it was stronger than
ever."

"When ... ? But I ..."

"It was clear that you still wanted nothing to
do with me, and I was told that you were called
'The Female-Hater.' I tried to turn my mind from
you, but you were always in my thoughts. I heard
your praises sung for your work in the reform societies, and of your concern for the poor, and for the
child laborers, and ... and I loved you even more
for that." She sighed.

"But you always seemed so happy."

"I was determined not to wear my heart upon

my sleeve. And since there was no hope with you, I . . . But by the Season's end I knew it was no use. I could never marry anyone else. I thought I would have to die a spinster."

He was too incredulous to speak.

"Then, when Godmama came, well, it was the answer to a prayer. She said she might be able to arrange for you and me to be at Witley for a visit during the same time, and that with luck a romance would grow out of it. She explained that you were shy around women and that I should not take it amiss if you were silent or reserved. When I arrived, she told me I must be amenable to your every invitation, for a rebuff might frighten you away forever." Amabel shook her head with a reminiscent smile. "She didn't need to be afraid of that—I would have gladly gone out barefoot in the snow if you'd suggested it."

Then there had been no point to his having tried to portray himself as masterful. The irritation with his grandmother had already begun, but he discarded it in favor of a more important thought. "But the way I've been treating you for the past several days—"

"—frightened me to death. I thought you had decided I was too forward when I told you that I loved you the other day in the nursery and that you were trying to decide how to be rid of me. I finally had to go and talk to Godmama because my spirits were so low. She told me that I must act as warmly to you as ever and not be afraid to let my love for you show, that your shyness was simply making things difficult for you. She said that love must be tenacious or it cannot survive."

The familiar words served to make the anger which had been simmering within him boil over at last. "She has treated us like a pair of fools!

She has never given me credit for having the sense to manage my own affairs, and here is the result. She has maneuvered us into a romance as if we were two wooden-headed puppets. I can never forgive her for this, never!"

The force of his wrath surprised Amabel. After a moment or two she stretched out a cautious hand, and taking his, gave it a squeeze. He looked up at her, his eyes full. "I am sorry."

"I don't see why you should be." Her voice was low, her tone serious. "Whatever the method, I am to marry you and you me, and that is all I have ever wished."

He shook his head. "But she could have simply told us. She could have told me that you had a fondness for me already . . ."

Her expression remained grave. "Forgive me for asking, my love, but even if you had known, would you have been able to converse with me and spend time with me as you did—without the benefit of your grandmother's lessons?"

It was a new thought and it arrested him momentarily. Another instant later and he shook his head again. "Perhaps what you say is true. But I still cannot forgive her for leading me to deceive you so unnecessarily—for making me appear to be what I was not."

She smiled a little. "I don't mean to begin our engagement by disagreeing with you constantly, but I don't see that I *was* deceived. I know that you don't think that you are brave or noble or strong or decisive, but there are those of us who do. As for 'silent,' well, you do talk freely about subjects that interest you, but I would never call you loquacious."

He frowned at her words. She squeezed his hand again. "Don't you see? She was merely giving you the confidence to act like yourself with me, the confidence to talk to me."

"But you don't realize, this whole campaign for Valentine's Day—waking you, the flowers, the card, the . . . they were all part of my *grandmother's* plan, not mine. Even the idea of sneaking you from the ballroom into the garden and . . ." He dropped his head, ashamed.

She took his other hand. He looked up and met that clear blue gaze. "I've already told you I am delighted with the result. As for the rest . . . well, I shouldn't say it, but I believe no gentleman would ever give a girl flowers without being prodded by another female at some time or another. I always have to tell Father when it is Mother's birthday, so that he can buy a gift for her. They are things you would know to do if you had sisters or a mother of your own."

"That reminds me!" Shocked at his own forgetfulness, he withdrew the ring from his pocket. "It was my mother's."

A sigh escaped her as he slipped it on her finger. "How beautiful." Her eyes were bright. "I know that Godmama must have thought of this, for it must mean a great deal to her. And she knew how much it would mean to my mother and to me."

The last vestiges of his anger had evaporated into the night air. "Grandmother said there was something special about Saint Valentine's Day, that miracles were possible. She must be right, for I still cannot quite believe that you love me."

There was one obvious way to convince him, and she lost no time in making the effort. He crushed her to him, but was distracted by her shivering. "I have kept you out here far too long. You must be frozen." He began to lead her to the house. "As soon as we go inside, I will seek out your father and speak to him."

She smiled at him lovingly. "I think that perhaps we should go find the marchioness first. I mean to thank her, for surely no romance was ever sponsored by so capable a Cupid."

A Waltz Among the Stars
by Mary Balogh

SAINT VALENTINE'S DAY. It was the worst day of the year. Even worse than Christmas. Christmas at least was for families, and there were always family members—and plenty of them—with whom to cheer himself. Always family members with whom to mask the absence of that one person.

But Valentine's Day was different. It was a day for lovers, a day for two people, a day when relatives and friends counted for very little. Just that one other. That one dearly beloved other.

Anna-Marie. Dead for almost two years already. Married in January, dead before March turned to April. Married in haste because she was dying and they had both wanted her to die as his wife. And Valentine's Day, when she had sat propped up in bed against her pillows, almost as pale as they, presenting him with an absurdly large red velvet heart trimmed with copious amounts of white lace. And laughing with him over it until she tired and fell asleep, her head on his arm.

And the library downstairs afterward, when he had set the large heart down on the desk and cried for the first time—racking, painful sobs, admitting to himself finally that the miracle he had hoped for and prayed for was just not going to happen.

Just two years before. Last year he could

remember only as a haze of pain intensified even as his year of mourning drew to its end. And this year the dull ache of the approaching day and its reminder of love lost and of emptiness and loneliness.

Caleb White, Viscount Brandon, noted at a glance from the window of his traveling carriage that Durham Hall was finally coming into sight at the end of the winding driveway. The sun was shining off its long mullioned windows, making them appear to be glazed in gold. He had never been there before, but all the reports he had heard of the splendor of the Duke of Durham's principal seat had not been exaggerated. First the twin stone houses at the gates, one occupied by the porter. Then the square stone dower house with its neat garden, followed by the dense forest with occasional glimpses of grazing deer and follies and distant lawns. And now the house itself.

He was glad he had agreed to come. A week-long party in honor of Saint Valentine with the promise of plenty of company. And the possibility that at the end of the week he would be betrothed to Lady Eve Hanover, the duke's daughter. It was a match favored by both his own parents and hers. And it was one he had agreed to consider seriously.

He was acquainted with the lady. He had danced with her a few times the year before during the Season in town, and he had twice been a member of a party that had included her, once to Vauxhall and once to the theater. She was pretty, amiable, charming. He had scarcely noticed her. But then, he had noticed no one else either. He had still been raw with pain over Anna-Marie.

But it was time to live again. And time to love again too, or at least to make a marriage and work

on bringing contentment to his wife and to himself. It was time to start begetting sons and daughters. He would be thirty on his next birthday. And
he wanted children. It was all he had ever
wanted—a wife and children in the quietness of
his own home. And Anna-Marie, of course. She had
been his father's ward, nine years younger than
he. He had loved her from the moment of her
arrival at their home, a thin and wide-eyed waif
of an eight-year-old. Yes, Anna-Marie had always
been a part of his dreams.

But it was time to put aside old dreams and to
live again.

Lord Brandon glanced out of the window as his
carriage slowed almost at the top of the driveway
and drew to one side. A child—a little boy—was
tripping along at the other side of the road, alter-
nately hopping on one foot and landing on both
feet. He stopped at the approach of the carriage
and glanced up curiously. A handsome dark-
haired, dark-eyed child. The viscount smiled and
raised a hand. The boy waved back.

And then the man saw that the child was not
alone. A lady walked a short distance behind him,
a lady dressed modestly, though not inexpen-
sively, in blue cloak and bonnet. A lady who also
looked up and met his eyes for a brief moment
before he touched his hat and the carriage passed
her.

Beautiful. She was beautiful, he thought. But
the carriage was rounding the formal gardens, and
the great double doors at the top of the marble
horseshoe steps were opening to reveal liveried
footmen and the duke himself moving between
them to descend the steps.

Yes, the viscount thought, he was glad he had
come. It was February the eighth. He would be at

Durham Hall until at least the sixteenth, perhaps longer if the suggested betrothal became a reality. He would be surrounded by other people, and his days doubtless would be filled with activity and merriment. Perhaps he would be too busy to think. Perhaps this most painful of all times of the year would be over before he had time to brood.

He smiled and raised a hand to the Duke of Durham.

Saint Valentine's Day. Always the worst day of the year. Many times worse than Christmas. At Christmas there was always Zachary and his child's exuberance. And there was the house to decorate and the baking to participate in and a thousand and one other things to be done to occupy her time and her mind.

Worse too than July 28. The Battle of Talavera. Spain, 1809—eight years before. She had been at her Aunt Sophie's in Bath on that date, awaiting Zachary's birth. The anniversary of that day and that battle was always painful, for Zach had been killed there, though she had not known until the end of November, two weeks after their son was born. Everyone had kept the news from her—for more than two months since it had filtered through from the Peninsula. It had been strange, unreal, during those days of joy in her child, grief over her lover, to know that he had been dead since July and she had not known it. She had tried, in vain, to remember exactly what she had been doing on that day.

But Valentine's Day. It was a day for lovers, a day for two lovers, all the rest of the world excluded. Zach had left for Spain hurriedly, unexpectedly, the day after Valentine's Day eight years before, upsetting their plans for a summer wedding. They had become lovers on Valentine's Day, in a last bittersweet farewell, and he had left her with the most precious love gift of all.

Lady Barbara Hanover, leaving her father's house after a brief afternoon visit to her mother, glanced ahead of her to where her son was skipping along the driveway toward the dower house where they lived, singing tunelessly to himself. Her brother, William, had just promised him one of the spaniel's puppies after it had spent a suitable amount of time with its mother, and Zachary was entirely happy. He was blissfully unaware of the approaching anniversary—the anniversary of his conception.

But Lady Barbara was not unaware, even though there were six days yet to go. There were guests at the house, several of them, almost all of them young, single, and eligible. They were to be there for more than a week. It was a Valentine's party. And probably a betrothal party too. The Viscount Brandon, eldest son of the Marquess of Highmoor, was coming as a prospective suitor for Eve. And Eve was prepared to accept him, since he was wealthy and well-connected and handsome. Though he was quiet and humorless, Eve claimed. He would not perhaps be the most amiable of husbands, but . . .

Eve had shrugged and laughed.

Barbara had never seen the Viscount Brandon. Or any of the other guests at the house. She had never mingled with the *ton* at all, even though she was the elder daughter of a duke. She had been scarcely eighteen when her great disgrace had happened. She had never had a come-out Season. Her mother had just informed her, gently enough—though she had not needed to be told—that it would perhaps be as well to keep herself from the house and from the sight of Papa's guests during the coming week. Even William had told her that he would come to fetch Zachary to see the puppies the next day—to save her the walk up from the dower house.

"Zachary," she called ahead to her oblivious son, "watch the carriage, sweetheart. Move over to the edge of the road."

She had thought that all the guests had arrived. Obviously there must be one straggler. Her son stopped, looked up in curiosity at the strange and grand carriage, and waved to whoever was inside.

Lady Barbara had time only to notice the crest on the side of the carriage and to look up into a pair of blue eyes that were still twinkling from the smile their owner must have given Zachary, and the carriage had passed.

"Who was that, Mama?" her son asked, looking back at the carriage.

"I think probably the Viscount Brandon," she said.

"He waved to me." Zachary sounded surprised. He did not know very many adults except his mother and the servants at the dower house. Those he did know, with the exception of his Uncle William, had a tendency to ignore him or to frown disapprovingly at any signs he gave that he was not deaf and mute and immobile.

"I wonder if Cook has those jam tarts ready," Lady Barbara said. "Shall we hurry along and see?"

Her son resumed his tripping progress along the driveway.

The viscount was indeed very handsome, she thought, though she had only those smiling blue eyes to judge from. Kindly blue eyes, smiling at a child. She felt a sudden envy of Eve. Eight years was a long time. Such a very long time. It was becoming more and more difficult to remember exactly what Zach had looked like or what his voice had sounded like. Sometimes she tried desperately to recall what his kiss had been like and what his body had felt like when she was conceiving Zachary.

She could barely remember. Perhaps she could not remember at all. After so long it was difficult to know what had actually been and what she had embellished in her imaginings.

Valentine's was a difficult time. She was forgetting Zach and she did not want to forget him. She had loved him all through her girlhood, though her parents had never encouraged their friendship, since he had been the son of a mere baronet of moderate means. They had only grudgingly agreed to the marriage after Zach had inherited a sizable fortune on the death of a great-aunt. Now Barbara had nothing by which to remember him except Zachary, who mercifully looked very like him. Zach's father had died less than a year after him, and an unknown branch of the family now lived in their former home.

She was forgetting Zach, and she was restless and longing for something to which she could not—or dared not—put a name. And Valentine's Day was always the worst day of all. She dreaded it and wished it past already.

She quickened her steps with gladness when the dower house came into sight. Home. And it was a chilly day despite the glimpses she had had of primroses amongst the trees.

The ladies unanimously declared that it was too cold a day for riding farther. It was the wind, Miss

Sterns said with a shiver. It cut through one to the bone.

And so William Hanover, Earl of Meacham, led the way back to the stables with the Honorable Miss Woodfall, and the gentleman helped the ladies to dismount amidst much laughter and chatter.

"A cup of hot tea will never be so welcome as now," Lady Eve said, smiling at Lord Brandon, who had just lifted her from the saddle. Her cheeks were glowing from the exercise and the chill air. With her green riding hat and its jaunty feather curling about one ear, she looked extremely pretty. "I shall order the tray as soon as we are inside."

"I could think of something more sure to warm the insides than tea," Sir Anthony Hutton said, and there were cheers from two of the other gentlemen.

"Well, perhaps," Lady Eve said, releasing her hold of the viscount's shoulders. "If you are very good, Anthony. But where are you going, William?"

The Earl of Meacham was mounting his horse again. "I promised Zach a treat," he said.

His sister nodded without replying and turned to lead the way to the house.

"I shall come with you, if I may," Lord Brandon said. "The air feels too good to be abandoned so soon."

"He is just a child," the earl said. "But come by all means if you wish, Brandon."

There was the perverse need to be away from the crowd after less than a full day of being with them, the viscount thought. And yet he was enjoying himself. The duke and duchess had welcomed him warmly, as they had all their guests.

Lady Eve had greeted him with a smile and a look in her eyes that had suggested that she would welcome his suit. And the other eleven guests were an amiable lot who appeared to have come with the intention of enjoying the week to the full. Viscount Brandon was acquainted with most of them.

It was clear already that he had done the right thing to come, that his expectations for the week were not to be disappointed. He was looking forward to the activities of the remaining seven days of the house party. And he was looking forward to his betrothal, which was appearing to be an almost certain thing if he wanted it. It would be good to have another woman on whom to focus his attentions.

It would be good to put Anna-Marie finally to rest, a dearly cherished memory but no longer a present pain.

But there was this need to be away from the group for a short while. A need to ride in the fresh air for longer than the half-hour of the group ride.

"I like children," he said, swinging himself back into his own saddle and grinning down at Miss Sterns, who told him that he must be a glutton for punishment. He assumed that she was referring to the weather rather than to the fact that they were going to take some treat to a child.

"He lives at the dower house," Lord Meacham explained as they turned their horses' heads for the driveway. "I promised to bring him up to see the puppies. One of them is to be his when it is weaned. Children need pets when they have no brothers or sisters."

"And even when they do," the viscount said. "My mother always complained when I was growing up that if she was not falling over children, she was tripping over dogs or sitting on cats. I always rather pity people who come from small families. There was never a dull moment with the nine of us—ten with Anna-Marie."

"Your wife," the earl said.

Lord Brandon nodded. "And you have had only one sister with whom to fight," he said. "A shame."

The earl did not reply.

The walls of the dower house were covered with ivy, the viscount noticed, looking more closely at the house than he had from his carriage window the afternoon before. The garden was full of rose-bushes. Doubtless it would be a riot of color later in the year. He sat his horse outside the gate at the earl's suggestion while the latter dismounted and walked up the cobbled path to knock on the door and disappear briefly inside.

He emerged a couple of minutes later with the little boy the viscount's carriage had passed the day before.

"Uncle Will," the boy was asking, "am I to ride up with you? When may I ride my pony again?"

"Soon," the earl said. "As soon as the weather warms up a little more, Zach."

"But as soon as the weather warms," the boy said, "you will be going. Mama says you will be going to London for the Season."

"Make your bow to the Viscount Brandon," Lord Meacham said. "This is Zach, Brandon."

"Happy to meet you again," the viscount said with a smile. "You are the lad who almost ran my horses down yesterday."

The boy chuckled as his uncle lifted him to his horse's back and mounted behind him. "But they were bigger than I, sir," he said, "so I moved out of the way."

The lady who had been walking behind the boy

the day before appeared in the doorway. His mother? Lord Brandon touched his hat and inclined his head to her, though Meacham did not offer to make introductions. She looked steadily and unsmilingly back at him and inclined her own head slightly.

"Will the puppies be awake today, Uncle Will?" the boy was asking.

"Puppies sleep a great deal of the time," the earl said. "We will have to wait and see."

She was slender and graceful, not very tall. She was dressed in a simple green wool dress. Her hair was honey blond and combed smoothly back from her face. He had not been mistaken in his first impression that she was beautiful. The child did not look like her.

"Bye-bye, Mama," the boy called as the horses turned back up the driveway.

She raised one hand and smiled. And looked ten times more lovely, if that were possible. So she *was* the boy's mother. The father must be very dark.

She wandered restlessly and finally sat down to her embroidery. But there was too much silence surrounding her. She set her work aside and picked up a book. But her mind could not focus on the adventures of Joseph Andrews. She closed the book with a sigh and went to fetch her cloak. She would see if any more daffodils had pushed above the soil to brave the cold weather and proclaim the approach of spring.

The thought that Zachary was seven years old already was a little frightening. In another few years William would send him away to school and she would see him only during the holidays. Before she knew it, he would be grown up and

William would find him employment somewhere. Somewhere where she could live with him and care for him, perhaps. But then he would wish to marry eventually, and she would not live with him and his wife.

They were foolish thoughts. She bent and saw that, yes, her eyes were not deceiving her. A spring-green shoot was breaking its way through the soil. Foolish, when Zachary was still only seven years old. Little more than a baby. Foolish to wonder in panic what she would do when she was entirely alone. Many people were alone. They survived. They somehow made meaning out of life.

There were sounds of a horse's hooves on the driveway. Just one horse. William was bringing Zachary back. The Viscount Brandon was not coming with him this time. She was glad. He was a handsome man. She had not been deceived in that one impression of smiling blue eyes the day before. Handsome in a way that somehow intensified her loneliness. Not handsome in any way that set him quite apart from all other men and that made women nervous. And not handsome in any haughty manner. Just good-looking and amiable-looking and . . . attractive.

Barbara shook her head, straightened up, and shaded her eyes to watch the approach of her brother's horse. Except that it was not his. She could see that at a glance, sun or no sun. And it was not William either. It was the viscount with Zachary up before him. She could hear her son's voice prattling.

"Mama," he called when they were still too far away to allow him to talk at normal volume, "I know the one I want. He was awake and squeaking because he could not walk on the straw without tripping and falling. He has the roundest little nose. Uncle Will says I may have him."

Barbara walked slowly to the gate. The viscount touched the brim of his hat and smiled at her.

"Lord Meacham was caught up in the panic of a lame hunter," he said. "One of his favorites, apparently. I offered to bring your son home to you, ma'am."

"That was very kind of you, my lord," she said. "I hope it has not been too much trouble."

"We have been having a spirited conversation, have we not, Zach?" the viscount said. "Or rather"—he grinned, so that Barbara felt an uncomfortable breathlessness—"Zach has been delivering a spirited monologue about the superiority of his father's horses over all others."

Barbara felt herself flushing. "I talk to him about his father," she said. "I want him to know his father and to be proud of him, even though he never saw him."

The smile disappeared from the viscount's face. "I am sorry," he said. "I did not know . . ."

"He died at Talavera," she said. "Four months before Zachary's birth. He was a great hero, was he not, sweetheart?"

"I am sorry," the viscount said.

"It was a long time ago." She was wishing that she had stayed inside the house so that Zachary could have come in without the necessity of this meeting and conversation. "Will you come inside, my lord? I shall have some tea made."

"Thank you," he said, smiling at her again. "I would like that. Caleb White, Viscount Brandon, at your service, ma'am."

He had dismounted and was lifting Zachary down to the ground.

"Famous!" Zachary said. "I am going to show

you my boat, sir. It really sails. Mama says I may take it out to the lake the next time we walk that way."

Did he know? Barbara wondered, noting that he was not very tall. Her head reached to above his chin. And his eyes were indeed blue, not that gray color that some people liked to pretend was blue. A light and very distinct blue. And brown hair, which looked, as far as she could tell beneath his hat, as if it was probably too long for fashion. Did he know?

"Barbara Hanover, my lord," she said.

He hitched his horse to the fence and came through the gate after Zachary. "Mrs. Hanover," he said. "Your husband was related to the duke?"

"I was not married to Zachary's father," she said quietly, turning to lead the way to the house. "The duke is my father. I am William and Eve's elder sister." She did not look back to note his expression.

"I made it myself," Zachary said.

"The boat?" the viscount said. Barbara wondered if he wished he could turn back without appearing impolite. "That was clever of you. How did you do it?"

"Actually," Zachary admitted, "Ben helped me whittle the wood. And Mama helped me with the sail. But I did a lot of the work."

"That is what counts when you are a lad," the viscount said. "To watch and learn and do as much as you can so that when you are a little older you can do something all alone."

"I shall go and fetch it," Zachary said, turning toward the stairs as soon as they entered the house.

"Wash your hands and comb your hair while you are up there," Barbara said, and then wished she had not done so. She did not wish to be alone with the Viscount Brandon. She led the way into the parlor. "It was kind of you to bring him home."

"My pleasure, ma'am," he said, taking the chair she indicated after she had seated herself. "I never subscribe to the theory that being with children is tedious. And perhaps it is as well that I hold that view. I have fourteen nephews and nieces already, and there is no sign yet that they have stopped coming."

"Oh," she said. "You come from a large family?"

"When I have just mentioned the number fourteen," he said, his eyes laughing at her, "one would hope that I am not about to say that I have one poor sister. I have five, ma'am, two older and three younger than I—all married and mothers already. And one of my brothers is married too. I did not know that Meacham and Lady Eve had a sister."

"I am the skeleton in the family closet," she said.

He looked steadily at her. "Are you?" he said. "But you have a lovely son."

"Yes," she said. She raised her chin in an unconscious gesture of defiance. "He is all I have of Zach, and I am not sorry."

"I can understand that," he said. "I have no such memento of my wife. I envy you."

Her eyebrows rose in surprise—at two things he had said. "You have been married?" she asked.

"Two years ago," he said. "Very briefly. We knew that she was dying before we married. But we married anyway. I wanted the honor of being her widower."

"Oh," she said, "how I envy you. Zach was a

cavalry officer. He had to leave for the Peninsula with very little warning. There was no time . . ."

"I understand," she said as Zachary came back into the room, a crudely carved boat clutched proudly in his hand.

Barbara poured the tea, which had just arrived, and watched as Lord Brandon set one arm about her son's shoulders and gave the toy his full attention. He listened to the lengthy and muddled account Zachary gave of the making of the boat, and asked questions about it.

"I would like to see her make her maiden voyage," he said at last. "When is it to be?"

"Her?" Zachary chuckled.

"Of course," the viscount said. "Ships are always female. Did you not know? Have you not given her a name yet?"

Zachary was giggling.

"Perhaps you should give her your mama's name," Lord Brandon suggested. "The *Lady Barbara*."

Zachary giggled harder. "Do you like it, Mama?" he asked.

"I would feel deeply honored," she said, meeting the viscount's dancing blue eyes across the room and puzzling over Eve's description of him as a humorless man.

"And when is the maiden voyage to be?" the viscount asked. "That means her very first voyage, Zach."

"Tomorrow," the boy said decisively. "At the lake. Can we go tomorrow, Mama?"

"I suppose so," she said. "If the weather is kind."

"In the afternoon?" the viscount asked. "About this time? I shall be there."

But he would not be able to, Barbara thought.

He was a guest at the house. Eve had a dizzying number of activities planned. Besides, he must not be seen to be consorting with her or her son. Papa would be furious and Mama upset and Eve annoyed. Even William would be displeased. She would have to live with the discomfort of their disapproval for a long time after the house party was at an end.

Besides, Viscount Brandon was no ordinary guest. He was intended for Eve. The thought was depressing in some inexplicable way.

"Well," Lord Brandon said, getting to his feet after finishing his tea, "I must not keep you any longer. I appreciate the tea and the warmth of the fire, ma'am. And I am impressed with your boat, Zach. Until tomorrow?"

"You must not feel obliged," Barbara said, rising and following him from the room to the outer door. "I know that there is a busy schedule of events planned at the house."

"Are you to attend any of them?" he asked. "There is to be a ball on the evening of Saint Valentine's Day."

"No," she said.

"By choice?" he asked. But he frowned when she did not immediately reply. "I am sorry. That was an impertinent question. Good day, Lady Barbara. Zach?"

"You will be there tomorrow?" Zachary asked anxiously. "Promise?"

Barbara opened her mouth to say something to her son, but the viscount spoke first.

"It is a promise," he said. "I could not allow the *Lady Barbara* to make her maiden voyage without my being there, now, could I?"

He smiled at them both and strode away down the path to his horse.

Barbara stood looking after him, hardly listening to the excited prattling of her son beside her. It was February 9, she thought. Just five days away from the day for lovers. She felt her loneliness as a heavy and very physical sensation.

If only, she thought as he swung up into the saddle and turned to touch his hat to them. If only . . .

The following morning was taken up by a ride to Woville Castle, five miles distant from Durham Hall, and luncheon at an inn close by. The weather cooperated. The sky was a clear blue and the air warmer than it had been since Christmas, although the breeze was fresh.

Lady Eve was in very high spirits. Viscount Brandon had heard it said that she might have married any of a number of eligible suitors during her first Season the year before. And he could believe it. Just her position as the only—no, as the *younger*—daughter of the Duke of Durham would have ensured her success. But her beauty, her smiles, her exuberance, would have won her admirers even without her dowry and her title.

She was behaving well. This was her house party, since her brother seemed unconcerned with laying claim to it himself, and these were her guests. She was treating the ladies with kind friendliness and the gentlemen with an easy familiarity that never descended into vulgarity. She called almost all of them by their first names, though not the viscount, and flirted with each of them in an offhand manner that left none of them offended when she turned to another to flirt in like manner.

Only with Lord Brandon did she not flirt. There was a subtle difference in her treatment of him

and a slight proprietary air in her dealings with
him. She rode with him during much of the morning's outing and sat beside him at luncheon. It
was very clear to him that she had decided to have
him, though not by word or gesture did she indicate that she expected his offer.

She was unlike her sister, he thought as she
laughed at something another of the guests had
said during the ride home. A little alike to look at,
it was true. Her hair color and complexion were
similar. She was a little shorter than her sister
and a little plumper. But the greatest difference
was in nature. Lady Eve was lighthearted, gay,
gregarious; Lady Barbara was quiet, dignified,
proud. Lady Eve was pretty; Lady Barbara was
beautiful. And several years older, of course.
Talavera had been fought in 1809. She had said
that both Lady Eve and Meacham were younger
than she.

It seemed for a while that they would not be
home in time for him to keep his appointment
with mother and son. Everyone lingered over luncheon and then Hutton suggested that they visit a
Norman church that was only three or four miles
distant. If he was not to break his promise, Lord
Brandon thought, he would have to make some
excuse to leave the party and return alone. But
fortunately a chorus of female voices declared that
they had done quite enough riding and exploring
for one day, and they all turned toward home.

"I am going to take a stroll to the lake," the
viscount told Lady Eve as he lifted her from the
saddle after they had reached the stables. "I feel
the need to stretch my legs after so much riding."
He had spoken only after she had made the
announcement to the whole group that tea would
be served directly in the drawing room.

She looked a little annoyed for a moment before smiling at him. "I would accompany you, my lord," she said, "except that my guests would think it rag-mannered of me to abandon them at teatime."

"And you would need a maid to accompany you," he said. Her hand for some reason was in his. He squeezed it. "I shall see you later?"

He felt almost guilty as he strolled off in the direction of the horseshoe lake to the west of the house. Almost as if he were doing something quite clandestine. Perhaps he should have mentioned why he was going to the lake. He had no reason and no wish to keep his rendezvous there a secret. But he guessed from the evidence he had gathered so far that Lady Barbara, even though she lived on her father's estate, was not considered to be a full member of the family. He guessed that her family would not look kindly on her consorting with one of the guests from the house. And since she must be dependent upon them, he supposed that they could make life unpleasant for her if she did something to arouse their disapproval.

He could not quite imagine any of his own sisters being ostracized by the rest of the family under similar circumstances. Rather, doubtless they would all fall upon yet one more child in the family with great glee. But then, it was hard to imagine any of his sisters unmarried and with child. He knew he would be angry if any such thing had happened to any of them—angry at the man who had so carelessly caused their disgrace.

They were standing on the bank of the lake, mother and son, Lady Barbara looking out over the water to the still bare trees at the other side, the boy looking anxiously back toward the house.

He visibly brightened and waved vigorously as the viscount came into sight.

"Famous!" he yelled when Lord Brandon came within earshot. "You came, sir. I knew you would. See, Mama? I said he would come."

She turned and smiled at him. She was wearing the same blue cloak and bonnet he had seen her in before. "I heard that you had all gone to Woville Castle," she said. "I was trying to make sure that Zachary was not overly expectant of your coming."

"I promised," he said. "Your son knows that gentlemen do not break promises, do you not, Zach? Is the *Lady Barbara* ready to sail?"

"Over there," the boy said, pointing excitedly to their right. "The inlet is sheltered. The wind would blow it out to sea if we tried to sail it here."

"Ah, yes," the viscount said, squinting out across the water. "Clever of you to have noticed. Let us go, then. Ma'am?" He offered his arm to Lady Barbara.

There were problems. The boat listed so heavily to starboard when Zachary first tried to sail it that it was in danger of capsizing altogether. And when the sail was adjusted, it was not willing to pick up any wind at all, so that it seemed as if the boat was going to scrape ignominiously against the shore for safety.

Lord Brandon first knelt on the bank beside the boy and then sat cross-legged on the ground, heedless of the cold or possible damp of the ground. He worked patiently at the boat, making several minor adjustments while Zachary watched with anxious disappointment and his mother stood quietly behind.

"There," the viscount said at last. "Try it now."

The boat bobbed and spun on the water, took a

few seconds to decide whether or not it would do what it was supposed to do, and then caught the breeze in its canvas and sailed bravely out across the few yards to the opposite bank.

"Hoorah!" Zachary leapt to his feet and jumped up and down in his excitement. "It does work. I knew it would. Just look at it, Mama. Look at it!"

The viscount stood up and brushed grass from his coat and breeches. "We forgot one thing, Zach," he said, ruffling the boy's hair with one hand. "We forgot the champagne to break over the hull before she sailed. But no matter. The *Lady Barbara* scorns the consumption of alcohol."

He laughed as the boy darted around the bank to meet the boat at the other side and start it on its return journey.

"Be careful," his mother called. "Don't go too near the edge, Zachary."

But the child was too excited to listen to any adult. He started his boat out on its way and raced back around the bank again to the point at which the craft would come to land. He would be fortunate if he did not end up having a ducking, the viscount thought, striding toward him. And a ducking in February with a stiff and fresh breeze blowing would not be an enjoyable experience. He knew. It had happened to him once. Though he had been pushed, of course, by a younger brother—though none of the brothers who had been close enough to have done it had ever owned up to the dastardly deed.

He was not a moment too soon. The boy was reaching out too early for his boat and one foot was already slipping from the bank when Lord Brandon shouted at him and reached out a steadying hand. Zachary also screeched, feeling his balance going.

The viscount opened his mouth to deliver a caution on carelessness and its probable consequences, when he heard a muffled scream from behind and turned to see Lady Barbara, rigid with terror, both hands pressed to her mouth. His body must have screened her view of what had been happening. But she must have heard the two shouts. He strode toward her as her son, behind him, hauled in his boat and stepped back from the bank.

"All is well," he said. "I had a strong hold on him, ma'am. He did not fall in. He is quite safe."

But she had lost control of herself for the moment. Her face was drained of all color and she stared at him with wide and dazed eyes. Her hands were shaking over her mouth.

"It is all right," he said, reaching out and taking her reassuringly by the shoulders. "He is quite safe, Barbara. And I would not have let him drown, you know. The worst that could have happened was that he would have been soaked. Boys invariably survive such discomforts."

"He is ... He is ..." But her teeth were chattering. "He is all I have," she said as he drew her against him and held her there, his arms firmly about her. "I have nothing else in the world. Only him."

"I know." He spoke quietly against her ear and rocked her in his arms. "But you must know that I would not have allowed him to come to harm, Barbara."

"I am sorry," she said, relaxing in his arms, the rigidity going from her body. "I am making such a cake of myself. I'm sorry."

"No," he said. "He is your only son. I understand."

He pictured himself with a son or daughter if

only Anna-Marie could have lived so long. And he knew that that child would have been precious both for its own sake and for the reminder of the love he had known with its mother. And once again he felt the stabbing of a certain envy of Lady Barbara Hanover.

"Mama," Zachary's voice said, "did I frighten you? But the boat is super, is it not? Wait until I tell Ben. And Uncle Will."

"Zachary." She pushed herself from the viscount's arms and stooped down to draw her son into a fierce hug. "You foolish boy. Oh, I should spank you hard. What did I tell you when we were coming here? What did I tell you?"

"Not to get too close to the edge," he said sheepishly. "I would not have fallen in, Mama. I was being careful." He looked up to the viscount, who widened his eyes and winked at him.

"Oh," she said crossly, straightening up, "you think to convince me, do you? Did you at least rescue my namesake?"

"Here it is," he said, holding up the dripping boat.

"Good," she said. "It is time to go home. I am sure that Lord Brandon must be eager to get back to his tea at the house. Thank him for coming."

"I shall escort you home," the viscount said. "Would you care to ride on my shoulders, Zach?"

His shoulders were always a coveted perch among his nephews and nieces. Young Robert had actually bloodied Andrew's nose over the privilege at Christmastime and been forced to walk every step of the way home from the mill as a result, while Andrew rode triumphant and red-nosed.

Zachary was no exception to the general rule. Within a few seconds he was astride the viscount's shoulders, his boat clutched in one hand, and Lord

Brandon was left with the suspicion that he had maneuvered Lady Barbara into a shared walk that she had not planned and maybe did not wish for. And he was giving himself a two-mile walk that he had not expected.

Why? he asked himself, when tea and company and Lady Eve awaited him at the house. But the answer was not difficult to find. He had found something of a kindred spirit in this woman who had loved and lost and who clung to her memories, more tangible than his own. And he had held a woman in his arms for the first time in two years and she had felt good there. He felt a curiosity to know her better, to know more than the mother whose love was focused so totally on her child.

"Talavera," he said. "That was early in the wars. And he had just arrived there?"

"Yes," she said. "He was so eager to go. He could hardly believe his good fortune when the orders came through. He tried to hide some of his elation from me, of course, because we were to have been married in the summer and he knew I would be disappointed at the postponement. But he was happy to be going and I would not show him my unhappiness or anxiety. I am glad now that I did not."

"Did he know about the child?" he asked quietly.

"I don't know." She smiled somewhat sadly. "I had only one letter from him. But that was too soon. I did not hear again, and my letter was not among his effects that were returned to his father. I don't know. I like to believe that he knew."

"One of my brothers fought at Waterloo," he said. "He was fortunate to escape with only flesh wounds, but it was a month before we heard, and even then it was only that he had been wounded.

We knew that so many died of wounds and the fever. Another month passed before my father and I could get over there and find him to bring him home. I know the anxiety. It must have been a dreadful time for you, especially with the added burden of your condition."

"Yes," she said. "They did not tell me until after Zachary was born." She smiled up at her son, who was gazing about him, not listening to the adult conversation. "It is a marvel how someone can be taken away and another given to take his place."

"Yes," the viscount said. "You loved him." It was a statement, not a question.

"Yes," she said. She looked at him, quiet for a moment. "You knew that your wife was dying when you married her? How long did she live?"

"For two months," he said. "She was bedridden the whole time, poor Anna-Marie. Mercifully there was little pain. Just the terrible weakness and weariness of consumption. But she was always a frail girl, though sweet and patient and cheerful. She never once complained or raged against her fate. Unlike me. I almost bled to death after putting my hand through a pane of glass the day of her death."

"I am the fortunate one, am I not?" she said. "I do not know how I would have lived without my child. But I suppose I would have. You have lived."

"For a long time," he said, "one does not even want the pain to go away. It seems disloyal to be without pain, to allow an hour to go by without thinking of the one who has gone. And there is a certain fear of forgetting, as if that would prove that one had not really loved at all. But life is wiser than we, it seems. Pain eases. One laughs again. Eventually one is ready to live again."

"Yes," she said.

He looked down at her. But he could not ask the question. It would be impertinent. Did she have anything or anyone to live for except her son? Was it possible for her to resume life as he was resuming it? Did the fact that she was an unwed mother doom her to living on the fringes of life forever after? Was there no end to her disgrace, as there was an end to his grief?

"To dance," she said wistfully before he could say anything, looking ahead to where the dower house was just coming into sight. "How lovely it would be to dance." But she seemed to realize suddenly what she had said. She flushed and looked up at her son. "He must be getting heavy. Zachary, do get down, sweetheart, and run ahead and open the gate. Will you come inside for tea, sir?"

"I have been gone longer than I intended," he said, swinging the child down from his shoulders. "I think I had better return to the house. But thank you."

He could think of no excuse to see her again. And did he want to see her again? He had come to participate in the gaiety of a house party, not to indulge in bittersweet memories with someone who had had experiences comparable to his own. He had come to pay court to Lady Eve Hanover, not to develop a friendship with her elder sister.

But yes, he did want to see her again, he realized as they stopped walking and he looked down into her beautiful face. And he knew suddenly what gave it its beauty. Eight years before, she had probably been exceedingly pretty, as her sister was now. But in those eight years, suffering and love had etched character into her face, and calmness and knowledge of life into her eyes. And she was beautiful as a result.

"Perhaps I will take you up on that invitation tomorrow instead, or at least one day before I leave," he said. "If I may?"

Her eyes smiled at him. "You will be welcome, sir," she said. "But you must not feel honor-bound to come. I know that these are busy and enjoyable days at the house."

"Don't scold him too roundly when you have him alone," he said, his eyes twinkling down at her. "Boys are ever heedless. It is what being a boy is all about."

"I had noticed," she said.

And without realizing it, he had taken her hand in his. He squeezed it, hesitated, and raised it to his lips.

"I am sorry about Talavera," he said.

"And I about that wasting illness," she said.

"But life goes on." He squeezed her hand again, released it, and waved to Zachary, who was swinging on the gate. He turned and walked almost regretfully back along the driveway toward the main house and the gaiety of a Valentine's house party.

He did not come the next day, of course, but it did not matter, as she was not really expecting him. It was true that she postponed her weekly visit to some of her father's elderly dependents during the afternoon, but then, she had promised to go through the linen cupboards with her housekeeper one day, and that was the day. Besides, her son had discovered that he enjoyed arithmetic, and she had to spend some time upstairs with him, giving him columns of figures to puzzle over.

He would not come. She was not expecting him.

He was a kind gentleman and he had taken a liking to Zachary and given him pleasure at the lake. He had worked patiently with the boat until it sailed. She could still picture him sitting on the cold grass, frowning over the toy while Zachary knelt beside him watching, the top of his head almost touching Lord Brandon's cheek.

And he had been kind to her too. For eight years she had had no dealings with anyone except her family and her father's tenants and laborers and the people of the village. She would have expected a gentleman, and a nobleman at that, to recoil in embarrassment and disgust as soon as he discovered who and what she was. The viscount had not only continued to treat her with courtesy, but had shown her sympathy and understanding too.

Was it any wonder that she was falling in love with him? It would be very strange if she were not. Poor starving fool, she thought as she sorted through linen, weaving dreams about the only gentleman to take notice of her in eight years. About Eve's future husband.

Suddenly she was glad of the fact that she and Eve were not close, that Eve avoided her whenever possible, as if her disgrace might be somehow infectious. She would not want to be close to her sister once she became the Viscountess Brandon. She wondered if Eve would be happy with him. More important, she wondered if he would be happy with Eve. And she understood finally why her sister had described him as she had. Eve would not fully appreciate kindness and gentleness.

Barbara hugged a pile of linen sheets to her and stared off into space. She could feel his arms strong about her, the unexpected strength and firmness of chest and thigh muscles. She could hear his voice murmuring soothing words into her ear. She could smell his cologne and the warm masculine smell of him.

Poor starved fool, she thought again, and returned to her work with renewed vigor. She would probably not see him again. She doubted that she would be invited to the wedding. And she would not wish to attend even if she were.

He came on the evening of the following day. It was dark already. Zachary was in bed. She was sitting in the parlor working on a shawl for Mrs. Williams, who was old and felt the cold constantly even through the summer months. And she was remembering Valentine's Day eight years before and the watch case she had embroidered with a red heart for Zach. And the silver heart-shaped locket he had given her and the promise to have his miniature painted as soon as possible for her to keep inside it. It was still empty.

She heard the knock on the door, and her hands paused at her work as she waited for a servant to answer it. It could be any number of people, she told herself, even at this late hour. There was no possible reason for her heart to beat so painfully. There was no reason to believe that it would be he.

But it was. She rose as her manservant announced him and he came striding into the room, smiling at her. He was dressed for evening in a form-fitting coat and silk shirt and elegantly tied neckcloth. He looked quite devastatingly handsome, she thought, inwardly mocking her own reactions. She was behaving like a schoolgirl.

"This is a very improper time to pay a call," he said. "I came to apologize for my failure to appear either yesterday afternoon or this. I am afraid you were quite right. Almost every minute of each day has been planned for. Boredom will certainly be no one's worry this week. Having said that, I shall take my leave immediately if you wish."

She should send him away. His presence alone in her home was improper. But what did propriety matter to her reputation? Besides, she did not want to send him away.

"Will you take a seat, my lord?" she said formally, indicating a chair close to the fire. "I shall ring for tea."

"Please don't on my account," he said. "I have eaten and drunk far too much in the past few days." But he crossed the room to the chair and waited for her to sit down before doing likewise. "How is Zach? Has he fallen into any lakes in the past two days?"

"No," she said. "But he has explained at great and tedious length to Ben, our manservant, and to William, early this morning, how you made his boat seaworthy. You have become his great hero, you know."

He grinned. "It is what comes of having a whole army of nephews and nieces," he said. "I seem to trip over them wherever I turn during our family gatherings. I suppose because I am unencumbered by wife and family myself I seem fair game to those who cannot attract a mother's or a father's attention."

Barbara thought it probably had more to do with a certain kindliness of manner and willingness to treat children as if they were people who mattered, but she did not express her thoughts aloud.

"There are to be charades later," he explained. "But the ladies had important business to transact after dinner. Something to do with hearts and valentines, I gather, something involving a great deal of merriment and secrecy. The gentlemen were banished to the billiard room. I escaped."

She smiled. "You do not like a constant round of entertainment, my lord?" she asked. "I thought that was why people spent the Season in London and visited places like Bath and Brighton and went to house parties."

"But one can be so ferociously enjoying oneself," he said, "that one has no time to simply enjoy oneself." He laughed. "And if you can make sense out of that, you must be very clever indeed."

She laughed too. "I am very clever, then," she said. "But is it not very wonderful, sir, to be able to ride with other people and converse with them and play games with them and dance with them at will?"

"Yes, it is." His smile on her was gentle. "The important words being 'at will.' I suppose it is no more pleasurable, though, to feel forced into entertainments than to be forced to stay away from them. Is that what has happened to you?"

She drew the shawl toward her and resumed her crocheting. "I am content with my life," she said. "I have this home and everything I could possibly need. And I have Zachary. I could not give myself over to pleasure when I have a son to bring up."

"Is that it?" he asked. "Your home and your son?"

She did not think of telling him that his question was impertinent. She thought about it. Was that all? No, there was more. She would soon lose her sanity if there were no more.

"My father allows me to visit his tenants and laborers," she said. "I like to call on the sick and the elderly. Some of them like to be read to. Some

of the older people like just to talk, to remember
the old times when they were young. And their
own families are often too busy with their daily
work to listen. The elderly are often lonely, even
when surrounded by family."

He was smiling when she glanced up at him.

"And yet you want to dance," he said.

She looked up at him again, startled. "I was
foolish to say that," she said. "I suppose all of us
sometimes long for the stars. But that does not
mean that reality is unbearable or even
unpleasant."

"When did you last dance?" he asked.

She smiled. "Almost exactly eight years ago,"
she said. "At the Valentine's ball at the house. The
world was mine, except that Zach was going away
the day after and I feared that I would never see
him again."

And so she had gone out walking into the night
with him and stepped inside the pavilion on the
lower lawn with him to escape the coolness of the
night air, and their kisses had grown more desperate until she had been down on the floor of the
pavilion, his coat beneath her, and he had been
pushing with frantic and inexperienced hands at
her skirts and she had reached for him with equal
desperation and equal inexperience.

"He must have been dark and handsome." The
viscount was smiling at her. "And tall too? His
son is going to be tall."

"And tall too," she said. "He was all that a
giddy eighteen-year-old found dashing and irresistible. And a cavalry officer to boot."

"Did he love you?" he asked. "Would he have
come back to you?"

"Oh, yes," she said. "He would have come back.

He would have been pleased about Zachary,
though distressed for me."

"Valentine's Day is painful for you too, then,"
he said. "I married in January. Anna-Marie died
before the end of March."

"Ah," she said.

Lady Barbara had never married her lover, he
thought, but she had conceived his child. He had
married Anna-Marie, but their marriage had never
been consummated. She had been too ill. He had
made the decision not to distress her by trying to
take his conjugal rights. He had shown his love by
abstaining.

He got to his feet and held out a hand to Barbara. "Dance with me now," he said.

She looked up at him in astonishment and
laughed. "Dance?" she said. "Here? Now?" She
looked about her foolishly. "But there is no
music."

"Do you not sing?" he asked. "I can do tolerably
well myself."

She laughed again. But somehow she was on her
feet, and her hand was reaching out toward his.

"You will never have waltzed," he said. "Have
you seen it done? Have you heard of it?"

"The vicar's wife says it is a very improper
dance," she said.

He grinned. "You may judge for yourself in a
short while," he said. "You place a hand on my
shoulder, thus." He raised the hand he held and
placed it on his shoulder. "And my hand rests at
your waist, as so. I take your other hand in mine
like this."

"This is absurd," she said, suddenly embarrassed and aware of the emptiness of the room
and the closeness of her guest.

"Very," he said. "All dancing is, if you really

think about it. But you want to dance again. You have said so."

"I would like a star in my pocket too," she said. "But I never expect to find one there."

"And just as well too," he said. "It would doubt-less be a mite heavy."

It was more than absurd, she thought several minutes later after he had taught her the steps and was dancing with her, humming a tune at the same time. It was ridiculous. It was thoroughly improper. It was exhilarating and wonderful.

She stepped on his foot and heard herself giggle.

"Ouch!" he said, and his blue eyes twinkled down into hers as he stopped humming and lost the beat. "If this were a fairy tale, I would be able to snap my fingers and a full orchestra would appear. Alas, this is not a fairy tale."

"Oh, yes, it is," she said, not at all realizing what she was saying until she heard the words. They had stopped dancing.

"Yes," he said, "it is." And he bent his head and kissed her on the lips.

He had meant it to be just a light gesture of affection. She realized that afterward. Of course that was all he had meant. He had called on her, coversed with her, danced with her. He was about to take his leave. He had kissed her, much as a brother might kiss a sister or one dear friend another.

But she lost her head and immediately pressed her lips closer to his. And then her body was against his and her arms up about his neck, the fingers of one hand in his hair. And his arms came all about her as they had two days before at the lake and his head angled against hers and his mouth opened over hers and he was licking at her lips with his tongue.

She heard herself moan as her mouth opened and his tongue explored its way inside.

And then his mouth was moving away from hers and down over her chin and along her throat. His hands were finding her breasts.

Poor starving fool. Her own thoughts came back to her and she pushed hard against his shoulders and turned her back on him.

"Barbara," he said after a moment's silence. "I am so sorry. I had no intention of allowing that to happen. Please believe me. That is not why I came here. I am so sorry."

She was so ashamed. She hid her face in her hands and closed her eyes tightly. She had not known a man in eight years, had had no dealings with any in all that time. And now she had met a young and good-looking man—the man who would be betrothed to Eve before the week was out—and she had grabbed for him as if there were nothing more important in life than being touched by a man, than lying with him. For a few moments she had behaved exactly as she had behaved eight years before in the pavilion. Except that then she had been eighteen years old and she had been with someone she had known all her life and loved for all of two years.

She thought she would surely die of shame.

"Please leave," she said.

"Barbara . . ."

"Please leave."

She kept her eyes closed and her hands over her face until she heard the door open quietly and close again. Even then she did not move immediately.

He wondered at what exact moment he had fallen in love with her. When he had first seen her walking along the driveway behind her son? When he had held her and soothed her at the lake? When he had danced with her and she had stepped on his foot and giggled like a girl? When he had kissed her?

Or perhaps there was no exact moment. Perhaps all his encounters with her, few though they had been, had contributed to his knowledge the morning after that kiss that he loved her.

Or perhaps he did not love her at all, he thought. Perhaps it was that he was lonely and that he had recognized her loneliness and responded to it. Perhaps it was nothing more than that.

But Lady Eve could soothe his loneliness. Any number of women who would be only too eager to receive the addresses of a wealthy viscount and heir to a marquess could soothe his loneliness. And yet with Lady Eve, with all the other guests at Durham Hall, he felt lonelier than he had for the previous two years.

No, it was not just need that drew him to Lady Barbara Hanover. It was Lady Barbara herself. There was a quiet maturity about her, an acceptance of life, an absence of bitterness despite the cruel treatment she had received at the hands of fate, an inner strength. Those qualities drew him like a magnet. And her beauty. And the slender, graceful body.

She was as different from Anna-Marie as it was possible to be. Anna-Marie had been tiny and fragile and timid and adoring. He had realized long before that his feelings for her had been as much paternal as loverlike. He had wanted to shield her from the inevitable clutches of death. He would have gladly died for her if he could. But he had loved her and always would.

And now he loved Lady Barbara Hanover. Except that he had no business loving her. He was a guest at the home of the Duke of Durham, and the duke did not even publicly acknowledge her. He himself was there on the understanding that he was Lady Eve's suitor, and she obviously had every intention of having him. It would be awkward to do nothing about developing that relationship after all. It would be impossible to choose her elder sister instead.

And he had insulted Lady Barbara horribly the night before. Kissing her like a gauche schoolboy and losing his head as soon as his lips touched hers. Allowing the kiss to become intimate and suggestive. Touching her, fondling her through the thin fabric of her dress. Wanting her.

God! How much more insulting could he possibly have been? It had been as if he were telling her that he considered her a woman of easy virtue merely because she had once loved too well and too unwisely. He should never even have called on her at that hour of the night.

What must she think of him? He had felt her need. It had almost overwhelmed her—and him—for a few moments. But that was of no consequence now. He had started the whole thing by going there, by dancing with her, by kissing her. She was a woman of dignity. He would be fortunate indeed if she even allowed him to apologize.

His thoughts and his feelings gnawed at him all morning until the time when Lady Eve and her lady guests led the gentlemen into a downstairs salon and displayed to their interested gaze a table of large ornate hearts at either side of the room—seven on each table. Before dinner that night, each of the gentlemen was to pick up one heart from the table on the right. The lady whose name was written on the back of the heart was to be his valentine for the next day. Each lady was to pick a heart from the table on the left. The gentleman whose name appeared on the back was to be her valentine for the next day.

"In a moment we ladies will leave," Lady Eve announced, "so that you may each write your name on the back of a heart, gentlemen. But remember that you are gentlemen and must not peep at the hearts of the other table."

"But what if my valentine does not choose my heart in return?" Mr. Stills asked. "Will it not be a trifle confusing?"

The ladies laughed merrily. "Therein lies the fun," Lady Eve said, clapping her hands. "Tomorrow could prove to be a most interesting day."

All the hearts were quite different from one another, the viscount noticed. Doubtless there would be some whispering and dropping of hints between then and the time before dinner when the choices were to be made. The choosing of a valentine might not be quite as random as it would appear to be.

But the idea was fun. He had to admit that. He grinned at Lady Eve as she smiled brightly at him, and winked at Lady Caroline Weaver as she whisked herself from the room behind the other ladies. He chose a rather lopsided heart whose base had been cut clumsily with careless scissors, and wrote his name large on the back of it.

He would slip outside, he decided as he left the room. There must be almost an hour before luncheon. If he hurried, he should be able to ride to the dower house and back in that time and make his apologies. There was little else he could do. He could not call on her for tea as if nothing had happened between them the night before. If he went out through a back entrance, perhaps he would avoid company.

He was almost at the back entrance of his choice when he literally collided with a servant coming down the back stairs. He caught her by the arms to steady her.

"I do beg your pardon," he said.

But she was not a servant. It was hard to know what Lady Barbara was doing coming down a servants' stairway—no, perhaps not so hard—but there she was anyway. She focused her eyes on his chin.

"I was not looking where I was going," she said. And then, unnecessarily, "I was calling on my mother."

"I was on my way to the dower house," he said.

"There is no need." She had not once looked into his face. "It was all my fault. I would prefer to forget about it."

"No," he said, and somehow he had possessed himself of her hand. "No, Barbara, I should not have put you in such a compromising position. I apologize most humbly."

She looked up into his eyes then, such an agony of something in her own that he unconsciously gripped her hand more tightly. But there was no chance to say more. Someone else was coming down the stairs, and he drew her to the door and outside.

"Zachary is in the stables with the puppies," she said. "He will be wondering why I have been so long."

Which was as foolish a thing as she could have said, he thought. What boy, alone in the stables with horses and dogs and puppies, would ever think of wondering why his mother was spending such a long time with his grandmother? He offered her his arm.

"No." She shook her head. "You ought not to be seen with me, my lord. My father would not like it."

"A gentleman being polite to his own daughter?" he said, falling into step beside her and clasping his hands behind his back.

"You are going to marry Eve," she said. "You are, are you not?"

"I have made no formal offer," he said.

"But you will." Her pace had quickened. "You will discover soon enough that I am acknowledged only as a dependent. William is kind to Zachary, and my mother still receives me, but to my father I am no longer his daughter. Stay away from me, my lord. If you think to befriend Zachary and to be kind to me, you will find yourself in an untenable position after you are married."

"I was not being kind last evening," he said. "I am sorry, Barbara. I did not mean to be insulting. I was playing with fire, coming late as I did and then dancing with you."

She smiled unexpectedly. "At least I have danced again," she said. She looked up at him fleetingly. "It was wonderful."

"Tomorrow there will be an orchestra at the house here," he said, and then wished he had not spoken.

"Yes," she said.

Zachary was sitting cross-legged in the straw, his chosen puppy sleeping in his lap as he stroked with one finger between its eyes. The mother looked quite unconcerned, glad perhaps to have one less puppy to worry her constantly.

"Mama," the boy said excitedly when she appeared in the doorway of the stall with the viscount. He scrambled to his feet, holding the puppy in the palm of one hand. "Uncle Will says I can take him home tomorrow. Because it is Valentine's Day, he said. What is Valentine's Day?"

"It is a day to show love," she said.

"I am going to care for him until he follows me everywhere," Zachary said. "I am going to train him to fetch and to sit up and beg. Uncle Will says that the first thing I will have to do is train him not to make puddles on the floor."

"Yes," she said with a sigh while the viscount chuckled.

"Hello, sir," Zachary said. "Will you come tomorrow to see him? I want to show you my drawings of horses. Mama says that one looks just like my papa's horse when he left for the wars. Mama says I am a good artist."

Lord Brandon rubbed the backs of two fingers across the child's nose. "I shall call for a few minutes," he said, "if it is all right with your mother."

"Oh, it will be all right with Mama," Zachary said confidently. "Won't it, Mama?"

She looked up at the viscount's chin again. "You will be busy," she said. "But Zachary would be pleased if you can find a moment to come."

And you? he wanted to ask. But it was a pointless question. It would draw merely a polite response. It was a good thing the boy was there, he thought, even though he had turned away to set his puppy down carefully beside the mother dog and was laughing at the squeaking of his waking pet. And it was a good thing that the voices of grooms told him that they were not far away. He might have drawn her into his arms otherwise. She looked so very tense, so very unhappy.

She had been warm and soft and yielding and

passionate the night before. She would be a calm and a gentle and a warm companion. And it was so long since he had contemplated a relationship with a woman. It was so long since he had had a woman. Even his marriage had not brought him that sensual satisfaction that he craved.

But her son was there. And the grooms were there. And it was just as well.

"I shall do my best to find a moment," he said. He bade her and her son a good morning and turned back to the house. He sensed that she did not want him to walk home with them.

He wished suddenly that he had been invited to Durham Hall as just an ordinary guest. If that were so, he would know his course and he would pursue it without hesitation. But it was not so. Although no formal offer had been made, he had been invited there as the prospective husband of Lady Eve Hanover. Surely it would be arranged that she was his valentine and he hers the next day. He would be expected to pay court to her all day and to make his offer either during the evening or on the following day.

He was not committed, of course. There was nothing to stop him from leaving Durham Hall a free man. But there was everything to stop him from turning his attentions to the girl's sister.

Yes, it was as well that he had been stopped from acting according to instinct in the stables a few minutes before. It would be well for him to find it quite impossible to call at the dower house the next day. Except that the promise had been made to the boy.

And except that he knew he would move heaven and hell to make that brief visit.

* * *

"Do you approve of our little game, my lord?" Lady Eve looked up into Lord Brandon's face as they strolled with the rest of her guests through the trees toward one of the follies later that afternoon. Her eyes sparkled with fun and merriment.

"Now I know why you and the other ladies were absent for so long last evening," he said. "You must have made two hearts apiece."

"Right," she said. "One would think that a heart is a heart, would one not? We were amused to find that all were different when we were finally finished and compared efforts."

The viscount smiled. This was exactly what he had been expecting.

"Mine were short and fat," she said, laughing, "and extravagant. I used twice as much lace as anyone else. But I ought not to be saying this, ought I?"

"That depends, I suppose," he said gallantly, "on who your listener is."

"But it is all to depend upon chance," she said. "Or upon fate or Cupid. What did you think of the hearts on the gentlemen's table?"

It was very tempting to lead her deliberately astray. And yet she was pretty and good-natured and favored him. He had come with the full intention of courting her. Had he not met her sister, the chances were that he would be entering wholeheartedly into this game of chance that was not intended to be left to chance at all—not as far as Lady Eve Hanover was concerned, anyway.

"That one of them was lopsided," he said, "but otherwise perfect." It was not strictly true, but close enough. There would be some chance left in the game. More than one heart had been less than symmetrical in shape. He had not noticed another with a clumsy cut at its base.

"You and I will be first to choose," she said. "You as the gentleman of highest rank and me as hostess."

"Not your brother?" he asked.

"William feels that as host he should be last," she said.

"At least," he said, "he will not have the agony of a decision to make."

She laughed.

And so when the ceremony began later that evening, before dinner, with the duke and duchess as amused spectators, Viscount Brandon had seven hearts to choose among, while everyone else watched, the gentlemen joking, the ladies tittering and bright-eyed.

Perhaps even then he would have given in to temptation if he could. But there was no mistaking the short and fat red heart with its two rows of pleated lace. He pretended to ponder before picking it up, turning it over, and smiling and bowing to Lady Eve. She blushed as everyone else exclaimed and applauded.

She was not so fortunate. There were three lopsided hearts on the other table, one with the scissor cut at the bottom, another with the lace crooked at the center, and the third quite perfect apart from the lack of symmetry of its two halves. Lady Eve smiled and picked up the last of the three and turned it over.

"Sir Reginald Brock," she said with a dazzling smile for that gentleman as he bowed and looked thoroughly pleased with himself.

She was perfectly well-bred, the viscount thought. Not by the flicker of an eye did she show disappointment, if indeed she felt disappointment. She touched him on the sleeve while Miss Woodfall made her choice.

"Would you believe that there were three lop-sided hearts?" she said.

The viscount frowned and shook his head rue-fully. "But at least," he said, "I had the good fortune to draw your name."

She smiled again.

Valentine's Day was, as Lady Eve had predicted, one of good fun. For her careful planning of the Valentine's game had ensured that no couples were paired for the entire day to the exclusion of all others. No gentleman had had the fortune—or misfortune—of choosing a valentine who had also chosen him.

Viscount Brandon found the situation to his liking. For while he gave his attentions to Lady Eve all day, seating himself beside her at luncheon, he found that the Honorable Miss Mowbury was intent on luring him into her company and that Lady Eve was flirting quite determinedly with Sir Reginald Brock.

And the day was much to his liking, too. It was fun, exhilarating, busy. There was all the anticipation of the ball, which would bring other neighbors to Durham Hall. He could enjoy himself without in any way feeling trapped.

Trapped? He smiled ruefully to himself as he went to his room to fetch his greatcoat after luncheon. Had he definitely decided, then, that he did not wish to offer for Lady Eve Hanover? She was as charming and as lovely and as eligible as she had been a week before, when he had been contemplating this week in the country and its probable consequences with some pleasure.

Yes, he had decided. Of course he had. Circumstances made it almost impossible for him to pay court to Barbara. But he could not marry Eve when he loved her elder sister. Perhaps in the future, he thought. Perhaps after a year or so, when his prospective courtship of Lady Eve had been forgotten, when perhaps she would have married someone else. Perhaps he could come back.

He walked through to his bedchamber from the dressing room and opened a drawer next to the bed, which held nothing except a large red velvet heart with lace that had yellowed with time. He smiled and waited for the stab of pain. But it did not come. Only a sweet nostalgia, a faint longing for what might have been. She had been dead for a little less than two years. Dear Anna-Marie. Could the heart mourn no longer than that?

He set the valentine carefully back into the drawer where he had placed it on his arrival at Durham Hall and thought of someone who had not danced for eight years to the day, except for an awkward waltz in a small parlor to the accompaniment of his humming. Of someone who wanted to dance again, to live again. Of someone who was alive and warm.

He shook his head and went back to his dressing room for his greatcoat. There was to be a drive to the village. Most of the guests, himself included, were eager to ransack the limited resources of the shops there for small Valentine's gifts. One for Lady Eve. None for Barbara. It would not be proper. She would not be willing to accept it. Perhaps something for her son instead.

He left the room and hurried down to the hallway, which was loud with chatter and laughter.

Barbara did consider going to visit Mrs. Williams on the afternoon of Valentine's Day to deliver the shawl she had finished the evening before. But she had been there yesterday afternoon, taking a basket of cakes and a book to read from. It would be strange to call two days in a row.

And she considered walking into the village to buy some new silks for her embroidery. But she had bought some just the previous week and told Miss Porter that she now had all the colors she needed for weeks to come. It would look peculiar if she went back so soon.

Besides, William delivered the puppy just after luncheon and brought word that Eve and most of the guests were themselves going into the village to shop. And of course there could be no leaving Zachary anyway. He was so very excited over his new pet and needed to share his excitement with someone more important to him than his nurse.

And truth to tell, she did not wish to go out and miss the viscount's visit. The chances were that it would be very short. It was even possible that he would not come at all, but she thought he would. He was a man who seemed to feel it important to keep his promises to children.

She would stay, she decided. After all, the few minutes of his visit were all she would have of Saint Valentine's Day. A foolish and a disturbing thought.

And so she was at home when he came, in the nursery with her son and the puppy, which was trying to scamper beneath the furniture away from the busy hands of its new master. He was smiling and cheerful and very handsome, and her heart turned over inside her.

"Well," he said to Zachary as her son rushed across the room to greet him. He ruffled the boy's hair. "How many puddles so far, Zach?"

"Only two," the boy said. "He drinks milk from

a saucer. You should see his tongue, sir. It is all pink. Shall I hold his mouth open to show you?"

"Hm," the viscount said. "Would you like your mouth held open so that someone might view your tongue or your teeth?"

The child laughed. "I am going to teach him to do tricks," he said.

The viscount looked up at Barbara and grinned. "I suspect it is going to be like having another child in your nursery for a while," he said.

"May I ring for tea?" she asked.

"I cannot stay," he said. "I decided to walk home from the village instead of riding in one of the conveyances with everyone else. But I must be back for tea. It seems to be obligatory on this particular day. And there is a ball to get ready for."

She smiled, disappointed, and glad that this encounter would not be prolonged.

"Zach," the viscount said, "where is that picture of your papa's horse?"

The boy raced across the room to fetch it, a drawing of a squat black horse whose hooves all rested solidly on the bottom edge of the paper.

"Ah, yes," Lord Brandon said, "a cavalry horse if ever I saw one. What was his name?"

"Jet," Zachary said without hesitation. "He was my papa's favorite, was he not, Mama?"

She nodded.

And then, almost before she had caught her breath from his arrival, he was taking his leave, handing a parcel he had been carrying to Zachary and smiling as the boy opened a package of sweetmeats.

"I am sure they must be strictly forbidden," he said. "But remind your mama that this is Valentine's Day. Let her have one."

"You did not need to bring him a gift," she said as she accompanied him down the stairs. "But thank you."

He stopped to look down at her before leaving the house. "It is almost over," he said quietly. "A few more hours and it will be February 15. Just an ordinary day, posing no threat at all."

But this is the fourteenth, she told him only with her eyes. *This is Valentine's Day and you are going to be dancing with Eve this evening to the music of a whole orchestra while I have only my fading memories of Zach and my painful dreams of you.*

She said nothing. She thought that perhaps she smiled.

He set light fingertips against one of her cheeks. "Happy Valentine's Day, Barbara," he said.

She watched him hesitate before bending his head and kissing her lightly on the other cheek.

She smiled again as he turned to leave the house. She said nothing. She could not. She was waging too fierce a battle against tears. She did not believe she had ever felt more lonely in her life.

"Mama." Zachary's voice came down the stairs. "He has made a puddle again."

He, Barbara thought, turning back to the stairs, was going to have to acquire a name soon. Not to mention a few indispensable skills.

The ballroom at Durham Hall was decorated with flowers from the hothouses. And with the bright silks and satins of the ladies' gowns and the gentlemen's evening coats and waistcoats. The ballroom was not large. As a result it looked almost as crowded as any London squeeze.

Viscount Brandon was not quite sure just how much the duke and duchess were expecting his offer for their younger daughter. They had been gracious to him and all their guests, and impeccably courteous. And yet at dinner, he noticed, a formal occasion attended by some of the neighboring gentry as well as the house guests, and one at which dinner partners were assigned rather than chosen, he was seated beside Lady Eve and was therefore to lead her into the opening set of the ball as well.

She glowed and looked rather like an angel, he thought, dressed all in white satin and lace, her blond hair styled in countless smooth and shining ringlets. He felt that every gentleman present envied him and expected that he would take full advantage of his position as her favored suitor.

"I do think Valentine's Day is the most wonderful day of the year, my lord," she said to him as he led her onto the floor and they waited for the orchestra to begin playing. "Would you not agree?"

He smiled at her and agreed. Her words came from a blissful inexperience of life, he thought. And he wished for her sake that she would always feel the same way about this day.

And yet he could not force himself to enjoy the ball. He danced each set, smiled and conversed, gave every appearance of enjoying himself. And he thought of someone sitting quietly at home, someone who should be here as the elder daughter of the duke. And someone who was probably longing to be here. Someone he longed to go to.

Mrs. Averly excused herself before the end of the third set, since part of her hem, which had come down as a result of a collision in a vigorous country dance previous to that particular set, was proving troublesome and must be repaired. The viscount smiled and let her go and wandered from the room to enjoy the unexpected few minutes to himself. His steps took him to the conservatory, on the opposite side of the hall from the ballroom.

And there he surprised and embarrassed both himself and a couple locked in close and some-what indecorous embrace. Brock and Lady Eve.

"I do beg your pardon," he said, inclining his head and half-turning to leave. They had sprung apart and she was plucking at the bodice of her gown.

She laughed and shrugged her shoulders. "It *is* Valentine's Day, my lord," she said.

"And I had the good fortune to be chosen as Eve's valentine," Sir Reginald added with a flash of white teeth. He was tall and blond and had been a favorite with the ladies all week.

There was perhaps a little anxiety in Lady Eve's expression, Lord Brandon thought as he looked steadily at her. And a little defiance too. He grinned at her.

"Continue where you left off," he said. "I shall make sure that the door is securely fastened behind me."

"Thank you," Lady Eve said, and the defiance was quite unmistakable in her voice now. It was almost spite. "That is very good of you, my lord."

"Eve, darling . . ." Sir Reginald was saying as the viscount shut the door quietly.

He was, of course, only a baronet and only mod-erately wealthy. Not a rich viscount with pros-pects of becoming an enormously wealthy marquess. But he was handsome and charming. Perhaps she would settle for him, Lord Brandon thought. Or perhaps tonight's *tête-à-tête* was merely flirtation in the spirit of the day.

But he did not care. All he knew was that she had just done him an enormous favor. All he knew was that he wanted to shout with laughter and with exuberance and joy.

The Duke of Durham was talking with two of his neighbors. The duchess was beside him. Viscount Brandon waited until the neighbors turned away before crossing the room. He bowed and smiled at the duchess and turned to her husband.

"Sir," he said, "may I beg the favor of a private word with you at your convenience?"

He was aware of her grace clasping her hands to her bosom. He saw the broad smile on the duke's face as he clasped a hand on the viscount's shoulder.

"No time like the present, my boy," he said. "No time like the present. Come to my study. I have known your father for years," his grace said, his voice jovial as they left the ballroom and made their way to his study. "We were at school together and at university. A madcap fellow. Never a dull moment. He was the last one anyone would have expected to settle down and raise himself a large family. But he took one look at your mama and changed like that." The duke snapped his fingers and laughed heartily. "And who can blame him? A charming lady, Brandon. Charming. The toast of the *ton*."

The viscount could not quite picture his plump and placid mother as the toast of the London Season, though he had to admit that even after well over thirty years of marriage and eleven children, including the two who had died in infancy, she still had a pretty face.

"Now." His grace rubbed his hands together and turned a jovial smiling face on his guest. "What can I do for you, my boy?"

"I believe that your permission is not necessary," Lord Brandon said. "But I am asking for it, sir. I would like everything to be done properly. I would like your blessing on the offer I am about to make your daughter."

The duke's eyebrows shot up. "She is but nineteen, Brandon," he said. "Had you thought her of age already? But of course, my boy, I am more delighted than I can—"

The viscount interrupted him. "I am hoping that your *elder* daughter will do me the honor of becoming my wife, sir," he said.

The duke stopped mid-sentence, and his jaw hung inelegantly for a moment. "Barbara?" he said.

The viscount inclined his head. "I love her," he said. "I hope to persuade her that she returns my regard."

"You have met her?" The duke's eyebrows drew together. "Why, the hussy. She has my express orders to—"

"Her behavior has been exemplary," Lord Brandon said. "It is I who have gone out of my way to arrange meetings with her and her son."

"And has she thought of telling you," the duke asked, "that the child is a bastard?"

"That the father died fighting for the honor of his country before he could marry her, yes," the viscount said.

The duke scratched his head. "You want to marry Barbara," he said, as if the truth of what he was hearing was only beginning to sink into his mind. "Your papa will not like it above half, my boy."

The viscount grinned unexpectedly. "But both he and my mother—especially my mother," he said, "would doubtless be delighted to be presented with another ready-made grandson without having to wait nine months or longer after the wedding."

"Well, bless my soul," the duke said. "Take a seat, then, boy. We have a few things to talk about here. The matter of dowries and settlements and such. Barbara! When her grace and I both expected that it would be . . . Well, bless my soul."

Zachary had gone to bed long before, assured that his puppy would be returned to him in the morning. She had had to insist on Ben's taking it for the night, since it was likely to cry for its mother and the unfamiliarity of its surroundings for the first little while. And doubtless Zachary would take it into his bed if allowed to keep it for the night, and his sheets and blankets would be soaked in the morning.

Barbara had tried to settle to her book, but the adventures of Joseph Andrews had no more power to hold her attention than they had had all week. She went upstairs and fetched the silver locket and the linen handkerchief, which was lying on the chest beside her bed.

The locket sprang open to her touch upon its catch. But it was as empty as it had ever been. She wished, as she had wished a thousand times before, that she had a picture of Zach. Though portraits never did justice to the original, of course. Nothing did. No picture could have captured the youthful eagerness and energy of Zach, his boyish good looks that would have developed in time into undisputed handsomeness. But there had been no time. He had died one month before his twentieth birthday.

Poor Zach. So much zest for life. So many plans and dreams. All smashed to nothingness by a French shell. But the pain of the thought, the rawness in the throat, the bitter sense of loss, would no longer come. They had not come for a long time. Only the restlessness and the frustration of knowing that she was tied to that one girlish and passionate love for the rest of her life.

She would not call it a mistake, for Zachary was never a mistake. And never regretted and never unwanted from the moment of his conception, even after she had been told of Zach's death. Not a mistake. Only this unending bond to a long-dead love.

She closed the locket and held it regretfully in her hand for a long moment before setting it down beside the handkerchief. And she picked the latter up, carefully opened its folds, and looked down on the sugared sweetmeat lying there.

And the tears came and dripped onto one corner of the handkerchief.

He would be dancing now. With Eve. Smiling at her with those kindly blue eyes. Perhaps he had already asked her. Perhaps the announcement had already been made. Perhaps he had a new Valentine's Day to remember to ease the memory of the single one he had spent with his wife. Perhaps all was celebration at the house.

She wished him happy. She closed her hand about the handkerchief and sweetmeat and shut her eyes. She wished him happy. And he would be. Eve was a good girl. Heedless and flirtatious, it was true. But the errors were on the side of youth and exuberance. Under the influence of her husband she would mature well.

Her husband. Viscount Brandon. Barbara felt his fingertips light against her one cheek again and his lips warm against the other. He had wished her a happy Valentine's Day.

Oh, God! She threw back her head, her eyes still

closed, and felt hot tears running down her cheeks
and dripping onto her dress. Had the pain been
this sharp when she had lost Zach? This unbearable? But it must have been. Of course it must.
Zach had been her world and she had just borne
his child. Life was perhaps merciful in that way,
she thought. Just as pain and grief faded, so did
one's memory of just how dreadful they had been.

And would this pain fade too? And its intensity
be forgotten? Of course it would. She had but to
be patient. But what was ahead of her? Nothing
but emptiness and more emptiness. She set the
handkerchief aside and gave in to despair and self-
pity. She spread her hands over her face and cried
and cried.

She was coming downstairs half an hour later,
having bathed her face in cool water and combed
her hair and picked up her embroidery bag, when
there was a knock on the outer door. She stood
quite still, waiting for a servant to answer it. It
could not be. There was a ball in progress at the
house. He was with Eve. He was probably
betrothed to her already. It could not be. But who
else could it be?

He was wearing a black evening cloak and beaver hat, which he removed and handed to Ben,
bidding him a good evening and asking if Lady
Barbara was at home. Beneath the cloak he looked
even more magnificent than he had looked two
evenings before. His brocaded coat was burgundy,
his waistcoat and knee breeches silver silk, his
linen and stockings a sparkling white. There were
copious amounts of lace at his neck and wrists.
Diamonds sparkled from among the folds of his
neckcloth.

"I am here, Ben," she said, "thank you."

And he looked up at her and smiled and she saw

nothing else as her servant withdrew to the back of the house again. She did not know if she returned the smile or not.

"Good evening, my lord," she said.

She was dressed very plainly in comparison to the ladies he had just left in the ballroom at Durham House. She wore an unadorned long-sleeved, high-necked silk dress of dark blue. Her hair was dressed neatly and simply. She had been crying. There were no telltale red marks on her pale cheeks or about her eyes, but he knew she had been crying.

She looked beautiful.

"Good evening, Lady Barbara," he said. He felt suddenly anxious, unsure of himself. If his guess was correct, this was a painful anniversary for her. Her son must have been conceived on this day eight years before. Had she been crying for her dead lover? "I seem to be making a habit of calling at improper hours."

She came down the remaining stairs. Would he know that she had been crying? That she had been crying for him? She felt mortified. She wished he had not come. Had he come to tell her of his betrothal? But why would he do that?

"Will you come into the parlor, my lord?" she asked him. "Shall I have tea brought up?"

"Not for me," he said, following her into the parlor.

She wished he had refused both invitations. She wished he had stated his business and left again. And she wondered desperately if his visit would be as short a one as that afternoon's, if he would leave before she could grasp onto his presence for one more memory to carry into the emptiness ahead.

Perhaps his visit was an intrusion on this day of all days, he thought. Perhaps she wished to be alone with her memories. Perhaps she would be insulted by his ill-timed attentions.

"Am I disturbing you?" he asked.

She shook her head and indicated the chair he had sat in two evenings before.

"You have been crying," he said, and she shot him a glance, doubly mortified. "Is my presence here distressing to you, Barbara? Would you prefer to be left alone? Or can I lend a sympathetic shoulder to be cried on?"

"It was nothing," she said. "It is over now. Are you not dancing?"

"Later," he said, smiling. "There is plenty of time left." Though he knew that he would do no more dancing that night unless she danced with him. Was he intruding? "You loved him very much?"

"Zach?" She looked up at him with luminous eyes. "Yes. I thought I could not live when he went away. And I thought I would surely die when I knew he was dead. It did not seem possible for this world to go on without Zach in it. He was so full of life and laughter. But of course the world did go on and I lived on. I had no choice. I had Zachary."

"I am sorry," he said. "If only we had lived through different times, perhaps there would have been no wars to take so many young men and to widow so many young women."

"I was not married to him," she said, lowering her eyes to her hands in her lap.

"Oh, yes, you were," he said. "In your heart you were. Unfortunately you also had your family's censure to live with, since they appear not to have seen that. But it is true, Barbara. Have you been grieving for him tonight?"

So that was why he had come. Out of kindness. She might have guessed it. He had thought that she would be grieving for Zach, and he had come to offer company and perhaps some comfort. She loved him for his kindness. If there had been nothing else, she would have loved him just for that.

"I think I have been trying," she said. "There is a locket. An empty locket, since he never had a chance to have his miniature painted to put inside. The sight of that emptiness always used to be able to bring on the pain. It no longer does so. Too much time has passed."

Her tone was regretful. He knew exactly what she meant.

"And you have been crying over the fact that you can no longer cry?" he asked, smiling.

She smiled back. "I would have loved him all our lives," she said.

"Yes," he said, "as I would have loved Anna-Marie."

Ah, yes, this was another reason for his coming. His wife, so much more recently lost than Zach. He needed to spend at least a few minutes of a festive evening with someone who would understand because she had suffered a similar loss.

"Yes," she said. "But we did love them while they lived, and that is what really matters. It would be even more dreadful to lose loved ones and have to live with the guilt of knowing that we had not loved them as we should while they lived."

"Are you ready to love again, Barbara?" he asked quietly. He unconsciously held his breath.

She laughed softly and smoothed her hands over the silk of her dress on her lap. "I gave up the right when I lay with Zach and conceived his child," she said.

"Is the ability to love a right that can be lost or discarded, then?" he asked.

She smiled down at her hands. No, it was impossible that that was why he had come. She must not even begin to think such a thing. She was a fallen woman, he the heir to a marquess. She must not invite unnecessary pain. She raised her eyes to his.

Such misery and such suffering he saw there that his smile faded. God, what was it? He crossed the room to her and was down on his knees before her chair and taking her cold hands in his before he realized what he was doing.

"Barbara," he said. "I am ready. I did not think it would be possible, or not quite so soon anyway. I was prepared to make a marriage of convenience. Or perhaps not quite that—a marriage of affection, let us say. I did not know that I was ready to love again. Not until I met you."

Tears sprang to her eyes and she bit her upper lip. "Don't," she said. "Please don't. You must know how vulnerable I am, how lonely. You must know the temptation you are pressing on me. But I will not take another lover. Not even if I were ten times more lonely."

If he had not been directly before her, blocking her path to the door, and if he had not had such a strong grip on her hands, she would have fled the room and left him to find his own way out of the house and back to the ball and Eve's waiting arms. She hated him at that moment. She hated him because she wanted him so much and she knew she could have him with just one word.

"Lover," he said. "Yes, I want to be that to you, Barbara. And friend. And father to Zach. And your husband." He watched her face closely. He could not guess at her thoughts. He watched two tears trickle down her cheeks, and resisted the urge to take her into his arms. "I have come here to ask you to do me the honor of becoming my wife."

She was on her feet then and pushing past him. She stopped in the middle of the room, her back to him. She was laughing, though there was no amusement in the sound.

"Do you not realize what I am?" she said. " 'Whore' is the word that has been used in my hearing more than once. Do you not realize what Zachary is? 'Bas—.' "

He caught her by the shoulders and spun her around to face him. "You are a woman who loved unconditionally," he said. "Zach is a product of that love. You have never let those labels destroy your pride, Barbara. Why remember them now?"

"Why?" she said. "Because you have just asked me to be your viscountess, daughter-in-law of your father, the Marquess of Highmoor. Because you have asked me to take a place in respectable society at your side and to allow my son to become your stepson. Do you not realize the utter impossibility of what you ask?"

"There is only one fact that would make it impossible," he said. "Only one, Barbara. If you do not love me. Sometimes in the last few days I have thought that perhaps you do or that perhaps you can come to do so, given time. But perhaps it has just been your loneliness or your sympathy with my past with which you can identify. Or perhaps it is just friendship and can never be more."

Her hand was against his cheek suddenly, though she could not remember lifting it from her side and placing it there. "I have one of the sweet-meats from Zachary's box wrapped in a handkerchief upstairs," she said, looking directly into his blue eyes. "I know that I will keep it there for the rest of my life, along with the silver locket Zach gave me on this very day eight years ago."

His hand was over hers, holding it against his cheek. "Say it, then," he said. "Say it, Barbara."

"What is the point?" she said. "I cannot marry you. We both know that. And I will not lie with you. I will not. Ah, please don't ask that of me, for I might say yes, you know."

"Say it," he said. And his eyes burned into hers and exultation was growing in him.

"I love you, then," she said. "There. Are you satisfied? I love you, my lord."

"Caleb," he said. "Cal."

"I love you, Cal," she said. "Now, will you return to the ball? I am ready for bed." She looked distressed. "Alone. Will you leave?"

"Yes," he said, and her heart plummeted right down inside her slippers and she realized how much damage his visit had already done and just how sleepless a night she was facing. "In a little while. There are some matters to be dealt with first." He felt rather like whooping with joy, but it was too soon yet. And that misery was back in her eyes.

"What?" she said.

"This, for a start," he said, and lowered his head and kissed her.

Yes, it was true. Even if she had not said it in words, he would have felt it in her body and tasted it on her lips and in her mouth. She was his. Hot and passionate with physical need, but warm and tender too with love. Her fingers dealt gently with his hair even as her body pressed to his own from shoulders to knees and then drew back from the waist up to allow his hands to cover her breasts.

It was true. He kissed her, held her, fondled her, and fought to keep the control that would prevent him from making this evening merely a repeat experience of eight years before for her. He wanted her on their marriage bed, his ring on her finger, his signature beside hers in a church register before he took final possession of her body. Before he impregnated her with the first of their children.

She did not care any longer. She was in his arms and they were warm and strong about her, and his mouth was hot and demanding over hers, his tongue firm and seeking. And she could feel his need as powerful as her own. She did not care. For she had spoken the simple truth. If he asked, she would say yes. And he was asking. Demanding. Soon, in a moment, he would lift his head and either lay her down on the carpet or lead her upstairs to the greater comfort of her bed. And either way she would lie down with him.

Perhaps she deserved that label after all. But label or no label, she did not care. Not any longer. He had said that he loved her. She loved him. That was all that mattered.

He lifted his head and she opened her eyes slowly. And she wondered even at that late moment if she would have the will to send him away.

"And this, second," he said. "Will you marry me, Barbara? Your single state and Zach's existence aside, and your mental image of my father beating us both about the head with a big stick and of society gasping in horror. All those things aside, my love, because really, they do not matter at all. Not one iota of one iota. Will you marry me?"

"Cal," she said. "Cal, it is a fairy tale. Fairy tales are not reality."

"This one can be," he said. "With one little word, Barbara. Yes. Say it. If you do not, you know, I will build me a willow cabin at your gate. Do you know Shakespeare?"

"And camp there until I do say yes?" she said. "Yes, I know the play."

"You said yes," he said, grinning down at her and tightening his arms possessively about her.

"I did not," she said.

"You said 'Yes, I know the play.'"

"Cal."

He rubbed his nose across hers. "The sunshine has started to come back into my life," he said. "Don't take it away again, my love. Not unless I cannot bring it back into yours."

"Oh," she said, and she hid her face against his shoulder.

"What does anything else matter?" he asked. "Only the sunshine, Barbara. That is all that matters."

"And you will not one day regret that you have chosen to wed a fallen woman?" she said. Her voice was muffled against his coat.

"How could I regret turning my face to the sunshine?" he said.

"And you will never regret taking on Zachary?"

"The puppy will doubtless have stopped making puddles by the time we are married and Zach turns him loose on my carpets," he said. "That is the only detail that might have me a little anxious."

She laughed against his shoulder.

"This is better," he said.

She looked up at him, and he was dazzled suddenly by the sunshine.

"Well?" he said.

"Yes," she said.

"Yes?"

"Yes."

They smiled into each other's eyes for a few moments before he tightened his arms about her once more, lifted her from her feet, and swung her twice around.

"Then it is settled," he said, setting her down on her feet again. "Just as soon as ever the banns can be read. I wish it could be sooner. And third . . ."

She looked at him expectantly, and he drew the diamond pin from his neckcloth with its head of tiny diamonds arranged in the shape of a heart. He had bought it in London, intending to give it to Lady Eve if his plans to court her had brought them to a betrothal on this day. He took Barbara's hand and set the pin in it.

"It will keep better than a sweetmeat," he said. "Happy Valentine's Day, my love."

She raised her face to his, radiant with love and happiness, and kissed him.

"And now I can return to the ball," he said.

"Yes." Her smile faded a little. "Yes, you must. You will be missed."

"With you," he said.

She looked at him blankly.

"Will you want to change?" he asked. "To me you look lovely enough to eat, but I know that ladies are very particular about such matters. I can allow you half an hour to get ready if you really must."

"To go to the ball?" she said. "I cannot do that. You know I cannot. But it does not matter." She smiled more determinedly at him. "I shall go to bed and dream of you and hope that this part too is not a dream."

"Twenty-nine minutes," he said.

"Cal . . ."

"Your father is expecting you," he said. "And probably your mother too."

Her smile faded right away.

"I asked your father for you before I came here," he said. "The settlements have all been agreed upon. All that was left to do was for you to accept me. Your father is to make the announcement before the end of the ball—if we get there in time. You have twenty-eight minutes."

"He would not," she said. "Papa hates me. He has had almost nothing to do with me in eight years, apart for paying all the bills here."

"The dowry he offered with you was many times larger than I expected," he said. "I do not need a dowry. I have a fortune of my own with which to care for you. But he insisted. No daughter of his would go to a husband without bringing a respectable dowry with her, he told me. And it was no more than was to be settled on you at his death."

Her eyes widened.

"And I have been told in no uncertain terms that the only thing I will be required to bestow on Zach is a father's love," he said. "A sum quite as large as your dowry has been established for his education and settlement in life, a sum that would have been his in trust on your father's death, even if I had never shown my nose in this county."

"William?" she whispered.

"I believe fathers take their daughters' troubles harder than anyone else," he said. "Your brother, I believe, has been your father's eyes and hands in the past eight years. Though I am sure he is fond of you and the boy in his own right."

"Oh," she said.

He set his head to one side and looked closely

at her. "You are not about to cry again, are you?" he asked.

"Yes, I think so," she said, dashing a hand across one cheek. "I am not usually such a watering pot, I do assure you, my lord."

"Cal."

"Cal."

"I think you must be down to twenty-four minutes," he said. "Go." He bent his head and kissed her swift and hard on the mouth.

She went.

She felt very inappropriately dressed in her rose-pink silk. It was the best she had. She had not had need for any fancy evening gowns for many years. She wore Cal's pin at her bosom and the small diamond earrings she had been given on her eighteenth birthday. She had coaxed her hair into curls at her temples and ears.

And she was terrified. Almost shaking with fright. It had been eight years. And she was to face her father, her mother, William, Eve, all their guests, all the neighboring gentry, who had done little more than nod to her after church for years past. Her betrothal was to be announced. She was to dance with Cal. He had said so.

She gripped his arm after a footman in the grand hall had taken their cloaks, and was reassured by its firmness and warmth. She received his brief kiss gratefully, heedless of the presence of several of her father's servants.

"I am terrified," she said.

"I know," he said. "You look lovely, Barbara. I love you."

His blue-eyed smile, his hand over hers, calmed her. She raised her chin.

"That's my girl," he said, and he led her in the direction of the ballroom.

She could never afterward remember the following half-hour with any clarity. She knew that her father opened his arms to her and that she went into them, forgetting all about bitterness and blame and pride and a long estrangement. And she knew that her mother hugged her as if intending to break bones. And William was winking at her and Eve looking shocked. And there were neighbors too, and people she had never met before. Her father was presenting her to some of them, Cal to others.

And the announcement of her betrothal. And exclamations. And more hugs and kisses. Even eventually from Eve. And the growing conviction that it must after all be a dream, that it was too perfect and too bizarre to be real.

But there always, beyond the noise and the confusion and laughter and hugging and exclaiming, was Cal. Cal steady and smiling and kindly. Cal with pride in his face and love in his blue eyes. Love unmistakable.

And she was more convinced than ever that she dreamed.

"You have come late," her father told them when all the excitement of the announcement seemed finally to be dying down—except in her heart. "We keep country hours here, my boy, and do not dance until dawn as you do in town. The last set is about to begin."

"A waltz, I hope," Lord Brandon said, smiling at his betrothed.

"Probably not," the duke said. "But it will be, my boy. My elder daughter and her fiancé must have their wishes granted on this particular evening." He strode away in the direction of the orchestra.

"Not a waltz," she said in some panic. "I will make a spectacle of myself, Cal. I will tread all over your feet."

"I want you to look into my eyes the whole time," he said, leading her onto the floor. "I want you to pretend that we are dancing among the stars, Barbara. And it will not be entirely pretense. That is what we will be doing. Stars were not meant to be put in pockets, you know. They were meant to be danced among."

He smiled slowly into her eyes, drawing an answering smile from her. The music began and she held his eyes determinedly and almost immediately forgot her terror and her inexperience with the dance.

They waltzed among the stars.

The Light Within
by Carla Kelly

THE SCURVY PLOT that set in motion the elopement of the season was precipitated by the deposit of kittens upon the doorstep of 11 Albermarle Road, the City, two days before Valentine's Day, in the Year of Our Lord 1816.

Perhaps to call it an elopement is to put too strong a face upon the matter, although many insisted that Thomas Waggoner had last been seen in a fervent embrace with a beautiful woman. But no one really knows. There are those in London's best houses who still wonder whatever became of Lord Thomas Waggoner, second son of the late Marquess of Cavanaugh and brother to the biggest rake who ever cheated his tailor.

Among the *ton* who discounted the elopement theory were those who believed the rumor that Tom Waggoner had taken holy orders and thrived, shriven and shorn, on some remote isle of Micronesia. Others declared that he had taken the king's shilling yet again and served this time as a mere private in one of his majesty's far-flung regiments.

Absurdities mounted among those who still remembered Lord Thomas. One family friend even claimed, years later, that he was sure he had seen Thomas, Quaker from his broad-brimmed hat to his plain black shoes, striding bold as life down a street in Nantucket, America, with a small boy perched on his shoulder, an army of stairstep children behind him and a rather pretty lady at his side.

"And we remember how susceptible all Waggoners since Adam have been to a pretty face," the man had insisted. "And Lord, she was a beauty, what I could see of her around that Quaker bonnet."

It was a piece of nonsense, everyone agreed. No one considered it for a moment. Still . . .

"He will ruin us, Chattering," Thomas Waggoner declared to his valet, who was surveying Lord Thomas' wardrobe and frowning. "It distresses me no end. I swear I would take to the bottle if the vile brew were not so expensive."

"It does seem that Lord Cavanaugh is making serious work of the family fortunes," the valet commented, his eyes still on his master's outmoded clothing. "Sir, by a glance in this closet, one can see how long you have been soldiering."

"Oh, I do not care," Thomas said, flinging himself back on his bed and propping his hands behind his head. He smiled to himself. "Look at that, Chattering! I can put my arm behind my head now. And you thought I would never be able to do that again."

"Pardon, sir, it was the regimental surgeon who said that, not I," the valet declared firmly. "I, for one, have infinite faith in your capacity to come about."

Thomas grimaced and gingerly straightened his arm. "But it does hurt." He held his arm up over his head and opened and closed his hand. "How nice to still see fingers at the end of this pesky arm."

He folded his arms on his chest, corpse-fashion,

and eyed his valet. "I would have left the brigade, had I known the seriousness of Charles's idiocies."

The valet turned to fix the same look of concentration on his master that he had awarded the outdated waistcoats and jackets. "You would never have left your men, my lord, and you know it. It took a saber cut of iniquitous proportions to do that."

Thomas nodded. "So it did." He sighed. "I shall not dwell on that, Chattering, for it only makes me dismal." He managed a slight smile that rendered his face young again, as long as one did not look too closely at his eyes. "Do you think Charles's latest dolly-mop would scare off if I acquainted her with his precarious finances? And I do have a little money of my own. Perhaps she would remove her hooks from Charles for some coin of the realm."

The valet shrugged. "You could try, my lord," he said, the doubt evident in his voice.

"Perhaps I shall," Thomas Waggoner said. He closed his eyes and rubbed his arm.

"Lord Cavanaugh's man let it drop to me only this morning that he is taking his ladylove to the opera tonight."

Thomas opened his eyes wide. "Charles at the opera? I wonder what it can mean?" he murmured. "It sounds to me that he is tiring of his honey and means to inspect the opera dancers." He closed his eyes again. "But even Charles would not take his current amour on a hunting expedition. We have some breeding, Chattering."

"Of course, my lord," the valet said, even as he inspected the ends of his fingernails.

Thomas raised himself to rest on his good elbow. "Do you know, I could waylay his fair damsel. Of all things, Charles hates to be kept waiting.

If he is already less interested, this could put an end to the affair, if I know my brother."

Chattering nodded. "But there would only be another one to follow."

Thomas lay down again. "I am sure of that, my man, but even Beelzebub himself must surely pause a bit between dirty dealings. Perhaps I could reason with Charles, and if not I, then our solicitors."

He sat up. "I shall do it! I shall write a pretty note to ... to ... Have you any idea what her name is?"

The valet recoiled, and shook his head emphatically. "Really, my lord! Probably any flowery phrase will do. And while I am thinking of it, shall I order flowers to accompany it?"

"Gracious, no!" Tom said firmly. "What a waste of money!" He thought a moment. "I have a better idea. A stroll through the kitchen only this morning put me in mind of it, and it's something dumb that Charles would do. No, my good man, no flowers. Prepare a basket, though, and I shall kill two birds with one stone."

"Very well, my lord."

Thomas Waggoner rubbed his hands together. "Perhaps I shall kidnap her and deposit her in some remote part of the landscape."

"I am sure that would be illegal, my lord."

Thomas nodded. "Then I shall have you do it, Chattering."

"My lord!"

Blessing Whittier did not answer the doorbell for some moments. She had removed her shoes and was lying on her bed, staring up at the ceiling, when the doorbell jangled. She felt remarkably disinclined to answer its summons.

Her feet ached from standing upon them all day, and all day the day before, waiting for an audience with a lord of the Admiralty, any lord of the Admiralty.

She sighed and sat up, rubbing her ankles. No matter how early she and her mother-in-law arrived at the building with the three massive pillars, there was always a crowd before them, composed mainly of naval officers and others with petitions.

No one ever offered them a chair. "It is because we are Americans," Patience Whittier had whispered to her at the end of that first endless day.

"Perhaps they are not Friendly," Blessing had said, her small joke bringing a dimple to her cheek, even as her feet ached and her mortification grew.

"Thee is a trickster," Mother Whittier had said, a smile on her own face. She raised her chin. "We can outwait them, my daughter. It is a talent we Friends have. And it is not as though we have a choice, is it?"

And so they had waited, day after day, for an audience. Her spine straight, her eyes demurely lowered, Blessing had counted over and over the black and white tiles in the floor of the Admiralty antechamber. She ignored the rude stares of the officers, the jokes not quite loud enough for their ears, but meant for them all the same. When she felt bright-headed from all that standing, she leaned against her mother-in-law and considered the Light Within.

So great had been their weariness that afternoon that they had splurged for a hackney. They sat in silence, side by side, on the journey from the Admirality House to one of the City's shabbier

streets. Blessing touched Patience's hand as they
neared their rented rooms.

"Does thee think we have come upon a fool's
errand?"

She was startled to see tears in her mother-in-
law's eyes. "I begin to fear it, my dear. They will
not see us, that is obvious, and it is our poor fortune that our ambassador is not in the country
right now."

Patience looked down at her clasped hands.
"But we will not surrender yet, Blessing. We have
come too far, and the issue is too important. We
will wait in that antechamber until someone will
see us."

Blessing recalled her thoughts to the moment
and raised her eyes to the ceiling again. It was not
as though they were asking for the moon, stars,
and George Washington's teacup. "It is only a
paper, my lord admiral," she said out loud. "You
need merely direct some piddling clerk to search
the records and bring us written verification that
the British Navy did sink the *Seaspray*, whaler out
of Nantucket."

Tears came to her eyes, and she wiped them
on the hem of her dress. "My lord admiral," she
whispered, "it was only a small ship on a great
ocean. My father-in-law captained, and my husband was his second, but you need not concern
yourself with that. We only need a paper."

She lay back down and stared up at the ceiling
again, her hands tight fists at her sides. "Aaron, I
can scarcely remember thy face," she said. "Has
it been so long?"

To the best of their knowledge, the *Seaspray* had
been blown out of the water—try-pots, harpoons,
and all—in the first year of the war with England.
Another whaler, the *Jennie Birdsong* out of Boston,

had watched from a prudent distance at the Arctic whaling grounds, and then grabbed for the weather gauge and beat a hasty retreat when the warship swung about. "Mind, we're not sure, Mistress Whittier," the captain had told her months later, "but it looked like the *Seaspray*."

And then the lawyers had descended on her and her mother-in-law, spouting their "whereases" and "therefores" and Latin until Blessing wanted to escape the room. All she remembered was that they stood to lose their home and the Whittier Ropewalk to the ship's partners unless they could confirm that it was an act of war and not mere accident.

The doorbell jangled again and Blessing got up, straightening her cap, tucking her hair under it carefully. I am sure there is no place for lawyers in the kingdom to come, she thought. I am wicked to think that, but I expect it is true.

She hurried down the grimy hall and opened the front door upon a neighbor lad who held a basket with two kittens. With a sigh of relief he thrust it into her arms.

"Coo, but I'm glad you're home," he said. "I dislike the idea of dumping these, or surprising me mum."

"Oh, I cannot . . ." she began as she stared down into two whiskered, inquiring faces, all white and gray perfection. Blessing smiled and tucked the basket on her hip so she could touch their velvet ears. "There must be some mistake."

The boy shook his head vigorously and clapped his cap back on. "There was gent, a nice-looking gent, walking up and down at the head of the street. He asked me if I knew of a beautiful lady on Albemarle Road." He blushed and looked down at his feet. "The mort next door, she's a pretty tart, ma'am, begging your pardon, but she's not an eye-popper like you."

"Heavens!" Blessing exclaimed, her face as red as the errand boy's. "No one has ever called me beautiful before," she said, even as she thought of Aaron and his words of love murmured from such a distance of space and time that she couldn't even be sure he had ever said them. "Well, no one recently."

The boy grinned at her. "And I like to hear you talk, ma'am, even if me mum warns me not to speak to the Americans." He tugged at his cap and looked down into the basket. "The gentleman, he said I was to make sure that you saw the note. Good day to ye."

"And to thee," Blessing said as she smiled and closed the door, the kittens in her arms.

Patience was coming from her room, her hand rubbing the small of her back. "What has thee there?" she asked, coming closer, and then laughing out loud at the kittens, which by now had taken exception to the basket and were scrambling up the front of Blessing's dress.

"I will share this blessing," Blessing said as she handed the white kitten to Patience. "I am sure it is someone's idea of a joke," she said, and then sat down on the floor, the other kitten in her lap. She let it go, and it wobbled on unsteady legs. "The lad claims there is a note."

She looked in the basket and pulled out a note, sealed with a dab of wax and inscribed with a strong hand. "Here is the answer to our mystery."

As the kitten climbed into her lap again and dropped immediately into slumber, Blessing broke the seal and stared at the short note. " 'My dear,' " she read, " 'come walking at the end of Albemarle Road at seven of the clock, and we will settle this little matter to your advantage, I am sure. Cavanaugh."

She looked up at her mother-in-law. "Cavanaugh? Cavanaugh? Mother, is that one of the Admiralty lords? I seem to recall the name."

Patience sank down onto the low stool beside Blessing. She took the note from her daughter-in-law's hands. "I am not rightly sure. Does thee think so?"

"I cannot imagine what else it would be," Blessing said, her practical nature in charge once again. "Perhaps the Admiralty feels that diplomacy is best served by this kind of discretion."

Absently Patience removed the kitten that was attempting to climb her cap. "How odd these British are!" she exclaimed. "Is there any wonder that we thought to separate from them?"

"As to that, I do not know, Mother," Blessing said. "As I think of it, I am sure that there is a Cavanaugh numbered among the lords of the Admiralty, and I will be there this evening." She touched her mother-in-law's face. "Don't thee be so alarmed! If this is how the British choose to carry out delicate matters of state, I say let them, if it means we could be on a ship bound for Boston in a few days."

Patience nodded. "I am so anxious to be home!"

Blessing gently replaced the slumbering kitten into the basket, got to her feet, and held out her hands to her mother-in-law. "Then remove that frown, dearest. What could possibly happen that is worse than standing day after day on marble floors?"

If she had any doubts of her own, Blessing Whittier kept them to herself through their frugal dinner and their moments of silent contemplation in the sitting room. She was meditating upon her own sins, wondering why a ragbag neighbor boy's assertion that she was an eye-popper should cause her such pleasure. *I am only grateful Patience did not hear him,* she thought, and the dimple came to her cheek again.

She stroked the gray kitten, its stomach bulging with pabulum, which had found its way to her lap again. The little beast purred and rolled onto its back. "Think how good they will be for mice in this wretched place," she said to Patience, who also contended with a similarly well-fed kitten in her lap.

Patience smiled and rubbed under the chin of the white one. "I will remind thee that the mice which are part of these furnished rooms are bigger than these kittens." She glanced at the clock. "And now it is hard upon seven, Blessing. Do you think you should go?"

Blessing set the kitten on the lumpy sofa. She tucked her hair carefully under her cap again and settled her bonnet firmly on top. She pulled her cape about her shoulders and peered out the window. "I wish it were not so foggy, Mother. I shall be swallowed up in this pea soup the moment I leave."

"Don't go, my dear," Patience urged.

Blessing kissed her cheek. "Only think how fine it will be to feel a heaving deck and know that this paltry round of seasickness will be carrying us to Boston!"

In the narrow street, she looked back at the house once, marveling how rapidly the fog settled about her. She nearly turned back once, then shook herself for her want of spine and set out at a brisk pace to the junction of Albemarle and Hose.

The street was deserted. Everyone with any sense is indoors, she thought as she pulled her cloak tighter about her. And so I should be. I will give this quixotic Lord Cavanaugh five minutes and no more.

The words had scarcely crossed her brain when she heard horses' hooves. A carriage with a crest on the door loomed out of the fog and stopped before her. A man, black-cloaked like herself, opened the door and pulled down the step.

"Come, madam," he said, holding out his hand.

"Are you Lord Cavanaugh?" she replied, stepping back from the carriage, and wishing all of a sudden that it was bright daylight and the street crowded with its usual complement of vendors.

"Come," the man repeated. "Lord Thomas will make this worth your while."

As she hesitated, Blessing wondered at the tone of disgust that entered the man's voice. Are we Americans so hated abroad? she thought as she hesitated a moment more, and then held out her hand and allowed the man to help her inside.

The horses leapt into motion, and Blessing grabbed for the strap that swung so wildly. She hung on, her eyes growing accustomed to the gloom.

As she watched, wide-eyed, the man seated across from her removed his hat and swabbed his face with an immaculate handkerchief. When he finished, he shook it at her. "I told Lord Thomas it must be illegal to kidnap young persons, but he did not listen."

Blessing stared at him. "What!" she managed as the horses careened around the corner and she clung to the strap.

He ignored her outburst and folded his arms.

"So I told him, miss, I think too much war has addled his brain."

"Let me out at once," Blessing ordered. "Thee has no right to do this. I am an American citizen," she declared, raising her voice to be heard above the horses. "That ought to mean something to thee."

The man stared at her and groaned. Out came the handkerchief again for another vigorous swab of his head. "Oh, Lord, now we have created an international incident," he said, his tone much put-upon. "But no one told us Cavanaugh's light-skirt was a Yankee!"

Blessing gasped again. She administered a ringing slap to the little man's face, looked out the window, decided against jumping, and curled herself into a ball in the far opposite corner.

She rode for hours, or so it seemed, cocooned as they were by the fog and the artificial stillness it created. Other than a sniff and a wounded look in her direction, the little man in black ignored her after muttering something about looking for employment elsewhere.

The horses raced on through the foggy streets. The sound changed, and she knew they were in the country. The fog lifted, but she could see no more than the dark outlines of trees, and houses spaced farther and farther apart.

When she could force herself to think beyond her immediate fears, Blessing considered her situation in rational Quaker fashion. I cannot lose my virginity, she thought; that's been gone these three years and more. If they kill me, I know there is a much better world beyond, and Aaron is there. If they mean to hold me for ransom, they will soon see their mistake. I only wish I could give a reassuring report to Patience.

They careened down a narrower lane, one where the bare branches of February trees brushed against the carriage. The lane showed signs of neglect, being graveled here, muddy there. They lurched along and Blessing held her breath, waiting to be overturned. Tears stung her eyes as she thought of the high hopes with which they had sailed for England. She glanced over at the man who crouched in the other corner of the carriage.

"Does Lord Cavanaugh mean mischief?" she asked hesitantly.

"Lord Cavanaugh always means mischief."

"Oh, dear."

They must have traveled a mile at least before the carriage rolled to a stop. Blessing peered out the window at a small house, brightly lit, with the door wide open despite the chill in the air. A tall man stood on the steps, silhouetted black against the light. She gulped. And to think I believed that Lord Cavanaugh would help me, she said to herself.

"Come, miss," said the man in the carriage. He held his hand out to her.

"No," she replied, her voice quiet but filled with determination.

The valet lunged for her as she hurled herself from the carriage, gathering her skirts for a run down the road.

"Please, miss!" the valet wailed, even as the man on the steps ran to the carriage. The tall man grabbed her by the arm and she shook him off, wondering as she struck out at him how someone with such an open, friendly face could plot so nefariously against a widow with only a small bone to pick with the British empire.

She squeaked in surprise as he grabbed her and threw her over his shoulder. She dragged her fingernails up both sides of his neck and then clutched at his hair.

When he would not let her down, she flailed out, striking him on the arm. His breath went out of him in an *oof!* as his legs buckled under him and he sank right down on the driveway.

Her knees scraped the gravel, but Blessing was on her feet in a second, her hair wild about her face, her bonnet flung somewhere in the dark. She sucked in her breath and drew back her leg to kick him, when she remembered with a start who she was.

Blessing looked down at the man who clutched his arm and writhed on the driveway, the bloody tracks of her fingernails across his neck. She put her hands behind her back in embarrassment and came closer, to find herself pushed aside by the valet.

"Are you all right, my lord?" the little man asked, his face pale and anxious in the moonlight. "Oh, let me help you." He bent closer. "My lord, she is an American!"

"That explains a lot," gasped the man on the ground. He stared up at her and allowed the little man to help him into a sitting position. "Good God, woman, was that entirely necessary? I'm sure you needn't fear for your virtue."

He looked at her closer then, his unbelieving eyes taking in her plain black cloak, her gray dress, and the demure fichu of white linen twisted now about her neck. He stared down at the linen mobcap which he still held tight in his hand.

"Thee is a very bad man," she said, her hands still behind her back.

"Oh, God," he breathed.

"And I will thank thee not to take the Lord's name in vain," she said as she took hold of him by the arm and tugged him to his feet. When he swayed on his feet, she gave him another shake. "Thee should know better than to kidnap helpless widows." She took the cap from his fingers and dabbed at his neck with it. "Our founder, George Fox, enjoined us not to resort to violence, Lord Cavanaugh," she said, "but I gladly made an exception in thy case!"

He could only stare at her, his mouth open, then transfer his gaze to the little man in black who stood in miserable silence beside her. "Chattering, remind me never to send you on an abduction again," he murmured, taking the cap from her hand and holding it to his neck to stanch the bleeding. "You have botched it."

To Blessing's amazement, the little man burst into tears. "But there she was, sir, standing at the corner of Albemarle and Hose."

The tall man touched his arm and winced, holding it steady by the elbow. "Obviously, Chattering, there is more than one beautiful woman on Albemarle Road." He shook his head and held out his left hand. "My dear Miss . . ."

"Mrs. Whittier," she replied, taking his hand.

He rolled his eyes. "Worse and worse! Mrs. Whittier, there has been a dreadful mistake. Will you permit me to explain?" He motioned toward the house.

Blessing released his hand. "What is this place?" she asked, suspicion high in her voice.

To his credit, the man did not flinch. He took a deep breath and grinned. "It is the iniquitous love nest of Lord Cavanaugh, who, I profoundly assure you, I am not. The only danger you will encounter within is that certain numbness that comes from staring overlong at really poor art reproductions."

She smiled. "I had hoped to find a lord of the Admiralty here."

He offered her his good arm. "And I had hoped to have a serious discussion with my brother's ... ah, yes, Lord Cavanaugh ... my brother's latest amour. Obviously we are both doomed to disappointment."

She nodded. After a moment of contemplation that the tall man did not interrupt, she took his arm.

"Let us discuss this turn of events, Mrs. Whittier. Oh, Lord, I hope your husband will not call me out. I am a dreadful shot these six months and more."

"He will not call you out," she replied, suddenly shy. "Let me help you, sir."

She grasped him more firmly by the elbow and steered him up the stairs and into the sitting room, where he sank onto the sofa, his eyes closed.

He was handsome in a rangy way that appealed to her, his hair black as an Indian's, his cheekbones high. His nose was arrow-straight and there were creases about his rather thin mouth. He was dressed quite casually in buckskin breeches and an open-throated linen shirt. His fingers were long, and the veins on the backs of his hands stood out distinctly, as though he had lost weight in recent months and not yet regained it.

"Sir?" she inquired when he did not open his eyes. "Are you all right?"

He looked at her then, a slight smile relieving the severity of his face. "I am well enough," he replied. "I was just wondering where to begin. Perhaps if you went first, we could get to the bottom of this quicker. Chattering, do you think my dratted brother keeps anything as prosaic as tea in this bordello?"

"I am certain he must, my lord. After all, he is an Englishman, even if he is a rake."

Blessing laughed out loud, and then put her hand to her mouth in embarrassment.

"We do have our standards," the tall man murmured, and reached into his pocket. He removed a small penknife, which he tossed into her lap. "I never thought I was squeamish, but do me the favor of cleaning out those devilish sharp fingernails of yours, Mrs. Whittier."

She busied herself with removing the bits of bloody tissue from under her nails. "Do tell me your name, sir," she said when there seemed to be no end to the silence. She peeked a glance at him to observe him gazing at her, a half-smile on his face. "Sir?"

"Oh! Yes." He put his hand to his heart. "If you do not mind, I will remain seated. I am Thomas Waggoner, brother to Charles Waggoner, Earl of Cavanaugh."

"And is *he* a lord of the Admiralty?"

Thomas shook his head. "He has been called many things, my dear Mrs. Whittier, but lord admiral is not among them."

"I thought he was, does thee see, else I never would have answered that note."

He nodded. "The note I remember well, because I wrote it. But I do not understand your obsession with lords admiral. One scarcely meets a stuffier lot."

Over scalding tea Blessing told Thomas Waggoner what had brought them from Nantucket, Massachusetts, to London. Her voice faltered when she mentioned Aaron Whittier and his father, and the *Seaspray*, lost these three years and more.

Lord Thomas touched her hand. "I am sorry, Mrs. Whittier."

"It is not thy fault," she replied quickly. "The Lord works in ways we cannot discern."

"So he does," Thomas agreed, taking a sip of tea.

"When I received that note that said I would be given what was due me, I thought . . . Well, we thought perhaps this Lord Cavanaugh chose not to go through official channels. I am sure this matter is an embarrassment to the British government." She looked up at him. "Foolish, wasn't I?"

He nodded, but his eyes were kind. "The Admiralty lords are much too prosaic for kittens, Mrs. Whittier. Tell me, are they a burden? I can reclaim them."

She laughed and shook her head. "So far, they are the one bit of real joy in this whole wretched affair, Mr. . . . er . . . Lord Thomas." She set down her teacup and folded her hands in her lap. "And now you tell me there is no Lord Cavanaugh on the Admiralty Board."

He thought a moment. "There is a Lord Ravenaugh," he said.

"Ravenaugh, Cavanaugh," she said. "Yes, that was my mistake." Blessing rested her chin on her hands. "But I am no closer to solving my problem, am I?"

He set down his cup and folded his arms across his chest, contemplating her. "It could be that you are closer than you think, my dear Mrs. Whittier. Have you heard of Thaddeus Calcingham, Lord Renfew?"

She nodded. "He is another, is he not?"

"In very deed. He is my late mother's uncle. I think I can solve your problem tomorrow. A note to Uncle Calcingham will grease the wheels of naval inquiry amazingly."

He looked up when the valet entered the room. "Chattering, allow me to introduce Mrs. Whittier to you."

"Blessing Whittier," she added, and held out her hand. "I am sorry I was so rude to thee."

"Blessing, is it?" Thomas said, his eyes merrier than she had seen them yet that evening.

"I was the first daughter after five sons," she explained. "We Friends value our daughters as well as our sons, Lord Thomas."

He smiled. "Well that you should. Have you any children of your own, Mrs. Whittier?"

She shook her head. "Are you married, sir?"

"No." He leaned forward, resting his elbows carefully on his knees. "And it's just as well. I am certain my brother is taking the Waggoners down to utter financial ruin. Thank God I do not have a wife and children to muddy the waters."

She reached out impulsively and touched his arm. "Oh, sir, discomforts are less unpleasant when they are shared."

He blinked and stared at her, the smile coming back into his eyes. "I never thought of it that way. Seriously, Mrs. Whittier, beyond a small sum which I had hoped to tempt Charles's beautiful doxy, I am worthless."

Blessing tightened her grip on his arm. "No one is worthless. Thee cannot be serious." She shook his arm. "I do not wish thee ever to think so again. Promise me," she said, her voice urgent.

Startled, he nodded. "I promise thee," he said softly. He looked up at Chattering, who had been watching him. "Are we ready for the return trip, my man?"

The valet yanked out his white handkerchief

again and, in the gesture rapidly becoming familiar to Blessing, dragged it across his bald head.
"My lord, we must have jarred the axle on the
way down that wretched lane. The coachman says
he can fix it in the morning, when the light is
back."

Thomas Waggoner sighed. "You know times are
harsh for the Waggoners when Charles can't even
afford to maintain the road to his love nest." He
looked at Blessing. "I am afraid we will be spending the night here, Mrs. Whittier."

She got to her feet quickly. "I dare not leave
my mother-in-law wondering what has become of
me." Tears came to her eyes. "We have only each
other, and she will be prostrate with worry if I do
not return." She reached for her cloak. "I am sure
I can walk."

Thomas Waggoner took the cloak from her. "We
are some little distance from town, madam." He
looked at Chattering again. "What do you say to
the postboy riding my horse back to London with
a message for . . . for . . ."

"Patience Whittier," she supplied.

"I am sure that he would, my lord." Chattering
broke into a rare smile. "He would like to ride
that hunter of yours."

"I am sure he would, too!" Waggoner stood up.
"It's the only item of value I possess anymore.
Very well, then. Chattering, see if you can find pen
and paper somewhere about this den of iniquity,
and we will let Mrs. Whittier compose a satisfactory note."

"I suppose I have no choice," she said, far from
satisfied.

"I wish you did," he answered apologetically,
"but events would dictate otherwise."

"Very well, then. I shall write," Blessing said.

The note was less than satisfactory, she decided after two attempts and coaching from Lord Thomas, who seemed, to her irritation, to find the situation amusing. She stabbed the badly mended pen in his direction.

"Thee claims thee is not a rake, but I say thee is too easily entertained!" she muttered as she began again.

He looked at her with wide eyes. "Madam, I am not a rake, but I am still a Waggoner, and we *are* easily entertained. It's in the blood," he offered as further explanation.

"Then take thyself off so I can finish this. Thee is a serious annoyance."

He threw back his head and laughed, then propped his feet on the dining-room table where they sat and folded his hands in his lap. "I have finished *my* composition to Uncle Calcingham," he said, unable to keep the note of injured virtue from his voice. "I do not know what is so difficult about informing your mother-in-law that you must spend the night in a love nest with a rake's brother. And so close to Valentine's Day," he added for good effect.

Blessing laughed in spite of herself. "Well, as long as the news does not travel to Nantucket," she said at last.

"How could it possibly?" he replied. "Some of us I could name seem to relish making mountains out of molehills."

A smile on her face, she addressed herself to the note again, remembering how Aaron used to say much the same thing. I suppose it is true, she thought as she wrote, reread, and then folded the missive with a sigh.

Thomas left with both notes. In another moment she heard a horse galloping down the lane. She got up from the table and went in search of the bedroom.

It was a small house, and she found it quickly. A candle burned on the bedside table. Gingerly she felt the mattress.

"I am certain that the mattress is in excellent working order," came Thomas' voice from the doorway.

She could tell without even looking around that he was grinning from ear to ear. Her face fiery red, she returned some noncommittal answer.

He came closer. "Beg pardon?" he murmured.

Blessing leveled him with a frosty stare that only made the smile wider.

Thomas went to the bureau and opened a drawer. "It appears that you will find any number of nightgowns."

She came closer and gasped. "I would never wear one of those iniquitous gowns!" she exclaimed, staring at the little patches of lace and silk.

He closed the drawer, his back to her as his shoulders shook. "Mrs. Whittier, I am sure that is the reaction of many of the women who have been here before you. They probably never wore these either."

She burst into laughter. "Thee is not good for me!" she protested.

"Ah, but thee is good for me!" he said, and bowed himself out of the room.

She closed the door and locked it with a click, listening to Thomas' laughter on the other side. "Some people . . ." she said out loud so he could hear.

Blessing knew that she would never sleep, but she undressed, found a nightgown a little less iniquitous than some of the others, and crawled into bed. The mattress was perfect, she had to admit. She snuggled herself into the bed and was asleep in minutes.

She woke an hour later, thinking of Thomas Waggoner and his injured arm. She pulled the pillow against her stomach, resting her chin against it. I suspect there is no other bedroom in the house, and so he must be contending with that sofa, she thought. Mother Whittier would say I am thoughtless indeed.

Blessing lit the candle and went to the dressing closet, where she found a wrap. She tied it firmly around her and went to the door, unlocking it and tiptoeing into the hall.

Thomas Waggoner, his eyes haggard, was sitting on the sofa, holding his elbow with his other hand. He looked at her in surprise and straightened the sheet about his bare legs.

"What on earth?" he began.

"Get up," she said. "Thee may take the bed and I will sleep here. Thee cannot rest this way on a narrow sofa. I am sorry I did not think of this sooner."

"I won't hear of it," he said.

She sat down on the sofa with him. "Then I will sit here until thee comes to thy senses."

He glared at her and then leaned back. "I would be more comfortable in a bed," he admitted, "but I hate to wish this sofa on you."

"It is of no concern to me, Lord Thomas," she said, getting to her feet again. "I am much shorter than thee, and the only pain I feel is when thee cracks thy miserable jokes."

He smiled. "Very well, Mrs. Whittier," he said. "I capitulate. Now, close your eyes and I'll do a better job with this sheet."

She saw him settled in the bed and reached

across for the extra pillow. "Would this be better tucked under thy arm?" she asked. "How should I do it?"

"Chattering usually helps me," he said. "Yes, yes, just prop it there." He relaxed and closed his eyes. "Much better. I fear you will not do as well."

She only smiled and blew out the candle. "Good night, Lord Thomas."

Blessing woke in the morning to the fragrance of bacon cooking. She sat up and stretched, rubbing the small of her back. It was a wretched couch indeed. She pulled on her wrap and tiptoed to the bedroom to reclaim her clothes.

It was empty and the bed was made. She dressed quickly and followed her nose to the kitchen, where Lord Thomas was concentrating on the bacon. He looked up to see her in the doorway, and waved the bacon fork at her.

"Crispy or chewy, Mrs. Whittier?" he asked.

"Crispy," she replied, tugging at the curls that would not behave and wishing that she had not sacrificed her cap to Lord Thomas' wounds last night.

"An excellent choice, madam," he said, "considering that I have long since passed the chewy stage. Chattering, is that bread toasted yet?"

"Yes, my lord," the valet replied. "Mrs. Whittier, if you would set the table, I think there is silverware in the dining room."

"We have discovered that Charles and his ladyloves don't spend much time in the kitchen either," Thomas said, and turned back to the kitchen stove before she could scold him. "Chattering had to borrow a frying pan when he went to the farm nearby for bacon and eggs."

Blessing set the table, wondering how Patience was faring in London, and spent a moment at the window in silent contemplation, staring out at the bleakness of February. She thought of Aaron, something she rarely did, because remembering him was too painful. Hugging herself with her arms, she recalled other mornings—too few of them—when she and Aaron would read to each other from the Old Testament after breakfast.

She closed her eyes and leaned against the window frame, wishing herself home, back where friends and neighbors would greet her and not ignore her and look away because she was Quaker and an American too. She longed for the fragrance of the sea and the sound of water lapping on pilings. . . .

"You may be able to ignore bacon and eggs, but I am constitutionally unfit for such asceticism," said the voice behind her.

She whirled around in surprise. Thomas Waggoner was seated at the table, a napkin in his lap. He grinned at her, and then his face became serious.

"But you weren't thinking of bacon and eggs, eh?" he asked, his voice gentle. He glanced out the window, where bare branches scrubbed the glass. "Dreadful useless month, my dear Mrs. Whittier. Thank God there is Valentine's Day to relieve it."

She took a cue from his light tone and joined him at the table. "It is not a holiday we Friends celebrate, Lord Thomas," she said, taking the platter from him and sniffing it. "You are certainly good with eggs, my lord."

"I can cook over campfires in caves, in abandoned Spanish monasteries, and in dens of iniquity."

She laughed. "And I can pray over it, sir, just in case."

Her blessing on the food was soft, his "Amen"

hearty. They ate in companionable silence. Thomas finished first. He pushed his plate back and leaned back in his chair, crossing his long legs and contemplating her.

"Mrs. Whittier, this has been frightfully inconvenient for you," he commented. "Any other lady of my acquaintance would have shrieked and fainted last night."

She looked at him over the rim of her teacup. "And are *you* such an antidote, sir?" she asked quickly, before she thought how improper it sounded.

He laughed out loud, bringing the chair back to the floor with a thump. "You are a bit of a rascal, my dear, aren't you?"

"I am not," she protested. "Sometimes I speak before I think."

He grinned at her, and she blushed.

Thomas got to his feet and stretched. "Well, I, for one, am grateful for your kindness." He pulled her chair back for her. "Neither of us realized a successful outcome from this venture, but I have met my first American, and you might yet be satisfied by my Uncle Calcingham."

He saw her into the parlor and then went outside, whistling to himself to check on the progress of the carriage.

He was back before she had opportunity to tidy the room beyond straightening one or two of the poor art reproductions that he had disparaged last night, and wondering where she might find a dust cloth.

"Mrs. Whittier, your carriage awaits. If you do not object, I will ride with you. Indeed, I must, considering that the postboy left last night with my horse."

"Of course I do not object," she replied as she

allowed him to help her into her cloak. "If your Uncle Calcingham fails me, you can suggest some other avenues I might attempt. Bribery is out, I must add. I have scruples." She made a face. "And little cash, anyway."

"I shall put my mind to the matter, Mrs. Whittier," he replied, and promptly fell asleep when the carriage began to roll.

Blessing sighed and settled herself, wondering where Chattering had taken himself off to, and deciding that he had chosen to ride with the coachman. How odd, she thought. He should have known he would be welcome in the carriage.

The ride back into London seemed to go much faster on the return trip. Lord Thomas Waggoner woke up, winked at her, and then directed his gaze out the window.

It should have been an embarrassing ride. Blessing had never been alone before with a man who was not a relative, but even in silence Thomas Waggoner seemed to give off an air of warmth. I wonder, sir, she thought, are you used to taking care of people? He had mentioned the army, and his wound had obviously been a result of last year's horrendous struggle at Waterloo. She shuddered, unable to imagine war.

And then she was struggling to stay awake, thinking herself intolerably rude as she nodded and dozed and then jerked awake again.

In another moment Thomas had left his seat facing her to sit at her side. "Mrs. Whittier, I insist that you rest your head upon my shoulder before you pitch forward and crash onto the floor," he said firmly, and she opened her mouth to protest. "I fear I would be in serious trouble with your mother-in-law, and probably the American embassy, should I return you in less than impeccable condition."

Blessing did as he requested, burrowing comfortably into his shoulder. She thought to object when his arm went around her, but it seemed a waste of good breath.

"Tell me, Mrs. Whittier, what is Nantucket like?" he asked finally as they struck fog again and the carriage slowed.

She considered Nantucket. "It is all blue sky, white dunes, sea gulls, and the coldest water, even in summer," she replied. "And there is always the smell of hemp and tar and salt herring."

He made a face. "You miss the smell of rope?"

She nodded, her head against his shoulder. "I miss the ropewalk, Lord Thomas," she said. She sat up to see him better. "Have you ever seen a ropewalk?"

He nodded. "Once before in Portsmouth, before we shipped out for Spain. I never saw such a long, narrow building. Fascinating, I might add, how the strands twist and twist and produce the most prodigious cables. Noisy, too, with all that rope turning.

"I run the Whittier Ropewalk," Blessing said, unable to keep the note of pride from her voice. "Patience has not the constitution for business, and one of us had to take over when . . . Well, it is the other family business. Not as prosperous as the *Seaspray* was . . ." Her voice trailed off.

"You run a business?" he asked, his voice filled with respect. "I have often thought such a thing would be great fun." He chuckled. "Don't tell any of my relatives. They would sniff and call me baseborn."

Blessing's chin went up. "Work is a very American enterprise, Lord Thomas. I can recommend it to anyone." She moved away from him a little. "After a day of supervising in the ropeworks, I am too tired to repine over my situation."

"Who runs it now?" he asked quickly, to fill in the silence that threatened to choke her.

"My cousin William Peabody," she said, her voice light again. "But he was to have returned to Harvard, and only stays on in sufferance now. We had thought to have this matter cleared up much earlier."

"And now you shall," Waggoner said. He put his arm around her again and pulled her to rest against him. "You'll be on the next ship bound for Boston, I'll wager."

"Yes, I expect so," she agreed, and wondered why the notion did not inspire total delight.

She slept then, to be shaken gently awake later. The carriage had stopped. The door was already open, and Chattering stood there. Blessing allowed Lord Thomas to help her down. He walked her to the door, looking around him.

"Not a very promising street, Mrs. Whittier," he commented. "I am sure Aaron would not have approved."

" 'Twas cheaper than hotel rooms," she explained. "No, I do not think Aaron would have approved either."

He was in no hurry to leave her at the door. "Tell me, do you know where this other beauty on Albemarle Road lives?" he asked.

"I wish thee would not call me a beauty," she scolded, feeling the spots of color in her cheeks.

"Well, the other antidote, then," he said with a laugh. "My dear, do you ever look in mirrors?"

"No!" She stared at him in confusion. "*Who* is the family rake?" she asked pointedly.

He staggered back as though she had shot him,

and she laughed. "I have never had the slightest inclination to be a rake, Mrs. Whittier, but I do have two functioning eyes! All this aside, I would still like to find this damsel and talk to her."

"She lives next door with a veritable dragon I can only assume is a chaperone," Blessing replied. "I am not so sure she is a lady. She wears overmuch powder and rouge, and her laugh is memorable, to say the least."

Blessing stopped. It was hardly necessary for Lord Thomas to know that she had heard that laugh, and other sounds, any number of times through the thin walls of her bedroom. The sounds should have repulsed her, but they only left her hugging her pillow and feeling lonelier than she could have expressed in words. No need for Lord Thomas to know anything of this.

He looked at the house next door, vaulted the iron railing that separated the two doors, and knocked. He cocked his head toward the door and listened, and then knocked once more. No answer. He joined her again. "Well, I shall think of something," he murmured, and took her hand again, kissing it. "Good day, Mrs. Whittier. I trust you will have good news from the Admiralty House before this day is over."

He saw her into the house and then waved to her from the carriage window as she stood there in the entrance watching him depart.

Patience hugged her and cried, then blew her nose and demanded an explanation over tea and biscuits.

"I told thee it was a strange scheme," she reminded her daughter-in-law when Blessing finished her recitation.

Blessing sighed. "So it was. I was foolish and God was merciful."

Patience nodded, and kissed Blessing again. "But now you think we might hear at last from the Admiralty?"

"That is what Lord Thomas says."

"Can he be trusted?" Patience asked, her eyes anxious. "I am desperate to be home again, daughter."

Blessing nodded, remembering the strength of his arm about her. "He can be trusted."

By mutual agreement, both ladies retired to their respective bedchambers. "Even after that letter last night, I am sure I did not sleep above twenty minutes," Patience assured her.

The fog had burned away and the sun was quite high in the sky when Blessing's rest was disturbed by another jangle at the doorbell. When it would not stop, she dressed quickly, tugging her curly hair under her cap as she ran down the hall.

She opened the door upon Lord Thomas Waggoner, looking fresh as the flower in his lapel and bearing one more kitten in his arms. He winked at her, to Blessing's acute embarrassment, and bowed as best he could with the kitten.

"I seem to have overlooked one more little nuisance, Mrs. Whittier," he said. "It was mewing and mewing all around the kitchen this morning when I went belowstairs to beg a snack from the cook. It would have wrenched tears from your eyes."

With a laugh she accepted the kitten and carried it inside, setting it down on the floor where the other two kittens had congregated when the doorbell rang.

"Sir, how am I to return with these to Nantucket?" she inquired, half-amused, half-exasperated.

"Perhaps you will feel compelled to remain

here," he said, his voice offhand. "At least until they have grown."

"I will remind thee that I have a ropewalk to run," she said. "The strands do not twist by themselves! Shut the door if thee is coming in."

He closed the door behind him, looking about with some disfavor at the dingy hall and its faded, tattered wallpaper. "I wanted to tell you that I have been to the Admiralty House."

"And thee got in?" she asked, her eyes wide.

He widened his eyes in imitation of her. "I am an Englishman, my dear, with some good report from my army days. I won't say they exactly stood aside and bowed, but I did see my uncle, and he will help you."

Blessing clapped her hands. "Thee is a wonder!"

He smiled modestly. "We Waggoners have that effect on some. You may ask any woman within a fifty-mile radius."

"But that is thy brother," she accused.

He nodded. "I cannot pretend to trade upon his . . . his . . . skill."

"No need to say more," Blessing interrupted hastily.

Thomas Waggoner was looking about him again, an expression of dissatisfaction on his face.

"I have a much prettier parlor in Nantucket," Blessing said, reading his thoughts.

"I suppose you have a view of the sea?"

"Oh, yes, my lord. Everyone does."

They just stood in the hall, Lord Thomas with his hat in his hand, and Blessing wondering if her cap hid all her uncombed curls.

"Mrs. Whittier, you could do me a great favor," he said at last, after obvious hesitation. "How would you feel about attending a Valentine's costume call this evening at my brother's house on Curzon Street?"

"I ... I could never, Lord Thomas," she protested. "We Friends don't mind a gathering every now and then, but not in costume."

He thought about it a moment, eyeing her gray dress with its tidy lace collar. "Suppose I were to come in costume and you wore what you have on now. You do look fine in gray."

Blessing blushed. "I never think about it."

He smiled at her confusion, and put his hat back on his head. "You probably never do. Do consider my offer, my dear. I will come by for you at nine o'clock."

"But ..."

Thomas had to resist the urge to whistle as he strode down Albemarle Road and hailed a hackney coach. He considered the matter. Walking would be cheaper, but the victory of convincing beautiful Blessing Whittier to attend the costume ball deserved some reward.

And by great Jehovah Lord above, she was a beauty. He leaned back in the coach, a smile upon his face. I have never seen such luminous blue eyes, he thought, although they were a trifle stormy last night. His hand went to his neck, grateful that his high collar hid the worst of her nail scourings. She's not a woman to rile, he thought.

He had never seen such perfect skin. Blessing Whittier would never need to resort to potions and powders. She was one of those women, he decided, who would probably grow more beautiful with age and children. I have always wanted a large family, he thought, allowing his mind to roam freely. Damned unfashionable, I suppose, but there you are. I like children.

He sighed and tugged his thoughts back to the present. I couldn't support a family of sea bream in my present circumstances, he thought, and here I am mooning about a regular tribe of Abraham. Oh, Lord, Charles has just got to be brought up to snuff.

He tapped on the roof and the coach slowed.

"Take me back to Curzon Street," he said.

Charles was awake and sitting up in bed as Thomas came into the darkened room and threw back the draperies.

"Have a heart, brother," he gasped as he covered his eyes with his hands. "Is it noon yet?" he asked.

"Noon and then some," Thomas said as he sat himself down on Charles's bed. "I wonder that you have not been jerked awake by all the servants scurrying around, making ready for your party!" He leaned closer. "And how you managed to convince our solicitors to advance you any blunt for a party, I cannot fathom. Charles, don't you comprehend that quaint old expression 'under the hatches'?"

Charles removed his hands from his eyes and gazed at his younger brother with an expression of serenity that made Thomas want to shake him. "You seem to think I have done nothing to bring us about," he murmured. "I wish you would trust the head of the family, dear boy."

Thomas laughed, but there was no mirth. "All I have noticed since my return from Belgium—on a stretcher, I might remind you—is you turning losing cards and sniffing after questionable women."

"Jealous, Thomas?" Charles said, his eyes narrow and his voice soft.

"Damn you, Charles," Thomas said, his voice equally soft. "Don't you care what's happening to the family name?"

Charles sighed and stretched out his hand for the bell rope. "I was going to tell you tonight, you crosspatch, but I suppose it will not wait."

"*What* will not wait?" Thomas asked.

"I am to be married." Charles shuddered, and then smoothed the hair from his eyes. "So do not think I have been idly standing by wringing my hands and waiting for the creditors to carry us off to the workhouse."

"There's not a family in London with a father so dead to reason that he would allow even his most distempered daughter to come within a block of you."

Charles laughed and threw back the covers. "Thank God for Northumberland," he said. "I have met an earl's daughter from that wretched place, and she will have me."

Thomas stared at his brother. Charles laughed and threw a pillow at him. "Lord, Thomas, if you don't look like a trout hooked and tossed up on the bank! Angela—and she truly is an angel—agreed last night at the opera." He paused and raised himself on his elbow to look at his younger brother. "You may wish me happy, Thomas."

Thomas did no such thing. He frowned and paced to the window, where he stood, hands in his pockets, staring out at the activity on Curzon Street. As he watched, tradesmen staggering under the weight of potted trees and cases of champagne formed a veritable parade into the servants' entrance below. Charles joined him at the window. He clapped his hand on Thomas' shoulder. "I had no trouble convincing our solicitors to extend me credit upon my expectations." He gave

Thomas a little shake. "And what better way to celebrate Saint Valentine's Eve than with an engagement party? Think how surprised my guests will be."

Thomas said nothing for a long moment. When he did speak, he tried to keep his voice casual. "And where does this paragon, my future sister-in-law, reside?"

"On Albemarle Road," Lord Cavanaugh replied promptly, and then laughed, his voice indulgent, as though he humored a much younger child. "And now you will tell me that Albemarle Road is not quite the thing for the daughter of an earl."

Thomas nodded, his eyes still on the street, not trusting himself to look at Charles. "Yes, that's probably what I would say. How perspicacious you are, Chuck."

Charles went to his dressing table. "Yes, I suppose I am. I wonder that Mother was always so insistent that you were awarded all the brains in the family." He turned around to regard his brother. "I did ask Angela Davenport—ah, yes, the Northumberland Davenports—that very thing. The dear girl assured me that it was her father's idea."

Thomas held up his hand. "Don't tell me, Charles, but let me guess," he said, his voice rising despite his efforts to control it. "Papa Davenport thought that such a humble address would surely shield his daughter—his super-wealthy daughter—from a legion of gazetted fortune hunters."

Charles nodded in perfect accord. "One would almost think you knew the story, Thomas," he murmured as he turned back to contemplate his face in the mirror.

"Heavens, no!" Thomas said, failing utterly at control. "I'm sure that without overmuch exertion you could find this little faradiddle scratched on a clay tablet in Babylonia! Are you such a flat, Charles?"

"Jealous," was all Charles said. "Shut the door quietly when you leave, Thomas. I have a bit of a head this afternoon."

Thomas slammed the door behind him, but took no satisfaction in Charles's anguished shriek. His face set, his complexion pale, he hurtled down the stairs and out the door, scattering tradesmen and hothouse flowers on Curzon Street.

In a fury at his brother, he walked, his head down, to St. James's Park, where he threw himself onto a bench. His stomach churned; he felt the burning sensation of unshed tears as he stared at the nursemaids strolling by with their little charges, and small boys braving a chilly wind to launch their vessels on the pond.

I am ruined, he thought.

Blessing Whittier had stood for some minutes at the door after watching Thomas Waggoner leave in the hackney. As kittens nipped and purred around her ankles, she asked herself again:

"Did I *really* tell Lord Thomas that I would attend a costume ball with him?"

She could never have done such a thing, she thought as she knelt to appropriate one particularly insistent kitten. "Has thee no manners?" she scolded, and then massaged the little one under its chin. "No more do I," she said. "Dear me."

Blessing was wide-awake now. She walked slowly into the sitting room, kittens trailing, and sat cross-legged on the sofa.

"I would like to be home in Nantucket. Rope is so uncomplicated," she announced to the kitten in her arms. "And I suppose thee will insist upon coming too."

The other kittens climbed the sofa and arranged themselves in her lap. *If we can truly save the ropewalk, I can let Mother Whittier know somehow that I would not object to marrying again,* she thought as she rubbed each kitten and increased the crescendo around her. *Of course, it will likely be to a widower with a ready-made family, but I can be content with that. I wonder, does Lord Thomas have blue eyes or gray?*

She was admiring the kittens in her lap and contemplating serviceable names for them when the doorbell jangled again. She was on her feet and down the hall in a twinkling, smiling to herself. *He must have found another kitten somewhere and means for me to keep it company,* she thought as she flung open the door.

It was the porter from the Admiralty House.

"Oh!" Blessing exclaimed, and stepped back, to the irritation of a kitten. She recognized him as the man who sat behind the high appointment desk. For almost a month she had watched him gaze out across the throng of petitioners and naval officers with a look of extreme distaste on his face that must have frozen into unpleasantness years ago and could not be altered.

"Mrs. Whittier?" he asked, removing the stocking cap he wore. There was nothing in his voice of disdain this time, and she came cautiously closer.

She nodded in acknowledgment, but did not let him in. He handed her a thick packet stamped with wax.

"Then this is for you, from Lord Renfrew," he said, and bowed as he backed away.

She watched, openmouthed, as he seated himself again in the government vehicle outside the door and spoke to the driver. Slowly she closed the door and stared down at the package in her hands.

She wrinkled her nose. The packet was bound in canvas and sealed with tar, and she knew that it was a ship's log, or at least a part of one. She pulled it from the protecting canvas and traced the words on the cover with a hand that trembled. HMS *Dare*.

She ran down the hall, calling for Patience and tugging at the red cord that bound the log.

Soon she sat on Patience's bed and opened the folded sheet that accompanied the log. She held it out to her mother-in-law, but Patience, tears in her eyes, pushed it back.

"Oh, I cannot! You read it, my dear."

" 'To the Mrs. Whittiers: This excerpt from the first and second weeks of August 1812 should satisfy your solicitors,' " she read. "Mother, it is signed and stamped!"

Patience was looking at the far wall. "Read the entries," was all she said.

Heads together, arms about each other's waists, Blessing and her mother-in-law read each entry of the log of the *Dare* during the very week that hostilities opened between England and the United States. Her voice faltering at times, Blessing read how the *Seaspray*, unaware, was caught in the Arctic whaling ground. In the dispassionate, spare style reminiscent of her own dead husband's log entries, she read the nameless captain's encounter with the whaler, the explosions, and then the men hunted down who had fled into the whaleboats. "Survivors, none," he had written with a bold flourish. "Salvage, naught."

Patience sat a long time gazing at the papers. She leaned against her daughter-in-law. "We are the better for knowing, Blessing," she said at last. "And we have proof for our creditors that it was an act of war. That should satisfy the solicitors." Tears welled in her eyes. "I only wish I felt better about it, my dear."

They cried together one last time; then Patience folded the papers, running her hand over the tarry bag. "Thee may sleep now, my husband and son," she whispered. "And we *will* run the ropewalk." She looked at her daughter-in-law for reassurance. "Blessing, can we make it turn a profit?"

"Mother, we can try," Blessing said, swallowing her tears. "I will continue to supervise the rope-making. We need to find a salesman."

Patience hugged her again. "Do you know, we owe thy young man such a debt."

"Mother, he is not my young man!" Blessing protested. "I only wish he would stop bringing me kittens."

Patience picked up the newest arrival, a striped mixture of the other two. "I suppose thee will yip and wail if we do not take thee along," she said, stroking the tiny kitten that purred so loud it shook. "Blessing, let us pack our trunks. We could even leave tonight for Portsmouth, if we hurry fast."

Blessing put a hand to her mouth. "Oh, dear, we cannot," she said. "Mother, you will not believe this, but I have promised to attend a Valentine's Eve costume ball at the Marquess of Cavanaugh's house this night."

Patience gasped, and the little kitten arched its back. She opened her mouth to protest, and then looked down at the canvas parcel in her lap. She touched it. "Well, perhaps it is the least thee can do," she said. "A costume ball, did thee say? Blessing, thee grows quite wild with dissipation."

"I . . . I told him I should never," Blessing said. "He has a way of doing precisely as he wishes. It is a vexatious habit, Mother."

Patience only twinkled her eyes at her daughter-in-law.

"I cannot imagine anyone of our acquaintance behaving in such fashion. Can thee?"

"Mother!"

She was ready long before she heard the carriage outside the door, and Lord Thomas' knock.

"Never?" he teased as he helped her into her cloak. "How glad I am you changed your mind."

"I owe you this," she said, and then put her hand on his arm as she remembered. "Oh, Thomas! I mean, Lord Thomas. The note from Lord Renfrew came only this afternoon!"

"And?" he prompted.

"Mother Whittier has the log and a page proof, signed and stamped. It was the HMS *Dare* that sank the *Seaspray*."

He was silent, watching. "It is hard to know," he said at last, his voice quiet.

She nodded and lowered her eyes. "They were hunted down like animals in their little boats."

He bowed over her hand and kissed it. "I am so sorry, my dear."

She let him continue holding her hand. "I need not spend any more of my nights wondering, and that is some consolation."

"I am sure that it is." He thought a moment. "Tell me, because Uncle Calcingham will ask me, I am sure. Was the porter who delivered the package polite?"

She opened her eyes wide. "Unusually so! Oh, when I think how rude . . ." She stopped in confusion. "Oh, but that is unimportant." She leaned closer. "How did thee know?"

"It was something you said . . . or maybe didn't say. Men who prey on helpless widows excite my censure. Even if you are American, and lately a belligerent," he added with a twinkle in his eyes. "I told him myself that if he did not treat you with good English courtesy he would never work again."

"Oh!" she said, her voice solemn. "I could never be so bold."

He only smiled, and offered her his arm.

She took it and then took a good look at him for the first time. "Lord Thomas, thee looks fine as a new penny!"

He handed her into the carriage. "I wondered when you would notice," he said, climbing in beside her and tapping the side with the elegant ebony cane he carried. He seated himself and brushed at the front of his gray coat. "Since you would not—or could not—go in costume, I had to, of course. Tell me, my dear Blessing, did William Penn really wear a rig-out like this?"

She nodded, her eyes merry again. "I suppose he did. Thee would be a trifle outmoded now, but not by much. Thee would scarcely be out of place walking down Orange Street in Nantucket, nodding and tipping thy hat to my neighbors."

"So glad thee approves," he aid, his eyes straight ahead, some lingering sadness or longing on his face. "I hope this costume ball is not a purgatory for you, but you will recognize Charles's light-o'-love, and I really would like a word with her before Charles is able to detach himself from his other guests."

"It is the least I can do, after all thee has done

for us," she replied, her eyes on his face. "But what will thee do?"

"I had thought to pay her off to leave Charles alone, but what does my brother tell me this very day but that she is an earl's daughter from Northumberland, come to town. Do you think this possible?"

"No, Thomas, I do not," she said, forgetting his title at last. "She ... she must be saying that to tempt him into an unwise marriage." She gasped as the knowledge took root. "She must suppose *him* to have a fortune!"

"This is odd, indeed, Blessing," he said, taking her hand. "She thinks to marry him for his money, and apparently he labors under the delusion that she is wealthy, if a trifle eccentric." He eyed her. "I wonder who will be the more disappointed?"

"Thee, I think," she replied slowly. "Thy brother is thoughtless beyond measure, but thee sought to save the family name, didn't thee?"

"I did," he replied. "I seem to have some memory, even if Charles does not, of days when Waggoner, Marquess of Cavanaugh, was a respected name and title."

"Perhaps thee will be able to avert some disaster," she said as they turned into Curzon Street and the carriage rolled to a stop behind others in a long line of guests. "My, for a rake, thy brother can command the attention of many people!"

He managed a wry smile. "We Waggoners have been well-known since William the Conquerer as impeccable hosts." He moved restlessly, stretching his long legs out in front of him. "If I can convince Charles ..."

He turned to her, his eyes pleading. "Blessing, I am certain that it would take only a few years of judicious management. Perhaps Charles would

have to sell his place in town, but what is that, if
he can hang on to Cavanaugh? It is the prettiest
estate in Kent, or at least it used to be."

"Oh, Thomas," she said, taking his hand.

"Waggoners have been born there since the time
of Queen Bess," he said, his eyes on the carriage
in front of them. "It is my home, and I mean to
save it."

"I wish I could help. I truly do," she whispered.

He remembered himself, and squeezed her
hand. "What you're doing is enough. Just point
out the fair damsel to me, and I will try my best
to dissuade her."

The carriage moved forward. "And if thee does
not succeed?" Blessing asked in a low voice.

"Then I am ruined, my dear," he said. "No self-
respecting woman will have a second son with no
prospects." He managed a crooked grin. "Even if
Charles's amour throws him over, he'll find someone desperate enough, maybe a millowner's toothy
daughter who'd like a title, no matter how shop-
worn. And then it still will never be the same
again." He sighed and patted her hand. "It's a bit
daunting to think of facing the world with a bad
shoulder and no prospects."

Impulsively she kissed his cheek. "The worst has
not happened yet, Thomas. Thee may very well be
able to convince thy brother of his folly and save
thy home. If I can help in any way . . ."

He smiled at her, his good humor restored. "Just
stand by me, fair one, and I will feel a little more
indomitable."

"Done, sir," she said as the carriage moved forward again and the postboy opened the door.

Clutching tight to Lord Thomas in his severe
Quaker garb, Blessing entered the Marquess of
Cavanaugh's residence at 11 Curzon Street. She

looked about in delight at the winking chandeliers reflected in the expanse of mirrors, and the graceful sweep of the staircase that lifted to the floor above. Masked ladies and gentlemen strolled about and greeted each other. She sniffed deep of the perfume and pomade.

Thomas stared too. "I did not think that even our solicitors would be so generous," he muttered, holding her close to him as a party dressed as Napoleon's Life Guards strode through the hall, their bearskin shakos brushing the lower chandeliers.

He shuddered at the sight of them, and then loosened his grip on her. "No one who was there that day at Waterloo would ever dress up like that. God, how I hate war," he said, more to himself than to her.

Blessing looked at him in dismay, powerless to erase the desperation from his eyes. She stood in front of him a moment, straightening buttons that were not out of place, and then placed her hands on his chest. "But thee is a fine Quaker gentleman," she reminded him. "Thee can have nothing to do with war anymore."

He shook himself visibly, and regarded her seriously. "Thee is right as always, Mrs. Whittier," he said. "How am I doing?"

"Excellently well, Thomas."

He bowed to her, an elegant bow that made her put her hands to her flaming cheeks.

"Does thee dance, Mrs. Whittier?" he asked.

She shook her head. "No! And do not think that thee can coerce me."

"I would never try," he protested, and then grinned at her. "Well, not above three or four times a day, I am sure."

She looked beyond him to the door, and there was the beauty of Albemarle Road.

In spite of her own stringent upbringing, Blessing Whittier blinked and stared at the spectacle before her. No matter that Angela Davenport had cluttered her face with too much powder and rouge; no matter that her laughter just edged on shrill; in that bit of silky gauze that clung to her generous frame, Miss Davenport was a sight to behold.

"Look over there," she said unnecessarily. Thomas was already staring at the woman in the foyer. Blessing felt a momentary irritation. "But thee doesn't need to look so hard, William Penn!" she admonished, and tugged at his sleeve.

"I am sizing up the enemy," he whispered back, not taking his eyes from the overblown sight before him. "Tell me, Blessing. Do you think that is one of the nightgowns you refused to wear last night?"

Blessing opened her mouth to protest, and then looked into Thomas' laughing eyes. "Thee is a rogue," she said, her voice low but distinct. Several guests did look around, and she blushed when they laughed. "Well, thee is," she insisted. "That is she, if thee ever had any doubts. And Lord bless us, she managed to shake off her chaperone."

Thomas nodded and watched the woman's stately progress from the door to the center of the hall, where she stood alone and stripped off her gloves, well aware of the eyes upon her, some appreciative, some wary. She looked around for Charles Waggoner, who stood across the hall at the card-room door, his back to her.

Thomas took Blessing's hand off his arm. "Wish me luck," he muttered as he stepped forward with a smile, holding out his hand to the woman.

"My dear, I am Thomas Waggoner," he said, and bowed over her hand. "Charles's dull brother."

Angela tittered, her silly laugh grating on Blessing like fingernails on slate. Well, Blessing thought grimly as she watched Thomas Waggoner's graceful bow, at least after this night I need not suffer that laugh through the walls of our apartment. I will be on a ship to Boston.

In another moment Angela was hanging on Thomas' arm, leaning toward him as he made a joke, and then laughing louder.

"You needn't be so charming," Blessing murmured under her breath as the couple swept past her. She shook her head at her own discomfort. Thomas, thee could probably sell tomahawks to Indians, she thought as they moved down the hall.

Angela's laughter had captured Lord Cavanaugh's attention finally. With a bow to his gentleman friends entering the card room, he hurried into the hall to stand beside Blessing. He looked after his brother thoughtfully, and then turned his attention to Blessing.

"Two Quakers, eh? Now, where would my slowtop brother ever dredge up a lady as tempting as you?"

He put his hand on her waist, and Blessing moved out of his reach. He reached for her again, his hand clasping her more firmly. "Let us follow them, my little Quakeress."

"Get thy hands off me," she said between clenched teeth.

Charles threw back his head and laughed. "Oh, and is *thee* an actress too? How far does this charade go?" He touched her under the chin, his fingers rough. "Where *did* my brother find you?" he murmured, his lips close to her ear.

When she did not answer, Charles laughed again and pulled her closer, tugging her along the hall after his brother. "I think he is up to no good, my dear. What do you say we find him?"

When she continued to pull away from him, he released her finally, but continued in the direction his brother had gone. "Actually, I suspected that he would try to make my dearest Angela cry off even before we announced our engagement." He patted his coat pocket. "Let's see whom she believes."

He surveyed the closed doors. "Now, where . . ." he began. "I know. He has gone into the library. He knows that is a room I never think to enter." He opened a door and peered inside. "And I was right. Come, come, let us enjoy this little scene."

Angela Davenport and Thomas Waggoner stood close to the fireplace. Thomas was leaning forward and gesturing with some energy, but as soon as Charles Waggoner entered the room, Angela hurried toward him, awarding him a lingering kiss that made Blessing look away.

Her hands possessively on his shoulders, Angela stared back at Thomas, who stood with his lips tight together in an uncompromising line.

"Is he really your brother?" Angela asked.

"If I can believe my late mother," Charles replied, and then sighed heavily. "Alas, every now and then there is a stuffy Waggoner. I cannot account for it, but there you are."

Angela formed her lips into a pout. "He claims that you have no money at all." She twined her arms around Charles's neck. "I told him that was silly. I mean, just look about this room!"

"I suspect even the books are mortgaged," Thomas said, his words clipped short.

Charles fixed a stare on his brother over Angela's shoulder that was not lost on Blessing. "Of course it's silly, dear heart," he purred.

Thomas made no move to come closer, but his voice carried, and Blessing felt a little shiver at the command in it. "I was merely suggesting to Miss Davenport that she might wish to visit our solicitors in the morning, Charles."

Charles yawned. "Thomas, you are too tedious! Angela has better things to do than visit a dreary solicitor's office." He kissed her. "We have so many wedding plans to make, don't we, my sweet?"

"Well, I suppose," Angela said after another glower at Thomas. "But he did say . . ." Her voice trailed off.

Charles patted his pocket again. "Besides, my angel, I have something here for you which ought to put a stop to any foolish notions about my worth."

Angela clapped her hands and then reached into Charles's pocket. She drew out a green velvet case. Blessing looked around in surprise as Thomas sucked in his breath.

"Charles, you wouldn't dare," he began, and moved closer.

"Oh, wouldn't I!" Charles said. He opened the case and Blessing leaned closer for a look.

A many-stranded diamond necklace winked at her, all fire and ice. As Blessing held her breath, Charles lifted it from the velvet nest and put it around Angela's neck.

"Diamonds for a lady," Charles said, his eyes on his brother.

"Damn you, Charles," Thomas said.

Blessing hurried to his side. "Not a scene now, Thomas," she urged.

He shook her off. "Yes, a scene now!" he shouted

at his brother. "You would give the Cavanaugh diamonds away? My God, Charles, you're certifiable!"

He was so angry he shook. Charles merely smiled at him serenely, and then winked at Blessing.

"My dear, take Miss Davenport closer to the light of the fireplace. I think the clasp is not sufficiently in place."

"No," Blessing said as she took Thomas by the hand. "I won't."

Charles raised his eyebrows. "You're a managing baggage," he said, his voice soft.

She ignored his insult and leaned closer to Thomas. "And thee will control thyself," she said.

The brothers glared at each other. After a moment of vast discomfort, Angela shrugged her bare shoulders and flounced toward the fireplace, muttering something under her breath about "people of class with no manners."

"I have a mind to call you out," Thomas said to his brother.

Charles only smiled. "You can't even aim a pistol with accuracy anymore, Thomas dear, unless you've suddenly achieved ambidexterity." With a supercilious smile that made Blessing want to rend him from collar to boots, Charles came forward in conspiratorial fashion. "Besides, dear brother, they're only paste anyway. I am depending upon Angela's aging father, the earl from windy Northumberland, to cock up his crusty toes. Then I shall redeem them, and the devil of a lot more."

"Paste? The Cavanaugh diamonds?" Thomas gasped. "Good God, Charles! How long?"

Charles attempted to stare down his brother's fierce gaze, but found himself regarding Angela preening herself in the mirror over the fireplace. "Oh, years and years," he said vaguely with a wave of his hand. "Tom, it's devilish hard to maintain horses the year around."

Thomas turned away, his eyes closed. He bowed his head, and Blessing found herself close to tears. She thought suddenly of the ropewalk that she had nurtured and led along through the days of her grief at Aaron's loss. How would I feel if it were suddenly taken from me? she thought as she rested her hand on Thomas' shoulder. To her surprise, he reached over and grasped her fingers. His hand trembled, and her heart went out to him.

"Then we are ruined," Thomas said, his voice scarcely audible.

Charles threw up his hands in exasperation and came around to face his brother. "Thomas, haven't you heard a word I have said? I am to marry into this juicy family." He frowned at Angela. "I suppose she is a little, well, less genteel than Mama would have wished. But, Thomas, she's rich."

How callous you English are, Blessing thought as she watched the brothers. She dabbed at the tears that spilled onto her cheeks and sniffed audibly.

For the first time, Lord Cavanaugh seemed to really take note of her presence in the room. His eyes narrowed as he watched her.

"And who, pray tell, are you, to intrude upon this tender family scene?"

Thomas turned around slowly, as if suddenly old beyond his years. "She is my friend," he said simply.

Charles grinned at his younger brother and raised his eyebrows. "So that's what you call them? Thomas, you needn't split hairs in such hardened company." He took Blessing's other hand, and before she could withdraw it, kissed her fingers. "I want to know how you convinced a Haymarket doxy to dress in Quaker gray. When you tire of her, just hand her down."

Before she could stop him, Thomas dropped her hand, hauled back, and struck his brother at the point of his jaw. Angela uttered an unladylike oath as Charles's eyes fluttered back in his head. A quizzical expression on his face, he sank to his knees and pitched forward, unconscious.

Angela threw herself on her knees beside the recumbent marquess. She shook him, and then turned him over, hugging him to her ample proportions. "Charles," she murmured over and over. When there was no response, she began to sob.

Thomas regarded his bleeding knuckles ruefully. "I have always wanted to do that," he said, more to himself than to Blessing. "I do not expect you to understand, but it felt so good." He grinned at her. "I won't do it again," he promised.

Thomas strolled to Angela and knelt beside her. Humming to himself, he pulled back one of his brother's eyelids. "He's still in there," he said, and turned to Angela. "My dear Miss Davenport. I don't know how to break this to you, but that necklace you are wearing is paste. Charles is truly to let. He had thought to marry you and replenish the family fortunes, but we both know that's a taradiddle, don't we?"

Angela opened her eyes wider and pulled Charles closer to her. "Whatever do you mean?" she asked.

"I took a stroll to the registry office this afternoon. The only earl from Northumberland who could possibly be your father died five years ago and left his fortune to his housekeeper."

Angela raised her chin and tried to stare him

down. She looked away first. "That dratted house-keeper," she said between clenched teeth. "I thought the old scarecrow would at least mention me in his will." She looked at Blessing, her eyes imploring. "And he was me dad, even if it was not a regular affair."

Blessing shuddered and went to the window.

"You're petitioning the wrong party, Angela," Thomas said mildly. "Blessing is more scrupulous than the Waggoners, thank goodness, and obviously the Davenports too."

Charles began to stir, but he did not open his eyes. Thomas regarded him for a moment. "And you just picked Lord Cavanaugh out of a hat?"

By now Angela had lowered Charles Waggoner to the floor. "The old earl mentioned how rich you were." She touched the necklace. "Can you blame a girl for trying?"

Thomas smiled back, his affability restored. "I suppose not. Pity you picked someone so improvident." He helped Angela to her feet and directed her toward the door. "Don't be discouraged, my dear. There are any number of choice spirits present here this evening who would love to, ah, make you their valentine. Oh, and keep the necklace, by all means, my dear. Happy hunting, Angela . . . Angela . . ."

"Scrooby," she sighed. "That old buzzard never would admit I was his own flesh and blood." She poked Charles with her foot. "I hope I am a wiser girl, Lord Thomas."

"Glad the lesson was so instructive," Thomas commented as he closed the door behind her.

His expression thoughtful, Thomas watched her leave and then turned to Blessing. "All's well that ends, my dear," he said. "Oh, and look, Charles is coming about. Well, thank heaven for that! I would hate to have disabled such a boil on the rump of humanity."

Hands in his pockets, he stared down at his brother a moment. He sighed and turned away. "Come, my dear, and let me take you home. The emergency is over for the moment, I suppose."

They rode in silence. Thomas stared out the window, his thoughts miles away. Blessing knew that if she even made the smallest pleasantry, she would burst into tears, tears she would be hard put to explain away.

The carriage pulled up in front of 11 Albemarle Road. Thomas helped her down and stood beside her. "I suppose you are leaving soon?"

She nodded, careful not to look him in the eye. "Tomorrow we go to Portsmouth on the mail coach."

He held out his hand. "Glad I was able to be of service, Mrs. Whittier," he said, his voice casual, offhand.

She started to say something—what, she could never recall—when he grasped her by both shoulders, pulled her close, and kissed her soundly.

He needs consolation, was her first thought, and then she did not think anymore as she caressed the back of his neck and stood on tiptoe to make consolation easier. From her lips he explored her neck, and then traveled up the line of her jaw to her lips again. She clung to him.

And then he was holding her away from him and looking at her as though he wished to memorize her face. She looked at his own dear face, more austere than she would have liked, and too solemn for his own good, but unspeakably important to her.

"May I write to you?" he asked finally, when he could speak.

She nodded. "Care of Whittier Ropewalk," she whispered, and touched her fingers to his lips one last time.

Without a backward glance, she ran up the steps and into the house.

Hours later, morning found her still staring at the ceiling, willing the sun to rise faster so she could leave sooner. Dry-eyed now after a night of tears, she contemplated her rope-bound trunk. Patience must never know, she thought. It would make her so uncomfortable that I even considered for one minute what I have spent a whole night wrestling with. I dare not hurt someone so kind to me.

Blessing was dressed and waiting for Patience to check through the house one last time when the doorbell rang. She leapt to her feet and ran to answer it.

The neighbor boy stood before her, cap in hand, holding out a package done up in frills and ribbons. He gestured with his head. "From that gentleman. You know."

Blessing smiled her thanks and tore off the wrapping paper. The boy watched, interested, and then sniffed and stepped back, muttering something about gentry and their strange notions of Valentine's Day.

Her heart marching at the double quick, she opened the box and burst into tears.

"I'd cry, too, miss," the boy said.

A valentine, tarred and made of rope, lay nestled among tissue in the box. She dried her eyes on her sleeve and picked up the card. " 'Happy Valentine's Day,' " she read out loud. " 'A whiff of this every now and then ought to stave off the pangs of homesickness until thee is safely home in Nantucket. As ever, Tom.' "

The boy watched a moment in uncomfortable silence and then cleared his throat. "Ma'am, I think he's still waiting at the head of the street for a hackney."

With a cry, she dropped the box, picked up her skirts, and ran to the corner of Albemarle and Hose.

He stood where the lane turned, hands in his pockets, head down against the early-morning mist. He looked up and smiled as she approached, but made no move.

"It's silly, I suppose," he said.

"It's beautiful," she assured him. "I've never had a valentine before. It's not something we Friends do."

He bowed in her direction, his voice light. "I will see that you have one every year, then. That should shock your neighbors."

She watched him. His tone was light, bantering, but his eyes reflected some new misery she had never seen before. She touched his arm. "Something has happened," she stated.

He nodded, at a loss for words. When he could speak, he gazed over her shoulder, as though he could not bear to look into her eyes. "I shouldn't have left Charles alone when I took you home last night."

Blessing drew in her breath and clutched his arm. "Oh, surely he did not . . ."

He shook his head again. "Oh, no, no! Nothing that dismal, my dear. Charles is too much of a coward to lift a hand against himself." He laughed, the sound bitter. "A hand!" He took a deep breath. "My brother lost the Cavanaugh estate and our house in town on the turn of a card last night at that dratted Valentine's party."

Blessing put her hands to her mouth. Speech-less, she shook her head.

"He always swore he could turn a good hand. Well, now he has done it," Thomas said as he stepped into the street to hail a passing hackney. The vehicle stopped and the driver opened the door. Thomas climbed inside before Blessing could stop him and closed the door.

"But what will thee do?" she managed to say as the driver seated himself again and looked down at her, no patience in his eyes.

"Stand away, miss," he ordered.

Blessing stamped her foot. "I will not!" She opened the door. "What will thee do?" She asked again, her voice more insistent.

"Pack, I suppose," Thomas said, not looking at her.

"Thee knows that is not what I mean!"

He took her by the hand. "I do not know, my very dear Mrs. Whittier. Do you know anyone who wants a broken-down soldier?"

I do, she wanted to say. Blessing let go of his hand but did not move away from the hackney. She took a deep breath.

"Thee must listen to thy Inner Light."

Thomas looked at her. "What?" he asked, his voice incredulous. "I tell you that the Waggoners have ruined themselves and you rattle on about 'inner light'?"

She backed away then, her hands behind her back, feeling all the embarrassment of her differ-ence. All the humiliation of the last few months in England washed over her again, and she wondered what she was thinking.

"Yes, thy Inner Light," she repeated stubbornly. "Thee has one. It will tell thee what to do." She hesitated, her face red, and plunged ahead. "Does thee ever pray, Thomas?"

"Not since Waterloo," he muttered.

She raised her chin. "I recommend it."

She stepped back then and waved the driver on.

Thomas did not look back. Blessing watched the hackney as it careened down the street crowded with early-morning merchants and the tattered sprites of Albemarle Road, staggering home after a late night.

Thee will likely never see him again, she thought as she started back to their rented rooms. Tears came to her eyes. She stopped and stood where she was until she had some measure of control over herself. It would never do for Patience to see how much Thomas Waggoner had come to mean to her in less than three short days. She would call me impetuous, and she would be right, Blessing thought. She sighed. And he is not a Friend.

Patience, well-covered in cloak and bonnet, stood on the doorstep, holding the wicker basket of kittens. A hackney waited in front, their luggage already inside.

Silent, her face composed, Blessing retrieved her rope valentine where she had dropped it in her hurry to chase after Thomas.

"He is certainly an Original Item," was Patience's only comment. A smile lurked around her lips. "Does thee think it is a good length of cable?"

Blessing forced herself to enter into the spirit of Patience Whittier's gentle joke. "Not as good as Whittier Ropewalk can do, Mother," she said.

Patience was too kind to continue her scrutiny. She set down the kittens. "Unless thee has some additional pressing duty in London, I suggest that we shake the dust off our boots and go home."

Blessing nodded. She put on her own cloak and bonnet. Taking up the kittens that mewed in their basket, she followed her mother-in-law to the hackney. "And I will try a bit of my own medicine and listen to the Inner Light," she whispered under her breath.

If she felt disinclined to speak much on the journey by mail coach to Portsmouth, and to say still less while they waited in the inn for the *Josiah Dabney* out of Boston to finish stowing cargo, Blessing could only thank Providence for Patience's forbearance. Several times her mother-in-law seemed on the verge of conversation that could only prove difficult. Each time, she stopped and did not ask questions. Her soft-spoken reminders to Blessing to eat her dinner, and not stand on the dock so late contemplating the waves, carried no reprimand.

Patience's voice was gentle as always, her eyes full of sympathy. Blessing knew without saying a word that Patience was fully aware of her personal agony. Someday when I have passed this difficult point, I will thank her for her circumspection, she thought as she leaned on the ship's rail finally and watched the topmen lower the mainsail.

She gazed seaward and took an appreciative sniff. The smell of hemp and tar was all around her now, reminding her of home, but even more forcefully of Thomas Waggoner.

"What will thee do, my dear?" she whispered. "Where will thee go?" She waited for the captain to give the command to weigh anchor. The sailors on the deck waited too, resting their arms on the capstan, their eyes on that worthy who stalked the poop deck.

"Why do we not go?" she asked Patience crossly.

Patience had turned her gaze to the far shore. "I think there is a Johnny-come-lately passenger," she said, her hand shielding her eyes from the sun on the water. "Thee would think he would know about winds and tides and urge the waterman to row faster."

"Perhaps he is a lubber, Mother," Blessing said, her eyes on the water.

In another moment she heard Patience chuckling to herself. Patience touched her arm, her voice filled with amusement, and tremulous with another emotion.

"Look, my dear, oh, do look!"

Mystified by Patience's curious insistence, Blessing crossed the deck to the lee side. Patience was leaning over the rail now, waving.

"Mother, whatever . . ." Blessing began, and then stopped, her eyes wide. She clung to the rail and stared at the sight below her.

Clutching his saddle, an expression of real preoccupation on his face, Lord Thomas Waggoner sat in the harbor dinghy that pitched beside the *Dabney*. He was looking dubiously at the chains hanging over the *Dabney* as the waterman gestured to them.

Blessing could only stare. Patience took in the situation and turned to the boatswain, who was motioning impatiently for Thomas to hand up his saddle and then climb the web of chains.

"Thee does not understand," she was saying calmly. "He cannot climb the chains because of an old injury. Waterloo," she added for good effect.

"I've already stowed the chair," said the boatswain, one eye on the captain, who glowered down from the poop deck.

"Then throw him a bowline," Patience said. "He has the wit to know what to do with it."

The boatswain did as Patience Whittier suggested. In another moment, Thomas Waggoner, his arms still tight around his saddle, was deposited on the deck. His duffel followed, and the captain boomed out, "If his worshipful lordship is happy now, we will weigh anchor." His Yankee voice was heavy with sarcasm.

Blessing took the saddle from Thomas and handed it to a seaman, who whistled at it and took it below. "Thee'll have to excuse the captain," she said, her attempt at calm undone by the quaver in her voice. "I think we Yankees can be every bit as rude as ye British."

Thomas straightened his coat. "I expect so." He nodded to Patience, who smiled back.

"Blessing, I had best go belowdecks and comfort the wretched kittens," she said, a twinkle in her eyes.

"Lovely lady, is your mother-in-law," Thomas said. "I wonder, do you think she likes me?" He led Blessing to the rail that faced the open water. "I'd rather not look back," he said as the sails boomed and the ship began to move. He looked down at the water.

"I did what you recommended," he said at last, and took hold of her hand. "I listened to my Inner Light."

Blessing let out the breath she had been holding and squeezed his hand. "And . . . and what did it tell thee?"

He laughed. "You won't believe . . . well, yes you will. Something very distinctly told me to sell my horse." He put his arm around her. "It gave me a pang, I can tell you. I rode her to Tatt's for the last time, and got my passage money."

"I'm sorry thee had to sell thy horse," she said. She hesitated a moment, and then put her arm around his waist. "I thought ... Didn't thee say thee had some money to bribe Angela Davenport with?"

He nodded. "I did, but I thought Charles could use it." He scratched his head. "Which brings me to a delicate bit of negotiation here, Mrs. Whittier of Whittier Ropewalk. I haven't a sixpence to scratch with, and will be needing employment. Do you think I could sell rope to Yankees?"

Blessing stood on tiptoe and kissed his cheek. "I think thee could sell lions to Christians, Lord Thomas!"

He winked at her, but shook his head. "No Blessing, it's just plain 'Tom Waggoner' now. Isn't there something in your Constitution about no titles?" He pulled her closer to his side. "I wonder, does the Society of Friends ever admit new Friends?"

"Those who truly believe, Tom Waggoner," she replied, her voice soft.

He smiled back and turned around for one last look at Portsmouth before it disappeared behind Harbor Island. His eyes clouded for an instant and he took a deep breath. Still looking at the receding shore, he raised her hand to his lips.

"Then let us voyage, my dear," he said. His eyes grew merry again as he turned to the windward side. "Does thee know, I was thinking on the mail coach, what does thee think about calling it 'The New England Ropewalk'? I mean, if it's as good as you ... thee ... says, then Whittier Ropewalk should cover the region."

She laughed out loud. He pulled her closer to him, even as the deck began to heave.

"I love thy laugh, Blessing," he said. "I hope to hear it for years and years to come." He leaned closer, his tone more confidential. "Does thee ever get seasick?"

"Not after the first day," she said, wishing that all the ship's hands weren't on deck, and the captain himself watching them.

He frowned. "Well, I will be. That was my last good suggestion for several weeks." He looked around, and kissed her again, to the cheers of the sailors clinging to the rigging. "I trust it will be enough to get me a job." He touched his forehead to hers. "I am planning to marry me a wife in Nantucket, and should be gainfully employed."

The Midsummer Valentine
by *Sandra Heath*

THE ROAD ACCIDENT would not have happened if it had not been Saint Valentine's Eve, because the wagon and its slow team of oxen would not have been on the turnpike at dusk, on its way to deliver extra flour to the baker in the Gloucestershire market town of Stow-on-the-Wold. In turn, the baker would not have required more flour if he did not hope to sell a considerable number of the sweet valentine buns that were as traditional to the fourteenth of February as hot cross buns were to Easter, and mince pies to Christmas.

Nor would the accident have happened if the middle-aged farmer, whose heart had never before been engaged, had not become so enamored with the pretty Stow widow that on impulse he had driven his whiskey the five miles from his outlying Cotswold farm to leave a valentine posy on her doorstep.

By the time the farmer climbed back into the whiskey to begin the drive home again, the brief winter afternoon was fast drawing to a close. The sunset had become little more than a swirl of blush pink on the western horizon, and there were very few people in the streets. The farmer and the flour wagon were destined to arrive together at the crossroad on the very edge of the town, with calamitous, but happily not fatal, consequences.

Also traveling along the turnpike toward the crossroad that day in February 1799 was a yellow post chaise hired in Harrogate, Yorkshire, by Miss Georgina Hartford, who was on her way to the nearby Gloucestershire village of Bourton-on-the-Water to stay with her married sister, Henrietta Churchill. Henrietta was expecting her first child in March, and had wanted all her family to be with her at such a happy time, but her mother was still unwell after suffering very badly with influenza, and her father was too anxious about his wife's health to leave her, and so Georgina, who was eager to be with her only sister, was being allowed to travel south on her own, with just her maid, Jenny Sowerby, for company.

The Hartfords did not usually resort to hiring post chaises, for they had a particularly fine traveling carriage of their own, but at the last minute there had been a problem with its springs, and so the chaise had been secured at a posting house in Harrogate. Driven at breakneck pace by two yellow-jacketed postboys riding postilion, the vehicle had so far accomplished the long journey in excellent time, but Georgina would have settled for a slower, more comfortable progress in the family carriage.

She was thankful that there were now only a few more miles to go to Bourton, which lay further south along the turnpike, beyond the fateful crossroad. As the lights of Stow began to twinkle through the gathering dusk ahead, there was no hint as yet that an accident was about to occur that would change Georgina's life. The chaise was not destined to be involved in the fracas at the crossroad, but it would nevertheless be forced to halt for a few minutes. Those minutes were to prove very momentous indeed for Georgina Hartford, for she would gaze into the clear gray-green eyes of the mysterious gentleman who had haunted her thoughts for nearly eight months now, since she had danced a cotillion with him at the midsummer ball at Harrogate assembly rooms.

Only a few brief words had passed between them before the dance, and none at all during the measure itself, but the cotillion required the giving and taking of favors and forfeits, and the handsome gentleman had boldly demanded a kiss. He had managed to steal not only the kiss but also her foolish heart as well, and he had left the assembly rooms immediately afterward without her even knowing who he was.

Georgina was twenty years old, with long silver-fair curls, a heart-shaped face, a creamy complexion, and dark-lashed lilac eyes that always seemed much larger than they actually were. They were shy eyes, their glance frequently seen from beneath lowered lashes, but at the same time they possessed a charm and gentle humor that revealed her to be a far from dull or trivial creature. She was proud of her hair, which was indeed her glory, and she wore it piled up in a knot from which tumbled several flattering ringlets. She had a small-waisted figure that was becomingly curvaceous, and she was considered to be very attractive indeed, but it was her twenty-three-year-old, dark-haired, dark-eyed sister, Henrietta, who was acknowledged to be the beauty of the family.

For the journey, Georgina wore a long-sleeved, high-necked gray woolen gown and matching three-quarter-length pelisse, the latter trimmed daintily with dark-blue braiding. Pelisses were very new and fashionable, and she felt very stylish indeed because there were not yet many ladies in

Harrogate spa who possessed one, even though the resort was of considerable consequence in society. On her head there was a dark-blue straw bergère hat tied beneath the chin with wide gray satin ribbons, her gloved hands were plunged deep into a gray muff decorated with dark-blue ribbon bows, and on her feet there were neat black japanned leather ankle boots. Her appearance was very *à la mode*, because the Hartfords were a family of some standing in Yorkshire, and money was by no means a problem. Their home was a large mansion set in a park on the outskirts of Harrogate, and through distant connections on Mrs. Hartford's side, both Georgina and Henrietta would inherit fortunes when they attained their twenty-fifth birthdays.

On the seat beside Georgina, Jenny Sowerby had fallen asleep, her head nodding to the rhythm of the chaise. The maid was well wrapped in a voluminous green cloak, and there was a dark-red felt bonnet on her wiry brown hair. She was a freckle-faced Yorkshire girl, and had been with Georgina for two years now, ever since Henrietta had married and left home.

The blush-pink remnants of the sunset were almost gone now, and the lights of Stow became brighter all the time. The chaise lamps picked out the hedgerow, revealing early pussywillows and catkins, for the winter had been unusually mild. During the day Georgina had seen the first lambs, and because the sun had shone so brightly from a clear blue sky, it had felt almost like spring. Now, however, with the bitter chill of a winter night descending over the Cotswold hills, she was reminded that there were many weeks to go before it was truly spring.

Georgina gazed out of the chaise's front window,

past the postboys riding so swiftly on the nearside horses. This was the first time she had been away from home on her own, except for brief visits to relatives in Yorkshire, and it was certainly the first time she had been so far south. This coming summer her parents were going to lease a house in London in order to launch her into society, just as three years before they had done for Henrietta. On that occasion, because she was deemed too young for London, Georgina had been sent to stay with an aunt in Richmond, and so she had missed the initial furor caused by John Churchill's entry into her sister's life.

With Henrietta's beauty and prospects, it had been her parents' earnest hope that she would make an advantageous match, perhaps into the aristocracy, but instead she had fallen in love with a Gloucestershire gentleman of only modest means. Dismayed at such a choice, Mr. and Mrs. Hartford had at first refused to countenance such an alliance, and had gone so far as to remove Henrietta from London back to Harrogate, ordering John never to approach her again. But true love won out, and John had determinedly followed them north, laying constant and ardent siege to the woman he adored.

Henrietta's wretchedness on being kept apart from him had alarmed her doting parents, who could not fail to see how thin and low she had become. In the end they had relented, and a year after first meeting, Henrietta and John had married in York Minster. They had been man and wife for two years now, and were blissfully happy together, a fact for which Mr. and Mrs. Hartford were more than prepared to forgive John his lack of title or fortune. All was now sweetness and light, and the Hartfords were as overjoyed as the young married couple that the birth of the first baby was now imminent.

Georgina gazed at the crossroad that now loomed ahead, visible in the lamplight from a wayside tavern. She hoped that one day soon she would emulate her sister and make a love match, but every time she wondered what her future husband might be like, her thoughts turned yearningly to the handsome stranger with whom she had danced that memorable cotillion on midsummer night.

The accident was now only a minute or so away from happening. The flour wagon and the farmer's whiskey were moving inexorably toward collision at the crossroad. The wagon was already preparing to turn off the turnpike into the town, and its lamps curved through the darkness as the oxen began their slow maneuver. The farmer was urging his horse along as swiftly as it could manage, for he had heard accounts of highwaymen in recent weeks, and wished to be safely home. With hindsight he wished that he had thought of the valentine posy a little earlier in the day, but he wasn't used to making romantic gestures, and it simply hadn't occurred to him that a loving gift of flowers might further his suit with the lady of his choice. The whiskey sped up through the narrow cobbled streets, and the farmer decided to save time by cutting through the yard of the King's Head tavern right to the crossroad. Two laborers who emerged from the taproom at that moment were forced to jump aside out of his way, and they hurled angry abuse after him. Incensed by their choice insults, he turned to wave his fist at them, and the whiskey hurtled out of the yard onto the crossroad, where the lumbering ox wagon was now completely straddling the way.

It was all over in a moment. The farmer's horse went down on its haunches as it strove to avoid the inevitable. The horrified wagoner shouted a warning, and the farmer forgot his fury with the laborers as he turned swiftly to the front and saw disaster looming. Frantically he struggled with the brake, just as the terrified horse managed to swerve violently to one side, snapping the shafts. The whiskey rolled over and over, catapulting the farmer through the air just before it struck the wagon, the wheel of which immediately collapsed. The farmer was pitched among the plump sacks it was carrying, and several of them burst, enveloping him in clouds of best white flour.

Finding itself unexpectedly free, the horse set off for home with its tail in the air, and as the sound of its frightened hoofbeats died away into the darkness, the wagoner began to jump up and down with fury, shouting every abusive word that came to mind. The two laborers hurried out from the tavern yard to see what had happened, and one of them knocked over a pile of empty casks, which rolled back down through the yard and then on down the cobbled street into the heart of Stow. The runaway casks made such a noise that they excited every dog in the neighborhood, so that the night soon echoed with yelping and barking. Windows and doors opened as the citizens wondered what on earth could be going on, and the peace of Saint Valentine's Eve was shattered by the pandemonium.

Georgina's chaise began to slow the moment the postboys saw the accident, but as they drew the vehicle to a halt at the side of the turnpike, a stylish maroon curricle flew past from behind, the high-stepping team of splendid chestnut horses gleaming in the light from its polished lamps. The curricle was driven with consummate skill by a fashionable gentleman in a tall-crowned black beaver hat and a caped bottle-green Garrick greatcoat. He was an expert with the ribbons, coaxing every last ounce of pace from the horses, so that the curricle positively skimmed over the road.

He did not glance at the chaise as he drove past, and Georgina could not see his face because of the brim of his hat and the flapping capes of his coat, but she did see how swiftly and surely he reacted to the scene at the crossroad, bringing the flying chestnuts to a standstill within a yard or so of the accident. Vaulting from his seat, he ran to help the winded flour-covered farmer from the crippled wagon, but as he did so he was immediately forced to hold back the furious wagoner, who was completely beside himself over what had happened. The farmer responded with matching rage, and it was all the gentleman could do to keep them apart.

A crowd of onlookers had now assembled, and there was much shouting and pushing as sides were taken and everyone tried to have his or her say. The wagoner and the farmer were so intent upon strangling each other that the increasingly exasperated gentleman was finding it virtually impossible to keep between them. At last he could stand no more, and suddenly pulled a pistol from his coat, firing it once into the air. There was instant silence, except for the barking of the Stow dogs, and beside Georgina, Jenny awoke with a start.

Using the pistol barrel to tip his tall hat back on his head, the gentleman coolly surveyed the two protagonists before replacing the weapon in his coat. The light from the wagon lamps fell across his face, and Georgina's heart almost stopped within her, for she immediately recognized her partner in the midsummer cotillion.

He was taller than she remembered, with broad shoulders and a natural grace that belied his physical strength. His dark hair was worn longer than was strictly the mode, and his gray-green eyes were shrewd and quick, their glance both compelling and authoritative. He was angry now, and as a consequence his mouth was set in an irritated line, but she knew that he had a warm smile.

Georgina gazed breathlessly at him, so startled by suddenly seeing him again that she could not move. Should she do something to attract his attention? But even as she wondered, she knew that it was out of the question. A proper young lady did not approach a gentleman to whom she had not been formally introduced, even though she may have danced a cotillion with him and forfeited her heart with a kiss. Society had very strict rules, and she had always been firmly drilled in etiquette, manners, and all the proprieties. She continued to stare at him, unable to bring herself to overrule her head by obeying the dictates of her heart.

Suddenly the chaise began to move again as the impatient postboys perceived that it was possible for them to maneuver around the obstruction in the road. They kicked their heels, urging the horses to the far side of the turnpike, where there was just sufficient room for the vehicle to pass behind the stricken flour wagon.

As the chaise drove by, the gentleman looked directly at it, meeting Georgina's eyes as she stared out at him. His lips parted as he recognized her, but as he took a hesitant step forward, the wagon suddenly collapsed still more, much to the alarm of everyone nearby. His attention was forcibly diverted as he swiftly pulled the farmer and the wagoner safely out of the way, but the chaise drove on, vanishing into the darkness of the open turnpike.

The wagoner now realized that his precious wagon was damaged beyond repair, and in the farmer he saw the cause of it all. With a furious flailing of his fists he launched himself upon the object of his loathing, and the distracted gentleman once again had no option but to do all he could to keep them from each other's throats. It was not until the town constables arrived that they were separated once and for all and hauled away to jail for causing a breach of the king's peace. By the time calm and decorum had been restored, Georgina and the chaise had long since vanished into the night.

Hurrying back to his curricle, the gentleman urged the chestnuts after her, bringing them smartly up to speed along the turnpike. Beyond Stow, where the land plunged down a long wooded hill, the turnpike divided into two, the more important left-hand branch leading to the town of Burford, and the smaller, right-hand one curving away through the beautiful valley of the River Windrush to the village of Bourton-on-the-Water. Reaching the fork in the highway, the gentleman reined in for a moment, glancing briefly along the Bourton branch before deciding upon the road to Burford as being the more likely. He urged his team on again, but each yard he traveled now took him further and further in the wrong direction.

Georgina was nearly in tears in the chaise. Why, oh, why, had she sat there like a fool? She could

have spoken to him! She blinked the tears away
as she gazed ahead out of the chaise's front window, past the postboys to the faint pools of light
cast by the lamps. There was still time to break
all the rules by ordering the chaise to turn around
and go back to Stow, and she wanted more than
anything to throw caution to the winds, but her
upbringing had been too strict, and she could not
bring herself to flout convention. And so she said
and did nothing, remaining inactive as the chaise
drove swiftly through the night toward journey's
end.

The River Windrush was a wide but shallow and
fast-flowing stream that in medieval times had
powered numerous fulling mills. It passed through
a picturesque countryside of villages, farms, grand
estates, and gracious parks that in daylight was
England at her glorious best, but now, in the February darkness was an invisible world of shadows.
Georgina stared wretchedly at the lamplight on
the road, and the tears had their way, wending
slowly down her cheeks.

She struggled to compose herself, for it would
not do to allow Henrietta and John to see that she
had been crying. Beside her, Jenny had no idea
that anything untoward had occurred, for she had
fallen asleep again as the chaise maneuvered
around the accident at the crossroad.

The tears had almost been mastered by the time
the chaise drove past a lodge and gateway that
resembled a castle barbican. Georgina knew from
Henrietta's letters that it was the entrance to Marriot Park, the country seat of the greatest land-
owner in the district, Sir Richard Marriot. His
family had owned many hundreds of Cotswold
acres since the time of the Norman conquest, and
their original home had been a plain and rambling

fortified manorhouse that had been enlarged over
the centuries, but in the time of Sir Richard's
father, Sir Jeremy Marriot, the old house had been
swept away. Sir Jeremy had been a great friend
of Horace Walpole, and an ardent admirer of Walpole's Gothic residence at Strawberry Hill, Twick-
enham. So great had been Sir Jeremy's liking for
the cathedral splendor of Strawberry Hill that
nothing would do but that he altered his own
property to match it. Thus ancient Marriot Castle
had become Gothic Marriot Park, a sprawling,
asymmetric edifice that was part palace, part
medieval castle, and part ruined abbey. It pre-
sided over the beautiful Windrush valley, its
stained-glass windows gazing across the rippling
water of the artificial lake that had been formed
by damming the river.

Georgina gazed at the entrance of Sir Richard's
fine estate, but then her thoughts returned to the
gentleman she had seen again on this Saint Valentine's Eve. Opportunity had been within her grasp,
but she had not seized it, and now she might never
have another chance.

The first building in Bourton village was the
Marriot Arms, an inn where horses and vehicles
could be hired. The postboys halted in front of it
to inquire of an ostler where they might find the
residence of Mr. John Churchill, and on being
directed, they drove on into the heart of the village, which was gathered around a wide green
through which flowed the omnipresent Windrush.
The village houses dated mostly from the sixteenth and seventeenth centuries, and were built
of the mellow golden Cotswold stone that made
this part of the country so very memorable. At the
far end of the green was the church, its tower a
silhouette against the night sky, and all was silent

except for the noise of the chaise and the chatter of the fast-flowing stream. The Windrush was about one foot deep and twenty feet wide, and was spanned by a number of single-arched stone foot-bridges, beside which were fords for animals and vehicles. The chaise splashed across toward the large house that was Georgina's destination.

Henrietta and John's home was three stories high, with steep gables that were topped by ornate finials. There were dormer windows set in the stone-tiled roof, and the mullioned windows on the lower stories boasted intricate lead lattice-work. At the front there was a flat-roofed stone porch on sturdy columns, and across a wide gravel area, where a carriage could turn with ease, there was a garden of shrubs, paths, and flowerbeds that ran down to the banks of the river.

As the chaise drew to a final halt before the porch, Georgina looked down toward the Wind-rush. Luck had tonight slipped through her fingers as swiftly and surely as the water flowed away beneath the village bridges. Tomorrow was Saint Valentine's Day, but there would not be a posy of flowers from the man who had stolen her heart, nor would there be a loving valentine verse con-fessing a passion that mirrored her own.

The chaise's arrival had not passed unnoticed in the house, for the door opened suddenly and a fair-haired maid peeped cautiously out. Seeing the travel-stained vehicle and its two female occu-pants, she drew quickly back inside to tell her employers that their guest had arrived. A moment later John Churchill came out, his good-natured face breaking into a welcoming smile as he saw Georgina. He turned to instruct the maid to bring

Henrietta, and then came to open the chaise door and help Georgina down.

He was a good-looking, tall, slender man with a pale, sensitive face and wavy reddish-brown hair. He wore a brown coat and fawn breeches, and there was a simple gold pin in his cambric neckcloth. There was something about him that Georgina had always found immensely likable, so much so that she had understood from the moment she saw him exactly why her sister loved him so much. When Mr. and Mrs. Hartford had been opposed to his suit, Georgina had supported him, and only Henrietta herself had been happier than she on the day of the wedding in York Minster.

Georgina flung herself delightedly into his arms, for a while forgetting her own unhappiness. "John! Oh, how good it is to see you again!"

"It's good to see you too, Georgina," he replied, hugging her tightly. "Was the journey very tedious?"

"Disagreeable in the extreme, but worth it all now that I'm here." She looked anxiously at him. "How is Henrietta? I trust the happy event has not anticipated my arrival?"

"Henrietta is very well indeed, and no, she has not yet been brought to bed."

Georgina looked past him toward the doorway as a diminutive figure appeared there. The former Henrietta Hartford was exquisitely beautiful, with short dark curls and shining brown eyes. Being so happily with child became her very well, for she had a glow that made her seem more lovely than ever, in spite of her round figure. She wore a loose rose muslin robe that had pretty lace trimming, and there was a little frilled cap on her head.

"Henrietta!" Georgina cried, running to embrace her, and the two sisters held each other for a long moment before Henrietta ushered her into the house, leaving John to assist Jenny and to supervise the unloading of the chaise.

Georgina walked beneath the stone porch, with its iron-studded door, and found herself in a candlelit stone-flagged entrance hall that in daytime was illuminated by four lattice windows in the wall above the door. The hall was oak-paneled, with a number of wall-mounted candlesticks, and it contained a heavily carved chest, a little table on which stood more candlesticks to light the way up the stairs at the far end, and a huge long-case clock that ticked in a slow, reassuring way. The oak staircase boasted handsome lion newel posts and passed up between more paneled walls on which was displayed a gleaming array of beaten brass and copper plates. The maid who had opened the door when the chaise arrived stood by the table. She was very neat and slender in a green-and-white-checked wool gown and starched white apron, and there was a mobcap on her plaited fair hair.

Henrietta turned Georgina to face her, and then took her hands earnestly. "How is Mother? Is she on the road to recovery?"

"She is definitely getting better, but it is a slow business. The influenza was truly very bad, and carried off many people in Harrogate. She sends you her love, and wishes me to tell you that she and Father will join us as soon as her physician pronounces her well enough for the journey. She longs to see you and John."

"And John?" Henrietta smiled a little wryly. "I did not ever believe that would be so."

"The past is well and truly over, Henrietta, and

I promise you that they now think very highly of your choice."

"As you always did, Georgina, a fact that John and I will always appreciate. Tell me, is Father bearing up?"

"He's in fine fettle, if still a little anxious about Mother. They are both very sorry to think that they may miss the birth of their first grandchild."

Henrietta placed her hands over her rounded abdomen and smiled. "Oh, Georgina, I couldn't be happier if I tried."

"I can see that."

"You look wonderfully well yourself, I'm pleased to observe," Henrietta said, surveying her from head to toe.

"But not quite as blossoming and—"

"*Embonpointe* as I?" Henrietta laughed. "I happen to think it suits me."

"Marriage itself suits you."

"As one day it will suit you." Henrietta raised a quizzical eyebrow. "Is there anyone yet, Georgina? A handsome young man who will be your valentine tomorrow?"

Georgina hesitated, wanting to confide in her about the man who meant everything but whose name she did not know, but then John came into the house, followed by Jenny, and then by the postboys with the first of the luggage from the chaise.

Henrietta looked curiously at her. "Georgina?"

"I . . . I'm feeling a little travel-weary, Henrietta. Could we talk later?"

Henrietta was immediately contrite. "Oh, forgive me. I shouldn't keep you chitter-chattering in the hall like this. I'll see that you're shown directly to your room, and when you're refreshed, you can join us for something to eat. I didn't know when you would arrive, and so I instructed the cook to be ready to prepare a meal at short notice. I believe it is to be *suprêmes* of chicken. We will await you in the parlor." She indicated a door further along the hall. "I've given you the best guest room at the front, because it has a boudoir, if that isn't too grand a name for a little chamber that will just hold a dressing table, a cheval glass, and a wardrobe. Your maid is to sleep with Katie." Henrietta beckoned to the maid in the green-and-white-checked gown. "Katie, please conduct Miss Georgina to her room."

"Yes, madam." Katie bobbed a curtsy and then lit a fresh candle from one of those on the wall before leading the way to the staircase, shielding the new flame with her hand.

Henrietta gazed thoughtfully after her sister. She knew Georgina well, too well not to guess that there was indeed a valentine in her life, and that that valentine was a source more of unhappiness than of joy.

John came to stand at her shoulder. "Is something wrong?" he asked quietly.

"I'm not sure," she murmured.

A little later, feeling much better for a wash and a change of clothing, Georgina was ready to go down to the parlor. She now wore a long-sleeved pale-violet dimity gown that had starched white ruffles at the throat and cuffs, and a silver-buckled belt around the high waistline directly beneath her breasts. There was a warm woolen shawl around her shoulders, its border embroidered with pale-green leaves, and her hair was pinned up in a pretty chignon at the nape of her neck, with a soft frame of curls around her face. Her only jewelry was a pair of amethyst earrings that trembled at the slightest movement.

She was in the little boudoir that Henrietta had mentioned, and candlelight swayed over the walls as she surveyed her reflection in the cheval glass. Behind her, softly illuminated by more candles, was the bedroom. It was dominated by an ancient four-poster bed that was hung with plum-colored velvet, and its ceiling was decorated with intricate plasterwork. Oak paneling covered three of the walls, but the fourth was whitewashed, lending a little very necessary light. More plum velvet was hung at the two tall windows that overlooked the village and the Windrush, and a log fire crackled in the hearth of the ornately carved wooden fireplace. The warm air was filled with the scent of roses from an open potpourri jar that stood before the flickering flames.

Jenny had been putting away the hairpins, brush, and comb, and now turned to her. "That's everything done now, Miss Georgina," she said in her broad accent.

"Then you may go, Jenny. Did Katie tell you where you will find your room?"

"Yes, Miss Georgina, and she said that the cook will have some supper ready for me when I have finished my duties."

Georgina smiled. "Then go there now, for I won't need you again tonight."

"If you're quite sure, miss?"

"Jenny Sowerby, I am quite capable of putting myself to bed for once."

"Yes, Miss Georgina. Good night."

"Good night, Jenny."

The maid bobbed a curtsy and then hurried out, closing the bedroom door quietly behind her. Georgina studied herself in the cheval glass again.

The room seemed suddenly silent, without even the sound of the fire, and as she looked into the glass she felt she could see a shadowy male figure standing next to her. He was tall and handsome, and dressed in formal black velvet, with a sapphire pin in the folds of his lace-edged silk neckcloth. It was midsummer night again, and she could hear his voice.

"I believe that you and I are to have this cotillion together, Miss Fitzwalter."

"I fear I am not Miss Fitzwalter, sir." Oh, the remembered confusion on looking into his eyes for the first time.

"Not Miss Fitzwalter? But you will honor me nevertheless?" His smile was disarming.

"Are you not obliged to seek the lady with whom you have really engaged to dance?"

"There is no Miss Fitzwalter, for this is merely a base male stratagem to bring about a dance with the loveliest woman here," he murmured, his gray-green eyes seeming to see right into her exposed soul.

On that occasion caution had indeed been thrown to the winds, for she had not demurred as he took her hand and led her to join the sets forming on the crowded floor. They had not spoken again, but she had danced on air. It had been midsummer night, and she had fallen hopelessly in love.

Georgina stared at the cheval glass, and gradually his image faded away, and she was alone again. She turned and left the room to go down to join her sister and brother-in-law in the parlor.

She heard voices as she approached the door, and paused as she realized that her sister and brother-in-law were not alone. The door stood slightly ajar, and she was able to peep discreetly inside.

The parlor was a long, low, rather cozy room, again with the oak paneling that was the mark of the house throughout. There was a beamed ceiling, and an immense carved wooden fireplace flanked by pilasters and topped with a mantelpiece that was supported on wooden statuettes. High-backed settles faced each other before the hearth, and there were a number of other chairs, their hard wooden seats made comfortable with tapestry cushions. Wine-red velvet curtains were drawn at the windows, where more tapestry had been placed on window seats that in daylight would afford a fine view down over the gardens to the river and the village. There were warm rugs on the uneven stone-flagged floor, and the room was lit by the fire and candles.

Henrietta was seated on one of the settles by the fire, her rose muslin robe blushing almost to crimson in the dancing light. At the far end of the room there was a table upon which were scattered a number of legal documents, and John stood there talking with a very fashionably dressed fair-haired gentleman of about twenty-five.

The newcomer was obviously a man of wealth, for his clothes were not only the height of fashion but also very costly. He wore a double-breasted tailcoat, pea-green in color and cut square above the waist, and his waistcoat was of a particularly fine gray-and-white-striped marcella. His white cord breeches fitted very closely, and his rather large white cambric neckcloth had been so stiffly starched that Georgina was sure it would crack if he turned suddenly. A diamond pin nestled in the folds of the neckcloth, and it glittered in the light from the candle on the table before him. A bunch of seals dangled from his fob, and there were a number of heavy gold rings on the hand he used to indicate a paragraph on one of the documents.

His face was rather Roman, with an aquiline nose, full lips, and light-blue eyes, and he had curled his fair hair in such a way that he resembled a long-gone Caesar. He smiled as he spoke to John, but there was something about him to which Georgina formed an instant and inexplicable aversion.

As she went into the room, Henrietta immediately looked up. "Ah, here you are at last, Georgina. I trust you are recovered after the journey?"

"I am, thank you."

The stranger's blue eyes raked her from head to toe before lingering on her face. There was no doubt at all that she met with his full approval, for he made the fact a little too obvious. Her instinctive dislike became more entrenched.

John smiled at her. "Georgina, allow me to present Mr. Maurice Mandeville. Maurice, this is my sister-in-law, Miss Georgina Hartford."

Maurice came around the table to greet her, taking her hand and drawing it to his lips. There was far too much warmth in his glance, and he held her hand for longer than was necessary. "I am honored to make your acquaintance, Miss Hartford," he murmured.

His voice was too silky by far. She wanted to snatch her fingers away, but did not like to do so for fear of appearing to offer an insult to someone who was obviously welcome in the house. She managed a smile of sorts. "And I am honored to meet you too, sir," she replied.

He released her. "I trust you will not think me forward, Miss Hartford, but I feel I must compliment you upon your gown. Nothing could become you more than that particular shade of violet, for in truth it brings out to perfection the color of your eyes."

"You are too kind, sir," she murmured, aware of Henrietta and John exchanging meaningful glances behind his back.

Determined to curtail any conversation he might have attempted, she excused herself and went to sit with her sister, leaving him little option but to return to the table and whatever business it was he had with John.

The moment she sat down, Henrietta leaned conspiratorially toward her. "I do believe that you have made a conquest, sister mine," she whispered.

"I would prefer not to have," Georgina replied in an equally low tone.

Henrietta was surprised. "Why do you say that? Maurice is very wealthy and eligible, and has an estate not far from here. He is Sir Richard Marriot's cousin, and considered quite a catch."

"A catch? Henrietta, please do not think of matchmaking."

"A match with Maurice would be very advantageous, and it is already quite obvious that he is smitten."

" 'Obvious' is the very word I would use to describe him."

"Why have you taken such an unreasonable dislike to him?"

Georgina glanced toward him for a moment. "I don't really know. I just find him unpleasant."

Henrietta studied her. "Could it simply be that you are not interested because you have found someone already?"

Georgina lowered her eyes. "Well, there *is* someone . . ." she began slowly.

"Ah! I knew it!" Henrietta declared triumphantly, but as she realized she had raised her voice a little, she immediately whispered again. "Do tell. Who is he? Do I know him? I know, it's Jonathan Fullerton, isn't it? I *knew* that one day—"

"It isn't Jonathan," Georgina interrupted. "It isn't anyone you know, and to be truthful, I don't even know him myself."

Henrietta was nonplussed. "That doesn't make sense."

"I know, but it happens to be the way it is. He—" Georgina broke off, for at that moment the two gentlemen completed their business and came to join them by the fire, taking the settle opposite.

Maurice's knowing glance rested on Georgina. "Are you here for long, Miss Hartford?"

"Several months."

"Then I am sure we will become well acquainted."

She trusted not.

He smiled, not sensing her reserve. "Will you be joining in the festivities this week?"

"Festivities? I don't understand."

"Didn't you know? My cousin, Sir Richard Marriot, is about to be betrothed, and a great junketing has been arranged. There is a fox hunt tomorrow morning, various shooting parties, a grand assembly for the entire neighborhood, and various other diversions, including a fireworks display, which I am reliably informed will be the finest ever seen outside London. There is an immense group of visitors at Marriot Park, with more guests still to arrive, and tomorrow night there is to be a costume *bal masqué* at which the betrothal itself will take place."

"I am afraid that I know nothing about it, Mr. Mandeville," Georgina replied.

Henrietta sat forward. "I was waiting until you arrived before telling you, Georgina. It's all very exciting, especially as the bride-to-be is one of London's most beautiful and influential ladies. Sir Richard is marrying Lady Celestine Vavasour, the daughter of the Marquess of Welborough, and the widow of Lord Vavasour. She is one of the patronesses of Almack's itself, and she is generally agreed to be not only beautiful and charming but also witty and clever as well. Oh, there has been such excitement here since we heard of it, and everyone is delighted that such a prominent lady is to be mistress of Marriot Park. I don't think Bourton has ever seen so many carriages and grand London folk before. I'm told that the drive at the big house is quite choked with elegant equipages, and that there isn't a room in the house that has not been allocated to a lord or lady. Our poor ears have been aching for days with the sound of shooting parties in the wood, and the Marriot hounds have begun quite a clamor in readiness for the hunt. The kitchens and servants' hall are open to all and sundry, and I shudder to think how many have supped to excess at Sir Richard's expense, but from the number of strangers who have been found sleeping it off in barns, I believe that news of the hospitality of Marriot Park has spread to all the neighboring counties."

Maurice laughed. "I believe that half of England has trudged to my cousin's door," he said dryly.

Georgina looked at Henrietta. "And tomorrow night there is to be a masked costume ball?"

"Oh, yes, indeed, but of course only society has been invited. It isn't going to be a thin affair, of that you may be certain, for I am told that upwards of five hundred will be there. Oh, I'd love to be going, but I fear I will have to rely upon Maurice to tell me all about it." Henrietta smiled at him.

He returned the smile. "I will do my utmost to oblige your curiosity, madam, indeed I promise to take along a notebook and pencil in order to write down full details of each and every plume."

"I will hold you to that promise, sir," Henrietta answered with a laugh.

At that moment there was a discreet tap at the door, and Katie came in, giving a neat curtsy. "Begging your pardon, madam," she said to Henrietta, "but the cook says that the meal is now ready to be served."

"Thank you, Katie."

"Madam." With another curtsy the maid withdrew again.

Georgina hoped that Maurice Mandeville was not going to join them at the dining table, and waited with bated breath as Henrietta turned courteously toward him. "Would you care to join us?"

To Georgina's immeasurable relief, he declined. "I fear I am expected at Marriot Park, indeed I should toddle off without further ado." He rose to his feet, turning to John. "Thank you again for being so reasonable about those fishing rights. I am in your debt, and if there is ever anything I can do for you, I trust you will not hesitate to approach me."

"I will bear that in mind, Maurice." John rose as well, to see him out.

Before leaving, Maurice took Georgina's hand again. "I am truly delighted to have met you, Miss Hartford," he murmured, drawing her fingertips to his lips.

"Sir," she replied, her tone and manner offering no encouragement at all.

John accompanied him from the room, and she heard them discussing the next morning's fox hunt, which it seemed they were both joining. She smiled at Henrietta. "So it's up at dawn to don the hunting pink, is it?" she asked.

"I fear so, with the consequent home-at-dusk-looking-bedraggled." Henrietta smiled mischievously. "He'll ache for days, but will pretend that he doesn't. Before we were married he was very much the hunting, shooting, and fishing fiend, but such activities no longer appear to hold the same attraction now that he has such an adorable wife to demand his constant attention."

"I will be sure to consult you before I go to the altar, for you are obviously a font of marital wisdom."

"I am indeed." Henrietta looked a little thoughtfully at her. "Are you going to explain about this mysterious sweetheart of whom you inexplicably know nothing at all?"

"Not now, for John will rejoin us at any moment. I will tell you at breakfast tomorrow, when you and I will be on our own."

"Very well." Henrietta looked toward the window as they heard the sound of Maurice riding away. "You could do a lot worse than Maurice, you know," she observed quietly.

"That is a matter of opinion."

"I'm sure you could snap him up in a trice."

"I have no intention of putting that claim to the test," Georgina replied.

She gazed into the heart of the fire, and it seemed that she could see the face of her midsummer gentleman gazing back at her. Tomorrow was

Saint Valentine's Day. If only his face were to be the first she gazed upon. . . .

She dreamed of him again that night. It was midsummer night once more, and she danced not only the cotillion with him but also every other dance. He was with her throughout, his glance warm, his voice soft as he whispered her name. And at dawn they walked through the summer mist in a garden of flowers, where fountains splashed and doves cooed a welcome to the approaching day.

He took her in his arms, pressing her close as he kissed her on the lips. She could feel his heart beating against hers, and desire flooded richly through her veins, making her feel as if she lacked substance. She could taste his lips, so sweet and firm, so ardent and filled with passion.

He cupped her face in his hands, his thumbs caressing her skin, and he whispered her name again.

She gazed into his eyes. "Tell me who you are. I must know your name."

But he was becoming indistinct, turning slowly to vapor, and vanishing into the morning mist that swirled all around. Tears filled her eyes, and her lips quivered as she tried to reach out to hold him, but he had gone, disappearing as if he had never been.

She awoke, and it was daylight. The early-morning sun of a beautiful Saint Valentine's Day filtered into the bedroom around the drawn curtains, and she could hear the birds singing outside.

A new sound disturbed the morning, the yelping of foxhounds and the steady clatter of many hooves as the hunt rode through the village. Flinging the bedclothes aside, Georgina hurried to draw the curtains back. She gazed across the sparkling Windrush and the village green toward the road, where the pink-coated riders were streaming past with the pack of excited, tail-wagging Marriot hounds.

She pushed her tangled silvery curls back from her face, keeping discreetly back from the windowpanes for fear of being seen in her nightgown. She didn't look at any of the riders in particular, just at the scene in general, but then, suddenly and inexplicably, her gaze was drawn to the face of one rider. Like his companions, he was dressed in a pink hunting coat, white breeches, and tall-crowned black hat, and he rode a large, rather restive black horse. He managed his awkward mount with the same consummate skill he had displayed the day before with the ribbons of his curricle.

Her lips parted breathlessly as she stared again at the man she had just kissed in her dreams. Her hand crept trembling to the lace of the throat of her nightgown, and her heart pounded in her breast as she watched him until he had ridden out of sight beyond the church.

As the sounds of the hunt died away into the distance, she remained motionless at the window. He was here in Bourton! He might be one of Sir Richard's guests, or he might even live somewhere in the neighborhood! Her lilac eyes shone with rekindled hope. It was Saint Valentine's Day, and his had been the first face she had seen.

Suddenly the February morning was different. The golden Cotswold stone of the village houses seemed to glow in the sunshine, and when she looked down at the garden in front of the house, she saw flowers she had not noticed the night before. Pink-blossomed daphne bloomed sweetly by the paths, and there was a bright yellow Austrian dogwood in full petal. Snowdrops spilled down the grass to the banks of the river, and a large tabby cat was sunning herself by a clump of early-flowering crocuses.

The bedroom door opened behind her, and Jenny came in with a cup of tea. "Good morning, Miss Georgina. Did the hunt awaken you?"

"I had just woken anyway," Georgina replied, returning to her bed and accepting the welcome cup.

"What gown will you wear today, miss?"

"The white jaconet with the blue spots," Georgina replied without hesitation. It was the gown she had worn last midsummer day before going to the ball.

Jenny hummed to herself as she went into the dressing room to open the wardrobe door.

Georgina smiled. "You seem in excellent spirits this morning, Jenny."

"I was given a valentine, Miss Georgina."

"Really? How did you manage that when you've been here for only a few hours?"

"Well, Katie, the maid, has a brother who is Mr. Churchill's groom, and he gave me a bunch of snowdrops." Jenny came to the doorway, blushing a little.

"He is evidently very much to your liking, judging by the pinkness of your cheeks," Georgina observed.

"Oh, yes, miss, I like him very much indeed."

As the maid went back into the dressing room to put out the gown and its accessories, Georgina sipped her cup of tea. Her thoughts had returned to the gentleman who now meant so very much to her. Was she to be given another chance? Would she maybe meet him again after all?

The blue-spotted gown, with its lavish trimming of lace and little blue bows, was very good to wear. It was tied beneath the breasts with a wide blue ribbon, and there were ribbons fluttering from her mignonette lace day cap. Her hair was pinned in a knot at the back of her head, with a single heavy ringlet falling past the nape of her neck. A pink cashmere shawl rested over her arms, and she held her skirts as she went down to take breakfast with Henrietta in the dining room, which looked out over the grounds at the rear of the house.

The smell of baking filled the air, for the cook had made valentine buns to eat hot with butter. Katie was dusting and polishing in the parlor. The door was open, and she sang as the worked.

> Good morning to you, Valentine,
> Curl your locks as I do mine,
> Two before and three behind,
> Good morning to you, Valentine.

She looked up as Georgina went to the dining-room door opposite. "Good morning, Miss Georgina," she called cheerily.

"Good morning, Katie."

The dining room was warm, with a fire roaring in the hearth. Oak paneling glowed richly in the morning light, and so did a display of magnificent silver on the immense Tudor sideboard that stood against one wall. Through the windows lay the long narrow strip of John's land that stretched back to the very edge of the village. Walled and secluded, it boasted some beautiful ornamental trees, and another walled area where the kitchen vegetables and herbs were grown. Doves fluttered around their dovecote, and a gardener was engaged in pruning the nectarine trees that grew against one of the more sunny stretches of wall. The tabby cat that Georgina had observed a short while before in the front garden now strolled down a path at the rear, her ears pricking with interest as an unwary robin flew down to the grass within tempting range. But as the cat darted toward it, the robin flew safely into the air again, and the cat philosophically resumed its stroll.

Henrietta was already seated at the dark oak table. She wore a long-sleeved white muslin robe sprigged with cherry-colored flowers, and there was a warm brown woolen shawl around her shoulders.

She put her cup down and smiled as her sister entered. "Good morning. I trust you slept well?"

"Very well, thank you," Georgina replied, going to kiss her on the cheek and then sitting down opposite.

"Well, since it is Saint Valentine's Day, I am afraid that breakfast consists solely of the obligatory buns," Henrietta said, indicating a dish of the warm shuttle-shaped delicacies.

"Buns which I happen to like very much," Georgina said, selecting a particularly large example and breaking it open to begin buttering it. "Did John set off in good time?"

"Before first light. The hunt rode past about an hour ago. Did you hear it?"

"Yes." Georgina continued to butter the bun.

Henrietta poured her a cup of coffee from the elegant silver pot on the table. "I'm pleased to say that married life has not blunted John's romantic spirit, for he gave me a valentine gift of silk stockings and a card that was all decked out with hearts, roses, love knots, and the plumpest Cupids imaginable. I believe he purchased it from an engraver in London last year, and has been keeping it ever since."

"I trust that you did not neglect your side of the bargain?"

"I did not. I gave him a particularly handsome pair of kid gloves, and I wrote him a little verse, but I will not tell you what it said."

"Because its fiery passion will shock my sensibilities?"

"Because it was so sweet and sugary that I am embarrassed," Henrietta confessed.

"I'm sure John liked it very much."

"He did." Henrietta eyed her. "By the way, I am not the only Hartford sister to receive a valentine gift this morning, for a secret admirer left a posy on the doorstep for you."

"For me?" Georgina looked at her in surprise. "There must be some mistake."

"No mistake at all." Henrietta nodded toward the sideboard, where a little posy of violets had been placed in a small porcelain vase. "There was a note with them," she went on. "It said, 'Violets to match your eyes, my lady fair,' and it was signed 'Incognito.' I'm afraid I had to memorize the message, because unfortunately it fell into the parlor fire, but I don't think we have to rack our brains very much to identify Incognito, do you?"

"Mr. Mandeville," Georgina replied flatly.

Henrietta nodded. "It must be, for he did go out of his way to admire the way your gown set off the color of your eyes, and he did make his admiration very clear."

"Very obvious," Georgina corrected.

"Violets are for sincerity, and they are sacred to

Venus," ventured Henrietta, evidently still hopeful that she could win her around to reconsidering Maurice Mandeville.

"Henrietta Churchill, I have no intention whatsoever of becoming Mr. Mandeville's valentine, and so would thank you not to attempt to further his cause with me."

Henrietta sat back in her chair. "Very well, I promise not to praise him anymore, provided you tell me about this other man you know but don't know."

Georgina nodded, sipped her cup of coffee, and then gazed dreamily out of the window as she related the story of the midsummer ball, of events on the turnpike the day before, and then of seeing the gentleman again that very morning.

Henrietta was startled. "He was actually with the hunt?"

"Yes."

"Could you have been mistaken? I mean, your window is some way away from the road, and—"

"I wasn't mistaken, Henrietta."

"Describe him in more detail, for it could be that I know him if he lives somewhere in this part of the country, although if he is simply one of Sir Richard's guests, then I will not have any idea about him."

Georgina told her exactly what the gentleman was like, from the devastating warmth and directness of his eyes and the inviting curve of his lips when he smiled, to the softness of his voice and the natural grace with which he moved.

Henrietta listened in silence and then smiled a little at the naked longing in her sister's voice. "Oh, my poor Georgina, you've quite fallen for him, haven't you?"

"Yes." Georgina's eyes were anxious. "Do you know him?" she asked hopefully.

Henrietta shook her head regretfully. "The only person I know who might be so described is Sir Richard himself, and I happen to know that he spent the whole of last summer in London pursuing Lady Celestine."

Disappointment engulfed Georgina. "Which means that my gentleman must be one of Sir Richard's guests."

"Well, I obviously do not know *all* the gentlemen in Gloucestershire, but I think it highly likely that he is a guest at Marriot Park."

"Oh, Henrietta, I wish I could forget all about him, but I simply cannot put him from my mind, and now that I know he is here, so near and yet so far away . . ."

Henrietta put an understanding hand over hers. "I know exactly how you feel, Georgina, especially after all the trials when John and I first met, but I must offer a word of warning."

"Warning?"

Henrietta hesitated, because she did not like to voice her doubts where the mystery gentleman was concerned, but for her sister's sake she felt she had to speak out. "I cannot help wondering why he resorted to such subterfuge in order to dance with you, pretending that you were a Miss Fitzwalter, and then left you immediately after the cotillion. It crosses my mind that the obvious explanation is that he is—"

"Married?" Georgina interrupted quietly.

Henrietta nodded gently. "If he was a bored husband with an eye for a pretty face, perhaps he hoped you were not quite the proper young lady you seemed to be. Perhaps he hoped that you would be responsive to a little flattery and that you would abandon propriety for the sake of a few stolen hours in his embrace. When he spoke to you, he would very swiftly have realized his error, and that would explain why he hurried away as he did, for he was no doubt on the search for more likely pastures." She smiled sympathetically. "Georgina, it has to be faced that your gentleman may be what Mother is pleased to term a 'detrimental,' and that for your sake it would be better if you did not find out who he is, or anything more about him."

Georgina was silent for a moment. "Is that what you really think?" she asked then.

Henrietta drew a long breath. "Obviously I cannot be certain, but I cannot deny a feeling of suspicion."

Georgina fell silent.

Henrietta felt guilty for having poured such cold water on things, and so endeavored to change the subject. "I have been wondering what we can do today," she said briskly, replenishing her cup. "This morning I have to call at the vicarage to discuss some particularly tedious parish matters, but I have nothing planned for this afternoon, and I thought it would be agreeable if you and I went for a walk. It's such a lovely day, and I know the woods will be particularly pleasant. We may even find some wild crocuses, for I know a spot where they grow."

Georgina tried to put the gentleman from her thoughts, and gave her a brisk answering smile. "I have no objection to a walk, but do you think you should when you are so near your—?"

"Georgina Hartford, I have never been in finer fettle than I am at the moment, indeed I've felt so well these past months that I vow I will have at least ten children."

"And make me an aunt ten times over? Heaven forfend. Oh, very well, a walk it is. Besides, after these valentine buns I shall be in dire need of the exercise." A thought occurred to her. "Actually, I wouldn't mind some exercise this morning as well. Could I go for a ride?"

"Why, yes, of course. You may take my horse. His name is Gulliver, and I'm afraid I've been forced to neglect him of late, so an outing would do him good."

Georgina smiled, and finished her breakfast. Her purpose in going for a ride was not entirely innocent, for at the back of her mind was a hope that she would encounter the hunt and maybe see her gentleman again. She did not believe that he was married or that he had any other guilty secret to hide, and she could not agree with her sister that it would be better if she did not find out anything more about him.

For the ride Georgina wore her new riding habit for the first time. It was made of a particularly becoming cerise wool, with a tight-fitting coat that had pretty gray piping on the bodice, collar, and cuffs. Her little gray beaver hat, which was a feminine version of the tall hats worn by gentlemen, sported a flouncy plume that had been dyed the same cerise as the riding habit, and she knew that she looked both modish and eye-catching as she rode out of Bourton and along a winding willow-fringed lane that led through the undulating Cotswold countryside. She could hear the hunt in the far distance.

Henrietta's horse, Gulliver, was indeed in need of exercise, for he had grown quite plump. He was a good-looking bay gelding, and appeared to be aware of his beauty, for he arched his neck and capered a great deal as she tried to keep him trotting in a straight line.

She had been riding for about half an hour, and the village had disappeared in a fold of the land behind her. The lane twisted between the willows, and each bend brought a different country scene, from sheep with their lambs in a stone-walled enclosure, and a farmer's boy driving some heifers into a farmyard, to some laborers clearing the ditch, and two little girls shooing geese from a field sown with spring beans. It was all very peaceful and beautiful, but she felt restless, hoping against hope that she would encounter the hunt and see her gentleman again.

As the lane curved again, she came upon an open field gate, from which a track led down a rolling incline toward a thick beech wood. On impulse she urged Gulliver through the gate, bringing him up to a much-needed and exhilarating gallop down the slope. He enjoyed the burst of speed, and was reined in only with difficulty when he reached the edge of the wood.

The track disappeared between the trees, and a light breeze whispered through the bare branches. In a few months' time the wood would be bright with bluebells, and soon after that there would be so much foliage overhead that there would be cool shade from the summer sun, but now, even on such a beautiful February day, it was a dull, almost dismal place.

Georgina was about to turn Gulliver around to ride back up the hill when she heard the gentle babbling of a brook. Gulliver heard it as well, and looked eagerly between the trees. Hesitating only a moment, Georgina decided not to deny him a little drink, but to be certain not to let him take too much. Kicking her heel gently, she allowed him to make his way toward the water.

The little stream flowed between overgrown banks, winding its way down through the trees toward the distant Windrush. As Gulliver dipped his muzzle into its ice-cold depths, Georgina dismounted to let him rest for a while. She leaned back against a tree trunk and took a deep breath of the winter woodland air, imagining how it would look here when the bluebells were out. She looked up at the lacework of branches overhead, for the birds were singing their hearts out. A smile touched her lips as she remembered that it was said that on Saint Valentine's Day all the birds chose their mates.

Suddenly she heard the hunt. The wavering sound of the horn seemed to be only about a quarter of a mile away on the far side of the wood, and from the noise of the hounds, they were in full cry. Were they coming this way? She looked hopefully through the trees, but gradually the sounds began to die away again, and she disappointedly knew that they were going in the opposite direction.

She was so intent upon listening to the hunt that she didn't hear a sound much closer at hand. It was Gulliver who first became aware of the horseman in hunting pink who had ridden up behind her and who had halted some yards away on the other side of the brook. The gelding raised his head from the water, whinnying softly to the other horse, and Georgina turned with a startled gasp. For the second time that day she found herself gazing at the man she so longed to know. Her heart missed a beat, and her lips parted as she stared at him.

He was as much taken by surprise as she, but then quickly recovered. "We meet again, Miss Fitzwalter," he said, a faint, almost disbelieving smile playing on his lips.

"It would seem so, sir," she replied, her voice barely above a whisper. She was all confusion, and an embarrassed flush leapt to her cheeks. She cast around for something to say. "You have been separated from the hunt?" Oh, what a lame remark to make, for it was plain that somehow he had become separated from the others! She wished she had not spoken at all.

He smiled again. "My saddle girth broke, and I had to return to Marriot Park for another." He urged his horse across the brook and dismounted next to her. He was so close that she could have reached out to touch him. His eyes were the color of the sea as he spoke again. "I'm glad it was no mirage yesterday, for I feared that I had imagined it when I saw you drive past."

"I . . . I was as surprised to see you," she replied, wanting to say so much, but not daring to say anything of consequence.

"Since we established last year that there was no Miss Fitzwalter, may I know your real name?"

"Georgina. Miss Georgina Hartford."

"Georgina. It suits you," he said quietly, his eyes seeming somehow warmer and darker than they had only a moment before. "My name is—" But before he could say anything more, a cock pheasant suddenly burst from the undergrowth nearby, fluttering and making such a noise that it frightened Gulliver.

The gelding was terrified as the bird flew low over his head, and he reared up immediately. The black horse was startled as well, but the gentleman kept a firm hold on the reins as it too reared and tossed its head. There was no restraint on Gulliver, however, and in a split second he had bolted, splashing wildly across the little stream and setting off at a gallop between the trees.

Georgina stared after him in dismay. "Oh, Gulliver!" she cried, watching helplessly as he disappeared into the wood.

Gathering the reins of his own horse, the gentleman climbed swiftly into the saddle. "I'll bring him back," he said, urging his mount after the fleeing gelding.

Hardly had he vanished in pursuit than she heard voices through the trees in the other direction, and she turned to see a party of six huntsmen riding down the track where she herself had ridden a short while before. She was dismayed to recognize her brother-in-law and Maurice Mandeville among them, and she stepped quickly out of sight behind a tree, for she wished to be alone when the gentleman returned with Gulliver. But in her anxiety not to be seen, she lost her footing on the damp ground beside the brook, and she gave an involuntary scream as she tried to prevent herself from falling into the water. Snatching at a branch, she managed to halt her fall, but not before her riding boots and the hem of her riding habit were soaked.

Her cry alerted the riders, and they turned toward her. She could not conceal herself now, for the cerise of her clothing was too obvious to anyone looking in her direction, and so there was nothing she could do but wait as they rode over to her.

Maurice Mandeville's warm gaze rested on her legs, for the riding habit clung almost improperly.

John dismounted and came quickly to her. "Georgina, what in God's name are you doing here?"

"Gulliver took fright when a cock pheasant

broke nearby," she said, shivering a little because the water was very cold where it touched her skin.

John was immediately anxious. "He'll have found his way back to his stable, and so I'll take you home."

"No," she protested quickly. "No, I can't possibly do that."

"Why ever not? Georgina, you're soaked through, and must be taken home to the warmth without delay. Let me lift you onto my horse."

"But someone has gone after Gulliver for me, and I'm waiting for him to return," she explained.

"Someone? Who?"

"I . . . I don't know his name," she replied. "He is with the hunt."

"Then he will understand if you do not court a fever by waiting," he said firmly.

Maurice had been watching her closely, and saw how very anxious she was to again see whoever it was who had gone after her horse. Oh, *how* anxious she was, which could only mean that the knight-errant concerned was very much to her liking. A finger of jealousy touched him, arousing the less pleasant side of his nature. If he could prevent her from a further meeting with the stranger who appeared to have caught her fancy, then that was precisely what he would do. He spoke almost casually. "Miss Hartford, please rest assured that someone will be here when the gentleman returns, for I will be more than pleased to oblige on your behalf."

"I am most grateful, Mr. Mandeville, but there is truly no need, for I am quite capable of—"

"My dear Miss Hartford, you cannot possibly wait here in wet clothes, for there is no saying how long the fellow might take," he interrupted smoothly.

She was not deceived, for she could read his thoughts in his cold blue eyes, and she loathed him more than before. But there was nothing she could do, for John was rightly determined to see her safely home, and Maurice Mandeville had neatly seen to it that she had no excuse for staying.

Without another word, she allowed John to lift her onto his horse, but as he mounted behind her, there were tears of frustration in her eyes. Why was fate so unspeakably cruel to her? She had been with the man who meant everything to her, but events had snatched him away before he had had time to tell her who he was. If only that wretched cock pheasant hadn't chosen to take flight, if only things had proceeded calmly, then she would have learned not only who he was but also much more about him. He had seemed as eager to know her as she was to know him. . . .

She blinked the tears away as John rode out of the wood and up the track toward the lane.

Behind her, the rest of the hunting party continued on its way, and Maurice Mandeville dismounted, making every pretense of meaning to wait as he had said. But the moment everyone had gone, he remounted and rode swiftly out of the wood. Georgina Hartford's rescuer, whoever he was, would return to find her gone.

Gulliver had indeed found his own way home, having set off at such a pace that the gentleman had lost him in the trees. Henrietta returned from the vicarage to find Jenny and Katie assisting Georgina out of her spoiled riding habit, and to hear of the incredible coincidence that had brought her sister and the gentleman together again, only to separate them immediately once more.

When Henrietta deemed Georgina to have recovered sufficiently from the mishap with Gulliver, and when a simple light meal had been partaken, the two sisters set off on the walk they had agreed upon at the breakfast table. Georgina again wore her blue-spotted jaconet gown, and over it she put on a sapphire-blue velvet spencer. Her hair was pinned up beneath a jaunty narrow-brimmed lemon silk hat that had a filmy blue gauze scarf tied around the crown, and the scarf lifted gently behind her as she walked.

There were ducks on the Windrush as they crossed over the stone footbridge, and Georgina smiled as she watched the birds paddling strongly against the river's swift current. She loved ducks, and always fed those on the ornamental lake at home in Harrogate. She resolved to feed them later, provided she could persuade Henrietta's cook to part with some bread.

Jackdaws soared in alarm around the nearby church tower, startled by a noisy group of village children who were running from house to house in the hope of being given some traditional valentine pennies, and a dog barked in a cottage garden, but apart from that everything was peaceful and quiet as the sisters reached the road and began to walk in the direction from which Georgina's chaise had driven the night before.

Suddenly they heard a carriage approaching from behind, and they turned to see a gleaming dark-blue vehicle drawn by a team of two elegant dapple grays. The coachman wore a powdered wig, and was dressed in impressive light-blue livery, giving the equipage an air of great style as it passed. It was evidently on its way to Marriot Park for the celebrations, for it was well laden with luggage. There were three gentlemen and a lady seated inside, and Georgina heard their rather drawling voices and laughter drifting out through a lowered window glass.

Henrietta watched the carriage drive on. "I truly wonder that Sir Richard has room for everyone," she murmured. "The house must be an intolerable crush now, but still they keep arriving."

"What is he like?" Georgina asked as they continued their walk.

"Sir Richard? The personification of charm and masculine beauty," her sister replied. "If I had set my heart on *him* a few years ago instead of John, I know that Mother and Father would have been overjoyed, for he is truly a gentleman who has every asset, both physical and financial. I believe that Lady Celestine Vavasour is a very fortunate creature, for she has snapped up one of the most devastatingly attractive men in all England."

Georgina looked at her in surprise. "Why, Henrietta Churchill, I do believe you're a little taken with him."

"There isn't a woman alive who wouldn't be, but I will settle for my John." Henrietta smiled.

They walked on past the Marriot Arms, and then left the road to take a little path that led through a strip of dense woodland between the road and the boundary wall of Marriot Park. The tree trunks were twined with glossy dark-green ivy, and here and there were the gold and silver of catkins and pussywillows. Tough woodland grass grew in clumps on the uneven ground, and there were tangled screens of brambles. Holly trees grew in profusion, some still sporting their scarlet berries, and in the nearby park there were splendid specimen trees from distant lands.

Birdsong echoed deafeningly all around, from the busy chirping of sparrows and the whistles of starlings to the harsh sounds of cock pheasants and the gentle cooing of wood pigeons. Georgina smiled. "It doesn't sound as if our feathered friends are simply choosing their mates this Saint Valentine's Day, for they appear to be arguing quite disgracefully."

"The course of true love, and all that," replied her sister with a laugh.

For several minutes they walked in companionable silence, but then they saw something that made them halt in immediate alarm. Concealed behind a thick holly tree that grew right at the side of the road, about fifty yards from the path, was a horseman with his tall hat pulled well down over his forehead, and a cloak that enveloped him completely, except for his rather expensive top boots. His horse was a fine strawberry-roan thoroughbred, and it was chafing at being kept in check. The man looked as if he was about thirty-five years old, and was well built. His skin was pale, but there was a dark shadow on his chin, as if he had not shaved for several days, and there was an almost desperate air about him as he stared along the road in the direction of the village. Another carriage was driving toward him, audible above the noise of the birds but not yet visible because of the slight curve in the road and the density of the trees.

As the two horrified sisters watched, the man pulled a kerchief up over the lower part of his face and then drew a pistol from inside his cloak. With the pistol cocked and ready, he gathered the reins in readiness to hold up the oncoming vehicle.

*   *   *

Georgina gasped and clutched her sister's arm. "Henrietta! We must do something!"

Her first instinct was to call out and frighten him away at the prospect of having witnesses to his crime, but then she saw how fearfully and instinctively Henrietta put her hands over her unborn child. Any thought of drawing attention to their presence immediately died on Georgina's lips.

She drew Henrietta behind a tangle of brambles, and they watched anxiously as the carriage drove unknowingly toward the ambush. They could see the vehicle now, and guessed that it too was conveying some of Sir Richard's guests. It was a handsome red barouche, its hood raised to keep out the winter chill, and it was drawn by four perfectly matched dun horses. The coachman wore a brown-and-gold livery that was echoed in the brown-and-gold coat-of-arms on the door panel. There was no doubt that it was the property of an aristocrat, and that it was about to fall prey to the waiting highwayman.

The barouche had almost reached the holly bush when the man kicked his heel and urged his nervous mount directly into its path. The startled coachman applied the brake, reining the plunging team in only a foot or so short of the menacing figure with the pistol leveled at his heart. With trembling hands the coachman made the ribbons fast and then raised his arms in surrender.

Ignoring him, the highwayman maneuvered his horse a little closer to the barouche itself and then called out, "Stand and deliver! Your heart and the rest of your life, my lady!"

Stunned, Georgina and Henrietta looked at each other and then returned their startled attention to the scene on the road.

The highwayman called out again. "Stand and deliver! Your heart and the rest of your life, my lady!"

After a moment the barouche door opened and a lady alighted. She was dazzlingly lovely, with bright chestnut hair, a peaches-and-cream complexion, and large blue eyes. She wore a full-length emerald-green silk pelisse that was tightly belted at the waist, and on her head there was a matching jockey bonnet from the back of which trailed a lace scarf that almost reached her hem. It was the latest thing to wear false white curls added to one's own hair, and two curling white ringlets tumbled from beneath the jockey bonnet, brushing against her shoulder.

She looked defiantly at the "highwayman." "Please leave me alone, Roger, for whatever there was between is now over."

Her voice was barely audible above the noise of the birds in the wood, and of one accord Georgina and Henrietta moved a little closer, slipping secretly through the trees until they could easily hear the man's reply.

"I am the one you love, and only your stubbornness and belated sense of obligation prevent you from admitting it," he said, tilting his hat back and then pulling the kerchief down from his face. His dark eyes were urgent and intense, and it was evident that he was truly desperate to win back his love.

The lady couldn't meet his gaze. "My mind is made up, Roger."

"How can you say that when we have been so much to each other? I will not let you do this, not when this is Saint Valentine's Day and I know that *I* am the one you really love." Tossing the pistol away, so that it fell to the ground only a little way in front of the two watching sisters, he dismounted and then took the lady's arms, forcing her to look at him. "Tell me to my face that you no longer love me, and I will leave you alone. But you must say it, for only then will I concede defeat."

The lady's lips trembled, and tears filled her lovely blue eyes. "Please, Roger—"

"Say it."

"I . . . I can't," she said, bowing her head.

The light of triumph was on his face as he put his hand to her chin, making her look at him again. "You do still love me, don't you?"

She nodded tearfully, and did not resist as he swept her into his arms to kiss her passionately on the lips. Then he drew back, looking ardently into her eyes. "You cannot possibly proceed with this madness. You must come back to London with me."

"But—"

"No buts, my love, for your place is with me."

She nodded again, closing her eyes as tears wended their way down her cheeks.

He kissed her once more, lingeringly this time, and then he assisted her back into the barouche before tethering his horse to the rear of the vehicle. After ordering the coachman to turn around and make all speed back to London, he climbed in with the lady and slammed the door behind him. The coachman, whose initial terror had now given way to bemusement, gathered up the ribbons, cracked his whip, and maneuvered the cumbersome vehicle around to drive back the way it had come. The offside wheels bounced up on the verge, and the barouche jolted a great deal, but as the coachman's whip cracked again and the team came up to a canter, a piece of luggage was dislodged from the back. It was a large trunk, and it fell heavily to the road, rolling over and over before coming to rest against the verge. The barouche drove on, and soon vanished in the direction of Bourton.

The sisters hurried from their hiding place to go to the trunk, but almost immediately Georgina had to halt, for she trod on something that almost made her fall. As Henrietta hastened on toward the road, Georgina bent to see what lay in the tufted woodland grass by her feet. It was the pistol, and as she picked it up she saw that it was a beautifully crafted saw-handled weapon, decorated with chased silver and marked with the owner's name and family motto. "Sir Roger Hamilton. *Nil desperandum.*" Never despair. Sir Roger certainly had not despaired; he had persevered, and in the end his perseverance had won him the lady of his heart.

Henrietta had reached the trunk, and found that the lock had been broken in the fall, so that it was a simple matter to look inside. It contained an elaborately frilled full-skirted gown of a style that had been fashionable at the French court about sixty years before. It was made of stiff ice-blue silk embroidered with silver and scattered with bows and artificial flowers, and with it there were various other items of apparel, including several garlands of pink velour roses, a dainty pair of high-heeled silver shoes, and a silver-veiled domino mask. It was evidently the lady's costume for the ball that night.

Henrietta straightened, beckoning to Georgina. "Come and see!"

Still carrying the pistol, Georgina hurried to join her, and her breath caught with admiration as she saw the folds of rich blue silk.

Henrietta gazed at it as well. "I'm sure it's French, for I once saw a portrait of a lady at Versailles wearing a gown that was very similar. Oh, just imagine what it must have been like to cope with all those frills and flounces. How much more fortunate we are now to have such simple muslins and lawns."

Georgina didn't reply, for an incredible notion had suddenly entered her head. The lady whose costume this was would not require it now, which meant that someone else could take her place! She, Georgina Hartford, could go instead, her identity completely hidden by the little domino. Maybe she would find her gentleman again! Her eyes shone with excitement as she looked at her sister. "Henrietta, *I* could wear this tonight and go to the ball!"

Henrietta was appalled. "That would be most unwise and improper, Georgina, and I will not hear of it."

"Propriety prevented me from speaking to my gentleman yesterday, and so—"

"No, Georgina! It's totally out of the question. Besides, why on earth do you imagine that you will be able to single out one particular gentleman among hundreds of guests who will all be masked and in costumes? Be sensible, Georgina, and forget all about it."

"Please don't forbid me, Henrietta, for I want more than anything to see him again."

"Even if I wanted to help you in this madcap plan, which I do not, I can tell you here and now that John would never permit it."

Georgina was carried away by the prospect of attending the ball. "John does not need to know, Henrietta. He could be told that I was unwell and had retired early to my bed."

Henrietta stared at her. "You really are serious about this, aren't you?"

"Yes. Henrietta, I simply *must* find my gentleman again, and I want you to help me. All you have to do is pretend that I have indeed gone to bed early."

"You're asking me to deceive my husband," Henrietta pointed out.

"I supported you and John when everything was against you, and now I'm begging you to do the same for me."

"That isn't fair."

"I know," Georgina replied with disarming frankness.

Henrietta looked crossly at her. "You are a wretch, Georgina Hartford, and right now I wish you were still at home in Harrogate."

"*Please* help me, Henrietta, for this man means everything in the world to me, and I will never forgive myself if I let another opportunity slip through my fingers. Now that I've spoken to him again, and I'm convinced that he is as interested to know about me as I am to know about him, I can't possibly shrink from doing everything in my power to find him again. I know that I may not succeed, but at least I will have tried. You do understand, don't you?"

Henrietta nodded resignedly. "Yes, I understand, but, Georgina, I still think it's a most improper thing to do. You will be an uninvited guest at Sir Richard's betrothal ball, and if you are discovered and your identity is made known, it will reflect very poorly upon John."

"I won't be caught," Georgina replied determinedly. "Please, Henrietta, just say that you will help me."

Henrietta hesitated, torn between her loyalty to

her husband and her desire to assist her unhappy sister find her heart's desire. At last she nodded. "Very well, I'll help you."

With a glad cry Georgina flung her arms around her neck and hugged her. Then she drew back quickly as they both heard a horse trotting along the road from the direction of the village.

They dragged the trunk into the undergrowth by the holly tree and pressed back out of sight just as the vicar of Bourton drove smartly past in his gig. He did not see them, nor did he sense their relieved gaze following him until he was out of sight.

Georgina pushed the pistol into the folds of the costume gown and then looked at Henrietta. "How can we get the trunk back to the house?"

"I'll send Thomas with the pony and trap. He will jump at the chance to do something for you, because he had taken quite a fancy to your maid. He gave her a posy of snowdrops this morning, or so Katie told me."

"If Thomas is Katie's brother, then yes, he did."

"Getting the trunk to the house is not a great problem, nor is getting you to the ball, for a chaise can be hired at the Marriot Arms, and the landlord is discreet, but I cannot help being very concerned about the whole business of your going alone to an occasion for which you have not received an invitation."

"No one will know, Henrietta, and if I see that invitations have to be shown, then I promise that I will turn around immediately and come home."

"I shall not rest anyway until you are home again."

Georgina smiled at her. "I will be all right, I know that I will."

"Let us hope so, for in spite of everything, we

still do not know anything about this mysterious gentleman who has swept you from your foolish feet.''

It was not yet time to prepare for her secret invasion of Sir Richard's masked ball, and to while away a few minutes, Georgina walked down the garden to feed the ducks, as she had promised herself earlier in the day. The sun was beginning to set as another brief winter afternoon drew to a close, and the church tower stood out against the crimson sky as she stood among the snowdrops and began to unfold the handkerchief in which she had brought the bread.

The ducks, never slow to perceive a treat, swam excitedly over, eagerly taking the tidbits she threw down. As she watched them, her thoughts were all of her audacious scheme to attend the ball. She knew it was wrong to even contemplate such a thing, let alone carry it out, but it was as if some madness had overtaken her. This was Saint Valentine's Day, the man she had fallen hopelessly in love with was so near and yet so far, and she could no more have turned her back on the prospect of finding him than she could have flown to the moon.

She felt guilty about having told fibs to John. He had returned early from the hunt because his horse had gone lame, and she had immediately embarked upon her plan, complaining of a headache that simply would not go away. Her guilt had increased because he had been so concerned, even ordering the cook to prepare her a herb infusion.

She had been conscious of Henrietta's reproachful eyes upon her as she drank the tea. She knew that her sister was very reluctant to help, but was

grateful that Henrietta had done all she could to
see that the plan proceeded without problems.
Thomas had been dispatched to bring the trunk
from its hiding place in the woods, and a chaise
had been engaged at the Marriot Arms, where the
landlord had been sworn to secrecy. He was
indeed a discreet man, for his adored wife owed
Henrietta several important favors, and Georgina
knew that not a word of her exploits would ever
pass his lips. All that remained now was for the
hour to arrive when she would change into the
costume, and then she would set off to intrude
upon Sir Richard Marriot's masked ball.

The sunset was magnificent, drenching the sky
in a glory of crimson, gold, and pink, and the air
was noticeably cooler as the winter night crept
nearer. She drew her shawl around her shoulders,
tossing the last of the bread to the ducks and then
turning to walk back to the house. But as she did
so she heard some horsemen riding through the
village, belatedly returning from the hunt to Marriot Park. She glanced across the river and the
green, and to her dismay saw Maurice Mandeville
among them. Not wishing to speak to him, she
hurried up through the garden, but he had already
perceived her, and called out as he rode swiftly
toward her.

She had no choice but to wait for him, because
by no stretch of the imagination could she have
failed to hear him call. The ducks scattered noisily
as he urged his horse through the Windrush and
then dismounted next to her.

"Good evening, Miss Hartford."

"Good evening, Mr. Mandeville," she replied,
her tone not inviting further conversation.

"I trust you have recovered from your mishap?"

"Yes. Thank you. Did the gentleman return after trying to catch my horse?"

"No. I waited for an unconscionable length of time, but I fear your knight in shining armor failed to return to your rescue." The lie slipped glibly from his lips, for he had not waited at all, and did not know whether anyone had returned. Nor did he care; it mattered only that his own desire for her was satisfied, and to that end he would have driven a wedge between her and anyone else upon whom she bestowed an even mildly warm glance.

She hid her disappointment. "Well, since I was not there anyway, I suppose it is not of any consequence."

"Not of any consequence? My dear Miss Hartford, the fellow proved himself to be a blackguard, for he left you helpless and alone. Hardly the conduct of a gentleman."

She didn't respond.

He gazed at her lovely lilac eyes and at the sweetness of her lips. She was perfection, and she had kindled his passion so much that he found it very difficult to just stand in polite conversation, when really he wished to sweep her into his arms and force his lips over hers.

"Should you not rejoin your companions, Mr. Mandeville?" she inquired, watching as the party of tired huntsmen rode on through the village.

"I can soon catch up with them," he replied. "Tell me, did you enjoy an agreeable Saint Valentine's Day?"

"Yes. Thank you."

"Was there a gift from a secret admirer?" he pressed.

She colored a little. "It is hardly proper of you to ask, sir."

"I merely wish to know if you are aware who 'Incognito' is?"

"I imagine that it is you, sir, but I am afraid that the valentine posy was a wasted gesture, for I am indifferent to you." She spoke bluntly, but knew that something dramatic had to be said in order to discourage him. She found him all that was unpleasant, and she resented the way in which he had interfered so deliberately in the woods that morning. She also resented his presumption in sending her a valentine posy when they had met only once, and briefly at that.

Anger lit his eyes at her words. "How very frank you are, to be sure," he murmured, a nerve flickering at his temple.

"You left me no choice, sir. I neither want nor welcome your attentions, and I would be grateful if you would desist."

He remounted without another word, snatching at his horse's mouth as he turned it to ride furiously back across the river and then on over the green.

She listened as the sound of his horse's hoofbeats dwindled away into the gathering dusk. Perhaps she had spoken a little strongly, but she was not sorry. He was odious in the extreme, and if she never saw him again, she would not be sorry.

She hurried back to the house. In a short while now she would dress in the costume and leave for the masked ball, and Mr. Maurice Mandeville had already gone from her thoughts.

It had been dark for hours now, and Georgina was supposed to be in her bed, suffering greatly from the persistent headache of which she had so convincingly complained, but she was standing before the cheval glass in her boudoir, gazing at her amazingly transformed reflection. It was not Georgina Hartford who stared back from the glass, but a French lady from the court of Versailles, in about the year 1740.

She wore a hooped petticoat and very tightly laced stays beneath the beautiful blue silk gown, and the abundance of silver embroidery gleamed in the light from the candles on the nearby dressing table. The gown's stomacher was adorned with silver bows, and there were more bows scattered over the rich frills of the skirt, together with several garlands of pink velour roses. Another garland was fixed over her left shoulder, and there were more of the roses on the cascade of lace ruffles spilling from the tight elbow-length sleeves. The gown plunged low over her bosom, and there was a separate lace ruffle around her throat. Her silk stockings were prettily gartered, and the high-heeled shoes gave her an extra height that looked and felt a little strange. Her hair was piled up in curls on top of her head, and her diamond earrings trembled as she turned first one way and then the other, seeing how best to manage the elaborate and heavy skirt.

Jenny had been looking out of the bedroom window, waiting for the chaise to arrive on the far side of the river, where it would wait away from the house in order not to alert John that something unusual might be in progress. As the vehicle drove quietly across the green from the direction of the Marriot Arms, the maid hurried into the dressing room. "The chaise is here, Miss Georgina."

Georgina's heart quickened, and she was filled with sudden doubt. Would it be wiser to call a halt to all this now, before it proceeded any further? But Jenny was already bringing the satin-

lined indigo velvet cloak that went with the costume, and as it was slipped around her shoulders,
the doubts faded away again, and her resolve
hardened.

Jenny tied the cloak at her throat. "Shall I tell
Mrs. Churchill that you are about to leave, miss?"

"Yes, but be sure not to let Mr. Churchill hear."

"Very well, miss." The maid hurried out.

With shaking hands Georgina picked up the
domino, which lay waiting on the dressing table.
The little mask was covered with silver spangles,
and they winked and flashed constantly. The lace
veil which was to cover the lower part of her face
was also threaded with silver, and it looked so
sheer and fragile that she could hardly believe it
would conceal her face, but she had tried it on
earlier and knew that it performed its task very
well indeed. She did not put it on now, but meant
to wear it the moment she stepped out of the
house. She prayed she did not encounter John, for
she did not know how she would explain her
unusual coiffure, or her immensely voluminous
cloak, or the fact that she wasn't languishing in
bed enduring the pangs of a headache.

Jenny returned. "Mrs. Churchill says you are
just to leave as you wish, Miss Georgina. Mr.
Churchill has fallen asleep by the fire, and she will
divert his attention should he awaken."

Georgina nodded, and then took a long breath
to compose herself. When she felt ready, she gathered her awkwardly full skirts and made her way
from the room. She went quietly down the stairs,
tiptoeing along the stone-flagged hall toward the
porch.

The winter air caught her breath as she emerged
into the night. An owl was hooting somewhere,
and she could hear the Windrush chattering over

its shallow bed. The domino felt cold as she put it on before raising her hood over her head. Her gown rustled excitingly as she made her way down to the footbridge, and the moon came from behind a cloud to shine on the silver spangles of her mask.

The landlord of the Marriot Arms was to drive her himself, and he climbed down from his seat as she hurried toward him. With a steady hand he assisted her into the vehicle, helping her with the many folds of ice-blue silk that seemed willfully determined not to squeeze through the narrow door. But at last she was inside, and the landlord resumed his place, swiftly urging the team away. The chaise drove across the green and then on to the road to Marriot Park.

As it did so, a stealthy figure emerged from the shadows near the house. Maurice Mandeville had been on his way to the ball in his carriage when he had perceived the curious sight of a chaise waiting on the village green close to the river. Curiosity had prompted him to halt his own vehicle, leave it in the yard of the Marriot Arms, and then come to observe what the chaise was up to.

Beneath his ankle-length cloak he was dressed as a Roman emperor, and his costume was a little flimsy for such a cold night. He shivered as he retraced his steps to the Marriot Arms. He had seen Georgina emerge from the house and put on her domino, and knew from that and the glimpse he had had of her gown that she was on her way to his cousin Richard's ball.

A cool smile played on his lips, for he intended to use his discovery of her activities to his own advantage. If she did not respond favorably to his advances, then he would take immense pleasure in exposing her as a trespasser.

*   *   *

Georgina's chaise swept in beneath the bastion gateway and followed two other carriages along the lantern-lit drive toward the brightly illuminated Gothic mansion. Every tree along the drive was adorned with lights, and so were all those in the park, and there were even lanterns on the little island in the middle of the lake.

Every room in the house was brilliantly lit, and none of the shutters were closed or the curtains drawn, so that Marriot Park was visible for miles in the Saint Valentine's Night darkness. The drive was choked with vehicles long before the steps of the main entrance, and there were so many guests arriving all the time that Georgina was anxious not to be observed making what might be a rather inelegant descent from the chaise because of the fullness and awkwardness of her gown. She attracted the landlord's attention, indicating that she wished to alight well short of the house, and so he drew the vehicle to a standstill in the shade of a spreading evergreen tree. She managed to climb down without exposing too much stockinged leg, and then removed her cloak, tossing it back onto the seat of the chaise.

The sound of carriages, hooves, and laughter was all around, and she could hear music drifting from the house. She watched as another vehicle halted before the main entrance and the guests it conveyed alighted. There were four of them, a Charles II, a Spanish lady, and a Harlequin and Columbine. The carriage after that disgorged two giggling, scantily clad nymphs, a stout Egyptian pharaoh who was having difficulty with his bulky headdress, and an even stouter John Bull, resplendent in scarlet tailcoat, wide-brimmed hat, and Union Jack waistcoat.

They all moved up the moss-strewn steps toward the arched doorway, through which dazzling light flooded out into the night. Inside she could make out the abundance of flowers that decorated every wall and corner, and the iron-rimmed Gothic chandeliers that cast their light over the crush of brilliantly dressed guests.

Her nerve faltered for a moment, but then she found herself remembering Sir Roger Hamilton's motto—*nil desperandum*—and with renewed resolve she began to hurry toward the house.

She did not look back at all. If she had, she might have seen Maurice Mandeville's carriage drawing up behind her own, and seen him alight in his Roman costume to follow her.

From the foot of the steps she could see clearly into the crowded entrance hall. There were bowls, garlands, festoons, and baskets of flowers everywhere, all of them hothouse blooms, from roses, carnations, and lilies, to camellias, hyacinths, and tulips. No expense had been spared, and the result was breathtakingly beautiful.

She went up the steps, picking her way carefully over the moss that had been laid with such precision. The sound of music, laughter, and conversation grew louder with each step, and she could hear stamping and clapping coming from the ball itself as a vigorous country dance was enjoyed to the full. Slipping in as discreetly as she could, she made her way around the edge of the hall to take up a vantage point by a column that was twined with garlands of camellias. Then she surveyed the gathering, wondering if one of the gentlemen could be the one she sought.

There were several who were tall enough. One was dressed as an Indian raja, in a crimson turban and cloth-of-gold coat, and another was a Robin

Hood, clad from head to toe in Lincoln green, but neither of them seemed quite right. Another possible gentleman was a Viking, with an obviously false straw-colored wig, drooping mustaches, and a helmet with enormous upturned horns. He was certainly of the right height, build, and deportment, but somehow she did not think that her gentleman would choose a costume that verged on the ridiculous. She scanned the rest of the entrance-hall assembly, but discounted a tall Henry VIII, a Peter the Great, and a pirate, who were respectively too plump, too fair, and too old. She did not notice the Roman emperor who was watching her, his blue eyes glittering behind his little black velvet mask.

Turning, she made her way through an archway draped with a heavy crimson velvet curtain and entered the lofty inner-staircase hall, where yet another press had congregated. Arras and arrangements of weapons adorned the walls, and there were gleaming suits of armor in all the corners, as well as on either side of the foot of the broad dark staircase that led up many flights and landings to a gallery on the next floor. At the far end of the vestibule were steps leading down into the great hall, which tonight served as the ballroom, and from whence issued the sound of a *ländler* as the ball moved on to the next dance.

She was just beginning to study the taller gentlemen in this second press, when to her dismay she saw a lady detach herself from a group by the staircase and come purposefully toward her. The lady was about thirty years old, and was dressed rather daringly as the goddess Diana, with a leopard-skin and a quiver of arrows over her shoulder, and a half-moon headdress in her honey-colored hair. She moved with feline grace in her flimsy white

white gown, and her eyes shone conspiratorially from behind her little sequined mask. It was obvious that she recognized Georgina's costume and intended to speak to the lady she believed her to be.

"My dear, I must commend you on your wig-maker, for I could really believe those blond tresses were your own," she murmured, pausing to adjust her quiver. "So you stood firm after all," she went on. "I must say I'm rather surprised, for I would have wagered on poor Roger's powers of persuasion, especially as you've left it until disgracefully late to put in an appearance. There's been much whispering, I'm afraid, with rumor flying everywhere, and you-know-who has had a face like thunder for some time."

Georgina didn't know what do to, for the moment she spoke, the lady would know from her voice that she wasn't who she was supposed to be. Her mind was racing. Roger? It could only be a reference to Sir Roger Hamilton. But who was "you-know-who"? For the first time she began to wonder who exactly the lady was who had run off with Sir Roger.

Diana had not yet noticed anything odd. "Are you absolutely set on this?"

She paused, evidently requiring a reply, and Georgina plucked inspiration from nowhere, pretending to have a dreadful cold that altered her voice. She feigned a sneeze, and then spoke in a croaky, barely understandable whisper. "Forgive me, but I fear I have a terrible cold."

"Oh, my poor darling, you sound absolutely awful!"

"It is only a temporary indisposition."

"Now I think you braver than ever. Brave, but wrong."

"Wrong?"

"In my opinion this is all a monstrous error of judgment on your part, for you and Roger were made for each other. I must say that when there was no sign of you, and no hint of when you might arrive, I was convinced you'd seen the light after all. Still, I suppose you know what you're doing."

"Yes, I do." Georgina was anxious to escape before the conversation took an even more awkward turn and she gave herself away. "If you will excuse me, I think I see someone I wish to speak to," she murmured, not giving the woman a chance to say anything more and pushing away through the crowd.

The goddess Diana was somewhat offended at being cut so obviously, but then she shrugged and returned to the group she was with. As she did so, she brushed past Maurice Mandeville, who had observed her conversation with Georgina. He hardly glanced at the lady, for he was still intent upon Georgina. He would seize the first moment to get her alone, and then she would swiftly regret having spoken to him as she had earlier.

Georgina paused at the top of the steps that led down to the great hall. She accepted a chilled lime cup from a footman, and then observed the scene below. The hall of Marriot Park might have graced a medieval castle, for it was immense, with a hammerbeam roof, a dais at the far end upon which the orchestra played, and a stone-flagged floor upon which moved a sea of masked, costumed dancers. Tapestries hung on the carved oak walls, heavy iron chandeliers were suspended from the vaulted ceiling, and there were still more flowers, so many that Georgina suspected Sir Richard of denuding every market garden in the county. Finishing the refreshing lime cup, she placed her glass on a little table and then went down the steps, observing the dancers all the time. Was her gentleman among them?

The *ländler* came to an end, and the master of ceremonies announced a cotillion. It was the very cotillion she had danced under such memorable circumstances last midsummer, and the melody was one she had heard constantly ever since, but only in her dreams. The past returned suddenly as she stood at the bottom of the steps watching the sets forming.

She closed her eyes for a moment, recalling that magical night, when her whole life had changed because of a stolen kiss.

"I think you will not deny me this dance," said a smooth voice close to her ear.

With a gasp she whirled about, for there was no mistaking to whom the voice belonged. "Mr. Mandeville?"

"The very same, Miss Hartford."

"But how did you know—?"

"I saw you leaving your sister's house." A cool smile played on his full lips. "The dance, madam?"

She was so horrified at having been found out that she allowed him to take her hand and lead her to join the last of the sets. "Please let me leave, Mr. Mandeville," she begged him, her lilac eyes imploring from behind her domino.

"All in good time, my dear. All in good time," he replied.

The cotillion began, and she moved in a daze of alarm and uncertainty. The remembered notes washed over her, and she followed the precise pattern of the measure, which led inexorably toward the giving and taking of favors and forfeits. Tears shone in her eyes, for this was not midsummer night, it was Saint Valentine's Night, and she was with the wrong gentleman, the wrong gentleman in every way.

Maurice watched her as she danced. How exquisite she was, and so suited to her elaborate gown because she was so dainty and had such a small waist. His desire for her increased with each note of the cotillion, and when the moment came at last when he could demand a forfeit, he was so overcome with ardor that he pulled her almost roughly into his arms and kissed her passionately on the lips.

She was so shocked that for a moment she could not move. The other dancers in the set exchanged uneasy glances, for such a kiss went far beyond the bounds of what was acceptable in a dance. Then Georgina found her strength, and with a supreme effort wrenched herself away from her assailant, dealing him a stinging blow to the cheek before gathering her skirts and running from the crowded floor.

The incident caused a considerable stir, and several other sets stopped dancing as everyone turned to see what was happening. Maurice's face had reddened with embarrassment, because in spite of his disguise his identity was very clear to all those who knew him, for after all he resembled a Roman emperor even when not in costume. He realized that he had been caught conducting himself very shabbily indeed, and he was anxious to smooth the matter over as quickly as possible. With a swift bow he retired from the floor, not following Georgina, but making instead for the adjoining chamber, where a supper was about to be served. As he reached the arched doorway, he observed a statuesque lady dressed as Britannia. Her filmy white robe left very little to the imagination, and she gave him a flirtatious smile, not having seen what had happened on the dance floor. Georgina faded immediately from his fickle mind, and with a return smile he advanced upon the new object of his desire. Miss Georgina Hartford was too troublesome by far, whereas Britannia gave every indication of being very available and interested.

Conscious of the stir in the great hall behind her, Georgina fled up the steps to the inner-staircase hall. All she could think of was going home to Henrietta, but as she reached the hall, she was dismayed to find that it was now such a crush that pushing through it was virtually impossible.

Fighting back tears, she began to make her way as best she could through the crowd, being careful to keep her eyes lowered for fear of catching someone's glance. The last thing she needed now was another encounter with someone who thought he knew her because of her costume.

Suddenly a man called out to her. She wasn't sure if he said a name, she was only conscious that he was looking directly at her and that he was anxious to speak to her. He was tall and slender, and was dressed very richly as a nobleman from the time of Richard II. He wore a long peacock velvet coat trimmed with black fur, and the golden girdle at his waist was studded with jewels. A splendid golden livery collar rested across his broad shoulders, and on his head there was a soft black velvet hat from which trailed a long crimson scarf that was arranged around his neck. His face was concealed by a black mask, but his manner was tense and angry as he came purposefully toward her.

He thought he knew her! Dismay cut freshly

through her, and she cast urgently around for somewhere to run, but all directions were a press of people, except the staircase. Gathering her skirts again, she fled up toward the next floor, and she heard the medieval nobleman shout again, but still she did not know what he said; she was too anxious to escape to hear.

Four passages led from the gallery at the top, and she selected one at random, fleeing down it just as her pursuer reached the second landing behind her. The passage was brightly lit, and as she ran thankfully around a corner, she knew that the man following would have no idea which way she had taken. She paused, her heart pounding. She could still hear the ball. The cotillion had ended now, and a minuet was in progress. She listened for a moment, but there was no sound of anyone following her.

She hurried on along the passage, off which there were many doors. She opened one or two, and found crowded card and music rooms beyond, but at last she opened one and looked into an empty chamber. It was the library, as brightly lit as the rest of the house, but for some inexplicable reason there was no one there. Quickly she stepped inside, closing the door behind her and then leaning weakly back against it. She still had to escape from this house, but for the moment she was safe from discovery.

She looked around the library, where the late Sir Jeremy Marriot had excelled himself in his indulgence in things Gothic, for the room was an almost cathedral shrine to literature. The glass-doored bookcases were arched, with a trefoil decoration in each apex, and there were stone columns such as those that lined the aisles and naves of churches. A handsome carved wooden screen stood to one side, ready to be pulled across to shield the room from drafts, and there was an immense writing desk in the Norman style. The armchairs were wooden, and heavily carved, and the room was lit by floor-standing iron candleholders such as might have adorned the solar of a medieval castle.

The dark-green curtains at the windows had been left undrawn, so that she could see her reflection on the glass, against the starlit darkness of the Saint Valentine's Night sky. A log fire roared in the huge stone fireplace, and its dancing light flickered over her as she moved further into the room.

Something drew her attention to the high mantelpiece, where there was a delicate ivory-framed miniature of a lady in an almost transparent muslin gown. She was standing by a marble pedestal, and behind her there was a Greek landscape, with ruined temples and a wide blue sky. The lady had beautiful chestnut hair, and Georgina recognized her immediately, for it was the same lady who had that afternoon been held up by Sir Roger Hamilton's highwayman, and whose gown Georgina was wearing now.

Georgina stared at the miniature. What was it doing here in Marriot Park? Who was the lady? Then, slowly and inexorably, her gaze was drawn up from the mantelpiece to the chimney breast, where wall-mounted candleholders cast a bright glow over another portrait, a full-size likeness of a gentleman. Her gentleman.

Her lips parted on a gasp, and she put a shaking hand on the back of a carved wooden chair. She gazed at the portrait, for there was no mistaking the identity of the subject. The painting was by Mr. Hoppner, one of England's most fashionable artists, and depicted her gentleman standing before a heavy brocade curtain with his left hand resting lightly on a table where several leather-bound volumes were piled rather unevenly. He wore a dark-blue coat, a wine-red waistcoat, a full neckcloth, and pale-gray breeches, and he looked directly out of the canvas, as if he was on the point of smiling. Mr. Hoppner had captured him to perfection, from the tilt of his head, the curl of his dark hair, and the clarity of his gray-green eyes, to the firmness of his chin, the hint of humor on his lips, and the tan of his complexion.

Georgina went hesitantly toward the portrait, for there was a little name-plate fixed to the bottom of the frame. *Sir Richard Marriot. 1798.*

She was so shaken that she took an involuntary step backward, reaching out again for the chair to steady herself. Sir Richard Marriot? Surely that could not possibly be . . . ? A thought struck her. The lady! Could she be Lady Celestine Vavasour? Georgina was about to go to the mantelpiece to look more closely at the ivory-framed miniature, when suddenly the library door opened behind her. Whirling about, she saw that the gentleman dressed as a medieval nobleman had found her after all.

The golden livery collar across his shoulders glittered as he entered the library and closed the door behind him. Her fingers closed tightly over the back of the chair as he faced her, his eyes in shadow behind his mask.

"Why did you leave it so late, madam?" he asked coolly.

The voice. It was her gentleman's voice, Sir Richard Marriot's voice. . . .

He continued. "I thought I was mistaken at first, for your hair deceived me, but I knew I could not be deceived by a costume I helped you choose. Why have you left it until now to condescend to arrive? Was it your purpose to make me appear the fool, or did you simply intend to keep me in a degree of uncertainty? Well, whatever your reason, I fear it is too late. There can no longer be any thought of a match between us, Celestine, for too much has happened in both our lives." He unwound the scarf of his hat, and then tossed the hat onto a table, before removing his mask as well.

Georgina stared at him, a thousand and one unspoken thoughts spinning around in her head. The man she loved was Sir Richard Marriot, and the woman who had run away with Sir Roger Hamilton was Lady Celestine Vavasour, Sir Richard's bride-to-be.

His gray-green eyes were more than just chill. "Have you nothing to say? I confess I begin to find your way of conducting matters a little tiresome, and I have most certainly ceased to blame myself for everything having gone wrong between us. It was not my neglect that caused you to dally with Hamilton, but your own fickle heart. I was a fool to ever believe you when you claimed to have ended it with him, and I was an even greater fool to have convinced myself that there was still sufficient between us for the match to succeed after all, but you stayed on in London, and several 'friends' have not wasted time in telling me of your continuing liaison with Hamilton. I wrote to you, advising you that the match was at an end, but your silence on the matter, and your arrival here now, suggest to me that either my communication did not arrive or you left the capital before it reached you. I have waited before making any public announcement on the subject, since I believed it courteous to have at least received a response from the bride-to-be before doing so, but I was on the very point of making such an announcement tonight when I happened to see you by the staircase." He paused for a moment, evidently trying to contain his bitter anger. "I'm sorry that you have brought our friendship to this low ebb, Celestine, and I confess to finding it beyond my comprehension that you should come here now, like this." He fell silent again, obviously beginning to notice something rather odd about her continuing silence. "Have you heard anything I've said, Celestine?"

She swallowed. "I . . . I'm not Celestine, Sir Richard," she said at last, her voice so quiet that it was barely audible.

He came closer, his eyes sharpening. "Not Celestine? Then who in God's name . . . ?"

With a shaking hand she removed the domino.

He stared at her. *"You?"* he exclaimed, taken completely by surprise.

"I know I have no right to be here like this, and I didn't mean to deceive you . . ." Her voice trailed away in embarrassment, because it was only too apparent that she had meant to deceive, for why else was she wearing Lady Celestine Vavasour's costume? She was clearly there under false pretenses, an intruder whose motives might only be surmised.

He studied her. "That *is* Lady Celestine's gown, is it not?"

"Yes." She lowered her eyes uncomfortably, the blush deepening on her cheeks. She felt very ill-at-ease and ashamed, and she was mortified to have unwittingly stumbled into such a very private and sensitive matter as the crumbling of his match with Lady Celestine.

"May I ask how you came by it?" he inquired.

She still avoided his gaze, for how could she possibly tell him the truth?

"Please tell me," he pressed gently, "for I think I have a right to know."

He was correct, he *did* have a right to know. Unwillingly she raised her eyes again, and began to tell him about the scene she and Henrietta had witnessed during their walk that afternoon, and about her exceedingly improper decision to wear the costume herself. She felt as if her face was on fire with embarrassment, and she wished with all her heart that she had never allowed such an ill-judged plan to enter her foolish head.

He remained silent throughout, and did not at first say anything when she finished.

Georgina felt more and more dreadful, as if she had deliberately pried, and had been caught in the act. "I . . . I'm truly sorry to have transgressed like this, Sir Richard, but I really did not know that the lady was Lady Celestine, and if you only knew how wretched I feel at having told you such things about her—"

"You haven't told me anything about her that greatly surprises me, Miss Hartford," he interrupted, smiling a little wryly. "Besides, I am sure you will have by now gathered that Lady Celestine's heart has not for some time been solely mine. The fact that she has now apparently decided once and for all to go to Hamilton is, if I am honest, a matter of great relief to me."

"Relief?"

"Yes, because I am no longer any more fully committed to the match than she." He held her gaze. "Why did you come here tonight, Miss Hartford? I cannot imagine that it was simply the excitement and risk that lured you, for you do not seem to be that sort of young lady. So, was there some other reason that was important enough to prompt such an out-of-character action?"

She wanted to tell him that he was the only reason, but the words would not come. They hung trembling on her tongue, but remained silent.

The ghost of a smile touched his lips, and he put his hand out as if to brush his fingertips against her cheek, but then his hand fell back again. "Maybe the time has come to be completely truthful, Miss Hartford, for although destiny has obliged us thus far by making our paths cross, it may not do so again. I have a confession to make, and if what I am about to say is a little forward and presumptuous, then I beg you in advance to forgive me, but I must say what is in my heart because I may not be granted another opportunity." He turned away, running his fingers through his hair as he went to the fireplace. He glanced fleetingly at Lady Celestine's little portrait, and then laid it facedown on the mantelpiece, as if to exclude his former love from overhearing. Then he pressed a log further onto the flames with his foot, before turning back to face Georgina again.

"Miss Hartford, I had not intended to go to Harrogate last summer, because I meant to spend all my time in London with Celestine. Then I found out that Hamilton had been approaching her, not without some success, and I confess that after my initial fury, I felt that a little of the blame was attached to me. I had been neglectful, and I knew it, and at the back of my mind I had begun to wonder if my passion for her was on the wane. I felt that I should remove myself from the scene for a while, and when chance brought me into contact with an old friend from my Cambridge days, and he invited me to stay with him in Harrogate,

I accepted without delay. That is how I happened to be at the assembly rooms on Midsummer Night." He hesitated, his eyes dark and warm upon her. "I saw you the moment you entered the room, and I wished more than anything to make your acquaintance."

Her lips parted, and she felt as if there was fire in her veins. His eyes seemed to caress her, and there was a softness in his voice that stroked her emotions, reawakening the desire that he had aroused from the first moment they met.

"Somehow I had to know you, Georgina, and so I resorted to the somewhat feeble ploy of inventing a fictitious Miss Fitzwalter."

She was trembling so much that she had to grip the back of the chair to conceal it. He had used her first name, and it had slipped from his lips as naturally and easily as if they had known each other forever.

He went on. "When we danced that cotillion, I fell further under your spell with each step, and when the moment came to demand a forfeit of you, I did not hesitate to steal a kiss. Your lips were so sweet, Georgina, and your perfume was all around me, bewitching me more and more as each moment passed. Then I was suddenly beset by guilt, for I had gone to Harrogate to think things over where Celestine was concerned, and there I was, committing as much of a sin as she. Remorse has a way of pouring ice-cold water over the hottest of passions, Georgina, and so I left the ball immediately. I also left Harrogate without further delay, and returned to London to see if matters could be put right with Celestine, for she had already accepted my proposal of marriage, and the whole of society knew that we were to be engaged on Saint Valentine's Day. She appeared to want to forget the awkwardness of the past, and so we tried to put it all behind us and look only to the future. But each time I kissed her, I thought of you, and each time I closed my eyes at night, you filled my dreams."

Georgina stared breathlessly at him. Her heart was pounding in her breast, and she drank in the warmth and desire in his eyes.

He continued. "It now appears that Celestine was far from certain about the match, for Hamilton did not entirely fade from the scene, although she was very careful not to allow the fact to come out. I could not put you from my thoughts, but I believed that things had proceeded too far with the match and that I was obliged to go through with it. Besides, although I may no longer have loved Celestine, I still had sufficient regard and affection for her to feel that our marriage would succeed. I left London to come here, and she should have followed a day or so later, but, as has become somewhat evident, she did not. Several of my guests here were moved to confide in me that they had seen her with Hamilton in London, and so I felt I had no option but to terminate the whole sorry business. I sent a courier to her residence in Berkeley Square, informing her of my decision and the reason for it, and requesting her to acknowledge receipt so that I could make the necessary announcement to my guests. There was no response, and I decided that that could only mean that she wished to cease all contact. I was about to inform my great gathering of guests that this was no longer a betrothal ball, but a celebration of Saint Valentine's Day, when I happened to see you, or, as I thought, Celestine. I couldn't believe my eyes, for even given her nerve and lack of all conscience, to choose to arrive as late as this seemed incredible. The rest you know—at least, you know most of it."

"Most of it?" she whispered.

"I have left out my joy on glimpsing you again yesterday when you drove past, my disbelief this morning when I found myself staring at you yet again in the woods near here, and my disappointment on returning after a fruitless horse chase to find you gone. It had not occurred to me that you might be somewhere in this area, for when I drove after you yesterday, I naturally took the Burford road."

"You . . . you followed me yesterday?"

"Of course. Georgina, you are the reason why I am less than heartbroken over Celestine, for you have stolen my every hour since midsummer last year. That is why I asked you why you came here tonight, for if your reason is as I pray it is . . ."

She gazed at him, and at last was able to open her heart. "I came tonight because I wished to meet you again. I did not know who you were, and I certainly did not guess that you might be Sir Richard Marriot. My sister told me that—"

"Your sister?" he asked quickly.

"She is married to John Churchill of Bourton."

He gave an incredulous laugh. "John Churchill? You had such close connections here all the time?" He came to her, putting his hand over hers on the back of the chair.

The warmth of his fingers was enthralling. She felt too weak to fight the tumultuous emotions that engulfed her, nor did she want to fight them.

"Tell me why you wanted to meet me again, Georgina," he pressed, his hand tightening over hers.

"Because you have filled my thoughts and heart as much as I have filled yours. Because I love you so much that sometimes I've felt as if my heart was breaking. Because—"

She said no more, for he stopped her words with a kiss. He pulled her almost roughly into his arms, crushing her so close that she could feel his heart pounding against hers. It was the kiss of her dreams, a fantasy that had become tangible fact, and she was swept away by an ecstasy she had never dared to hope would one day come to her. The valentine she had longed for was hers, a prize so precious that she was close to tears.

He felt her lips tremble beneath his, and drew back a little, cupping her face in his hands. "Oh, my sweet Georgina," he whispered. "No other Saint Valentine's Day will ever compare with this one, and now that I've found you again, I will never let you go." His thumbs caressed her warm skin. "I love you, you are life itself to me," he breathed.

"Hold me again," she begged softly, her lilac eyes shimmering with tears of joy.

Her body melted against his as he drew her into his arms once more. She was conscious of the thundering of her heart, and beyond, echoing faintly through the house from the distant ball-room, she could hear the orchestra playing another cotillion.

The Legacy
by Edith Layton

THE AFTERNOON WAS BLEAK, the sky was gray, and
the house and its furnishings so old and worn they
complemented the day rather than defying it. But
curiously, the elegant young gentleman awaiting
his host in the dim study was neither depressed
nor dissatisfied, even though his fashionable clothing was as much at odds with his surroundings as
his bemused smile was with the lowering day. The
leaded windows let in dreary February light, so
the room was lit only by a glowing fireplace,
which, considering its threadbare state, was a
kindness. But nevertheless the gentleman seemed
pleased. He glanced about, stretched out his glossy
boots in front of him, and sighed, content, as much
at ease with the room as he would be in his favorite old dressing gown—the paisley one that was
too worn for fashion but too comfortable to
discard.

Nothing here had changed. That was as rare in
this age of discovery, where war and fashion
changed a man's geography every time he turned
around, as it was at his own particular age, the
gentleman thought ruefully. For lately he'd discovered his friends and family changing even more
rapidly than the world around him was. He'd
returned from the wars by sea because Napoleon
had been busily changing familiar borders while

he himself had been trying to stop him from doing so, only to find the familiar borders of his own life entirely altered once he'd gotten home. His mama had married again. And though he couldn't blame her, widowhood having been no doubt as boring as it was unprofitable for her, it was odd to feel an alien in the home of his childhood. He'd suddenly acquired a father who seemed not much older than himself, and a mother who was suddenly a sexual being. At least his newly acquired father thought so, for the fellow, for all his dignity, was constantly leering at his new wife—when he wasn't cloistering himself with her in remote parts of the house. It was done in civilized fashion, of course, but since it was done at all, nothing could make it remotely bearable for the newly wedded lady's fully grown son.

There was no relief to be found at the home of his sister or brother either, since those worthies had become parents during his absence from England. And as parents, he soon discovered them to be as fully absorbed and occupied with pride of their progeny as they'd been with themselves when they'd been younger. As for his many friends . . . the gentleman sighed as he gazed into the fire, although his face showed nothing but his usual calm dispassion. Those of his friends that weren't wedded were trying to be—as though England had become some vast breeding ground since he'd gone away and returned. And yet even those that were not so occupied were not such friends as they'd seemed to be before he'd left them.

In fairness, he supposed that war changed the way a man looked at life too. Still, since he'd returned he found too many who'd remained at home too filled with trivialities to talk comfortably with, and too many who'd shared his experi-

ences too eager to talk about what he'd rather
forget now. Discontented and displaced, as out of
place in his homeland as he'd been on the alien
soil he'd tried to defend it upon, now he discovered himself pleased for the first time in a long
time. Because he could sit back in this drab old
room and forget, as it had, that time had changed
everything outside of it out of all recognition.

The room seemed to have cast a spell over him,
for even the voice that eventually awakened him
from his reveries was as familiar to him as his
own past was. Still, he waited a moment before
he looked up to its source. Having heard a memory speak, he was loath to face reality. He'd discovered to his sorrow that faces were temporary,
changing with time and troubles, as unreliable as
time itself was. But voices remained much the
same, and this one's cadences and tone were part
of the very fabric of his childhood. It was odd, he
realized as he arose from his chair, that such pee-
vish complaining tones were comforting, but they
were. When he looked up to his host, he discovered
something else was too, and then frankly grinned.
Perhaps vinegar was the best preservative after
all, because the wonder was that the face was as
unchanged as the voice. But then, he thought, perhaps it was only that old could scarcely get older.

"Good heavens!" the old gentleman exclaimed
in annoyance. "Sit down! Sit down! Took a ball
in your chest not a month past and you're standing for me?"

"Three months past," his nephew corrected him
softly, and sat again. He might have wished to
offer more, to actually embrace the old fellow and
hug him hard. But the Baron Blackwood had
already turned his narrow back upon his guest
and was rummaging through the drawer of his

desk before the younger man could offer his hand, much less embarrass him by any show of affection. He wasn't a touching sort of fellow, his nephew remembered, and hadn't even the excuse of years of homesickness to have given him such an unnatural impulse. No, he never left this house, it was that which had caused him to summon his nephew to it. But now he'd begun to accept that he might someday have to leave, if unwillingly, yet forever. And so he told his nephew at once.

He began his complaints without so much as a preamble about the weather or an inquiry as to his guest's own health. That was commonplace for him. Perhaps once the baron had been more conventional. But his wife had been dead for a generation, and his two sons carried off by a measles epidemic even before that, and as he'd kept to his house and his studies ever since, it was likely he'd gotten out of the habit of conversation. It hardly mattered. His nephew had always liked him anyway, perhaps precisely because he'd been the only adult male relative who'd never asked embarrassing and pointless questions, instead lecturing to him about whatever was on his own mind at the time they met. Since Uncle's consuming passion was archaeology, Valerian hadn't understood him very well in his early years, but the novelty of being asked his opinion about such exotic matters as ancient Roman earthworks, Celtic breastplates, and Pict war policies had been heady stuff to a growing boy. And whereas other adult male relatives had occasionally donated small coins or improving tracts as gifts, the baron could always be counted on to press all manner of interesting shards, broken medallions, and bits of clay and metal with undeciperable runes into his nephew's hands, in the manner of a slightly lunatic jackdaw, as tokens of his goodwill.

And goodwill there'd been, although two more different men would be hard to find. The baron was a small, slight, bald, and blue-eyed gentleman with a thin face distinguished mainly by its many wrinkles, a high querulous voice, and a remarkably deaf ear to anything that didn't interest him. Valerian Blackwood was tall, lightly but muscularly built, blessed with a full head of light brown hair, a lean handsome face made markedly handsomer by his watchful gray-brown eyes, possessed of a smooth tenor voice, and known to be more interested in hearing about others than volunteering information about himself. Mr. Valerian Blackwood, until recently Captain Blackwood of His Majesty's Light Hussars, was as interested in antiquities as he was in modern manners, no more, and not less, because he found many things interesting—not the least, his uncle himself. He liked the baron for his oddity as well as his intelligence, but would have been kind to him in any case, merely because he was his uncle. He'd never seen his uncle being kind or unkind to anyone: merely sublimely unaware of their emotions. True, the baron had once been a soldier too, long before his nephew had been born, much less bought his own colors. But he seldom spoke of any battle fought after 1066. In fact, uncle and nephew neither looked nor thought alike in the least, but there was a curious bond between them, though neither could say just why.

"And so although of course I knew he stood to inherit one day, I never refined upon it too much," the baron was saying in his usual high-pitched anxious drone, "but obviously he has done, for he wrote this damned impertinent letter when he discovered I'd donated a bit or two to the new British Museum—well," he huffed, as he passed the letter to his nephew with shaking hands, "as if a museum of antiquities could be based on a jumble of stolen Greek marbles! That's *Greek* history," he said with a sniff, in the manner that one might say "Martian history."

Valerian ran his eyes over the paper as his uncle whined on about the indignity of being asked just what he'd contributed. The letter was indeed, as the baron had said, and his nephew had suspected: a pompous, foolish, and unnecessary bit of presumption. Just as its author was, he thought on an interior sigh, and gazed up at his uncle as he paced the dim study.

"As I understand it," Valerian said, summarily interrupting the flow of complaints because he knew that was the only way to be heard, "my cousin has no grounds for complaint. The estate's entailed, so I imagine he could raise holy hell if you gave away a rug or a chair without his express permission. But that acquired by you yourself in the course of your life is yours to do with as you wish, is it not?"

His uncle stopped pacing and gazed at him shrewdly. The old fellow might be a nonstop complainer, and sublimely disinterested in modern life, but he was as sharp of wit as he'd always been. The family wisdom was that the Blackwoods went to their graves fully equipped with all their teeth and claws, no matter how ancient they were on that fateful day.

"Yes," the baron admitted, "in the usual course of things, that's so. But these artifacts were discovered here. On the grounds of the Hall itself. And so, my man at law says, the oaf has a say-so in the matter. He could claim that I'm disposing of his legacy. Well, he *is*. And I am. But he's got no interest in them. I suspect he's belligerent because he'll not get much more from me. And not just because I dislike him. No, no, I never earned a shilling to improve the estate, but neither did I squander one either. There simply never was much there. What there was, I spent on excavation—the barrow in the east meadow, the ruins of the villa out near the lake. This is historic ground. The only thing that bothered me was that there wasn't more to spend," he said, before with an altogether new and sly smile he added, "but as Bolton doesn't know the difference between a Roman pot and a Viking chalice, the riches he stands to inherit don't excite him in the least."

"Ah, well," Valerian said, "but as Bolton hasn't so much as a Roman cooking pot to ... ah, cook in, much less a chalice, I can see—if not sympathize with—his point."

"Of course you can't sympathize, you're rich as a Caesar yourself," his uncle said caustically.

"Oh, you see his point. Pardon me," Valerian said, "I hadn't realized you'd grown a partiality for the fellow."

"As soon as I would for any Vandal! No, no. I'm just stating facts. Your father was the craftiest in the family, his investments were nothing short of astonishing. Who would think tobacco and sugarcane would come to be worth more than statuary and texts?" he asked wonderingly. "But that's the way of the modern world, pleasure over knowledge," he went on in aggrieved tones, before he said accusingly, "and you not only inherited his fortune, but his acuity as well."

"Your pardon, Uncle," Valerian said with much mock humility, which his uncle ignored.

"You cousin Bolton's here now," the baron said

fiercely, as if it were truly a troop of savage Vandals occupying his guest room instead of his heir, "snooping and poking and prodding, wondering where I've hidden the silver plate and gold furnishings. He can't believe I paid what he calls 'good money' to excavate and unearth my 'pottery and crockery.' Almost comes right out and says I diddled him out of a fortune. Accusing me of all sorts. But I'm leaving him an estate in good heart and priceless treasures besides, although he can't see it—nor anything that isn't in his favorite tailor or jeweler's windows."

"And you sent for me so that I could help persuade him that all is in order?" his nephew asked softly.

"Aye!" the baron said, resuming his pacing. "Because you're almost of an age, though he's got five years on you. More than that, he respects you for all the wrong reasons: your fortune and fashion. Howbeit. You can do it. You must. His letter made me see I have to settle things before he takes over. I've always been concerned with posterity. Now I'm thinking about my own. I find there're things I wish to leave behind," he said fiercely, "but I have to get that sapskull's permission so I can."

"I'll talk with him tonight, after dinner. Does he still fancy himself a wizard at billiards?" Valerian asked.

"How should I know?" the baron asked with some irritation. "Hadn't clapped eyes on him in years before he arrived this morning. All I know is that he's more foolish than ever. Don't you run into him in town?"

"Now and again," Valerian admitted, "but then I usually run the other way. Well, then, shall I go to my room and change before dinner—my valet's likely unpacked by now—or should you like to take me around to see the place first? It's been years since I've been here too. I don't know a chalice from a chausable either, but nevertheless I'd like to see what's old that's new, sir, if I might."

"Still got charm to spare, I see," the baron said with a grimace, as if he were pointing out the fact that his nephew had some skin disease. "How is it you aren't wedded yet?"

Since he'd been wondering about that very thing of late, Valerian answered with less than his usual calm amusement.

"There were very few cotillions in the Peninsula," he said with a chill smile, "and though I found myself most grateful to my nurses for all the tender care they gave me when I was in hospital, I hadn't the urge to propose to any of those fellows."

"You were only gone four years, and you've been back three months. And you were home for twenty-two years before that," his uncle pointed out.

"Alas, I'm not impetuous," Valerian answered.

"But not disinterested. I hear you've already got a high flier in keeping," the baron complained.

"I'm not impetuous, but not dead yet either," his nephew answered coolly, for all he was astonished that his uncle knew something current as well as personal about him.

"Bolton may as well be," the baron sighed. "Been keeping some doxie in London for years now. Same one all this time—she's old as he is, fairly long in the tooth now."

"I thought you admired antiquities," Valerian commented as his uncle went on, "Not because he's devoted, mind you. Just lazy. So I invited a wife here for him."

After a second's silence his nephew asked idly, "Is her husband here too?"

"Bolton's going to have the title, the estate, the lot," his uncle said, ignoring his comment. "I'm leaving him everything but money, as I said. But without money an idiot like him will run the estate into the ground within a decade. So one of the things I'm going to get settled before I go is Bolton himself. He needs a rich wife; I've found him one."

"What a lot of excavating's been going on," Valerian mused. "Are you going to slip her into his bed? Or simply have her waiting with an armful of roses and a Bible by a convenient altar as he goes by? He has to agree to the union, you know, and he's remained stunningly single for all these years now. He is, as you say, lazy, and for all he's got his doxy in readiness, from what I hear, her duties are light. Not because he finds her unattractive, but because he's simply not terribly interested very often. How are you going to get the lad to the sticking point, sir? As you say, he already feels you haven't much to offer. Or have you actually been hoarding golden chalices against this day?"

"Don't talk nonsense," the baron said huffily. "What I have is you. That's one of the reasons I invited you here. You're going to talk him round to her, and it."

He waited for his nephew's response. But for once Mr. Valerian Blackwood, famed for his wit as well as his acuity, was silent; he only stood and stared at his uncle with his usually amused gray-brown eyes arrested and opened wide.

"I am," he finally managed to say, "a most unlikely Cupid, sir."

"Well, that's done," the baron said with something almost like pleasure in his thin voice. "Now,

come have a look at what I've got on display in
the muniments room, and then you can meet Miss
Exeter, and then we'll have dinner."

"Uncle," Valerian said firmly, "I'll do my best,
but I promise nothing."

"I ask nothing more," the baron said, leading
the way out of the study. "She's a good sort of
female," he conceded, "handsome as she is
wealthy, fair and buxom as a young Bodicea, actually," he said on a rusty laugh, "so it shouldn't be
difficult for you. Wait until you see the coins I
found beneath the mosaic at the villa."

But as Mr. Valerian Blackwood followed his
uncle, he remained silent, suddenly as anxious as
he'd been at dawn on days of battle, sensing a
trap, hearing something sinister beneath the birdsong, suddenly wondering if it wasn't someone
else who was playing the role of unlikely Cupid,
after all.

"Hist!" Bolton Blackwood said.

He didn't even hiss it, he said it, Valerian
thought wearily; that was part of the difficulty
with dealing with his cousin. Bolton stood in the
doorway to his room and accosted him as he came
down the corridor with a clearly enunciated:
"Hist!"

"Good evening, Cousin. You wished to speak
with me?" Valerian asked.

"Come in, come in. A word, for a moment, if
you would," Bolton said anxiously.

Valerian sighed, and nodding, followed his
cousin into his guest chamber. His lips curved
upward as he noted that Uncle had put his heir in
a badly furnished, damp chamber. But then he
straightened his face and his back and stood
before his cousin with every evidence of interest,

even though he anticipated very little of interest
to him. The male Blackwoods seemed to take their
looks from the female sides of the line, Valerian
mused. For his cousin looked nothing like Uncle
either, and yet he and Bolton had only their height
in common. Bolton was a tall, fattish gentleman
with thin blond hair and light blue eyes under
light brows. His face was not unhandsome, merely
not memorable; his plump lips, rosy cheeks, and
small nose suited his mother, whom he'd got them
from, far more than they did himself. He was
dressed neatly, in Brummell's prescribed fashion,
but it was a measure of the man that he scanned
his cousin Valerian's clothes with an anxious and
considering eye, noting his fobs and boots and the
cut of his jacket before he looked into his inquiring
eyes. Those eyes, on a level with his own, held the
usual polite and amused look which had always
caused Bolton both discomfort and envy, even
more so than his cousin's trim form, chiseled features, and thick lustrous hair always did.

"The old boy's been giving away half the kit in
the house," Bolton said without preamble, making
his cousin wonder if direct mode of speech was
the only thing that did run in his family. "I
mean," Bolton said, when he received no answer
but a calm stare, "everything."

"Come now," Valerian said reasonably. "I've
just returned from a tour of Uncle's treasure trove.
Corroded coins and broken mosaics, shield pins
with their jewels pried out centuries past, dagger
handles, and spearheads. It's fascinating stuff, to
be sure. But even museums prize better artifacts.
He loves them because he found them himself, and
here. I suppose they've some antiquarian value.
But there's not a precious gem or a sizable bit of
pure gold in the lot."

"Yes. well, that remains to be seen," Bolton said darkly, "but that's not the sum of it." And he added, to Valerian's skeptically lifted brow, "There're other things missing. The place is worn down, to be sure. But it's commonplace run-down, if you get what I mean. And that don't make sense. Damme!" he said with far more animation than Valerian had seen in him in years, "the furniture is old, but it ain't old Chippendale, do you see? And the rugs are old, but they ain't old Persian. And there ain't a tapestry in the house except on a chair back, and those are tatty old village-made things. The pictures on the walls are faded, but they ain't faded masterpieces, nor even murky old Dutch stuff like Prinny's collecting. Do you see? The baron's never paid no nevermind to the place. I know it. Come to think of it, neither did I, before now. I daresay you didn't either. What does a boy know of the value of art, after all? But I'm sure our ancestors knew. And I think," he said in a low, grieved voice, "that someone else does too.

"I'm not saying it's Uncle who's disposing of the goods in the open or on the sly," he said quickly, throwing up one plump hand as if in defense of Valerian's frown, "but he never paid much mind to the place, and he's old now. That's why I've come. Not so much to see to the bits and pieces he's packing off to the museum. But to cast an eye over the place to see who else might be stealing, and flogging the stuff—the good stuff—from here."

Valerian eyed his cousin in silence. For all the things that Bolton was not, he was not stupid. Foolish, as Uncle had said, true. But not precisely stupid.

Bolton's fair face showed the color of his distress as clearly as the dew of stress above his plump upper lip did."Will you help me, Cousin?" he asked.

Valerian's face showed none of his ruminations. It never did. His well-cut lips closed over any facile answers. In the past, Bolton had asked him the identity of his tailor, the direction of his tobacconist, and the name of his cologne. But never, in all the years of their acquaintance—and relatives or not, they'd never been much more than acquaintances—had he asked for help. And that, as it happened, was the one thing Valerian had always found it nearly impossible to refuse anyone.

"Very well. I'll try," he answered.

But first they had to make the acquaintances of their uncle's other guest.

The one room in the Hall that was in good repair, lavishly decorated and well-tended, it transpired, was the orangery. It was a huge brick-floored fantasy of a greenhouse, topped by a huge domed cupola, onion-shaped like the domes on the Prince of Wales's ongoing extravaganza at Brighton, but made of glass. It let in so much light it was gray-bright in the orangery even on this dreary February evening. At that, it was easy to forget the season, whatever the light, with the many miniature waterspills and falls babbling in among the several displays of tropical foliage and flowers. These were on the sides of the great round room. The centerpiece, the pearl at its heart, was a statue of Venus showing her exquisite profile— all the way down her marble body—to an ardent Mars, whilst Eros hovered over them with waters cascading from his arrow case to tumble down a tiered fountain, splashing the many varied orchids growing around them. But nothing graced the room so much as Miss Georgette Exeter did. On that, those three disparate males, the Baron Blackwood and his two nephews, were absolutely agreed.

She stood by the fountain, her blond hair blooming brighter than any blossom in the room. As she was half-turned from the gentlemen as they entered the orangery, they could see her profile was as noble and elegant as the stone Venus', and lower down, was not only more robustly fashioned, but made for far warmer purposes than art too. The tint of her rosebud mouth was the tenderest blushing shade of the lips of the nearby blooming orchids. And her eyes, when she opened them wide to see the gentlemen before she lowered long lashes over them, were the dulcet blue of summer skies. It was almost as if Nature had known nothing less would do.

Bolton Blackwood, always at a loss for words, stopped and stared. But as he was a gentleman, he did it with his quizzing glass before his astonished eye, and so did not appear to be gaping so much as assessing her as any gentleman of fashion might. Valerian Blackwood made his bow and then stood watching her, bemused. Until his uncle pinched his arm hard and whispered in a voice that the stone Venus could have heard, "And she's got money too."

She had everything, in fact, Valerian soon thought, except for conversation. Oh, she'd blushes aplenty, and soft giggles and pretty manners as well. But she had not delivered herself of a single complete sentence, any more than any of the lovely blooms around her had. But then, he thought in fairness, they'd scarcely given her a chance to speak, what with Bolton's hearty compliments and Uncle's constant nattering about his nephews' eligibility. The thing that bothered Valerian most was not the beauty's muteness, but his uncle's loquaciousness about his nephews—especially since he never specified exactly which nephew he was currently touting as the greatest catch in all England. That, and the additional fact that the beauty was guarded, like a rose by thorns, by a singularly astute-looking chaperone introduced as a devoted aunt, and that elderly lady's eyes were upon him, as though measuring him for a wedding suit.

If that was the baron's game too, Valerian wondered what he could be thinking of. For he didn't need the beauty's fortune any more than he needed her pale white hand in marriage. He'd only just returned to England, and wanted play, not permanence, from his female companions. He'd no inclination to such a commitment just now, and certainly never to a young miss who offered nothing but ravishment to the senses. His own current mistress wasn't half so handsome, but he'd wager she was three times as clever, in bed or out of it. Still, it would have to be a wager, since the poor beauty before him hadn't had a chance to do more than sweetly accept their compliments . . . and he himself, Valerian realized, hadn't even given her the opportunity to do that. And Uncle, he remembered as he smiled at the girl at last, might be a nag and an eccentric, but never was a fool.

"I see you're entranced by Uncle's flowers. Do you garden yourself, Miss Exeter?" Valerian asked on the heels of Bolton's comparing her to a "jolly blushing rose." His cousin seemed to believe courtship consisted of a volley of incessant compliments to the lady of his choice, which the lady was expected to parry with blushes and titters until, one could only surmise, she was either proposed to or propositioned. And perhaps he was right, Valerian thought sadly, when his simple question was answered only by the same sort of soft giggle that Bolton's gruff sallies had been.

"Miss Exeter had gardeners aplenty at home," her aunt said in response, "but she dearly loves flowers, do you not, my dear?"

"Oh, yeath," Miss Exeter said eagerly, "I do. Espethically rotheth."

Perhaps she only considered other females worth conversation, and so would answer only one of them, Valerian thought, as amused by the concept as he was, despite himself, enchanted by her pretty lisp. At that, he supposed it was only equitable, since he knew a great many gentlemen, Bolton among them, who considered only other men to be reasoning creatures.

"Ah, but what of Uncle's orchids?" Valerian persisted. "Are they not charming too?"

"Not my orchids," the baron protested before Miss Exeter could put in a blush or a word, "My gardener's. Fellow served under me in seventy-six. He was a good soldier, but good for nothing but posies now," he said peevishly. "He claims he can't dig for relics because he's got only the one arm now, but he digs roots and weeds smartly enough. He massacres anything else below ground," the baron complained. "I'd sooner let an ox near my excavations. Though he's nimble as an elf around daisies, he'd trample a thousand-year-old vessel to get to a new sprig for his gardens. He's got the place looking like a bower all summer, winter too. Orchids!" he scoffed, frowning at the flowers. "Pure ephemera. Useless for anything but looking at," he said, showing his disdain by sweeping his arm to include all the blooms, and in so doing, striking against a pale lavender orchid, bending its stalk and creasing and tearing its fragile calyx.

"Come, Uncle," Valerian said lightly, "what more would you require of a flower?"

"Or a beautiful woman?" Bolton said gallantly.

Miss Exeter blushed, and Valerian felt slightly ill, and as out of place as the orchids were in the cold February night.

Dinner consisted of five main courses, served with five fine wines, for however odd the baron was, he enjoyed a good table. The food occupied all of Bolton's attention; gentleman though he was, he'd never mastered the trick of attending to his food and his dinner companions at the same time. It was left to Valerian to keep the halting conversation going, since his uncle tended to forget everyone else at the table if the conversation didn't concern antiquities, and there was only so much his nephew could bear to hear about his recent Roman finds in the ruin on the hill.

"Mama will be here thoon," Miss Exeter said softly, in response to Valerian's question as the fish was being removed. "She couldn't leave home jutht yet. My brother hath a thlight indithpothithion, and thince my father thuccumbed to jutht thuch a thing, she ith tho nervouth that she put off her vithit until he ith well again. Even though he ith not coming with her," she added hastily, for she was, Valerian had discovered, a very literal-minded girl.

And a charming one, he conceded. Perhaps not terribly bright, but sweet, and so lovely, with her blue eyes and golden hair, that he discovered himself ready to make excuses for her lacks. After all, he thought, few other gentlemen would consider a complete absence of wit and humor precisely a lack at all in a beautiful, rich, and wellborn young lady. Bolton certainly didn't. From the worshipful looks he'd seen his cousin give the young woman, to his heavy-handed compliments to her, Valerian could see no reason for needing to play Cupid for the couple as his uncle had asked. Unless, of course, he thought, he'd been right in the first place and Uncle wished him to stay on until his own heart was engaged.

Which might take longer than a very long while, he thought. For he'd only been back on the town, relatively free from pain, for a few short weeks. He'd joined the army to belong to something when his father's death had left him unconnected and his mother's newfound freedom had become an increasing embarrassment to him. That certainly hadn't worked. Belonging to a group of men trying to stay alive against all odds had been absorbing, but not at all what he'd been after. No, he'd grown up instead, and had stopped looking for others to cure what needed to be remedied within himself. It was entertainment he was after now, nothing more, and absolutely nothing less. He wasn't out to cure his loneliness anymore. It was such a part of him by now he scarcely ever noted it, except when he thought about it, which, after all, he'd trained himself not to do.

Still, seeing how Miss Exeter sat poised now, slightly anxious and yet ready to hear his own next question—for she never volunteered anything without having been asked first—Valerian wondered if pity was enough of an inducement for him to offer for a wife. Because if he didn't ask, he was sure Bolton soon might. Looking at Bolton as he concentrated all his attention on his dinner plate, attacking his squab with gusto, Valerian sighed. If he asked, and she agreed, Bolton would give her his hand, eventually his title, and as many brats as he could. Then he'd take himself off to his mistress again, since a gentleman of Bolton's sensibilities wouldn't presume on his own wife, no matter how lovely, for satisfaction of desires for anything but heirs. And she, in turn, would give him her loyalty, her body, and as many offspring as she could. And never realize what other potentials there might be within that graceful, ripe, and lovely body; and never attain whatever possibilities there might be that lay hidden in that sweetly simple literal mind.

Perhaps, Valerian mused, glancing across the table to where the lovely chit awaited his next words with equal parts of apprehension and expectation upon her beautiful face—just perhaps pity might be enough . . . Or perhaps, he thought, alarmed, catching that fragmented thought, it might be that he'd had enough wine tonight.

When the ladies had retired, the gentlemen slouched in their chairs and cradled their glasses of port.

"She's smashing," Bolton said to the fireplace.

"Well, then, that's that," Valerian said, glancing at his uncle to see his reaction.

"Tha's what?" Bolton asked sluggishly, for he'd eaten and drunk as fulsomely as he'd complimented Miss Exeter earlier.

"Valerian here thinks you're about to offer for the chit. Are you?" the baron barked.

Valerian shot his uncle a look, for Bolton had lunged upright. He'd never seen a man sober faster, not even when he'd been doused with a bucket of cold water. Bolton's pale blue eyes went from watery inattention to a look his cousin had seen on the faces of men facing a firing squad.

"Never said so. Pretty thing. But early days yet," Bolton said, licking his lips.

His cousin was astonished. For a man of thirty-odd, who'd evaded matchmakers as cleverly as he had dunning tailors, that was as good as a declaration of intent. Because as any matchmaking mama could have noted, he hadn't precisely said no.

His uncle gazed at him thoughtfully. "Better look sharp then," he said after a moment. "A girl like that will be snapped up soon as she sets foot in London. Her father was a schoolmate of mine, so you've got a pre-Season preview here. You ought to make the most of it."

"Haven't said I *will*," Bolton grumbled, "said it's early days yet, and it is. Only saw her for a matter of hours. Don't even know if she likes me."

"That's not necessary for marriage," the baron said, and watched as his other nephew shifted his long frame as though his chair had grown uncomfortable. "I've thrown you together, you have to make the most of it. You've got two weeks before she travels on to London with her mama. Then you'll have hot competition, my boy. I've made sure you had a clear field here, at least. Don't even have a proper house full of guests so there won't be any fortune hunters to take the shine out of you. Well, damm it, sir," the baron said irritably at Bolton's wounded expression, "they know how to get around a female, it's their profession. Competition isn't your forte, Bolton, that's the truth with no bark on it."

"Well, then," Valerian said, arising and stretching gracefully, "I can see that I definitely oughtn't to add to it by my presence, one way or the other. I don't flatter myself that I would pose any problem for you, Cousin," he said with as much sincerity as he could muster, "but I'd definitely be in the way. A fellow needs to give his lady flowers and poetry, candies and compliments, as well as his undivided attention, in order to win her. I'll be on my way after breakfast in the morning, Uncle, Cousin," he said.

"No!" his uncle and his cousin cried at once, and then looked at each other. The baron inclined his head, giving Bolton permission to speak first.

"Ah, er, you wouldn't be in the way," Bolton said, perspiration showing on his round face even in the cool room. "I aint too used to young chits, you know. I might need some advice, you know," he went on, turning his face sideways to his cousin. Valerian noted that he'd begun to develop a tic in the cheek his uncle couldn't see. "Advice about what to do, you see," Bolton continued, "what to do about things *here*," he went on. "I'm not saying I'm going to ask for her right off, but I don't want to leave just yet, don't you see," he said pointedly, his eye twitching madly, until Valerian realized it was his cousin's attempt to tip him a wink that was causing the wild spasms in his face.

"Just so," the baron said. "You need to show him how to go on, Valerian. This would be a perfect opportunity for him. Valentine's Day is coming. What better time to win a maiden's heart? Can you write up a poem? One you didn't find in a book?" he asked Bolton suddenly. "Where would you get flowers? Raid my orchids?" he scoffed.

"There you are," Bolton said with relief, as if delighted to be so abused by his uncle. "I don't have a clue."

"So you'll stay," the baron said meaningfully, staring at Valerian, reminding him of his promise to see that Bolton's courtship prospered.

"Say you will," Bolton said, winking fiercely at

Valerian again, reminding him of his promise to see to matters of his purse rather than his heart.

"So I shall, I suppose," Valerian sighed, for the first time since he'd sold out almost wishing he were back in the Peninsula, where all he'd be expected to do was slay his fellowman and save his own life.

Valerian rode out the next day, after breakfast. But not alone, and not to return to his town house in London as he'd wished. He was accompanied by his cousin, and they were off to order up some flowers for Miss Exeter for Valentine's Day at their uncle's express command.

"I'd thought you despised flowers," Valerian told his uncle at the breakfast table when he was given his orders.

"So I do, when I think of them at all," the baron agreed between mouthfuls of porridge, "but females do not."

"You've got bowers of them here," Valerian persisted.

"Partnering your cousin has dimmed your brain," the baron snapped, "Even a good-natured chit like Miss Exeter doesn't want a fellow to simply shear off his uncle's greens and then hand them over to her. She wants something special and heartfelt."

"Been digging up volumes of Ovid in your excavations?" Valerian asked sourly, and when he received no answer, sighed and added, "Why must I accompany him on this expedition? Surely Bolton can point to a rose by himself."

"Don't be so sure. God knows what he'd order up for her. He's never courted a decent woman," the baron said, as Bolton, seemingly deaf to everything but the sounds of his own chewing, rounded up the last bits of egg on his plate with his toast. "There's a little shop in town near the church. Sells fruits and vegetables, preserves and such. See to it he doesn't order her a bunch of turnips. Oh. And have him write something flattering on the card."

"Flattering, but not fawning or anything like," Bolton corrected him now as he and his cousin rode into the village. "She's a beauty, all right, but I ain't necessarily going to dance just because uncle plays the tune."

As Valerian smiled and looked at him with dawning respect, Bolton nodded and said, "Aye, I'm keeping my eye on the main issue—what's become of my legacy. If it means I have to look smitten in order to stay on and keep doing so—well and good, it ain't hard. She is a charmer. And she's got a fortune."

"Look too hard," his cousin reminded him, "and you'll be looking down the aisle at a minister."

"Any objection to that?" Bolton asked warily.

"Me? Not in the least," Valerian said, eyeing his big blond cousin and wondering just what the fellow's game was. He didn't think Bolton capable of much deception. But he never thought he was capable of none. He'd been in the army too long for that.

"After we order up the flowers, I want to go back to the house. There's a one-armed fellow goes creeping about that I've got my eye on," Bolton announced.

"The gardener," Valerian said on a sigh.

"We'll see," Bolton said darkly as his cousin sighed again.

Bolton might well be capable of deception, Valerian thought bleakly as they rode down the small main street of the village, but he was certainly more capable of folly.

Sybil saw the two riders through her window. She could scarcely miss them. They were as unexpected a sight on the streets of town this windblown dreary February day as the flowers in her window were. They rode better horses than any of the local men were apt to do, but they themselves were more exotic than their fine thoroughbred mounts were. One was large, ruddy-faced and blond, and most imposing. He wore gentleman's clothing, but he might as well have been in armor, for he rode like a conquerer surveying the peasants, head high, with one gloved hand firm on the reins and the other knuckled in at his waist, in a show of confident languor. The other man, just as tall, was darker, slender, elegant and aware, and as watchful as a soldier riding into unknown territory, scouting it out for his commander. He wore no uniform but a fashionable gentleman's, but nevertheless she thought he looked very like her own father must have done when he'd two arms: one to hold the reins, and the other to rest lightly at his hip near to where his scabbard would have been.

They were obviously bound for the church; and most likely, she thought, in order to view in the sanctuary. The church wasn't famous but it was in some guidebooks, and was quite the oldest thing in the vicinity, except for the baron's finds. But his excavations had no roofs, and little to see, and certainly less on such a frigid afternoon, for even the baron had given up digging until spring.

But perhaps, Sybil thought, daydreaming as usual, but twice as fast because she'd something new and interesting to feed the omipresent dreams that whiled away her dull days, they were bound for the church to look up records of some ancestor, perhaps to find an heir to a legacy . . . perhaps a girl, for instance, who'd never known she was related to a duchess, and so was the long-lost heir to a fortune . . . and a castle . . . on the Rhine . . . no, Spain, she corrected herself quickly, it was warmer there . . . and . . .

She was genuinely startled when the bell above her door jangled as the door swung open. It brought in a blast of cold air and reality, and then unreality again; because when she looked up from her dreams, the two elegant gentlemen from her newest dream stood there before her in her shop.

The blond man looked around the small flower-filled room, his eyes searching everything but seemingly noticing nothing. She was disappointed to see that he was fairly thickset, his face bore a petulant cast better suited to a child than a conquerer, and in all he was not at all majestic, seen up close. But then she realized she was being stared at. She turned her head to gaze at his companion. The slender gentleman smiled at her. But though his smile was friendly enough, and showed a handsome display of even white teeth, it looked the sort of smile that wasn't given unless it was needful. He'd smooth light brown hair beneath his beaver hat, and even features set in a lean countenance. From this close he was far more attractive than he'd been from afar. But she couldn't judge exactly why, because his large gray-brown eyes were as observant as they were blandly colored— so much so she found she couldn't study his face at all when he was looking at her.

"Good afternoon," he said in a pleasant even tenor. "We were wondering if you'd some roses."

"I'm sorry," she said, for she was, "but they're all being forced for Valentine's Day."

"O cruel one," he said with a more realistic smile. "Sorry, Cousin," he remarked to his companion, although his eyes never left her face, "but we've obviously stumbled into a den of floral persecution. It seems there isn't a rose available, they're all off being molested."

The blond gentleman looked blank.

"But we've amaryllis and violets. And orchids, of course," Sybil said, dimpling as she bit back a smile.

"What? You've not got Amaryllis chained to a rock, and Violet being soundly thrashed?" the slender gentleman teased.

Sybil could no longer hide her amusement. "No, no," she said as he cocked his head to the side at the sound of her rippling laughter, "they're in fine fettle, I assure you. All we've done is cut them a little, and they're quite impervious to snubs, I assure you," she added, getting into the spirit of things.

Sybil and the slender gentleman laughed together, but all the while he watched her with something closer to secret glee than simple merriment. She'd always considered herself merely a medium-size girl with reddish hair and earth-brown eyes, and if she was vain about anything, it was the wave in her hair and the tilt to her eyes, and she'd never considered either attribute so remarkable as to make any gentleman stare. But she'd been brought up in a small village, and had long since decided that men liked her for her wit, and pursued her because there was a scarcity of unmarried girls in her village. Valerian saw a shapely young woman with brandy-snap eyes and chestnut hair, and a smooth white complexion to offset her delicate features. And he heard her wit and rejoiced in it.

But Bolton saw something else entirely.

He pinched his cousin's arm, hard. And then, realizing that he still wore his riding gloves so that Valerian hadn't felt a thing, he was reduced to prodding him in the ribs with his riding crop until he'd got his attention away from the young woman.

"Orchids," he muttered, lifting his light brows significantly when Valerian turned to look at him in annoyance.

"Roses," his cousin corrected him, and shrugging his wide shoulders, turned back to the young woman again.

"As it happens," Valerian said, "we've no need to put either Amaryllis or Violet to any further distress. We'd like some roses please, and we're willing to take them when their trials are over. We need them for Valentine's Day."

"Oh. But I'm terribly sorry," Sybil said, and she was, because he was the most enchanting gentleman she'd ever spoken to, and the thought of him not returning in time to collect his roses was as painful as the thought of whoever he was buying them for, "but they're all reserved. And no," she said quickly as she saw him about to speak, "no amount of cajolery or encouragement can loosen them up."

She laughed with him again, and then said seriously, and with regret, "We simply haven't enough to go around. But you've time. You might try Middleborough, that's a few miles to the east of us, or Slocum, a few hours' ride to the north. And of course, as you've almost two weeks, I'm positive you can send to London for some.

"In fact," Sybil said, thinking aloud, as she so

often did in the long days that she tended the store by herself, "I don't know why you didn't think of that first. Oh. Pardon me," she said, but as she wasn't a missish sort of female, she said it with chagrin and not a rosy blush, "I expect you were passing by and thought we could do . . . But I'm afraid we can't. We're only a local shop, with not half the resources one in a bigger town might have."

"The Baron Blackwood sent us," Valerian said softly. "We're his nephews. I am Valerian Blackwood, and this is my cousin, Bolton."

"Charmed," Bolton said absently, and then added, "Orchids," as he poked Valerian with his riding crop again and waggled his eyebrows.

"Oh!" Sybil said, curtsying, "I'm Sybil Prentice, sirs," and frowning so that Valerian found himself wanting to say anything that might erase the two lines that formed, marring her smooth brow between her puzzled eyes, she added, "I don't know why the baron sent you to us. We generally know our customers and their needs, and seldom have any excess—and we couldn't disappoint any of our usual clients . . . but . . . if you wish," she said more brightly, "we can send to London for you, and at least save you that trouble. Red or white? And how many do you think you'd require?"

"That is a problem," Valerian said as he continued to gaze at her. "What should you suggest? She's a young girl, lovely," he said in a low caressing voice, "surpassingly lovely," he went on as he stared at her, "surprisingly and enchantingly lovely, in fact. Shall it be white for her obvious purity, do you think? Or red for the passion she tries so hard to conceal? White, to signify the donor's blameless intentions toward her? Or red, for the color of his true love? Whatever they're to be, they must be fresh and fragrant, and as unexpectedly lovely as spring suddenly discovered in the midst of February—as she herself is."

Sybil found herself enthralled, staring into the depths of his moth-soft gray-brown eyes as he spoke. When he'd done, she recalled herself and then almost visibly shook herself back to awareness again. The slightest tinge of color appeared on her cheeks as she said, more sharply than she'd intended, "Perhaps pink, then? Not quite as passionate a declaration as red, nor so honest as white, perhaps, but under the circumstances—you did say she was young?—perhaps more politic?"

"An offering of compromise in the face of love? Fie, Miss Prentice," Valerian answered, grinning at her clever defense, now enjoying himself hugely.

"Compromise is always preferable to audaciousness, sir," she answered, lowering her lashes against the laughter in his eyes.

"Red being too forward too soon, and white too innocent a declaration in light of his obvious interest? Perhaps," Valerian mused, "but compromise wins no battles."

"It does, however," she said primly, "secure the peace."

"Bravo!" Valerian crowed, and as they laughed together, Bolton, confused and agitated, pointed a gloved forefinger and said, "What are you on about? Here, that bunch of orchids there is what I want."

"Orchids are never the thing for Valentine's Day," Valerian said absently. "We're ordering up roses for the lady."

"Orchids are perhaps more suitable for a more mature lady," Sybil agreed, remembering her duties and position, "and I'm afraid that though they're far sturdier than they look, they'd never last the weeks until the day."

"I'll take 'em anyway," Bolton persisted. "Nothing wrong with giving a lady flowers on a regular day, is there?"

"Why, Cousin," Valerian said with interest, looking away from Sybil for the first time since he'd seen her, "I believe you are smitten, at that."

"Well, never said I wasn't," Bolton said uncomfortably, avoiding his eye.

"Very well. And we'll order up a dozen blushing pink roses for your lady for Valentine's, as well. Is that all right, Cousin?" Valerian asked, as Sybil, who'd plucked the orchids up and begun to wrap them in silver paper, stopped to draw a breath of sheer relief as she heard whose lady the roses were for.

"Aye, fine," Bolton said distractedly, watching the orchids being tucked up in their wraps.

Valerian settled the bill and stayed on awhile to discuss roses with Sybil, and would have been content to stay on for hours more, discussing anything else that he could think up. But he finally had to take his leave, since Bolton was standing at the door all the while, clearing his throat repeatedly and shifting from foot to foot, as though he couldn't wait to be gone to present his bouquet to his lady.

So Valerian was considerably surprised when Bolton began to tear the paper from the orchids the moment they rode out of sight of the shop window.

"Here! Stop that!" he commanded, shaken from his contemplation of the past hour as he saw the orchids again. "It's frigid out here. You'll freeze their little purple heads off."

"Look!" Bolton said triumphantly, leaning over to wave a flower beneath his nose. "Don't know much about flowers, but I do know this one. Eh? Eh?" he said triumphantly as his cousin took the bloom in one gloved hand. He stared at the otherwise perfect orchid disfigured by a tear and a long brown crease across its bottom lip, where it had obviously been damaged.

"The same one uncle broke yesterday, or its twin, or I'm a blind man!" Bolton said with great satisfaction. "Now do you believe me? There's things being carried off from that house. This is only a rubbishy flower. Who knows what else of mine is being flogged in the village shops?"

Valerian's hand tightened on the flower until the creased petal was the least of its defects.

"Hey? Eh?" Bolton said. "And so now what do we do?"

"We look," Valerian said, spurring his horse, "for a one-armed man. And," he added grimly, for it was more than disappointment he felt, it was the pang of disillusion again, "his cohorts."

But first they had to finish an interview with their uncle. For he called them into his study the moment they arrived back at the Hall. Miss Exeter was already there, and the baron ushered them in too, rubbing his hands together, his reedy voice for once filled with pride, not complaint.

"Now, here, Bolton," the baron said, waving them to a long table covered with bits and pieces of metal, clay, and stone, "are some of the finds I'd thought to donate. Since you've a bee in your bonnet—no, no, no sense denying it just because Georgette is here, we've just been talking about it together—you think I'm robbing you of your inheritance. Well, and so, have a look. Whatever you wish to keep, you may. Whatever else, I want you to agree I may dispose of as I see fit. I've got them all listed here," he said, handing a paper to Bolton, "and when you're done with your inspection, I'd like you to sign it in front of my secretary, Mr. Lane, so it's all perfectly legal. Now, come, come, lad. Have a look."

"Don't know what I'm looking at," Bolton said, red-faced.

"Naturally not," the baron said briskly.

Miss Exeter gave Bolton a sympathetic glance as he glowered at the tabletop cluttered with artifacts.

"That's what I'm here for now," the baron went on with a show of outsize patience. "No sense wondering what I've given away after I'm dead and there aren't two men in the kingdom who know the value of my little treasures, is there? Now, then," he went on in a thin, high singsong— his usual lecturing mode, Valerian thought resignedly—"here's a bit of a buckle. Celtic. Comes from a belt, I'm sure. Unfortunately incomplete. Ah, but this is an almost-complete cup, same era, earthenware . . . who knows what elixirs it held in its glorious day? Mead? Water? Ale? Or some other unsung draft of our ancestors' brewing?" he asked with pleasure before he reluctantly moved on to the next piece, a bit of metal he claimed was part of a sandal, which he waxed rhapsodic about for some time—until Valerian moved things along by asking about a cracked pot near to it on the table.

Miss Exeter stood silently, watching and listening with awe that bordered on reverence as the baron displayed his finds. Bolton stood silently, scowling. And Valerian waited patiently.

Once the baron got to the part of the table with the Roman artifacts, he moved along more smartly: Roman history, he explained haughtily, not being his favorite avocation. Still, all that was antique ought to be reverenced, he said, although some ancient peoples scarcely deserved it. His uncle still considered the Romans unwelcome intruders, Valerian thought with enough humor to make the lecture barely bearable.

"Here! What's this?" Bolton said, awakening from his dumb silence, "gold, did you say?"

"Yes," the baron answered with a bitter smile, holding the half-coin he was discussing aloft, "but the only way you'd realize any worth from it would be to melt it down and sell it for weight in London. Of course, that way generations of school-children would never know what the Emperor Hadrian looked like. But you'd have a few more coins yourself, so do what you will." He shrugged his thin shoulders.

Bolton grew ruddier. "Never mind," he muttered, "rubbishing bit wouldn't be worth the effort. I say, sir, can we have done? I don't see anything I want."

"But there's gold here," the baron said with barely concealed spite, showing his nephew a piece of a plate and a strand of a necklace. "And here," he said, holding up a flat, thick bracelet, "gold, as well. Would you model it, Georgette, my dear?" he asked.

Miss Exeter held out one white wrist, and the baron slipped the wide band around it, where it hung, clumsy and dirty, an abomination on that fragile slender arm.

"Take it off," Bolton said in disgust.

"Yes, and hand it here," Valerian said suddenly. "I think it's a handsome piece. What's it worth, Uncle?" he asked curiously as he turned the heavy band round and round in his long fingers, where it looked far better than it had on a slight feminine arm.

Bolton looked interested, until his uncle answered.

"Worth? Oh, it's Roman," he said on a sniff. "There's no price that can be put on it, you see," he went on, clearing his throat, obviously about to launch into yet another interminable explanation of the inferiority of the ancient Romans, and why native Britons were so superior, as illustrated by a discussion of comparative arts and vices.

"Never mind!" Bolton said hurriedly as the baron began to sneer over the name "Hadrian" again. "I've heard enough. And seen it too. I'll sign the paper. I don't want these things—none of it. There's something else I want to discuss with you, sir."

The baron stopped speaking, crestfallen. And the kindhearted Miss Exeter shot a reproachful look to Bolton and begged the baron, "Oh, thir, pleath do go on. I thought it fathinating, truly, I did."

And so the baron's nephews excused themselves and went to cool their heels in deep chairs in their uncle's study, while he droned on and on about the days of Hadrian and his wall, and how very fortunate it was that bits of it were still in evidence on the grounds of his own Hall itself, as Miss Exeter listened, and cooed, unfortunately for them, in all the right places.

The man the two nephews finally located and cornered near a stand of tropical plants in the orangery stood tall, even though his interrogators towered over him. He was of medium height and age, but in good condition for a man of his years, and wore a gardener's smock. But his clothes were otherwise neat and clean, and the one hand he held his trowel in was covered only by fresh soil, not accumulated dirt. The other hand was missing. When he saw Bolton staring, he showed white teeth in a small smile, and glancing at his empty sleeve, said only, "I misplaced it at a place named New Jersey, sir, in the late unpleasantness there. It was not so popular or successful an effort as your recent one in the Peninsula, Captain," he said, turning to Valerian, "but it was as bitterly waged. The natives called themselves New Englanders, but they'd little wish to actually be such, as the baron and I soon discovered."

"Would I had been as successful as you say," Valerian said ruefully, before he added, "ah, but we both know a soldier can't pick his war's popularity or its success, can he? And please, the captain and I parted company the day I set sail for England again. Although I know some men enjoy being styled officers forever, I find myself quite pleased with the title 'Mister' these days; it involves a deal less ducking, not to mention bleeding. So you served with Uncle in the Americas?" he asked.

"I served under the baron then, and still do," the gardener said, nodding, "and like it better this way, by far. Now the things I put beneath the earth rise up again."

Valerian smiled. But Bolton's patience was at an end.

"Enough chitchat," he said. "See here, my good fellow, I found an orchid that was here the other day in a village shop the next day, and I'd like to know how it got there."

The gardener gave him a long steady look. "Are you a horticulturist too, then, sir? Should you like a closer look at this new one I just put in? It's rare, a nice bloomer too, if a little on the fragile side. But the amber tones are unique, as you must know."

"None of your insolence, my man," Bolton raged, "you know very well what I mean. How did it get there? And how many other things of my uncle's find their way to market?"

"I know of nothing taken from this house that shouldn't be, sir," the gardener said quietly.

"Now, see here, fellow," Bolton said threateningly, until he felt his cousin's hand rest lightly but firmly on his arm.

"My cousin is grieved, but not accusing you," Valerian explained, "although I'll grant it does appear so," he added, giving Bolton a cold look. "It's only that we did see a bloom from this room for sale in the village yesterday, and as he's our uncle's heir, you can see he has a certain proprietary interest in things that come from this house."

"Nothing's taken from this house that shouldn't be," the gardener repeated, looking Valerian full in the eye. "If you've a question as to the disposal of any articles, I suggest you ask the baron, sir. He is not young. But he is not addled."

"No, that's true," Valerian agreed ruefully, "though sometimes I believe we'd all be better off if he were."

"I say!" Bolton exclaimed, looking from one man's growing smile to the other's. "Are you going to let it go at that?"

"Certainly," Valerian said, nodding to the gardener as he steered Bolton from the room, and adding just loudly enough for the gardener not to miss hearing as he did, "I'm no fool either. Good God! Bolton, didn't you see? The fellow's still got his sword arm."

They heard appreciative chuckles from behind them as they left the room.

*   *   *

There were housemaids and footmen, stableboys and cook's helpers, the butler and a housekeeper and other household help to interrogate. And Valerian's opinion of his cousin's expertise at such sleuthing was no secret to Bolton, especially after his interview with the gardener. So then Bolton didn't understand why his cousin mounted up the next morning, leaving him to do the artful questioning, and Miss Exeter to their uncle's tutorage, while he rode off to see the village florist again. Still, Valerian's explanation—that all tracking must begin either at the source or the destination—sounded sensible enough, and was grudgingly accepted. Only his expression at his departure wasn't. For Valerian rode out in higher spirits than a man off to question a suspect ought to have enjoyed.

But he did enjoy it, all of it: the freedom, the foolishness, and the folly of visiting with a lovely and intelligent young woman, whatever excuse he made for it, however he knew he'd be bound to be disappointed again—by discovery of her complicity either in this scheme or in others. Because every female he'd met in the past years had been on the catch for something: marriage or money or both. He'd never anything to fear, he'd both to offer if he wanted to. It was only that he'd never wanted to give anything but money for his pleasure, and his pleasure was always diminished because he did. But this case was unique, because he didn't have to offer anything, only to listen and look.

He was as eager to visit Miss Prentice in order to see her face and form and hear her conversation as he was to discover her innocence or guilt. It was possible she was knowingly selling stolen goods. But again, it was also possible she'd no idea of it. And in a life that had been too filled with immutables and probables, the possibility of innocence was enough to send him off to the village with hopes—if not outright dreams. For he'd forgotten that he even had any of those left.

And it was so easy for him too. If she'd been a sheltered society lady, he'd have to offer at least the possibility of his hand in order to experience even such a tame delight as the mere pleasure of a visit with her; if she were a woman of the underclass, he'd only have to offer money. But luckily for him, she seemed to be a respectable workingwoman, and so it would cost him absolutely nothing but his time and trouble to have what he wanted of her today—her unchaperoned company. With a smile and a silent thanks to the modern world for having created such newfound freedom for women, he rode on toward the village. Of course he was aware of the danger of his situation and in his reasoning. But he'd been a good soldier precisely because he'd never refined upon danger, only faced up to it.

"I've a problem, ma'am," he announced as he walked into her shop.

The vicar's wife knew no one on earth could have a problem of the magnitude of the one she had. But she was definitely willing to stop discussing hers in order to listen to his. She was in the shop to decide which flowers to buy to decorate her tea table, and to purchase oranges for the bishops's delectation on his coming visit—and she wasn't sure of how many of which to buy, as she'd been telling Miss Prentice for the past half-hour. Because the display of flowers and fruit couldn't be so extravagant as to give the bishop false ideas about their economy, but neither should it be so paltry as to give a wrong idea of their ability to entertain. The handsome and elegant stranger that had just burst into the shop mightn't have a problem of *that* scope, but he was certainly worth hearing, if only so that she could repeat the tale frequently to other ladies in the village.

"Your pardon, madam," Valerian said at once, seeing the other woman in the shop with Sybil. "Excuse me, I can wait my turn."

"Oh, no," the vicar's wife insisted. "I can wait, I assure you, sir."

After a round of insistence and denials, Valerian was forced, in light of the fact that a lady must always have her say, to baldly state what he'd hoped to say after a pleasurable hour of teasing and jests.

"Ah, umm," he invented rapidly, for he found he couldn't even say that with the hawk-eyed lady watching him, "my cousin thinks that purely pink roses are too bland an offering, Miss Prentice. He thought, perhaps, a sprinkling of red and white in with them would do. What do you think?"

"My heavens, no!" the vicar's wife gasped. "Everyone know it's the worst sort of luck to mix red and white roses, sir. Some think it dates from the War of the Roses, and actually that makes sense, what with the misfortune of one side bearing the sign of the white rose and the other the red. Others believe it is because it signifies the red of blood and the white of bandaging, as does a barber's pole, but however it came about, it is decidedly considered a bad omen."

"You must be acquainted with my uncle, the Baron Blackwood," Valerian said wryly.

"Indeed, I am," the vicar's wife said, preening.

"Well, then," Valerian said hurriedly as he saw her draw breath for further explanation, "I suppose it will have to be pink with either white or red added. Perhaps yellow," he said quickly. "I'd best go tell him about this new turn of events and get his opinion on the matter. I'll be back," he said, bowing to both ladies, and after one sad and lingering look at the new way Sibyl had drawn her hair up from the nape of her neck, he left them.

But when he came back an hour later, after cooling his heels in the town livery, discussing fetlocks and furlongs until he was heartily sick of it, Mrs. Nelson was there, pricing pineapple. And when she left, he'd only begun to flirt around the corners of his topic while watching the shapely corners of Sybil's lips lift with each of his jests, when Mrs. Marlowe came in to buy a little nosegay to pick up her ailing neighbor's spirits. She was followed by Miss Hathaway, from down the street, who came to buy a few violets for her hall table. Mrs. Morris came in shortly after, to finger some lilies and ask their prices. By now Sybil realized it was her elegant male visitor, not her wares, that was attracting so much attention, and that made her smile even more. Until Valerian finally gave up, muttered something about pink and white being suitable, thank you very much, and left. Then she looked after him with such sorrow that Mrs. Morris actually bought a lily.

When Valerian returned to the Hall to dress for dinner, Bolton admitted he'd only gotten to interview the butler and the housekeeper and had only learned that the butler was as closemouthed as he was crafty, and that the housekeeper had problems with her legs, her heart, her veins and her two daughters-in-law. Valerian, while not admitting that he'd forgotten to look, did allow that he'd not recognized any blossoms from the orangery at the shop this time. In so doing, he realized he'd an excellent excuse for returning the next day, and brightened considerably as he addressed his soup.

They'd a quiet dinner that night, with Bolton sulking, Valerian musing on the coming day, and Miss Exeter's companion listening to the baron and her charge discussing various Viking burial rites.

But the next day Miss Prentice's little shop was even more crowded. It was so filled with various observant townsfolk that Valerian could scarcely have seen what sort of flowers it contained, even if he'd been looking anywhere but at Miss Prentice, and how well she looked in a new blue frock. It wasn't until the day after that that Valerian began to realize, from Sybil's sweetly helpless expression and the shrug she gave her shapely shoulders when she saw him, after he'd managed to wedge into her tiny shop, that he was the reason for the crowd.

It was true Valentine's Day was approaching, but that was no reason for the sudden silence that fell as the crowd parted like some biblical sea as he made his way over to tell her that Bolton had decided on all pink, after all, regardless of what he'd said the day before. No, Valerian realized, unless someone in the town was of royal blood and had recently died, there was no real reason that a flower shop should be so suddenly and increasingly popular. And though he'd never considered himself so fascinating as to draw a crowd, the way this particular crowd drew in its collective breath so as not to miss a word when he spoke convinced him of his newfound fame, even as Miss Prentice's sparkling eyes and barely suppressed amusement did.

* * *

"May I take you to tea this afternoon?" Valerian asked the next day, just as Sybil was approaching the door to her shop.

She had to stop a moment to catch her breath at the sight of him, not to mention the surprise he'd given her, suddenly appearing beside her from out of the mists of morning as he had, while her mind was elsewhere. He wore a greatcoat and a high beaver hat, and the look in his eyes did not belong to such an early hour of the morning. Or at least not in the circles she traveled in, she thought sadly—as she always did when she contemplated the differences in their ranks. As she had so often of late.

"You see, I surrender," he said. "The good folk of your town have routed me entirely. There's no way I can speak to you in your shop, and I do want to talk with you, about many things other than flowers. There's a tea shop just down the street. At three, then?"

He gazed down at her as she stared up at him as she stood with her hand arrested on the knob of the door to her shop. There were a dozen light things she could have said. And a dozen more proper things she should, and several more she wanted to say. But it was as though they'd already passed that unfamiliar stage of acquaintance, as if his eyes alone had already said so many things to her, the sort of things she'd heard him say in her imagination since they'd met. So she said what was foremost on her mind, what she knew was the last thing she ought to have, and later thought it was because of the unexpectedness of their meeting, and the strange, early hour of the day.

"Why?" she asked.

He stayed still, studying her carefully. The tip

of her nose was red with cold, and her face was white with distraction, but he never saw red and white so beautifully intermingled in any bouquet. But it must have been an unlucky thought, just as the vicar's wife had said. For when he spoke at last, still looking deep into her great worried amber eyes, he found himself saying the wrong thing.

"That's a very good question," he said.

"Because," she said, for having burned her bridges she was determined to say it all as the flames still roared in her ears, "you are a gentleman, you see. I've asked. A man of means and fortune and a place in society. And I am just a girl from this village. There's nothing wrong with that, of course, but most girls from your world who are my age—I am twenty—are going to balls and being presented at court and such. I'm convinced you'd never ask them to tea without a chaperone. I'm not saying you mean me ill. But still and all, though I'm well-bred, and quite bright, I think," she said in a rush, before she could stop herself, "I'm in no way the sort of female a gentleman such as yourself would take to tea for any reason my father would approve of, I think."

He remained very still.

"No, I mean you no harm," he said. "Teatime tomorrow, then? Please."

"Yes," she said.

And turned to unlock the door to her shop, feeling cold in the pit of her stomach, knowing she'd said the wrong thing, as he turned to go back to the Hall again, sick at having not said the right thing.

He interviewed some stableboys during the day, when he wasn't riding off in whatever direction the wind was blowing. And learned nothing he wouldn't have known even if he had been listening to what they said with more than half an ear. Then he passed his time writing to his secretary in London, authorizing him to pay a sum of money to a certain female—as severance. He wasn't being previous, he told himself, or even precisely anticipating anything. It was only that the more he thought about such a union, and he thought about it far more now than when he'd entered into it, the more it seemed absurd—if not obscene—in view of the sort of female he was spending even more time thinking about these days and nights.

Bolton harried chambermaids and chivied footmen, and was finally ordered out of the kitchen by the cook for his inquiries. He spent the rest of the afternoon fingering fabrics and inspecting walls, wondering what priceless antique chairs had been there before they'd been replaced by merely comfortable ones, speculating about what priceless paintings had hung where wallpapers did now. By dinnertime the only thing that was sure, as Bolton told his cousin ominously, was that some people knew something all right, but he didn't know quite what yet.

He passed dinner brooding over lost masterpieces. Valerian kept considering what his priorities in life really were, when he wasn't wondering how he could be worrying about something so profound when he'd only had a few minutes' speech with her altogether since they'd met, after all. And the baron and Miss Exeter had a spirited discussion about Pictish coming-of-age ceremonies.

"The problem," Valerian said when he'd got Sibyl seated opposite him at a table near to the window so that all the passersby could see what they'd have crammed into the tea shop to see if he hadn't, "is where can a gentleman go to speak with a lady? Just as you said," he added as she looked up from her gloves at his words and opened her lips to speak.

"Because you do have a chaperone, you know," he went on, gesturing to the window. "It is this whole town. And as I know you won't go out of town with me, how else can we come to know each other?"

She gathered up all her courage and asked what she didn't want to because she knew she had to, even though she dreaded losing the pleasure of his company, even if only just for this brief hour she'd been so eagerly and fearfully anticipating since she'd promised it to him.

"Why should we come to know each other?" she asked.

"You know far better than that," he said.

She did. So she smiled. And over tea, tried to tell him about herself, as he asked, when she wasn't asking him about himself. But they didn't get very far with that. When they weren't distracted by being caught staring at each other, they kept being caught up in digressions: foolish little stories about his childhood in Kent, and her first riding lessons, and his forgetful governess, and her best friend Charlotte's spotted dog.

When they met again two days later, they were both privately resolved to get down to cases. He told himself he already knew she had the faintest hint of a cleft to the left of center of her small chin, and a tiny spot over her upper lip that looked as if it were a spot of chocolate that he yearned to taste as well. But he really did have to know why she was selling orchids from the baron's orangery, for damn his soldier's eye, he thought, he couldn't help but notice that she still did.

And she resolved that even though she'd never seen such soft gray-brown eyes—for all he was pleased to mock them as "mouse-brown"—with the most caring, kind, and thrillingly disturbing expression in them that she'd ever seen in any man's eyes, still she definitely had to tell him she couldn't meet him like this anymore. Because even with the whole of England as her chaperone, there wasn't any future in it; she knew that as well as she didn't know what she'd do if she could never see him again.

He began by bringing up the subject of Bolton's valentine flowers. But they ended up interrupting each other, laughing and trying to tell each other about the worst Valentine's Day they'd ever passed. He told her about Miss Chivingham and the party she'd given when they were ten years old. And she told him about Mr. Harrington, and the wild proposal he had made—to her, her best friend, and then, in desperation, to Mary Price, and what she'd said.

When they stopped laughing they found themselves talking about other dreadful days. And somehow he found himself talking about the whole of it that day at Salamanaca, at last. Although he apologized profusely when he realized what he'd done by the tears in her eyes, he realized he didn't have to when she told him about that moment her father had wakened her to tell her that though the seven days of crisis of pneumonia had passed, so, too, with it, had her mother.

But teatime only lasted so long. And when he walked her the few steps back to her shop, he realized with equal parts chagrin and delight that he'd learned nothing of what he'd supposedly come for. So he at once asked her to come out to tea with him again in two days' time. Then she shocked him at last, although he had, in some way, been expecting it.

"No, I'm terribly sorry, you know I am," she said, "but I cannot, and I think you know that too."

"Yes," he said, and for the first time in their acquaintance touched her, putting out a hand to stop her as she walked away. "But I can't say what I must here in the street," he said.

Still, when he got her alone in the shop after they'd walked in, and he'd closed the door behind them, he didn't say anything either. He just took her in his arms and kissed her. And drew back and chided her gently for her lack of response. When she bridled and asked just what was wrong with it, he took her back again and kissed her lips, now opened to his in outrage, as he'd wished them to be, and then in wonder, as he'd scarcely dared to hope they'd be.

"The problem," he eventually said in a warm chuckle against her hair, forgetting any other than the most immediate one, "is how to convince you we suit, and that the only rank that I've ever had to be concerned with was when I was in the army."

"But we scarcely know each other," she protested as she breathed in the clean scent of him and waited for him to deny it as she would have if he'd said it to her.

But he only kissed her again, instead.

Bliss was all very well, but Sybil had a realistic turn of mind, even when her emotions were overturned to the point that she could feel caution slipping away as he touched her breast, and fear disappearing as he whispered her name as he did.

"I have a small dowry, and no social standing," she managed to protest.

"I have a great deal of money and some social standing, and I have a pocket watch that chimes the hour too," he said smugly, "so I win. What else do you want?" he asked, touching his lips to the delicious spot that tasted, he'd discovered, far better than chocolate.

"Oh . . . Valerian," she sighed.

"Oh, that paltry fellow?" he breathed before he kissed her again. "But you already have him.

"Now," he said, when he finally found the will-power necessary to just hold her close, "as to where I can find your father? You're going to marry me, you know," he said, "You have to. Half the village knows we've been standing in here alone with a 'closed' sign on the door. And no one needs to have a private viewing of flowers, except," he said, his eyes shining, "if one is look-ing at a perfect bloom—such as that on your cheeks when I do this . . . or this . . .

"To think," he said on a shaking sigh as he stopped kissing and caressing her and helping her to do the same to him, because there was no way he could go on to do what he wished now, "this all started because of flowers."

"Roses," she sighed.

"Orchids," he murmured absently, suddenly realizing that he did have her willingness, as well as the privacy to do at least some of what he wished, and wishing he hadn't the scruples, or at least the caution he did, so that he might try to, "all because Bolton and I wanted to find out why you were selling orchids and . . ."

It was, of course, the wrong way to phrase it. But it had to be said, after all, so it was as well that it slipped out when he wasn't thinking of any-thing stolen, but only of all that had been given so freely to him. He felt her body grow stiff before she pushed herself away and stared up at him.

"We saw the orchids and recognized them," he explained gently. "They were from the baron's orangery. Bolton's got a bee in his bonnet about his legacy being sold out from under him. It's not that he doesn't trust the baron so much as he can't believe he's got nothing of value to leave him, so he's started an investigation, and the orchids were the only thing he could be sure about, you see . . ."

"And you thought I was a thief?" she asked, tears starting to shimmer in her eyes.

"I didn't know. And then I supposed I didn't care . . . no," he said honestly, holding her by her shoulders and staring down at her gravely, "of course I'd care. Love is not blind. Not really. Only blindfolded, like Cupid when he shoots his arrows, so that it doesn't know where it's going at first. But then it does. For as I grew to know you, I knew you weren't a thief, and could never be one. I don't know how you came to the flowers, but I know it was an honest way."

"My father," she said carefully, watching him closely, wondering if this last thing he didn't know would be the one thing to end her beautiful living fantasy, "gave them to me. But he is entitled to them. He's the baron's gardener. And they're part of his wages. They're old friends as well as comrades in arms. And they can never agree on who saved whose life. The baron doesn't care for flowers any more than my father does for charity, so they worked out the arrangement by slow degrees. In all we spoke about, we never spoke about this. It wasn't a deliberate omission on my part," she said, even as she wondered, for the first time, if it had been. And then, as if in defiance of that, she lifted her chin and said, "But there it is. My father is a gardener now, however he came to it."

She stood very still, watching him. And saw the surprise, and then the amazement, and then the dawning laughter in his face. And then, gladly, gratefully, came back into his arms, where he wanted her.

"Lucky that my intentions are honorable, then—that *is* his sword arm that he still has, isn't it?" he asked.

"Want-wit, moonling," he said affectionately as he kissed away her tears. "As if it mattered. You didn't tell me, nor did I ask. We'd so much else to discuss, so many more important things, and still do. I don't know if you prefer mulberries to strawberries yet, or what your favorite color is. Shall he like me, do you think?" he asked, to stem her weeping, because he wasn't quite sure if she was sobbing or chuckling against his chest. But when she raised her face, he saw it was both. He kissed her again before she could answer, to turn it all to sighs.

"Yes," she said when he let her go again, "he does. He likes you very much. He mentioned it, as a matter of fact."

"Generous of him," Valerian muttered, "considering how Bolton treated him. But I never suspected him after I met him the once. But hear this," he said with absolute sincerity, giving her shoulders a light shake, "I'm glad I suspected you. How else should I have come to know you?"

"I sent you to her, remember?" the baron said with smug satisfaction when they made their announcement to him in his study the next day. "It hardly mattered if you suspected her of treachery, although that was delightfully convenient.

Suspicion brings people together—just think of Mark Antony and Cleopatra. Or rather, don't. Cleopatra can be excused, but you see how poorly he acted? Roman, after all," he said, shaking his head sadly.

"I knew you two would deal well together," the baron continued. "I told Prentice so. Yet I could scarcely introduce you, could I? My matchmaking would have scandalized you, Sybil, my dear, and would have definitely set Valerian's back up. No, I had to be devious. You see," he said, linking his hands behind his back so that he could deliver a lecture, as Valerian looked at Sybil and grinned, and she, a respectful girl, tried not to, "I told you I'd spent most of my monies on my excavations. Bolton was quite right, there were bits of art and furniture sold off, but years ago, to finance my excavations. Still, what were they but Da Vincis and Cellinis, Sheratons and Aubussons—modern art, after all?

"And what is money to you, Nephew?" the baron asked as he paced. "No, when I began to think about posterity after the impudence of Bolton's letter to me, I realized I had to leave you something of value even if I'd little you'd consider of value any more than Bolton did—if for entirely different reasons. He only wanted money. You . . . ah, you are a man of taste. It posed a problem. And too, I preferred that whatever I found for you be yours whilst I could still enjoy your enjoyment of it. If archaeology has taught me nothing else, it is that the past is truly buried and that one must appreciate life in the present.

"I pondered it. As I well know, something one finds for oneself is always more greatly valued than something handed to one. Then I hit upon it. I did put something of great value in your path for you to discover, did I not? Consider Sybil your valentine's gift—from a doting uncle," he said on a huff of a laugh at the very idea. "And he, yours from an old friend, of course, my dear," the baron added, catching a glimpse at Sybil's face, caught between flattery and annoyance.

"And oh, on that score, Valerian," the baron went on, "I'm giving you that Roman bracelet you admired as a wedding present. No, no," he said immediately, waving one thin hand, "don't thank me, it is not a thing one can price, but I believe you liked it, and so I should think Sybil would too."

"Indeed, I did, we thank you," Valerian said with an admirably straight face. "And now that you've got me so handsomely provided for, Uncle, and I've your blessings to boot, we have to deliver a sheaf of pink roses to Bolton so he can win his living inheritance: his—or rather, your—chosen bride, for him."

"Ah, well," the baron said as a tinge of color touched his paper-white cheeks. "I fear Bolton was too hesitant there. He was so taken up with his investigations, which, I repeat, there was no need for, that he shamefully neglected poor Georgette. I'm afraid she'll never have him, and yet I can only be glad of it, for she was far too good for him, you know."

"She's off to London, then?" Valerian asked.

"Ah, no, she's going to marry me," the baron said.

When the silence had gone on long enough to be deafening, the baron added in his most grieved and whining voice, "She has always longed for her father, you see, and so appreciates older men. So I should be pleased if you'd manage to close your mouth by the time you see her at dinner and offer her your felicitations, Nephew.

"And do restrain your sympathies, Sybil," the baron went on pettishly at the sight of Sybil's transparent distress, "for if you speak with her you'll understand that she's always been distressed at how the combination of her perfect beauty and natural lisp—which is a great trial to her, no matter how fashionable it is—has caused young men to treat her as a wigeon and disregard what she considers to be her considerable intelligence. It made her unbearably shy, and most unhappy. But no longer. She's fascinated by my excavations, you see, and it just so happens," he added with a smile that took years from his face, making him appear merely aged, "that she's got a dowry and income from her funds that will keep us happily digging for years."

"And so Bolton will eventually have his legacy, after all," Valerian murmured into his fiancée's ear, glad of the excuse to breathe in her fragrance again, but still not whispering softly enough to escape his uncle's sharp ears.

"I shouldn't get his hopes up," the baron snapped. "Georgette doesn't consider me old in that sense at all. It well may be that you'll be presented with a new infant cousin before you are a father, my boy."

"Then Bolton . . ." Valerian began when he'd control of his voice again.

"Will get the roses, obviously," the baron said.

It wasn't until Sybil and Valerian's eldest son was at university, and home on vacation one rainy afternoon, that he came upon his parents' wedding gift in the attics while rummaging for some oddments to entertain his sisters with. He took it to his cousin, who although only a year older than himself, was, in defiance of his father, already an authority in the field of Roman antiquities. It transpired that the bracelet, just as the baron had said, had no price that could be attached to it. Because it was, as the baron had always known, the Emperor Hadrian's own armband, and as such, it was, of course, priceless—although never as valuable to Valerian as his valentine's gift turned out to be.